ENTER THE BRETHREN

BARBARA DEVLIN

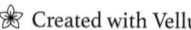 Created with Vellum

DEDICATION

This book is dedicated to my hero, my inspiration, and the love of my life, my husband Mike.
To my dear friend, talented author, and longtime critique partner, the late Judi McCoy. Judi believed in me long before I believed in myself. Her unwavering support and encouragement made me the writer I am today. Not a day goes by that I don't think of her, and I still expect her to call every Monday. How I miss Judi.

PROLOGUE

The Ascendants
English Channel
The Year of Our Lord, 1307

WANTED: DEAD OR ALIVE.

*a*rucard of Villiers shivered as he read the notice.

By papal decree, the Order of the Knights Templar had been banned, and Arucard, along with his four brother knights: Morgan, Demetrius, Aristide, and Geoffrey, was a hunted man.

"Alter course one point to westward, Pellier. Maintain heading nor'-nor'-west." The deck and the tops were alive with activity, and at the wheel were his most able-bodied helmsmen, yet he could not shake the unease investing the whole of his frame.

"Aye, sir, one point to westward, heading nor'-nor'-west," the quartermaster replied. "If I may, sir, whither are we going?"

"We sail for England, whither good King Edward II has outlawed torture." Arucard gazed sternward at the four ships hoisted in his wake. "With our sails abroad, we should make it with our necks intact."

"Do you think we will ever go home again, sir?"

"We have no home, Pellier." Arucard sighed and crushed the parchment in his grasp. "Philip has conspired to steal our legacy, as well as our fortune, but, in regard to the latter, he will be sorely disappointed when he reaches our empty stores."

"What makes you think the King will welcome us?" Pellier shuffled his feet. "Or do you plan to sail up the Thames and announce your presence, Captain? I fear we could be exchanging one noose for another."

"Well, we have two ship holds filled with priceless treasure to belay that fate." Yet Arucard prayed it was enough.

Pellier scratched his temple. "We have five ships, sir."

"And your point would be—what?" Arucard chuckled. "Worry not, old friend. We must hope that Edward is a sensible man."

"You are a sly one, Cap'n." The quartermaster smiled. "Yet, I would warn you. Do not let hope cloud your judgment."

"Hope is a good thing, Pellier." And so Arucard kept telling himself. "Wherefore are you so cynical? Have you previous dealings with the King of England?"

"No." Pellier rubbed the back of his neck and grimaced. "But I know powerful men, and they often charge a high price for allegiance and support, as you have discovered for yourself, of late."

"The booty resting in the other three ship holds ensures that we need no support, merely allegiance." At least, that was Arucard's ambition.

"Can you really separate the two, sir?" Pellier narrowed his stare.

Arucard frowned and, for the first time, let doubt creep into his thoughts. True to form, his steward on land and second in command at sea always asked difficult questions, but therein rested his strength.

Had Arucard chosen the right course?

Or was he leading his men into breakers?

"There is naught certain in this life." He studied the horizon and ignored the chill of desperation shivering along his spine. "But if we cannot live as free men, then we are already dead."

"Aye, Cap'n." Pellier dipped his chin. "But what you consider freedom might be vastly different from that of the King."

"Pellier?"

"Aye, sir?"

"Stop talking."

The quartermaster put up his hands, palms facing out, and laughed.

At that moment, Pellier descended the companion ladder, and Arucard tried, in vain, to ignore the hint of fear dancing a merry jig atop his shoulders. Gazing sternward, he focused on the four ships in his wake. Each carried a brother knight, men he long considered family, as her captain. If Edward turned them away or, worse, took them captive, the blame would rest solely with Arucard.

As a Templar, he had been naught more than a warrior knight. Yet, after the dissolution of their order, Arucard had been designated the leader of the outlaw mariners, much to his dismay. Seeking safe harbor in England had been his decision. If his grand plan failed, all in their haphazardly gathered brotherhood would suffer the consequences. Placing a hand over his heart, he lifted his chin.

"To freedom, my comrades." He swallowed hard. "May the price be such that we are willing and able to pay."

CHAPTER ONE

The Descendants
Jamaica
March, 1810

*R*evenge is a dish best served cold—or so the saying
went. Were she the meal, he would return to
feast again and again. Young and fresh, with a body made
for sin, she was the last thing he expected to find in Dalton
Randolph's cabin.

Trevor Reed Marshall, sixth Earl of Lockwood, hugged
the shadows and gazed at his lovely prey as she bathed.
Although he had ravished his share of the fairer sex on
numerous occasions, he could not recall ever remaining for
the cleanup. Of course, at the moment, there were many
things that escaped him, because it was quite difficult to
focus with a fully loaded cannon in his crotch.

That was the opening scene in the second act of the play,
which had begun two months ago, when Dalton made off
with Trevor's mistress. While men made sport of many
things, guarded doxies were sacred territory subject to the

rules of engagement.   Such breach of polite decorum demanded Trevor respond, in kind, which he was only too happy to do, given the ladybird in question. So he had his story committed to memory, knew precisely what he was going to say, but he paused to enjoy the fortuitous entertainment.

Temptation personified, she lifted an arm and squeezed a wet cloth to her skin, then stood to scrub a shapely thigh, and Trevor could have cried. With silent thanks to young Randolph for his taste in doxies, Trevor emerged from his hiding place.

Slowly, very slowly, he smiled.

Oh, yes.

To err might be human, but getting even—now that was divine.

"May I be of assistance, my dear?" He chuckled. "Wash your back, perhaps?"

The woman faced him, shrieked, and then dropped. Hunkering in the bath, her eyes were wide as saucers and just visible over the rim. Great heavens, had he not shaved that morning?

"W-who are you, and what d-do you want?" She cringed even lower, and he could almost hear the gears grinding in her brain. "Leave my chambers, at once, or I shall scream."

Although the barrel of ale laced with laudanum he had delivered as a boon from their captain would keep the skeleton crew sleeping for hours, he had not wished to invite trouble, so he stopped, palms raised. "Come now, dove, after what I just witnessed, you and I are already on intimate terms."

"I beg your pardon?" Her voice was high-pitched, as a frightened child. Just as quick, she lobbed a bar of soap at his head, which he avoided with ease. "Get out, you black-guard. I swear Captain Randolph will tar your hide."

"Will he, now?" Poor thing was not very convincing, though he fancied her spirit. "Nice bluff, but it might interest you to know that your benefactor is in port, partaking of Jamaican delights that rival your own. And I would wager he will not return until tomorrow."

"My benefactor?" The beauty peered at a towel draped on a chair that was just beyond her reach.

"One in the same." Trevor snatched the swath of cotton. "And he indicated you might be in need of a new guardian, after he lost a game of poker and incurred a few debts."

"Stuff and nonsense." She narrowed her stare. "You, sir, are lying."

Oh, she was a charmer.

"How can you be so certain?" he asked as he sat in the chair. "Men bet their ladybirds all the time."

"Perhaps." She snorted. "But Captain Randolph would never suggest such a ridiculous notion."

"Really?" He rubbed the back of his neck. "And why is that?"

"Because—" Her confidence faltered before him.

"Because—what, my dear?" There he had her.

"We are old friends." She shifted, and water splashed over the rim.

"How fortunate." Resting elbows to knees, Trevor leaned forward. "I would like to be your friend, too."

"You would?" She bit her lip. "Then you can start by handing me that towel and turning your back."

"Ha." He snickered. "Not a chance."

"Then you are not my friend." She frowned. "Would you have me remain, forever, in the bath?"

"No." He studied her ample breasts. "You may exit at any time."

"Without benefit of clothing?" The demirep clucked her tongue. "To use your words, not a chance."

With a chuckle and sincere appreciation for her moxie, he slapped a thigh. "Upon my word, but you are a feisty bit o' flesh."

"And you are too bold, sir." She folded her arms.

"Call me Trevor." How he ached to touch her. "And how should I address you?"

"As I do not intend to keep company with you long enough to require such pleasantries, sir, there is no need to make you free with my name." Soon, she would discover otherwise, as he had to take her in order to win retribution against young Randolph.

"Ah, but you are wrong, dove. I shall have you and your name before we dock in London."

"When first hell freezes." She averted her gaze, in an expression that harkened comparison with an offended debutante, not a whore. "And do not call me dove."

"I have seen longer odds and won the day, my dear." He shrugged. "And as you deny me the use of your name, what choice have I?"

"Your choice is to leave this ship, immediately." The water rippled when she fidgeted. "Captain Randolph will return shortly, and he will have your head for this affront."

"Really?" So it seemed he would gain far more than revenge, given the intensity of her inner fire.

"Any minute now, you shall see," she said as she stared at the door. Time ticked past as he allowed her a scarce second of false hope. "He is almost here."

Again, Trevor laughed. "I think not, dove."

"I know so."

"You posit a ruse, and you are not very good at it."

"I care not what you think." She stiffened her back, but violent trembling belied her true state. "And you seem foolishly sure of yourself, sir."

"Sure enough to know that my sire raised no fool, and we need to be on our way. So, should I help you from the bath?"

Confusion invested her delicate features, and just as Trevor stood, the doxy screamed. "Help! Someone, please, *help me!*"

"Bloody hell." Glancing left, then right, he searched for means to cork the damsel in distress. Quickly, he settled on a solution. Draped at the foot of the captain's bunk was a silk robe. Trevor drew the tie from the garment and stomped toward the ladybird. When she threw her hands up in a defensive posture, he bound her wrists.

"What are you doing?" She struggled in vain. "Let me go. Help—"

With a discarded cravat he muffled her protest.

"Sorry, dove, but I cannot risk further outburst." Trevor knotted the yard-length of linen at the back of her neck. "Once we gain the safety of my ship, I will free you to rain any number of curses on my soul. Now, out of the tub."

When the lady refused to comply with his request, only shook her head, he scooped her naked body into his arms, and the doxy kicked and squirmed.

"Somehow, I knew you would not cooperate." He thrust her atop the bunk and, before she could scramble away, wrapped her in the quilted coverlet, which left only one thing to do before he made his escape.

Trevor walked to the large desk positioned before the stern windows and retrieved a sheet of parchment. A familiar passage shot to the forefront of his brain, and he smiled at the sweet irony. Of course, a few minor alterations were required to convey his intent. Reversing the names, Trevor penned a missive similar to the one his nemesis had left in his wake.

Randolph,
I sincerely hope to savor your dove as much as you enjoyed mine. Your enchanting mistress will await you in London— unharmed, but a bit more experienced than when you last met. Thanks are unnecessary.
Happy Sailing,
Lockwood

After folding the parchment in two, he scribbled Dalton's name on the front and propped the note against the inkstand. "Perfect."

At that instant, his quarry fell to the floor in a clumsy heap. And the more she struggled, the more she entangled herself in the quilt, which resulted in a slew of muffled protests.

"Shh." He adjusted the blanket. "It is for your safety. The docks are filled with randy sailors, and we do not want anyone to see you in all your glory, my dear. Trust me, you would incite a riot."

The cabin door swung open, and a face he knew well peered around the edge. "Cap'n, what are ya doin'? We do not have all night."

"Quiet." He hissed at his first mate. "Is the hall clear?"

"Aye, sir."

Leaning forward, Trevor hoisted his new bunkmate as a sack of wheat atop his shoulder. His second in command took the lead, and together they crept down the hall, past the galley, and up to the main deck. With the stealth and ease of a lethal predator, he slithered amid the dozing watch members, with his precious cargo.

As they descended the gangplank, his lovely catch squirmed in his grasp, and Trevor placed a hand to her bottom, patting through the thick cover. A feminine shriek had him biting back laughter as he navigated the docks toward his ship. With a healthy dose of desire simmering in his veins, he thought to himself: *That was too easy*.

THE CHARMING COURTESAN wiggled amid the folds of the quilt. Soon, Trevor hoped to wiggle her into his bed, as he had no time to spare and could taste vengeance. Studying the unusual doxy from behind an oriental screen that shielded his bathing area, he was genuinely impressed when she used her teeth to loosen the belt knotted at her wrists. Once free of her bonds, she clutched the blanket to her chin in an odd display of modesty he could not quite understand. Whoever heard of a shy whore?

After inching to the edge of his bunk, she slipped to the floor and shuffled to his locker. Once again, she surprised him when she carefully enveloped herself in his robe, only dropping the quilt when she was securely covered. In an instant, her searching gaze settled on a priceless heirloom mounted on the wall. He wondered what she would make of the large sword, with its bronze hilt and ornate décor of incised "Adam & Eve" motifs. As she reached for the weapon, he stepped from his hiding place.

"You are not planning to use that on me, I pray."

"Bloody hell." She jumped and rotated to face him.

"My, my." He wagged a finger. "What naughty language from such a pretty mouth."

"You should have made your presence known, sir." The ladybird cast him a sweet little pout. "You scared me."

"My humblest apologies." He sketched her a proper bow. "There are a number of things I wish to do to you, but none involve fear."

Her mouth fell agape. "I...beg...your...pardon?"

The thrill of the chase burned in his loins, raw lust rode hard in its wake, and it was past time to get down to business. Trevor stretched to his full height and surveyed his latest conquest.

She had a delicate, heart-shaped face, a pert nose, and a succulent mouth he could devour for hours—and fully intended to at the earliest opportunity. Best of all, beneath his scrutiny, she favored him with the same wide-eyed, open-mouthed expression she adopted in Randolph's cabin.

"I-I was admiring the sword." She inhaled a shaky breath. "Is it yours?"

"Aye." Smiling, purposefully stalking her, Trevor was surprised when his captive, and she was his captive, held her ground. "It has been in my family for years."

"It is lovely." She took a half step in retreat.

"It is a sword." He stepped forward, closing the gap. "You are lovely."

Their eyes met, held.

"You think me lovely," she said, in a ghost of a whisper.

"Aye." A surge of triumph filled his senses when he spied a pink flush spreading in her cheeks. Soon she would be his. Before he realized it, he reached for her.

"What are you doing?" Panic marred her delicate features as she scurried to the opposite side of the cabin. "I demand that you return me to Captain Randolph's ship, posthaste."

"No."

"Then give me leave to—"

"Not possible."

"Why?" She raked her fingers through her long brown hair and paced before the stern windows. "You cannot keep me here against my will. That is a crime."

"My dear, I hate to disavow you of any notion regarding your worth, but never has a man been criminally charged for keeping a courtesan." He smirked. "I assure you, it is perfectly legal."

"You took me by force."

"Come now, let us not call it that."

"But that is what you did."

"Perhaps, but let us not call it that."

"You, sir, are without honor."

"Did I ever claim to possess such noble traits?"

"Blackguard." With arms folded across her chest, she lifted her chin. "I insist you free me this instant."

"By all means, my lady." Trevor nodded and bowed with a flourish, which had never failed to impress the fair sex. "You may go."

She flinched. "Are you joking?"

"No." He lied.

"So, I may take leave of your company?" Assuming a rigid posture, she adopted a confrontational stance, which was admirable, given her near naked state.

"If you so choose." He could only wish that all that fire lent itself to her trade.

With palpable shock and a wary expression, she swallowed hard, took two tentative sidesteps, and then halted. "Thank you."

As the fiery object of his desire turned, he reflected on her stubborn nature and savored her determination, however misplaced. "Yet, I can give you three good reasons not to venture beyond that door."

Over her shoulder, she eyed him with caution. "And they are—what?"

"One, we are at sea." He counted on his fingers. "Two, it is a long crossing to London."

"Have you a jolly-boat?" With an outstretched hand, she grasped the knob. "We could not have much of a start. I can row back to port."

"Three, you are the only woman aboard this ship. Ah, yes." Trevor snapped his fingers. "Four, you are naked, except for my robe, which I might add looks quite fetching on you."

"You must be the life of the ball." Her shoulders slumped, and she lowered her head and sighed. "Who are you, and why are you doing this to me?"

The sadness in her voice brought him up short, and uncharacteristic and unwelcome guilt nagged at his conscience, which he quashed in a flash. Perhaps a change in tack would improve his suit. "I have already told you who I am, and I should think you would be grateful for my intervention on your behalf."

"Grateful—for what?" She stared at him and clenched her fists. "Being kidnapped by an unconscionable rogue?"

"Dove, you should consider the theatre, because you have a flair for dramatics." How could he sway her, as he required her cooperation? "Young Randolph is a pup. And it is not as if you are Dalton's wife or some other important relation. Paramours are never permanent fixtures."

"How dare you." With a wicked glare, she shot daggers at him as she stomped a foot.

"Calm yourself, love." He would put that energy to good use, soon enough. "I merely paid you a compliment."

"By insulting me?" Her eyes flared.

"I did no such thing." Trevor pulled out a chair and sat, with his feet propped on the table to better enjoy the show. "I merely made an observation. And you have not been kidnapped. You have simply been re-let."

"Re-let?" She blinked. "How so?"

"As I said earlier, your guardian passed his responsibility to me," he explained.

"That cannot be true." She fumbled with the folds of the robe.

"Why?" Never had he found the fairer sex so captivating.

The doxy opened her mouth and then closed it.

"You believe yourself irreplaceable?" Trevor canted his head. "Do you not know, dove, that all courtesans are rented?"

"Perhaps we should begin at the beginning." The hesitant ladybird approached, pulled out the chair opposite him, and sat. "What, precisely, did Dalton tell you of me?"

"Well, to be honest, he denied your existence, until I informed him that his men had much to say on the docks."

"I see." She furrowed her brow. "And you forced him to acknowledge my presence?"

"Forced?" He frowned. "Now that is a harsh term."

"One suitable to describe our relations, thus far," quick as a wink she replied.

Once again, Trevor laughed. "I will grant you that."

"I am so happy to provide for your amusement, sir." The demirep huffed and folded her arms.

"Excellent, then we should discuss terms." Now her response garnered his fast attention. "What is your usual rate? Know that whatever you charge, I will double it."

"Terms? Rate?" She blinked. "For what?"

"Why, your surrender, of course." And his extra stout Jolly Roger prepared to board her main deck.

"My surrender?" The charming whore appeared stunned. "What, exactly, do you expect me to surrender?"

"All right, miss, I have had enough of your games." Trevor dropped his feet to the floor, leaned forward, and rested his elbows on the table. "Acting the innocent, which may prove stimulating in more seductive scenarios, has outlived its novelty and my patience. And it is time you gave me your name, as we are to be bunkmates during our voyage."

She bit her lip. After a few painful minutes, in which he was determined to wait her out, she finally responded, "You may call me Caroline, and I have no intention of sharing a bunk, or anything else, with you."

"How lovely to make your acquaintance, Mistress Caroline. Now, stop playing the injured party, set your price, and let us be done with it."

She shifted and clutched the folds of the robe to her throat. "But—"

"I know Randolph was your guardian, but I am your sole protector aboard this ship, and I find your reluctance puzzling, given that most courtesans change benefactors as men change breeches. If you approach our predicament sensibly, I am sure you and I can come to some understanding; an agreement that will allow us to pass the journey to London more...pleasantly." Then he seized upon a particular reward she would never reject. "And I give you leave to share the details of our liaison, including how you came to be in my custody, among your set, which should enable you to demand even more money from future customers. As it is, you should know that I am prepared to be very generous."

"Why?"

"Because I want you."

SINCE THEIR IMPROMPTU meeting in Dalton's cabin, the handsome kidnapper had steered her into one rogue wave after another. And despite her repeated attempts to land on her feet, Caroline had yet to gain her balance.

"You want me?" Now she was well and truly flummoxed. In an instant, gooseflesh covered her from head to toe, because, to her knowledge, no man had ever wanted her for any reason. "You cannot be serious."

"I assure you, my dear, I am very serious."

When Caroline stowed away on Dalton's ship, she had no idea of the consequences of her seemingly innocuous actions. One of her oldest and dearest friends, Dalton pitied her predicament when she explained her rationale. She had her reasons for fleeing London, and it was not as if her shame were a secret. Polite society could be anything but polite, so she had sought an escape from unwanted attention. In short, all she wanted was freedom--from the harsh scrutiny, the ugly innuendos, and the cruel comments.

"Mistress Caroline, I do not believe Bonaparte takes this long to negotiate."

"Sorry, Captain." She shook her head. The man thought her Dalton's paramour, and nothing could be further from the truth, but could she, and should she, enlighten the devilishly handsome stranger? "I am unprepared, at this time, to accept an offer—any offer, from you."

"I beg your pardon." Trevor sat upright. "Are you rejecting me?"

Were he a gentleman, she could not resist him. "When you put it that way, it sounds rather awful."

"It feels rather awful." He grimaced.

With a crisp linen shirt covering broad shoulders and buckskin breeches that disappeared into polished Hessians, her captor conveyed a boyish charm mixed with the confidence of an experienced mariner that, no doubt, melted many a female heart and garnered few, if any, refusals. A year ago, Caroline might have been vulnerable to such qualities, but not so, anymore.

"May I ask why you spurn me?" he inquired with a hint of ire.

Would that the answers to his query were simple, but she suspected he had neither the time nor the inclination to listen to her story. And even if he heard her out, would he sympathize with her situation and accept her choice? "You may, but, given the circumstances surrounding my presence aboard your ship, I feel no compulsion to comply with your request, Captain."

"I see." For a moment, he simply stared at her. "Perhaps, you should take a night to—"

"*Ooh*." Caroline almost jumped out of her skin when someone pounded on the door.

"It never fails." Trevor frowned and slapped a fist to his palm. "Come."

A gray-haired, bearded man ducked his head inside. "Cap'n, we're well found and away, and the crew is assembled."

"Excellent. Your timing could not be better." He waved a welcome and stood. "Come in and meet our guest. Madam Caroline, allow me to introduce my first mate, Mr. Loman."

"Pleased ta meet ya, ma'am." The crusty seaman bowed. "And call me George."

"Pleased to make your acquaintance, Mister—George." Caroline dipped her chin.

"I will send my cabin boy to accommodate your immediate needs, my dear." Trevor paused at the threshold and glanced over his shoulder. "I ask that you remain in my quarters, because you will be safe here, as no one enters without my expressed permission. I promise you will not be disturbed, and we shall continue our discussion in the morning."

Countless thoughts collided in her brain. Her captor was neither pirate nor gentlemen, but that had not meant he could be trusted. Whatever was she to do? "I do not look forward to it."

Alone, Caroline stared heavenward and whistled in monotone.

Well, had she not wanted to be free?

CHAPTER TWO

*S*nuggling close to an unexpected but much appreciated heat source, to ward off the chill of a night at sea, Caroline sighed, blissful and content. It took a few seconds before she realized what kept her warm. Despite her alarm, she knew screaming was a bad idea. And as she had not been accosted but, instead, slept uninterrupted, she saw no reason to be afraid. Careful not to move, she fully opened her eyes. Soft rays of morning sunlight filtered through the drawn curtains, bathing the quarters in a saffron hue sufficient to confirm her suspicions. She shared a bed with a man.

She should have been scandalized.

She should have been outraged.

She should have shouted her displeasure from the highest yardarm.

Instead, Caroline reminded herself he thought her a courtesan, considered her part to play, and could not resist lifting the covers for a quick peek.

When climbing between the sheets the previous evening, she had thought she would be sleeping alone.

Trevor had promised she would not be disturbed, so it was easy to assume he would be bunking with the crew—so much for assumptions. In future, she would be vigilant in clarifying such important matters.

At some point during the night she had curled beside him. The robe she had tucked snug about herself had parted, and her bare skin rested against his. The crisp hair on his chest tickled her breast, and his muscled arm draped across her waist.

Oh, dear.

Caroline wondered what her family would think if they could see her now, for all intents and purposes, nude, nestled beside an equally naked man. Her mother would no doubt swoon. Her brother would kill them, both, if she were lucky. However, she found him fascinating and frightening, at once.

Fascinating because he made her heart pound.

Frightening because he made her heart pound.

Though men had always seemed disinterested in her, she found them an intriguing lot. True to form, curiosity nipped at her senses until Caroline, at last, relented and risked a glimpse at his face. Though his eyes remained closed, she envisioned his piercing green depths, even as she studied his thickly lashed lids. Since it could not hurt, she availed herself of the opportunity to examine the rest of her rescuer's sun-kissed visage, and he was a beauty.

A wide forehead sat above arched brows. His thick and wavy hair, which fell unruly about his face, boasted more shades of brown than she ever knew existed and had gold highlights running throughout. She just resisted the urge to tame a wayward lock. A patrician nose sat amid chiseled cheekbones. His proud chin she knew so well, because she focused on it whenever his stare overwhelmed her, and that happened more often than she was willing to admit. But his mouth, now that was a marvel of unutterable perfection. What would it hurt to claim just one kiss from her captor? If only he were ugly.

In slumber, Trevor appeared harmless, almost boyish, but she knew better. He was a sleeping dragon that could breathe fire and warm her toes, and he had done so with a frequency she found quite unnerving. As she continued her detailed admiration of his lips, the corners of his mouth quirked. Peering up, she was caught by a pair of green eyes.

"Good morning, my lady," he purred. "I trust you passed a pleasant night?"

Inhaling, slow and steady, she tried to remain calm. But it ought to be a sin for a man to be so lovely, especially in the morning. Were she standing, Caroline was certain she would have melted into the floor, which brought to mind the danger her would-be benefactor presented. Could Dalton not have gambled with someone old and fat? Wrenching in a tangle of silk sheets, her hasty scramble ceased when his arm at her waist tightened as a steel band.

"No, do not run away." Trevor laughed. "I promise not to bite, at least, not yet. Besides, we have business to discuss."

"But—now? Here?" Clutching the sheet to her chin, Caroline righted herself and ignored the shiver of panic tickling her spine. "In bed?"

"Considering the topic," he said as he nipped the crest of her ear, "I cannot think of a more appropriate place."

The topic, she recalled, was that he wanted her to be his mistress. She had heard tales of wild abandon concerning her brother, his friends, and their courtesans, so her current predicament was not so much cause for concern in regard to her safety as it was for her reputation. The sole function of a mistress was to provide his relief. While she knew not the exact details, the mechanics, she had a general idea what was involved. Problem was, despite what he thought, she was no courtesan.

Oh, dear.

"Trevor—or should I address you as Captain?"

With a countenance she would characterize as...wolfish, he tapped a finger to the tip of her nose. "You may call me whatever you wish."

Several possible addresses popped into her head.

Rake.

Darling.

Mine.

Of course, that was neither possible nor realistic, even in light of her past humiliation, because her family would never consider Trevor suitable marriage material, not that she wanted to marry him. In a flash, images of her mother and brother appeared before her, and one word claimed her thoughts to the detriment of all else.

Forbidden.

"Captain, please, release me." Caroline squirmed in his embrace and tried not to contemplate the firm body pressed to hers. "It is very difficult to concentrate on the matter at hand while lying abed with you."

"Really? And why is that?" His baritone poured over her as honey on a hot scone, and the expression on his face was one of wicked thoughts, similar to hers no doubt. "Could it be that you want me as I want you?"

"Captain—I mean, Trevor, do you have to do that?" She swatted his hand, even as he stroked her flesh, in a pathetic attempt to cease the unwarranted but maddeningly delightful attention. "I cannot think."

In silence, Caroline rebuked herself and struggled to

suppress her reaction. What mystical power had the man possessed to affect her so? Good heavens, it was an effort just to breathe. What on earth had Dalton been thinking, divulging her presence to such a dangerous individual?

"All right, my lady." With a chuckle, he released his hold on her and crossed his arms behind his head. "If you insist on thinking and talking, pray continue."

Resituating her robe, Caroline scrambled to the foot of the bed and what she considered relative safety as her toes hit the floor. Of course, her frazzled sense of duty would improve if she could stop ogling his chiseled chest and broad shoulders. Could the man not put on clothes?

Because she could resist anything but temptation.

"Trevor, I am flattered by your offer—"

"Flattery was not my intention." He sat upright, and the sheet dropped to his hips.

Positive she would faint at any moment, Caroline blinked and turned her back to him. It should be a crime for a man to be so beautiful. She had known him a short while and yet he already made her want to be bad. Problem was, she was not sure what being bad with the handsome captain entailed.

"My singular thought was of the mutual pleasure and comfort we could share while journeying to London. I doubt a woman of your profession would be offended by the suggestion, and I do not think your benefactor would mind." He smirked. "In fact, he would be grateful you saw fit to compensate me in his stead."

Aghast, she peered at him. "C-compensate?"

"Yes." Trevor chuckled. "In lieu of funds for your safe passage to London. Actually, Randolph hinted he would be amenable to such an agreement."

Shoulders squared, Caroline faced him. "H-he did?" It

was too ridiculous. Dalton knew she could not give herself to that man. Perhaps her friend had been attempting a ruse, because the truth would have garnered both of them a sea of trouble. Drowning in a mix of confusion and fear, she chewed her lip, a nervous habit she had long suffered since childhood and had failed to break.

"My dear, sit down." Trevor flung the covers aside and tossed his legs over the edge of the bed. Stark naked, he walked to her. "You are as white as a ghost."

Temptation beckoned, luring her as a lodestone. In vain, Caroline staged a valiant battle against her own inquis-itiveness. She wanted to look; was compelled to let her gaze travel south of his belly button.

So she relented.

A one-eyed monster, thick and intimidating, stared back at her. Jutting, proud and formidable, almost angry, from a nest of brown curls, the mystery of flesh pointed straight in her direction.

Caroline swooned.

In her fogged brain, she told herself her reaction was justified. The only experience she had with the male form was from childhood. During the summer months, her brother and their friends swam *au naturel* in the pond near her country home. It had been harmless. Innocent. And as far as she could recall, none of the boys had ever appeared so healthy.

For a moment, she revisited fonder times and found sanctuary in the past. But the present ensnared her when Trevor hovered. Emitting a cursed shriek, she cringed.

"For the love of Christ, would you stop doing that?" He shoved off the bed and stormed across the cabin. "One would think I had assaulted you."

"I am sorry, but you did bring me here against my will,

or have you conveniently forgotten that?" Upon discovery that her errant captor had re-deposited her on the mattress, Caroline stretched and kept her eyes on his profile, lest she embarrass herself and faint again. "And I have not agreed to be your courtesan."

At his locker, he paused to pull on a pair of breeches. With unveiled impatience, he raked a hand through his hair and paced.

"I have met some unwieldy women in my day, but you are a contradiction." Suddenly, Trevor marched to the side of the bunk. With hands on hips, he glared at her. "By your chosen profession, you exist to pleasure men, and I only want to make love to you, a privilege for which I am prepared to pay a king's ransom. Do you not see that our tale will make you a legend? How is it that we are at odds?"

If only she could trust him.

If only she could tell him the truth.

"You are so sure of yourself, yet you know nothing of me."

"And I could say the same of you, Mistress Caroline." He appeared almost crestfallen. "What am I missing?"

"I simply cannot give you what you want."

He shifted his weight. "Why?"

Caroline needed an excuse, but her usual collection proved either irrelevant or inadequate, so she grasped at a straw. "Because you are a stranger to me."

"Since when does a doxy require familiarity with a client in order to spread her legs?" he asked, as he shrugged into a shirt. "You make no sense."

"As you have pointed out, I am unlike most women." Resisting the urge to shout denial, she seized the opportunity to advance her cause. "Perhaps, if you shared some personal history with me, I would be more amenable to your offer."

Trevor arched a brow. "Ask me a question I will answer."

"Are you a pirate?"

"Now you insult me."

Sighing her relief, she propped on an elbow. "Well, in light of your behavior, it was a plausible conclusion."

"Mistress Caroline, a pirate would not negotiate, as would a gentleman. A pirate would take you, with or without your permission, and give you overboard." He sat to pull on his boots. "Do you still think me a pirate?"

"No." All right, the threat to her person was not as dire as previously thought. So how could she resolve her predicament? The grand scheme she concocted had resulted in disaster, and Dalton's involvement could taint him, as well. She refused to sully her lifelong friend in scandal, so she had to devise a new game, one that would see her returned to London with no additional stain to her reputation. "Then why are you not in the Navy? That is to say, England is at war. Why do you not fight?"

"I served my commission with honor." Trevor walked to the washstand. "But I have had enough of war, and I have done my part for King and Country."

"I suppose I can understand your position." In silence, she calculated. There had to be a way out of her dilemma. "And you knew Dalton when you were in service?"

"Aye, and his elder brother Dirk."

Oh, dear. That could complicate her plan. "Are you much acquainted with the Randolphs?"

"No." He lifted a pitcher and poured water into the basin. "Not since I left the Navy."

Sweet relief. "Well then, Captain, I will make you a bargain."

He faced her, with his chin covered in shaving soap. "Madame, you have my attention, unreservedly."

Desperate times necessitated desperate measures, and Caroline was a desperate woman. "I will be your mistress until we get to London provided that, once we arrive, we part ways, never to see each other again."

Was it her imagination, wishful thinking, or had the charming seaman seemed rather put out by her proposal? "Done."

Well, maybe he was not so put out as she thought. "And one more thing—"

"How much?" He arched a brow.

"I do not want your money, Captain."

"Excuse me?" He cleared his throat, and now she was positive she had surprised him. "Then what do you want?"

Inhaling a deep breath, she squared her shoulders. "Your word that you will not force me to do anything until I am ready."

He shuffled his feet. "What the deuce does that mean?"

"It means that we begin with a kiss until I permit more." How much harm could he do with such limits?

With a sly smile that immediately had her rethinking her strategy, Trevor dropped his shaving brush into the basin, marched straight to her, wound an arm about her waist, hauled her against him, and planted his lips to hers.

And Caroline could only pray that she made the voyage to London, virtue intact.

~

DESIRE WAS A POTENT INTOXICANT.

Now Caroline understood why masters of the Renaissance wrote of it, why women lived for it, and why men killed for it. How unfair it was that the only man who wanted her, gentleman or otherwise, thought her a whore.

Standing at the larboard rail, clothed in a shirt and breeches borrowed from a member of the crew, because the cabin boy's togs were too small to accommodate her feminine curves, she inhaled the familiar and comforting scent of brine mixed with kelp.

Before her, the sky manifested a lustrous blue canopy, reflecting in the ocean surrounding the ship. Sunlight dappled the ripples and swells, shimmering as countless shards of the finest crystal. Beneath the surface, shadows danced an elegant waltz, allusive of the life thriving in the watery depths below. Wind whipped the rigging, crackling the air as it filled the canvas, and waves crashed against the hull, sounding thunderous roars as the *Hera* swam the seas.

Three days had passed since she enacted her bargain with Trevor. Three days of stealthy attacks, some inexpressibly tender, others not so much, but always in obeisance of her terms. Three days of assault on her senses and determination to avoid what he thought their inevitable fate. And although he had kept her off balance with his unconventional seduction, the remainder of their lives aboard ship had fallen into a reassuring routine.

They shared every meal, sometimes hosting Mr. Loman, and the irrepressible captain played a wicked game of poker, in which they bartered kisses most often claimed in his lap, because she had yet to win a single round. In the morning hours, while she bathed, he never interrupted her toilette, giving her complete privacy. And while he insisted she share his bunk every night, he had not once taken advantage of her when she was most vulnerable. When they climbed between his soft, silk sheets, he gave her his back, and she gave him hers.

So what frustrated her?

Two hands appeared on either side of hers, and she stiffened her spine before she could stop herself.

"Relax," Trevor said, with a rush of warm breath against the crook of her neck. Slowly, maddeningly, he trailed feathery kisses up the back of her ear.

Merciful heavens, the man could make a babe surrender its favorite rattle. "What are you doing, Captain?"

"Why, I am fulfilling our bargain, mistress mine."

"Yes, but, are you sure you should be doing that— there?" she inquired as he retraced his delicious path.

"If memory serves, we agreed to begin our liaison with a kiss, yet you devised no additional stipulations." He licked and then suckled her flesh in a delicate suggestion of more intimate entanglements. "Do you fault my placement?"

"I had thought that on the mouth was the usual custom," she said as she exhaled. "As it has been, thus far."

"Usual custom?" he said with a hint of good humor. "You make it sound like a chore, my dear."

"Well, it is my profession, as you are so fond of reminding me." She shivered, though it was quite warm.

"Point taken." He lifted his head and turned her to face him. "But I would count it the height of insult were you not to enjoy my attention."

She searched for something, anything, to say.

"You do enjoy my attention, do you not?" the infernal man had the nerve to ask.

Deny. Deny. Deny.

"Yes." Blast her lack of intestinal fortitude.

But the charming smile with which he rewarded her admission ceased all internal rebuke.

"Well, then, by your command, lady mine." And then his lips covered hers, his tongue flicking a sinful entreaty that she answered without hesitation, drawing her in to that elusive realm she had only visited in her dreams. But her dreams had been the stuff of girlish fantasy. Reality was far more intriguing. Had he known how he impacted her? Had he known how he made her feel? He was fire and ice at once, searing intensity and swirling sensation—

Catcalls and hoots brought them up short.

"Mind your stations!" Trevor shouted over his shoulder.

Oh, how her cheeks burned. "Captain, I have a small request."

"Beautiful lady, I am at your service." Must the insufferable man gloat?

"Make and mend day seems grossly insufficient to fill the needs of your crew." She anchored herself in a sense of purpose. "While I do not consider myself an expert tailor, I am rather handy with a needle and thread."

"What?" Trevor opened his mouth, and then closed it. "Am I to understand...that is to say...you wish to sew togs for my men?"

"Well, yes, I do." It was nice to addle him for a change. "I am unaccustomed to being idle."

"You know, for a kept woman, you seem awfully familiar with sea life." He narrowed his stare. "Where is your father, at present?"

"Dead." So much for her newfound confidence.

"Any other relations?" He adjusted the collar of her shirt. "A brother?"

Would die from the shock if he could see her now.

Caroline pretended to find the hem of her cuff infinitely fascinating. While she was willing to confess a growing fondness for her captain, she was unwilling to do more.

Men could not be trusted.

Bells sounded the noon watch.

"Mistress mine, I will consider your generous offer."

JUST WHAT WAS Mistress Caroline about?

Later that evening, at his station on the quarterdeck, Trevor stood mesmerized by the sight of his radiant captive. Well past the yardarm, the setting sun illuminated her hair as a halo, and what an angel was she. Dressed in an over-sized jacket, breeches, and boots, with her hair tied in the back, she could pass for a member of the crew to the casual observer. He caught his breath as she raised her face to the sky. For some reason he could not begin to comprehend, her unabashed delight touched him in ways he had not previously known, probably because she confounded his every attempt to understand her. So she wanted to mend clothes for his crew?

Whoever heard of a ladybird with a work ethic? Now she had to be an enigma. He knew captains who took their wives or mistresses to sea. That was nothing new or out of the ordinary. Personally, he had thought the idea one of sheer lunacy. Sharing his ship, much less his cabin, with a woman was something he had never before consid-ered, and he had not normally acted in such a rash manner. Bringing Caroline to his domain bespoke retalia-tion for the theft of his mistress, nothing more. Well, there was the fact that he wanted the lovely young courtesan.

He knew it the moment he found her naked, in a bath, in Randolph's cabin. Waking every morning to her guileless face was heaven on earth, because his sweet Caroline was quite fetching when she was sleep-tousled. Unlike most courtesans who often had a worldly, somewhat worn look around the edges, she was wholly...unspoiled. Indeed, nothing about her made any sense.

How in bloody hell had she resorted to selling her body in service to men as means for survival, because she seemed woefully unprepared for her occupation. Her continued devotion to her protector belied the cutthroat personality often associated with women of her profession, because most mistresses tossed aside one benefactor for another, without so much as a by-your-leave, if the price were right.

Yet she rebuffed his advances despite his generosity. For a whore, the subtle flinch, the hesitation in her response when he kissed her earlier denoted an uncharacteristic naïveté. To his abiding chagrin, she considered herself bound to another man, Trevor's nemesis. Her loyalty signified an invisible but nonetheless substantial barrier he would have to overcome, but not by force, to achieve his revenge.

He could apprise her of his identity, in truth. If she knew he was an English lord, she might look on him more favorably. She might be willing to negotiate a more lucrative arrangement if she knew he possessed sufficient wealth to sustain her. But that could be a double-edged sword.

If she knew he was a man of means and title, she could try to take him for a fortune. Or worse, she could attempt to trap him into marriage. A marriage he had not wanted. No, he would not enlighten her.

Women could not be trusted.

Consulting his charts, he confirmed their course. "Mr. Todd, steady as she goes."

The helmsman nodded. "Steady as she goes, sir."

"George?"

"Aye, Cap'n?"

"I need you to do something for me." Trevor paused and

scanned the horizon. What he was about to set in motion, not to mention his motives, perplexed him more than the beautiful demirep. If he let her, the woman would be his death. "No bloody questions. Not one bloody word. Just get it done."

"Aye, Cap'n."

"And if you wish to retain your teeth, I suggest you wipe that smirk off your face."

"Yes, sir."

"Check with the officers. If any should have need of mending services, gather their garments and have them delivered to Mistress Caroline."

CHAPTER THREE

*T*wo days later, Caroline returned to the cabin as Billy served the noon meal. Timid as a mouse, he excused himself and made a hasty exit. As she eased into her seat at the dining table, she spied another smaller table, with a basket perched atop and a matching chair, positioned in a corner near the stern windows. Inside the basket, she discovered a pair of scissors, a dented thimble, a collection of needles, and various colored threads. And on the floor, just to the left, gathered a mound of garments sporting all manner of rips and tears.

"Oh, my," she declared, as the door to the cabin opened.

"Well, well. What have we here?" Trevor laughed, as he assessed her predicament. "Your offer of sewing skills seems to have caused quite a stir, my dear. Perhaps it is a good thing that I limited your overture to the officers."

"No worries, Captain. I am stronger than I look." She indicated the ambitious stack of garments. "Make and mend is not for another few days, but I do not believe the allotted afternoon to repair their uniforms ever truly suffices."

At the washstand, Trevor stripped a soiled shirt, baring his impressive chest, and although she knew better than to risk a glance, she simply could not stop herself from staring.

"Please, Caroline, this is becoming quite tedious." He grimaced.

"I beg your pardon?" She met his too knowing gaze. "What is tedious?"

"Why must you gawk when I welcome your touch?" He flexed his muscles.

Mortified, she could only shrug.

Trevor grinned. "Come here."

"No." She shook her head.

"Come here," he repeated in a low voice that dared her to defy him.

Placing one foot in front of the other, she obeyed without complaint.

Why?

Caroline could not say.

Though she fought to maintain a calm façade, her insides twisted and turned. She wanted to flee, but she wanted to stay. She wanted to ignore, but she wanted to explore. Fear battled with desire, hesitation with wanton abandon, in a lethal struggle for control of her senses and conscience. Fire burned in the pit of her belly, its warmth suffusing her with a hint of derring-do.

"Go ahead," he said with a shameless grin. "As I said before, I will not bite...yet."

Now she feared she would melt through the floor. "What about our bargain?"

"Consider it a boon." He stuck his tongue in his cheek. "As you have been such a gracious loser at poker."

"How cruel you are to mock me so." Oh, how she

wanted to accept his offer. "I warned you I have never been good at cards."

"Then I suggest you keep your night job."

That one rejoinder, innocuously uttered, was enough to send her careening into reality. "I should sort the clothes, Captain."

"Coward."

Caroline was many things, but she was no coward.

With nary a thought, she set her open palms to his chest, splaying her fingers wide, marveling as his nipples hardened. How powerful she felt. Thrilling passion sang in her veins, searing her from top to toe. Her naughty captor groaned as she traced his sinewy valleys and ridges, sketching a tempestuous path to his belly button. Had she considered him dangerous? Slowly, very slowly, she kissed a single spot, somewhere between his erect nipples, which she silently claimed as her own, and Trevor rewarded her with a heartfelt sigh.

"Your skin is so hot," she whispered.

"And you unman me, mistress mine. Clutching her wrists, he gently pushed her away. "Any more, and I will break our bargain, here and now."

HE WOULD NEVER HAVE HER.

Despite his plan, despite his measured success with the coy courtesan, Trevor told himself it was sufficient that Dalton Randolph thought his chief rival tutored the shy ladybird in the sensual arts, during their journey to London.

That was revenge enough.

Standing on the quarterdeck, Trevor ignored the cool winds whipping through the sails, because his mind filled with images that had haunted his dreams for the past week, ever since he carried a chestnut-haired doxy aboard his ship.

Of late he had changed his tack with the resistant demirep. Instead of coming at her overtly, as he had done from the first, placing the lascivious arts at the forefront of their exchanges, he lured her with soft caresses and teasing kisses. He spent time talking with her, to invest himself in her affairs as he had done with no other woman, and his plan had been a brilliant triumph.

Not for a second could he mistake the subtle glances Caroline cast in his direction, the way she studied him when she thought he was not looking. Or how she arched into him when he took her in his arms and claimed her mouth. Problem was he feared his new strategy had worked on him more than it had worked on her.

Because Trevor had developed a genuine fondness for the demure mistress.

She was helpful.

Cook had at first resisted Caroline's presence in the galley, until she shared a few recipes that left the crew begging for more.

She was productive.

Her mending skills had the officers of the watch gushing effusive praise like a cargo hold of greenhorns.

She was...nice.

From an irreparable tunic, she had created a vest with numerous pockets for the many tools of the first mate's trade, and poor George blushed like a giddy virgin when Caroline gave him the custom-made garment.

In a mere sennight, the arresting young woman had earned a measure of respect from his men and, though he would deny it to his death, from Trevor, too.

No matter how he tried to rationalize his motive for bringing her aboard ship, the truth was he could not bear using her in so cruel a fashion, regardless of her profession. The unfamiliar and unappreciated sense of decency bloody well scared the hell out of him. So he contented himself in the knowledge that her former protector now suffered the torment of her loss.

"Cap'n!"

"What?" He blinked. "What is it, George?"

"Are ya deaf, man? I've called to ya three times." The first mate huffed. "Blast it all, Cap'n, pull yerself out of the clouds and take a long look at 'em! We're headed for foul winds."

Scanning the sky ahead of them, Trevor realized what had his first mate up in arms.

A dark cloud stretched low across the horizon, and they had steered straight toward it. There was no use altering their course, because the storm would be upon them before they could outrun it. The only option was to re-trim the sails, batten down, and hold the *Hera* steady.

"Damn." He scowled. "Where is Mistress Caroline?"

"She has yet to show a leg," the first mate replied.

"Assemble the watch, and I want the rigging inspected at once." Trevor perched at the top of the companion ladder. "And find out which members of the crew have helm experience. We could use an extra hand."

George inclined his head. "Where are you going?"

"To check on my bunkmate." He descended to the main deck and turned to the corridor leading to his cabin. As he passed the galley, he waved to the cook. "Serve an early lunch, and tell every man to eat his fill. I want the oven fires doused in two hours."

"Storm, Cap'n?"

"Aye."

"Bloody hell."

At the entrance to his quarters, he stiffened his back, grasped the knob, twisted, and stepped into what had been his private domain.

"Blast." Caroline, pretty as a picture and deep in concentration, sat at the tiny table he had rummaged from the fo'c'sle. To the undiscerning eye, she could have been his wife, busily mending one of his garments.

"Now that is not a very welcoming welcome," he said with more humor than intended.

"Oh, Captain." Her answering smile was pure angel. "You startled me, and that is never a good thing when I have a needle in my grasp."

"A lethal weapon, perhaps?" And he meant that in more ways than one. Why the devil must she be so damn decent?

"Not so much." She laughed, a lighthearted sound he found inexpressibly disarming. "How long have you been there?"

"Enough to know you are not having much luck with the repairs to my shirt." She favored him with a mischievous expression. "Shall I ask Billy to resume his duties?"

"Do not dare." She appeared offended by the mere suggestion. "While I must admit sewing was never my strong suit, I will not be upstaged by your cabin boy. It is just that I have stitched this tear three times, and I have yet to get it straight."

"Your devotion to the task is commendable, love." Trevor crossed the room and paused at the washstand. After pouring water into the basin, he grabbed a washcloth. "By the by, be sure to eat plenty for lunch, as it will be the last hot meal for a day or two."

"Has the weather turned?" she inquired without hesitation.

"Your knowledge of sea life continues to amaze me." He dried his hands and hung the towel on a wall peg. "Are you certain you have never served a man aboard ship—other than Dalton?"

"I promise, you are the second." Caroline retrieved the scissors from the basket and commenced cutting the crooked patch. "I believe you hinted at a storm, Captain. Are we in any danger?"

"It is a line squall." Trevor walked to his desk and assembled various charts. "And it looks to be a foul one."

"Oh, dear." She dropped the shirt in her lap and glanced out the stern windows. "Is there anything I can do to help?"

"I beg your pardon?" Once again she surprised him. With a bundle of maps tucked under his arm, he gathered his wits and strolled to the baffling whore. "What do you propose?"

"I do not know." The curious courtesan set her mending aside, rose from her chair, and shrugged. "But if you have need of me, I shall assist you, in whatever capacity you require."

There it was again, that sinking suspicion that his temporary mistress, who was not his mistress in truth, was something else entirely. But what woman would claim that occupation when she was not? It simply had not stood to reason.

"How many years have you spent in service to men?" He cupped her chin in his hand. "Tell me, Caroline, I will not be angry."

"Not so long as you might think."

Now he was getting somewhere. "If you are what you

profess, then I must know, was Dalton your first benefactor, on land and sea?"

"You could say that." She averted her stare.

Ah, that explained it. She was an inexperienced doxy, and a dangerous one, to boot. Youth and innocence were a potent combination, and she could demand a fortune in London for such qualities. Give her ten more guardians, and she might be ready for Trevor.

And he might be ready for her.

TWELVE HOURS HAD PASSED before Trevor returned to their cabin. And although Caroline had done her best to heed his advice, the constant pitch and roll, more pronounced than normal, made it impossible for her to remain in their bunk without clutching the mattress.

"My, but you look awful." She rushed to his side, wanting to do something, anything, to be useful. Since she could not give Trevor what he wanted most, she vowed to offer other assistance. For some reason she could not discern, his good opinion mattered to her. "It must be terrible up there, with the rain and wind. We need to get you out of those wet clothes before you catch a chill."

"Well, it is just my luck that you make such a tempting offer when I am too tired to oblige." He cast a lopsided grin, which scored a direct hit to her resolve.

Oh, those cursed blushes. "But you retain your sense of humor, I see."

Trading a towel for his soaked oilskin gear, she hung the outerwear on a peg. After he peeled his shirt from his damp flesh and tossed the soggy garment on the floor, she grabbed a second towel and blotted his back.

Trevor turned his head, arched a brow, sighed, and said, "Thank you."

"I am at your service, Captain." If he only knew how she wished to serve him.

"I know you are, but I am clueless to understand why." He rewarded her with a magnetic smile, impossibly sweet. "At the risk of offending you, I must say you behave nothing like a courtesan."

"No offense taken, and I should thank you." He could not know it, would never know it, but his awkward compliment touched her to the core. How could she tell him what he made her feel? Warm. Wicked. Wanton. When his hands fell to his waistband, she retreated. "If you give me a moment, I will fetch your tray."

She could not escape the cabin fast enough, because the handsome seaman was getting harder and harder to resist.

In what must have looked like a comedy of errors, Caroline tripped and stumbled her way to the galley and retrieved the captain's meal. It was, perhaps, her good fortune that the simple fare of dried beef, fresh fruit, and bread presented little chance of spillage, given the current conditions at sea.

Upon entering the cabin, she found Trevor sitting at the table, garbed only in his robe. After kicking the door shut behind her, she dipped and swayed with the motion of the boat and set the food before him. Slipping into the chair opposite her captain, she smiled. "Hungry?"

In an instant, Trevor snapped to attention, met her gaze, and pinned her to her seat. She expected him to say something, to shock her with a ribald comment, as he had done on so many occasions, but he simply sat there and stared. And how he stared.

While a storm raged beyond the stern windows, a

tempest of a different sort played hell with her nerves. In those all-too-knowing green eyes danced the promise of passion, blazing with intensity, the heat of desire, searing her from top to toe, and some mystical but nonetheless potent quality that defied recognition. "What led you to become a courtesan?"

Sword to the heart with deadly precision. It was as though he had doused her in the icy waters of the Baltic. He could not know it, and Caroline would die before she admitted it to a living soul, including her friends, but Trevor had hurt her just then. It disappointed her that he found it so easy to believe her a doxy, that there could be no legitimate explanation for her presence on Dalton's ship. Yet how could he know, as he remained unaware of her shame?

"You do not have to tell me, if you do not wish it." Her captain canted his head and furrowed his brow. "But I should very much like to know your history, if you care to share."

"It is a long story that will keep." She mustered a brittle smile. "You should eat and get some rest."

"Perhaps, another night." He appeared so hopeful.

"Indeed." She nodded once.

"Promise?" He swallowed hard.

Why would he want to know anything of her? Their agreement required that their acquaintance end upon docking in London. Of course, if they were never to see each other again, what could it hurt to divulge her scandal, as long as names were omitted to protect the guilty? "I promise."

They passed the meal in uneasy silence, the spell of desire broken, destroyed by his query. Afterward, Caroline gathered the dishes and conveyed them to the galley. When she returned to the cabin, Trevor reclined in the bunk, so she rounded the room, dousing the lanterns, one at a time. For a long while she stood at bedside, stealing glimpses, in the staccato flashes of lightning, of the man who haunted her slumber, as he tossed and turned with the ship. Finally, she sat on the edge of the mattress, reached out, and rubbed his scalp, back and forth in a soothing rhythm. Soon, his breath came, slow and steady, in deep sleep.

But sleep came not for her, so she kept midnight watch over her captain.

Mulling the circumstances that had placed her on Dalton's ship, she could not escape her demons. In a chair she eventually moved to the windows, she perched, with knees bent, hugging her legs. Beyond the mullioned glass, the ocean swirled and soared, foamed and sprayed, as a menacing manifestation of the pain and humiliation that tormented her every waking hour. And the skies above, dark and angry, rumbled and roared, as if to say: *You can run, but you cannot hide.*

Well, she had run, and in so doing had discovered that hers was a useless endeavor.

But she was accustomed to useless endeavors.

As a child, Caroline had been painfully shy, even among her lifelong friends. When choosing sides for Lady of the Manor, she was always the last one picked. A bit of a Long Meg, she preferred the youthful activities more commonly associated with boys, not girls, and that won her little notice from the opposite sex. And although her parents had hoped her awkward tendencies would fade with age, they had merely exhibited themselves in other ways.

At parties and dances, she sheltered in the shadows, hugging the wall or a convenient plant stand. Other than her childhood chums, no one sought her company. Eventually, she excelled in her ability to blend into the background. And just when she had despaired of ever finding a husband, one man paid suit with disastrous results, and she again faded into the landscape.

Not so anymore.

Trevor wanted her, had made no secret of his desire. Whether or not he knew it, he had fed her a tempting, oh-so succulent morsel of all that was achievable between a man and a woman, and Caroline wanted more. Yet she could not escape the familiar doubt that kept her at bay. Had they met in London, with so many beautiful ladies and young belles from which to choose, would he have shown her the slightest interest?

But should it matter?

In the middle of the Atlantic, she was the only woman aboard his ship, better odds she would never enjoy. What if she surrendered? What if she set duty, honor, and responsibility aside and yielded her virtue to the one man determined to claim it?

Perhaps that was her golden opportunity to move up from the rear.

Perhaps it was her time to stand.

A knock at the door startled her and brought Trevor alert.

"Come." He yawned and stretched.

George peered inside. "Morning, Mistress Caroline." To the captain the first mate said, "Sir, we're a wee before the first watch."

"How does she go?" Trevor rubbed his neck.

"We're on course, but the storm has slowed us down," he explained. "Ya saw us through the worst of it, tho."

"Sound the bells." The captain swung his legs over the side of the bunk. "I will be at post for the duty roster."

"Aye, Cap'n," said George before exiting.

"Should I fetch your breakfast?" she asked.

"There is no time." Trevor glanced at Caroline, her pillow, and then scrutinized her, as she remained at her self-imposed guard detail before the stern windows. "Did you not come to bed?"

"I did." She lied. "But all this tossing about made it difficult to actually sleep, and I did not want to disturb you, so I rose early."

"How very considerate of you." He narrowed his stare as he stood. "By the by, I passed a peaceful night, thanks to your handiwork. Where did you learn that particular skill?"

"My mother suffers megrims." She admired his stunning backside. "Massaging her scalp alleviates the pain, and I thought it might help you rest better."

"You thought right." Naked, Trevor opened his locker and pulled out a fresh shirt, draped it over his shoulders, and speared his arms into the sleeves. Then he stepped into grey breeches. "You know, given all you have done for the men, I would like to do something for you. Is there anything you can think of that might make your trip more comfortable? Mind you, we are at sea."

A week ago, Caroline had demanded her own cabin, but the captain declared there was no additional space available. But that was then. "I believe a kiss in payment will suffice."

He stiffened his back. "Forgive me, mistress mine, but you are not very good at bargaining."

"Why is that?" she inquired in a coquettish little singsong.

He chuckled. "Because I would expect a courtesan to demand something of value."

"And you believe your kiss holds no value, silly man?" Yes, she flirted shamelessly with her captain.

"Well said, my lady." Trevor arched a brow. "As for your question, a kiss can be of estimable worth, depending on the outcome."

"Ah, but that has already been negotiated has it not?" she asked, as he tugged on his boots. Delighted by his expression of surprise, she giggled. "So, shall I have my due, or must I call the master-at-arms?"

With nary a word he swaggered near, slipped his hand beneath her hair, and gripped her by the nape. Pulling her close, their noses a scant inch apart, Trevor suddenly froze. For what seemed an interminable pause, but was only a few minutes, he simply studied her, and she availed herself of their respective positions to do the same of him.

Myriad emotions danced in his countenance, some evident, others impervious to interpretation. But for his hold, she would have faltered beneath his intoxicating investigation. And though he touched her in a single place, she felt him everywhere at once. And, oh, what she felt.

"I could stare a lifetime into your eyes," Trevor said in the softest whisper. "You are, quite simply, the most beautiful creature of my existence."

Caroline went up in smoke.

Locking her arms behind his neck, she kissed her captain for all she was worth and garnered a pleasurable groan as reward. She moved her lips in a sensuous symphony, her tongue in a naughty rhythm meant to entice, almost begging Trevor to want her as she wanted him. How thrilling it was when he cocked his head and deepened their kiss, taking her even further into sweet oblivion, hugging her so tight that she no longer knew where she ended and he began.

Until he set her on her heels.

"Duty calls," was all he said.

A few minutes had passed before Caroline discovered she, alone, occupied the cabin, and she leaned against the table. From top to toe, her body burned, ached with a need she tried but failed to understand or command. Fire seared a line from her stomach to that never before touched space between her thighs. Like the falling rain, remnants of their passion lingered in the air, pooling on the boards at her feet. Caroline pressed her fingertips to her lips, still throbbing from the force of their shared bliss, and wondered how different their situation would be had they met in society's ballrooms. But should the circumstances of their acquaintance matter if they were temporary? That he thought her a courtesan seemed insignificant.

A new truth dawned.

If she gave herself to Trevor, she would be ruined—unmarriageable. And her brother would never force her to wed. From where she stood, indulging in the physical delights her captain offered seemed the perfect answer to her quandary, not to mention the man was gorgeous and willing to cooperate.

If she were smart, she would seize the gift of fate.

The weeks at sea would carry her into the twilight of her life. When she was old and gray, she could recall a time when she was desired above all else, when one man wanted her, and her, alone.

But she had to act fast.

At the very least, she surmised she had three weeks to give herself to Trevor. Three weeks to accept what he offered. On the thought, a wicked shiver coursed her spine.

Caroline strolled to the stern windows. The storm had eased but the ocean still churned. The turbulent weather matched her mood: tumultuous, hedonistic, and wildly unpredictable. No, she would not turn away from the virgin taste of passion. Bold and unafraid, she would charge his field. With unflinching determination, she placed a damp palm to the cold glass, but the chilled surface had done nothing to cool the heat simmering within her. Staring at her reflection, barely visible, she smiled.

"I will do it."

CHAPTER FOUR

$\mathcal{A}$s the storm ebbed and flowed, the following days passed in a fog of frustration. Trevor rose early and returned late, trudging into the cabin with a scarce glance in her direction. Sometimes he ate, and sometimes he merely flung himself, fully clothed, on the bunk. Just when they thought they had escaped the tempest, it gathered steam and raged again. But that was not the only thing raging.

Just how should a gently reared virgin launch a full-scale seduction?

While Caroline remained entrenched in the belief that her tack was true and equally certain her most intimate gift was destined to be his, she had no real idea how to entice a man. So she had performed in a manner she believed would make her desirable under the present circumstances.

Awaiting his arrival and his appetite, she served every meal with care, she mended his clothes, and she kept their quarters neat and tidy. In short, Caroline had done what she could to prove to her captain how useful she could be in every way—except one.

Must she do everything herself?

She had thought it a simple matter of kissing, which should lead to more intense relations. It seemed a sensible, logical conclusion. She had kissed his forehead, his cheeks, and had even kissed Trevor on the mouth as he fell asleep. Her reward had been an impressive snore.

How should one initiate debauchery?

As the tempest wailed for the fourth day, Trevor stumbled through the door. Soaked, eyes bloodshot, and face pale as a ghost, he collapsed in a coughing fit. After stripping the wet clothing from his skin, Caroline hurried to dry him.

"I am so c-cold." He shuddered violently.

"I know, and I am sorry." She blotted his hair. "I wish there was something more I could do."

Instead of leading him to the table to eat, she steered him toward the bed and tucked two blankets about him. Trevor accepted her fussing without a word, which heightened her worry, because her naughty captain always had a ribald response. After fluffing the pillows, she brought him some food and was alarmed when he ignored her.

"You have to eat, Captain." She offered him a beautiful apple.

"I am not hungry." He pushed away the tray.

As he turned on his side, she pulled the blanket to his chin, and he shivered. When she placed the back of her hand to his forehead, her concern grew in epic proportions. "Trevor, I think you have a fever."

"What of it?" He snuggled beneath the covers.

"You are ill." And she feared for his health.

"It does not signify." He closed his eyes.

"I beg to differ." If a chill took hold, he could be in grave condition by morning. "Have you a doctor aboard?"

"He quit on the last run to Jamaica." Trevor snorted. "Got leg-shackled."

"Have you any medical supplies?" Her mind raced, as she recalled Dr. Handley's cures for similar maladies.

"None that I know of, and I am in no mood for conversation."

"Then you will have to make do with me." Perched at the edge of the mattress, she massaged his scalp, hoping a good rest would go far to allay a serious infection. Yes, it was only a hope, but hope was all she had without a physician or medicine. Hot liquids would help, but it was not yet safe to light the ovens.

To her chagrin, her captain quivered even after he drifted into dreamland, and she considered possible remedies. A thorough search of the cabin yielded one additional blanket and a Garrick coat, which she draped over him, and yet he shook. Somehow, she had to warm him, else she could not rest. And then she paused, as an uncomfortable truth dawned in her brain.

Caroline cared for Trevor.

Once before, she had wagered her heart and lost. Could she take that risk again? The answer, when it came to her, seemed so elementary. Looking to the heavens, she whispered, "Thank you."

In a flash, Caroline undressed. For two seconds, she considered getting into his bed without benefit of clothing. Perhaps that might prompt Trevor to do the deed. Her cheeks burned as she envisioned her bare skin pressed to his. Just as fast, she quashed the image. If the man wanted her naked, he could bloody well do the job himself.

She had her pride.

After pulling on her silk robe, the same one she claimed the night Trevor had taken her from Dalton's cabin, Caroline slid between the covers. Curling up to his back, she wrapped her arms about his sinewy mass, bending her knees and tucking her legs to his buttocks. Using her body heat, she comforted him. Yet what she offered exacted a high price, as the green-eyed dragon seduced her with no effort.

That Trevor could lie innocent as a babe in her embrace and evoke such sensations seemed the height of unfairness. If only the blasted storm would end. With one last check of her captain, Caroline settled amid the pillows and soon surrendered to the realm of nocturnal fantasy.

And was brought awake in the early morning hours by a blustery gale of a different sort.

"What in bloody hell are you doing?"

"Ho-hum." She yawned and rubbed her tired eyes. He could not be serious. "I would think it quite obvious. And if you recall, you brought me here, against my will, to be your mistress."

"Did you...did I...did we—" With an expression of sheer horror, Trevor shot from the mattress as if he had been scalded.

"Did we—what?" She giggled.

He shuffled his feet. "Did we do what you do in trade?"

"I beg your pardon, no such thing occurred, as I am not in the habit of molesting unconscious men." Caroline folded her arms and snorted in disgust. "You were cold, and I sought to warm you. Nothing more happened." And she was not happy about it, but she was not going to tell him.

Tense seconds ticked past.

"I must say I am perplexed by your reaction." She swallowed her trepidation and pressed her suit. "We have a mutually agreed upon bargain, which you have promised, on more than one occasion, would lead to mutual pleasure."

"I-I said that, and I m-meant it." He sounded none too convincing, and he looked uncharacteristically nervous. "But I am needed on deck."

"You are not leaving this room."

"Duty calls."

"But you had a fever."

"Perhaps, but I am fine now."

"Get back in your bunk. " She folded her arms. "You need rest."

"I beg your pardon." He jutted his chin. "You are neither my wife nor my mother, and I am not a child to be ordered about."

"Delighted to hear it, because only a child would take such unnecessary risks, when we need you healthy and at the helm." She slid from the mattress. "Now, shall I fetch your breakfast?"

"I do not want any deuced breakfast." A fortnight ago, his sneer might have frightened her.

Caroline managed to muffle her snicker as he marched toward the door. What was she to make of his odd behavior? That aside, she had to admit the man had a first-rate backside. But she had not thought the crew would share her opinion.

"Captain?"

"What?" He speared his fingers through his hair.

"May I suggest you put on some clothes before you report for duty?"

Two days later, with the wind in his hair, Trevor assumed his station and assessed the damage to the *Hera*. On occasion, the sun filtered through the clouds, bathing the ship in warm, golden light. The tempest had passed.

On the main deck, the boatswain directed the crew in a thorough inspection of the canvas and rigging, as the sailors engaged in a refit, of sorts, at sea. In the middle of the action, Mistress Caroline occupied a chair, which had to be a maritime first. Small tears in the main upper topsail required darning. Quick to volunteer, she all but danced a jig when, after a nod of approval from Trevor, the leader of the watch accepted her offer of help.

Turning his attention to the charts spread before him, he plotted their current position with lethal accuracy. The storm had blown them off course but was no cause for alarm, because he would make the necessary adjustments and have them navigating the Channel in no time. After consulting his compass, he affixed small notations to the maps.

"Hoist the topsail," the boatswain bellowed.

"Merciful heavens, Cap'n, will ya look at that?" the first mate inquired.

With a palm pressed to the small of his back, Trevor stretched. "What is it, George?"

The forenoon watch ran up the repaired canvas and positioned it on the mainmast. There was nothing out of the ordinary about that, yet his first mate seemed transfixed, facing skyward, hands shielding his eyes from the glare of sunlight.

Mirroring his stance, Trevor followed his gaze. Jaw clenched, breath seized, chest tightened, gut wrenched, and he could not move. High atop the mast perched Mistress Caroline, balancing on the footropes, as she laced the sail to the yard. Had the damn fool woman not recognized the danger?

She could be killed.

Summoning every ounce of control within him, he descended the companion ladder and stomped toward the boatswain. It took a Herculean effort to suppress the urge to shout his displeasure, because he feared she might fall if he yelled. Unable to contain the fury in his voice, he barked, "Bo'sun."

"Cap'n, let me handle this." Grabbing hold of his elbow, George stayed Trevor. "Mr. Boyle, bring the lady down —now."

The crewman peered at Trevor, flinched, and dipped his chin. "Ma'am, the men can finish from there."

"Are you sure?" the ladybird asked from above, as she pulled taut a stitch and then looped another.

That had done it.

"Mistress Caroline, present yourself this instant." Trevor gritted his teeth. A single misstep would suffice, and his charming courtesan would be nothing more than a bitter-sweet memory. Had she expected to sprout wings and fly?

"Aye, Captain." After a final inspection of her work, she nodded, and then shimmied through the shrouds, clutching the ratlines for stability. As soon as her feet touched the deck, Trevor grasped her arm, giving her no warning of the tumult twisting his insides.

"What—" She emitted a plaintive cry.

The knowledge that his errant mistress was safe should have appeased him. It had not. The fear, the sheer terror coiling in the pit of his belly found a convenient outlet in his hand, which he let fly with a resounding *smack* on her bottom. The impact stung his palm and buckled her knees, and she would have fallen forward had he not held her.

Yanking her upright, with his fingers digging into her shoulders, Trevor shook her hard, and the emotions welling inside him roared at once. "What in bloody hell do you think you are about?"

Shock and humiliation eclipsed her expression, and Caroline reached for him. "I was only—"

"Hie yourself below." Trevor pushed her away with such force that she tripped. "If I so much as see your face on deck, I will blister your hide."

With head held high, she walked to the steps leading to his quarters and descended.

Her absence should have made him feel better.

It had not.

For a long while he stood there, second-guessing the weight of his actions and the implication of the emotions that held him captive in some invisible, but nonetheless real, prison.

Trevor could not move, until he surveyed the angry, almost mutinous, sailors surrounding him. "Carry on," was all he could say.

At his station, he noticed for the first time the sweat on his brow. A vision of Caroline's lifeless form, prostrate on the deck, flashed before him, and he shuddered. As if teetering on a precarious precipice, he leaned forward and placed his hands on the rail for support. Closing his eyes, he desperately tried to regain control and composure.

"Do ya want to tell me what that was about?" George chucked his shoulder. "Trevor, for God sake, what's the matter with ya?"

"There is nothing wrong." He bit back the bile rising in his throat. "Everything is fine."

"And who the hell do ya think yer foolin' with that, old friend? Ya ought to look at yerself. Yer as white as a sheet, not to mention the death grip ya got on that rail."

"Mr. Todd, I will take the wheel." Opening his eyes, Trevor cursed his white knuckles. "You are relieved."

The helmsman abandoned the quarterdeck quicker than normal.

"Cap'n, what's goin' on with the chit?" The first mate inclined his head. "I've never seen ya lose yer mind over a woman. That's it, isn't it?"

"Let it go, George, and make yourself scarce." Compressing his lips, he focused on the horizon. "I will stand watch until dinner."

Although the sun blazed a wide arc in the sky, time stood still as Trevor reran the earlier scene through his mind, over and over again. In each instance, his chest pounded, his throat tightened, and he labored to breathe. Gazing at nothing, he wondered what had happened to him, and what he surmised had not inspired confidence. But he would rather face a court martial than explore the possibilities.

How fate had to be laughing.

When he plotted to kidnap Dalton's mistress, his only consideration had been the punishment exacted in recompense for young Randolph's prior slight. The scamp had levied the first shot, and honor demanded Trevor respond, in kind. But he was no greenhorn in the games men played, and he should have recognized the threat Caroline presented the minute he actually saw her. What in bloody hell had inspired him to take her? And how fast could he get rid of her? One thing was certain; he could not face her. Not yet. Not after his uncharacteristic outburst.

So Trevor ate lunch with the crew, thinking it best to give the dangerous doxy time to calm down before he returned to his cabin. He was in no mood to dice with a weepy female, but it was his unpredictable reaction to her tears that truly frightened him. When he joined her for dinner, he would have himself in hand, and she would be ready to accept his explanation, whatever that was, for what had transpired on deck.

Not that he felt the need to explain himself.

Despite her recklessness in the rigging, Caroline possessed uncommonly good sense, as evidenced by her commendable desire to help with chores. She had not fussed over herself and had never complained. Neither was she given to histrionics, a trait he found offensive in so many of her sex. As captain of the ship, it was his duty to dispense discipline when needed. The courtesan had taken an unnecessary risk and had been punished, as would any member of the crew. The excuse sounded plausible.

She would understand.

And so it was with that rationale he descended the steps leading to his quarters. The tension in his shoulders eased, and he relaxed. As he passed the galley, Trevor's cabin boy gave him pause.

"A word, Cap'n?"

"Aye?" As he looked forward to settling matters with his charming captive, he swallowed his impatience at the delay. "What is it, Billy?"

"It is the lady, sir." Staring at the tips of his boots, the lad shuffled his feet in obvious discomfort. "She did not eat lunch."

"I am sure everything will be fine now." At least, that was what he hoped. What on earth would he do if the woman were still sobbing, offer her a handkerchief? Trevor frowned. "Serve dinner at eight. We will be ready."

Surely half an hour was sufficient time to wash, explain his position to Caroline, and partake of a pleasant meal. And he had a few persuasive weapons at his disposal, if the lady proved difficult. Perhaps they would share a few conciliatory kisses. He smiled at the thought.

At the entrance to his chamber, Trevor twisted the knob and crossed the threshold. Closing the door, he turned around—and ducked. The object on a collision course with his head connected instead with the wood panel.

Whack

Before he could sound the alarm, he caught a glimpse of another item and barely avoided it. Moving into the room, Trevor crouched again. Adopting a defensive posture, with his arms shielding his noggin, he sidestepped another bombardment. "Caroline, stop it."

"Go to the devil!" She launched another volley.

"I demand that you cease this childish behavior and talk to me." He crouched.

"Childish, indeed." Her blue eyes glittered with fire and ice, as she catapulted an additional attempt to de-brain him. "I should think you would expect it, as you spanked me in front of everyone."

As he evaded another attack, Trevor lowered his hands. "So help me, if you throw one more thing, I will do it again."

With high dudgeon, she stomped her foot. "You would not dare."

Snorting in surprise, he could not stifle a chuckle. No woman had ever defied his authority, and at that precise moment, ill timed as it was, he decided he liked it.

"I would dare," he said in jest, because, devil take it, Trevor could not resist her.

"Who do you think you are?" Drawing herself up, looking every inch a blueblood, though he knew she was not, the demirep pinned him with a narrow stare. "You do not own me, and I am not a member of your crew to be ordered about or subjected to your abuse."

"Come now, we both know I did not hurt you." Damn, he wanted her.

"That may be, but I am not to be disciplined as one of your men." Bloody hell, she was ravishing when she argued with him.

"I will grant you that, but you are aboard my ship." And his Jolly Roger roused with a vengeance.

"We both know how I came to be here." She pouted.

In that he could not argue. Gazing on the beautiful ladybird, poised with a book in her grasp, no doubt considering another shot at his head, Trevor could not be mad at her. And he was trying, with every ounce of strength, to summon anger, indignation, or ire—anything to keep the mistress at a safe distance. Unfazed and unapologetic, she stood before him, breasts heaving, thick hair jutting wildly, cheeks flushed in fury, and all he wanted to do was kiss her silly.

Every inch of her.

But that would violate his promise, and revenge had been won at the expense of young Randolph. There would be no seduction tonight, because he had sworn a personal oath that he would not take Caroline to his bed.

"We will continue our conversation when you are ready to discuss this as an adult." He crossed to the washstand, peering out the corner of his eye on guard for another barrage. "Dinner will be served soon, so I suggest you settle yourself."

"Rot you, Trevor." Her chin rose to impressive heights. "And do not ever touch me again."

"I love that *governessy* tone, and are you not going to eat?" He grabbed a towel as she marched to the bunk. "The ovens are lit, and we will have warm fare tonight."

"I shall do as I please," Caroline snapped. "And you may go to the devil."

"Suit yourself, madam." Movement on the floor caught his attention, and he retrieved a brass candlestick holder. A brief search yielded the mate where it had come to rest. Then he found the hairbrush they had been sharing. The next discovery was a bar of soap and, at last, a leather-bound tome.

Pursing his lips, he forestalled the laughter dancing on the tip of his tongue. It would take no genius to know his little hellion would not appreciate his good humor, and he was no glutton for punishment.

Someday, when the seas no longer entertained his roaming spirit, and he decided to fulfill the duties of his title, Trevor resolved to find a mate with a more docile temperament. An agreeable spouse, one who would give him heirs and content herself with being seen—not heard, was just the woman for him.

At present, however, there was work to be finished. Respite from the evening's drama resided amid a stack of logs requiring entries. Rolling up his sleeves, Trevor served himself a healthy portion of stew, sat at his desk, and opened the first ledger.

Hours later, he consulted his timepiece and closed the last journal. Plagued by a lack of concentration, it had taken him twice the usual effort to complete his tasks, and his distraction remained where she had been before, during, and after dinner, curled on her side, facing the wall, in his bunk. Why had he not given her alternate accommodations?

Caroline had not made a sound, had not moved an inch. What was he supposed to do with her? Well, if the ladybird expected an apology; that was not in his vocabulary or his character. Convinced tomorrow would see her set right, he turned out the lamps, undressed, and slid into bed.

In the solitude of night, Trevor wondered what had possessed him to strike her? She was correct in her assertion that he had no right to punish her, because she was a guest, albeit, one taken by force, aboard his ship. Yet he had acted before he had realized what he had done. Why had he lost control? Why had her jaunt among the ratlines sent him spiraling in panic? It was a puzzle that begged a solution.

But he would rather walk the plank.

A NEW DAY DAWNED, and Trevor found, much to his everlasting frustration, that Mistress Caroline could be every bit as stubborn as a man.

"Morning, sweet." Determined to make amends, he waited on her, for a change, setting a tray loaded with covered dishes on the table. "Breakfast is served."

A feminine sniff was her only response.

Such intestinal fortitude should be confined to the male species.

After inhaling a plate of fruit, bacon, and toast, he gathered his charts and glanced at her motionless form. The damn difficult demirep caused him no end of torment. Then again, she was a woman. Making a mental note to break for lunch, he decided he would coax her into eating that afternoon.

But despite his good intentions, things had not worked out as planned. The winds picked up, and the sails needed to be reefed, so Trevor lunched with the first mate and the helmsman on the quarterdeck. They discussed their current course and the time it would take to reach London. Once they anchored at Deptford, he would put the beautiful courtesan ashore and run in the opposite direction—never to see her again.

"Cap'n, a word."

"Aye, George, what is it?"

"I passed young Billy in the galley." The first mate scratched his head. "He tells me yer lady hasn't been eatin'. She did not break her fast, and her noon meal went untouched, as well. Is she ill, Cap'n?"

Trevor frowned. If he let her, Mistress Caroline would be his downfall. Lovely or not, the ladybird could not maintain her tack, and she had not eaten since the previous morning. Why he cared he was not sure.

"She is not ill, George, she is just being a woman." He exhaled in frustration. "Take over here, as I am going below."

"Aye, Cap'n."

Had he the time, he would have taken issue with the broad smile on George's face. But he was determined to remain focused on the task at hand. In his mind, he formed a suitable argument he believed would bring the demirep around—until he found himself before the door to his quarters.

Caroline was as predictable as the weather.

Upon entering his cabin, Trevor noticed the lamps had not been lit, which gave him pause, because it was a menial chore she had assumed and performed with unfailing efficiency. A check of the bunk confirmed his suspicions. The small female form had not budged from where he left her. At the knock on the door, he flinched. "Come."

"Cap'n, I have your dinner." Billy bowed his head.

"Set it on the table and light the candles. We will serve

ourselves." Hell would freeze before Trevor allowed anyone to witness what he knew must be done. "That will be all, Billy."

"Aye, sir."

At the washstand, Trevor splashed cold water on his face, stalling until his cabin boy exited. He had never dealt with an angry woman. In the past, whenever a lady got fussy with him, he simply took his leave. As they were at sea, that was not an option.

At last alone with his quarry, he sat on the bed, rested his palm to her hip, and gave her a gentle nudge. "Caroline."

"Go away." She wrenched free.

Rubbing his temples, he summoned patience and willed himself to remain calm, as he tried again. "Please, hear me out."

Silence followed, but he was not sure that was a good sign. There ought to be a codebook to decipher such behavior. "When I disciplined you in front of the crew, my intent was neither to hurt nor embarrass you. Seeing you in the rigging...you could have been injured or—" He could not say it. "I swear you took ten years off my life."

Staring at the ceiling, Trevor raked a hand through his hair and wondered if things could be any more difficult. "I am sorry I struck you." He swallowed hard, as uttering the words left a bad taste in his mouth. It was hell being a gentleman.

But his stubborn lady had not moved, despite his generous concession. "Believe me when I say I sincerely regret what happened on deck." Again he prodded her. "Caroline, please look at me."

All of a sudden, she rolled on her back, stared him straight in the eyes, and struck an imaginary but powerful blow to his gut. Remorse ripped through Trevor in direct proportion to the agony he spied in her tormented blue gaze. Inside him, something fractured.

He had caused her pain.

But he could make it right.

"I am so sorry." He cupped her cheek, as the heartfelt apology fell from his lips without hesitation. "I never meant to hurt you."

With something between a sob and a sigh, she asked, "Then why did you strike me?"

That was an excellent question for which he still had no explanation, and it was nothing he wished to probe. "As God is my witness, I do not know."

"You gave me permission to help the watch." She thrust her chin.

"To mend a sail, yes." Tapping a finger to the tip of her nose, Trevor smiled. "Not to climb the rigging."

"But you did not forbid it." How had he known she would argue her perspective?

"Because I did not think I had to, as I have never had a woman in the ratlines." He could only pray she accepted his flanking maneuver. "You scared the deuce out of me."

"I see." Caroline furrowed her brow. "So you thought I was in peril?"

"Aye." He should have guessed that his mere expression of regret would not appease the curious courtesan. "And if something had happened to you, I could not live with myself. You must understand, I am the captain, and the men rely on me to lead. This ship and her crew are my responsibility, so I must maintain control if I am to preserve discipline. But when I thought you were in danger, I lost composure, which put everyone at risk. Do you comprehend what I am trying to say? Can you apprehend my predicament?"

"Yes." Caroline dipped her chin. "I think I can."

Her all-too-satisfied countenance gave him the chills. It was as if she knew the answer to a riddle he could not solve. Against his better judgment, he studied her lips. How he ached to claim her mouth, but Trevor knew he would not be satisfied with a simple kiss. "Am I forgiven?"

Again, she nodded once.

"Excellent." Standing, he sketched his most elegant bow. "I would be honored if you would consent to dine with me, my lady."

To her credit, Mistress Caroline devoured every morsel he put before her—and that was no small feat, as he was determined to have her consume something akin to the four meals she had skipped. Teasing and cajoling, he plied her with wine until she pushed away her plate and begged for mercy. "I can eat no more, Captain."

"Then I have a surprise for you." Trevor walked to the door. Holding it open, he hailed two of his crewmen, who carried steaming buckets, with which they filled the bath.

"Saltwater is so harsh." Caroline wrinkled her nose and rubbed her forearms. "My skin may never recover from this journey." After his crewmen took their leave, she crossed to the bathing area, dipped a hand, and then touched a finger to her tongue. In an instant, her eyes grew wide. "How did you—"

"From the storm, though I cannot take credit. It was George's idea to have the men lash a barrel to the railing." Rocking on his heels, he delighted in her look of wonder, because pleasing her pleased him. "Given your hard work, you have earned a boon. Were we in London, I would find a more suitable gift, one worthy of your contributions. At sea, I am afraid a freshwater bath is all I can offer."

Caroline rewarded him with a radiant smile that left him breathless. Perched on her toes, she wrapped her arms about his waist and favored him with a delicate kiss on the corner of his mouth, which scored a direct hit to his loins. "Thank you."

And he just stood there, like a giddy schoolboy, painfully aroused, with his Jolly Roger at full sail. Mortified by the burn of a blush in his cheeks, Trevor shuddered and cleared his throat. "I will be back in half an hour, and we will share a brandy."

But not our bodies.

CHAPTER FIVE

*T*rue to his word, Trevor returned to the cabin precisely half an hour later. Anticipation surged in his veins, as had the unholy serpent in his breeches, when he entered the chamber. Despite the internal dialogue in which he had engaged, while prowling the decks, as a reminder not to seduce the courtesan, he was ready to devour a dish of chestnut-haired mistress. It required every ounce of his heretofore-vaunted self-control to restrict his appetite to the standard fare on the table.

After dinner, they shared bits of conversation and a bottle of his best brandy, and Trevor marveled at Caroline's knowledge of the ship and life at sea. Endeavoring to gain more insight to her past, and why he was interested he could not say, he probed her history with the stealth of a seasoned spy.

In less than two blinks of an eye, he confirmed her father had served in the Navy and had died in battle. Her mother and brother lived in London, and she intimated her elder sibling currently sailed on an extended voyage, though

she withheld the particulars. Trevor wondered if her relation were apprised of her situation—of the circumstances,
however grievous, which had led her to the life of a paramour. In secret, he cursed a family that, regardless of their
plight, would allow a diamond of the first water to under-
take such an occupation.

To his surprise and delight, he discovered Caroline
possessed the benefit of a useful education. Well-versed in
current affairs, she had viewpoints on everything from war
tactics to the social and moral strictures placed on women.
What he admired more than he wished to admit, however,
was her fervent belief in her right to voice her opinion.

In silence, he mused it would take an indulgent man to
wed the spirited woman. Just as quick, he corrected
himself. Men never married their mistresses—at least, not
men of his stature. And then he pondered what made him
think of marriage in the first place.

"Tell me something." Trevor shifted in his chair and
studied the contents of his glass. "How did you come to be
in the employment of Dalton Randolph? What twist of fate
landed you aboard his ship?"

Fidgeting beneath his scrutiny, Caroline tugged at the
folds of her robe and gazed into the flickering flame of the
candle on the table. Myriad emotions danced across her
face. Pain. Sadness. And he would give anything to read
her thoughts. In that moment, he realized he had touched
on a sensitive topic and was about to change the subject
when she spoke.

"I was trying to escape." Her voice matched her melancholy expression. "I wanted to run away."

Fascinated, Trevor leaned forward in his chair. "From
what were you running?"

"The past." She compressed her lips.

Various possibilities danced in his head. Could Mistress Caroline be a thief or a criminal of some sort? What a ridiculous notion. He propped an elbow on the table. "What did you do?"

She swallowed hard. "I fell in love."

Punch to the gut, completely unexpected. Cupping his chin in his palm, he opened his mouth and then closed it. Though hers was not the confession he had foreseen, because he presumed her situation had everything to do with solvency, or lack thereof, it was no less arresting. "Who was he?"

"A man," she said, with a ghost of a quiver. "Just a man, but he was special to me. He courted me without reserve, led me to believe he was in love, and wished to marry. So I gave him my heart, and I had such high hopes." Caroline choked on a sob, and her hand shook as she lifted her balloon of brandy. "And he betrayed me."

As she set down the glass, Trevor reached for her, clasped her fingers, and squeezed a reassurance. She had not looked at him, but he spied tears pooling, glittering in her blue eyes. "What happened?"

Still, she stared unseeing. "As I awaited a proposal, he announced his engagement to another."

Befuddled, he scratched the back of his neck. "I do not understand."

"Do you not? He used me to gain the attention and acquiescence of another." Caroline impaled him with a steely gaze simmering with anguish. "He never wanted me."

"Good God," Trevor exclaimed in disbelief. "What of your brother? Surely he called out the blackguard?"

"He was at sea." Her chin trembled.

"He bloody well should have demanded satisfaction when he returned." Trevor smacked a fist to a palm.

"He wanted to, but I would not let him."

"Why the devil not?" Even now, he seethed on her behalf.

"Because it would have only prolonged my shame." She rocked, back and forth, as she clenched her jaw.

"So your family did nothing?" He checked his tone, as the ladybird had not deserved his ire. "The bastard should have been forced to wed you."

"I would not have him marry what he did not love. And my family settled with his. My brother's broken knuckles and my former suitor's black eye attested to it. Polite explanations were made to cover my affront." She gave vent to a self-mocking snort. "A rumor circulated to the gossipmongers that I had conspired with my friend to bring his chosen lady to the altar, and suddenly I was a veritable saint."

"And that made it all right?" Trevor wanted blood for the unforgivable slight.

"No." She studied the rug.

"Because you were in love?" He held his breath.

"Actually, I am no longer certain it was love." Tears streamed her cheeks.

He exhaled in relief. "Then what was it?"

"I suppose it was the possibility that, at last, someone could want me."

"Forgive my confusion, but you think yourself unattractive?" Positive the charming paramour fished for compliments, he snickered in skepticism. "My dear, you are beautiful."

"I know what I am, I know how I look, and I make no apologies." Caroline shot out of her chair, and it fell backward to the floor with a thud. "My face is not fair, I stand too tall—I am neither petite nor graceful, and I have opinions, which I can, will, and do share. I will not lie to myself, or anyone else, and pretend to be something I am not. Now, if you will excuse me, I should like to go to bed."

Stunned by the revelation, by the force of her estimable declaration, Trevor remained in his seat, unable to move, as she marched to the bunk they shared and eased to her side. If it were anyone else, he would have questioned the sincerity behind the bold affirmation. But the ladybird's trembling shoulders and soft sobs she tried, but failed, to stifle told him her emotional distress was genuine. It appeared Mistress Caroline carried wounds as deep as his own, a fact that unnerved him for reasons he understood too well. And in that instant, she earned from him something no woman had ever claimed.

Respect.

O<small>H</small>, why had she told him so much of her past?

The sun had dipped below the yardarm, and Caroline had not vacated the comfort and refuge of the bunk. So much had transpired, and she reeled from the unplanned events. After her embarrassing confession the previous night, she had hid in the cabin all day, wanting nothing more than to avoid Trevor's sympathetic stare.

She did not want his pity.

Something else nagged her conscience. She had not told him everything; she had held something back. If she intended to give her captain her most intimate gift, she wanted him to know the whole, complicated truth of her circumstances. She had to, really, because she cared for him. Of late she compared what she experienced with Lord

Darwith, her erstwhile suitor, with what she now felt for Trevor. In all honesty, there simply was no comparison, so she remained steadfast by her choice. And, if he would have her, if only on a temporary basis, she would surrender.

"Still in bed, my lady?" Holding a tray of covered dishes, the green-eyed dragon kicked the door shut and smiled in that boyishly sweet expression that never failed to give her gooseflesh.

"I did not sleep well." She stretched upright.

"Believe I already knew that." He frowned.

"Did I disturb you?" How she wished he would make love to her.

"Not much," he said, setting the tray on the table.

"I am sorry." She re-secured the robe. "Will you forgive me?"

"Only if you consent to have dinner with me." He winked.

Oh, he was in a playful mood, and she was in a mood to play. But as Caroline eased into her chair, she second-guessed her plan. Picking at her food, moving vegetables from one side of her plate to the other, she searched for some way to broach the subject foremost on her mind.

"What can I do?" Trevor asked, his forehead a mass of furrows.

She snapped to attention. "I beg your pardon?"

"How can I make it better?" He seemed so earnest.

Cursing her suddenly absent courage, she contemplated his question. "I want to know about you."

As her host studied his clasped hands, Caroline reflected on her request. "Perhaps—"

"I suppose I should begin with what I love most." Trevor inclined his head and smiled. "Sailing."

Intent on learning all she could about the handsome

captain, before she divulged her last secret, she gave him her full consideration.

In a few short minutes, Caroline realized Trevor was a man very much like her brother. He hired experienced seamen, no landsmen, he cared for his crew, and his men respected him. Possessing knowledge of sailing that would rival her elder sibling's, he had made the rank of captain in the Royal Navy at the ripe old age of six and twenty.

"Tell me about the sword." She motioned with her hand. "The one hanging on the wall. I noticed it the night you brought me here, and if I recall correctly, you said it has been in your family for years. Does it have a history?"

"Indeed, it does, and it has a mate." Balancing the heavy decanter, he refilled their glasses. "But for you to understand the significance, we must journey to another time." Trevor tapped his fingertips together. "The weapon dates to the eighth century. It was a gift in observance of a marriage arranged to solidify ties between two warring factions."

"Your ancestors?" Fascinated, Caroline itched to press for more details, but something in his expression warned her she treaded dangerous waters.

"Exactly." He nodded once. "The images engraved on the hilt, Adam and Eve, were meant to symbolize a new beginning—a land of peace. The original pair were handed down from one generation to the next."

"But you said there were two." Puzzled, she scanned the vicinity. "What of the other?"

"Ah, yes. Eve." His face took on a harsh, hardened appearance. "Look closely, and you will notice the figure etched at the base of the hilt is male. The sword I have is Adam. When I was five, my mother took Eve and fled to France with her lover. I presume she needed money, because once on the Continent, she sold it. I have tried to recover the heirloom, but my solicitor has never been able to locate the weapon."

"Excuse me." Caroline blinked. "Did you say your mother abandoned you and your father?"

"Aye." He sighed. "Bear with me, because I was very young when it happened, but it began with another arranged marriage. There were no treaties signed or wars to be averted. It was the wish of a couple of old men, one being my grandfather, to unite their families, so they betrothed their eldest at birth."

"Your parents?" she asked, in shock.

"Eventually." He dipped his chin. "My father loved my mother, of that I am sure, but I do not believe she returned his affection. As was their duty, they wed, and I was conceived. About five years later, a distant relative came to stay with my parents. Whoever he was, I do not know." Trevor shrugged. "My mother fell in love with the man, and they engaged in an affair. When my father found out, he confronted them, and they sailed to France."

"Your poor father." Caroline rose from her chair and walked to him. "And you were only five, just a babe."

"I was sent away shortly thereafter to distance me from the humiliation and disgrace." Trevor quirked one corner of his mouth. "As for my sire, he drowned his sorrows in a bottle. I was at sea when he died. I hardly knew the man."

She placed her hand on his arm. "I am so sorry."

"Do not pity me." He glared.

How ironic was it that his thoughts mirrored her own.

"I do not pity you." Caroline cupped his cheek. "But I can sympathize with your disappointment."

So much anger.

So much pain.

Now she understood the gruff exterior, and why Trevor reminded her of someone very familiar. "Are we not a pair?"

"So it would seem, sweet lady."

Their eyes met, held.

And there it was, the promise of passion, igniting in a flash and burning in a steady blaze of heat and hunger in her belly. Trevor kissed her palm, and she was certain her knees would buckle at any moment. Lips parted, his tongue teased her flesh, his teeth nipped ever so gently. And through the hazy fog of lust, a reminder echoed in her brain.

At last, it was time to share the truth. "Trevor, there is something I would tell you."

"Now?" He looked his surprise.

"Yes." She rolled her shoulders. "You need to know—"

"*Boarders! All hands on station!*" The panicked call came from above deck. "*Boarders off the starboard bow!*"

Outside, cries of alarm from the crew rattled the timbers.

"Bloody hell." With a calm she found unnerving, Trevor released her, strode to his locker, and swung the door wide. He retrieved a sheathed sword and a large oak box with brass hinges, then walked to the desk and set the items on the blotter. After rummaging through the top drawer, he produced a small key, which he promptly used to unlock the box. Inside, on a bed of blue velvet, rested two perfectly matched flintlock dueling pistols.

"Do you know how to use a firearm?" he asked, as he lifted one and held it for her inspection.

"Yes." Caroline had not hesitated. Reaching out, hand shaking, she took what she considered an instrument of war.

"I will send Billy to stay with you, as he is too young and small to fight." Lethal weapon in his grasp, Trevor placed a finger under her chin and brought her gaze to his. "Lock the door behind him and permit no one entry but me. Do you understand?"

She managed to nod despite her ever-increasing fear. In a move that did not inspire confidence, he bent his head and set his lips to hers in a bruising kiss—as if he expected never to see her again.

And then he was gone.

For a few seconds Caroline stood dumbfounded. Overhead, pounding footfalls evidenced a furious clash on deck.

"Excuse me, ma'am." Billy shuffled into the cabin, wearing a scowl that she found quite amusing. "Cap'n ordered me to wait here with you."

"Yes, and we will do as he commands." She locked the door just as a hiss rent the air.

From the locker, Billy claimed another sword. "Oh, I say, I could skewer a few bloody pirates with this."

She flinched. "Now, just a minute, the Capt—"

"Hell's bells, but I am a man not a boy." He cast a mighty scowl.

"Billy, please, you must stay with me." Caroline raised her hands, palms facing outward, when the lad pointed the unsheathed, polished steel straight at her.

"You can sit here, if you want, but I am going to fight." With that, he unlocked the door, flung it wide, and charged into the hall.

"Billy, come back." She just stopped herself from giving chase. Quickly, she tucked the pistol in the waistband of her breeches and marched forth as a soldier heading into battle.

For all her brother Blake told her of combat at sea, nothing could have prepared Caroline for the scene she confronted. Crouched in the opening that led below decks, she surveyed the skirmish, unsure how to respond. "Oh, God, I never should have come up here."

The grating sound of metal striking metal reverberated in an eerie mosaic of sound as the fight reached a fevered pitch. Bursts of silver flashed in random patterns as lamplight flickered off the flat of the blades. The boarders had thick, overgrown beards disguising the lower half of their dirt-smudged faces. Scarves tied about their heads kept matted hair out of their eyes. What teeth the enemy had were yellow and rotting, and their clothes were torn and filthy.

They were pirates.

Just then, Billy went down, his body landing in a limp mass on the wooden planks in front of her. Caroline swallowed the urge to scream, until she met a menacing gaze, and then she choked out a plaintive cry. A chill traversed her spine as the rogue licked his lips, and he signaled his intent to engage her when he raised his sword.

"Well, well. What 'ave we 'ere?" The blackguard's voice slithered like a snake over her skin.

Since it was too late to change her tack, Caroline snatched the sword from Billy's lifeless form and stepped forward, lunging hard. Figuring her only hope for survival to be an aggressive attack, she drew on her fencing skill, derived from years of her brother's tutelage, and thrust in rapid succession.

Pitting her acumen against the pirate's brute strength proved a wise gamble. It was obvious the man had no formal training, unlike her. Where he was clumsy, she was agile. While his thrusts had power, hers had better aim. Her technique kept him off balance and more than compensated for her lack of brawn. Until she caught her adversary with a vicious riposte across the forearm, drawing blood.

After glancing at the red stain growing around the tear of his sleeve, he looked at her and growled. "You will pay for that."

Faced with a sudden punishing barrage, Caroline found herself on the defensive. The force of the villain's strokes proved impossible to parry, because she had not the strength to turn aside his weapon. Step by perilous step, he backed her into the railing. With a leap to the side, she changed directions, but it proved a temporary respite.

The rapid salvo resumed.

Caroline weaved left then right, trying to regain the upper hand. Another body hit wood, that time a pirate. Jumping, she slammed hard into another male form.

"Devil take it, woman, have ya lost yer mind? Get out of the way!" George shoved Caroline aside and took after the scoundrel she had been fighting.

She hugged the rail as around her the melee raged. The stench of blood mixed with sweat weighed heavy in the air, and corpses littered the deck. How many were dead or injured she could not know.

"You there, *en garde.*"

"You must be joking," was all she could reply.

To her amazement, she once again found herself engaging another foe. At first glance, she thought he was a member of the *Hera* crew. Clean-shaven, well dressed compared to his cohorts, he was younger than most. Still, his skill far surpassed that of her previous opponent. And as before, she was forced to retreat.

Having dispensed with his combatant, George pushed her clear and charged the boyish bounder. As a spectator, it had not taken long for her to realize the enemy maneuvered the first mate near one of the downed crewmembers.

Caroline tried to shout a warning, but everything

happened so fast. George stumbled, tripped, and fell back-wards, and his weapon rolled to the side, beyond reach. In horror, she gasped as the young pirate lorded over the first mate and, raising his sword high, prepared to thrust. At that precise moment, she recalled the pistol tucked in her waist-band. Without a second thought, Caroline grabbed the wooden butt and leveled the barrel. As the blackguard lunged, she fired.

The shot echoed, long and loud.

All activity came to a halt, and an uncanny quiet fell on the ship. The villain froze, a look of shock etched on his youthful face. The only sound heard was the clang of his sword as it hit the deck, then a thud as his body collapsed. Scanning the sundry crowd, she located Trevor on the bow, staring daggers at her.

A sinister laugh broke the silence.

The source was a rogue who had been dueling with her captain and was without doubt the leader of the motley crew. Unlike the others, he wore a white linen shirt, black breeches, and a beautifully shined pair of Hessians. He, too, was clean-shaven, but that had done little to dispel his menacing guise. A long, jagged scar traced from his left ear and across his cheek, disappearing under a leather patch adorned with a large ruby, concealing his eye. His ebony hair hung loose around his chiseled features. Though he might have been handsome at one time, he appeared a dangerous adversary.

"Have we met?" the pirate inquired. "You remind me of someone."

"No," Caroline responded, careful of her words. "I assure you, it is not possible."

"*Mon Ami*, you surprise me. Now you hire women in your crew?" The stranger eyed her as if she was wearing nothing more than her chemise. "I must say I approve of your taste. Throw in with me, and together we will wreak havoc on the seas."

Trevor snorted. "I will see you in hell first, Cavalier."

Caroline shivered as the rogue leader continued to stare. In a flash, he leapt beyond Trevor's reach and prowled in her direction, parting the adversaries who kept their weapons at ready. With a countenance of confidence, he gave his attention to the prone figure at her feet.

His smug smile faded.

Kneeling before his fallen comrade, he brushed a lock of hair from the dead man's forehead. When his gaze met hers, the humor was gone. Slowly, ever so slowly, he stood and brought the tip of his blade to her chin.

"Cavalier, do not harm her." Surrounded and outnumbered, Trevor maneuvered from behind several swords.

"He was my brother," Cavalier said through gritted teeth.

Paralyzed with fright, jolted by what she had done, Caroline wrapped her arms about herself. "I did not know," she blurted. "I am so sorry."

"Not yet." Though his voice was calm, his tone was laced with sarcasm and malevolence. "But you will be."

"Lanterns, *Mon Capitaine!*"

A sea of heads turned in unison. The orange glow of ship lamps danced like fireflies on the horizon.

"It appears luck is on your side, *Ma Puce*. I am a wanted man in more countries than you could ever hope to count. Back to the ship." Cavalier waved to his men. "We shall fight another day."

The pirate stopped short, as the last of his band of villains disappeared over the railing. A scowl of pure evil invested his features as he sketched an elegant bow.

"*Cherie*, do not fear I have forgotten you. I promise to

come for you one day, when I shall avenge my brother, but your death will be neither easy nor swift as was his." He smiled, and her gut clenched. "You will pleasure me at length until I tire of you. Then my men shall ride you till your back breaks."

"I did not want to hurt him." A shiver of terror nipped at her nerves, yet Caroline sensed there was more to his threat. "But he would have killed George."

"Brave lady." Cavalier narrowed his eyes. "Ever wonder how it feels to end your life as fodder for sharks? To be alive when they make that first tear at your flesh? To suffer the pain and agony, as they rip muscles from bone, knowing there is no escape? That is the death I promise you." With that, he raised his sword in mock salute and was gone before Trevor could reach him.

It was then Caroline noticed the malevolent silhouette. The lamps were guttered, rendering the vessel almost invisible. As a thief cloaked by a moonless night, the pirate ship stole away.

Trevor stood at the rail of the starboard bow, and she knew he was angry from the rigid set of his shoulders. With tentative steps, Caroline approached. "What is she called?"

"*Black Morass.*"

She waited, hoping he would say something, anything to alleviate the terror gnawing at her belly. When he proffered no such comfort, she turned and assessed the casualties. Grabbing the closest sailor, Caroline barked orders as if she were the captain.

"Fetch any medical supplies you can find. I need hot water, fresh not sea, and all the bandages in store. Oh, and get me something to clean the wounds. Is there any salve?" Before the poor salt could answer, she continued, "If we do not have salve then bring the captain's brandy—"

Trevor appeared at her side, and she almost screamed.

"Not one word." Caroline lifted a hand to forestall what she had no doubt was an impressive tirade. "Billy took your sword to join the fight. And for some reason I will never fathom, I ran after him. Right now, these men need attention, so you will have to beat me later." She paused. "Oh, and I need you to help me get the injured below decks. We cannot leave them here, and it would be easier to treat them if they were in one place."

With an expression of befuddlement, and green eyes shooting sparks, Trevor organized his crew. But she had to know, had to ask the question foremost on her mind, so she wrenched his shirtsleeve. "Who was that man?"

For a pregnant moment, he held her stare. "The one you killed was Henri Cavalier."

"I cannot think of that now." Caroline bit her lip and shook her head. "And the other one?"

"Jean Marc Cavalier." He rubbed the back of his neck.

She searched her memory. "I have never heard of him."

"Not surprising. He is the most ruthless pirate on the seas." Folding his arms, he frowned. "Cavalier slaughters crews and fires captured ships on a whim. He has been known to sell women and children as slaves on the Barbary Coast."

"Oh, dear." Caroline stared at her bloody hands. "And they were brothers?"

"They were."

She inhaled a shaky breath and rolled her shoulders in a failed attempt to dispel the shiver born of something more than the cool night air. "Will he come for me?"

"Aye, or die trying."

PERCHED at his station on the quarterdeck, Trevor stared at the yellow streak on the horizon heralding the new day. He had never made it to his cabin the previous night, because he preferred to remain on deck in case of another attack. Though it had not seemed likely that Cavalier would return, he was not going to take any chances.

He had also waited for Caroline.

Since she had not appeared on deck, it was safe to assume she still tended the wounded.

"Cap'n?"

"Aye, George." He glanced at his first mate. "What is it?"

"I can take over here, till Mr. Todd comes on duty." The crusty salt scratched his cheek. "The men are well at hand, so why do ya not get some rest?"

"I believe I will take you up on your offer." Trevor relinquished the helm. "What is the butcher's bill?"

"Seven dead. Three are ours, including Billy, and four bloody pirates. Eight wounded but yer lady says none serious. She's sleepin' in a hammock in the fo'c'sle so's to be near the men. Do not worry 'bout her though, the crew are watchin' over her." George paused. "Cap'n, she saved my life, ya know. That bastard woulda' killed me if she hadn't shot him."

Trevor clenched his jaw. "I know."

"Go easy on her." The first mate furrowed his brow. "She's puttin' on a brave face, but I seen her eyes. She's hurtin'."

"I know that, too." He had to deal with the willful paramour, but it could wait. And he was tired, bone-dead weary. "See to it she eats something when she wakes. I am turning in."

Trevor skipped down the companion ladder and proceeded to his quarters without delay. When he gained the comfort and quiet of his sanctuary, he collapsed, fully clothed, on his bed.

It was late in the afternoon when he woke. A quick check of the cabin told Trevor that Caroline had not returned from her makeshift infirmary. True to form, he knew, without doubt, the quirky demirep would work herself to exhaustion.

Muttering a curse, he stretched, swung his legs over the side of his bed, rose, and crossed the room. At the door, he called for Billy to prepare a bath and then remembered that his cabin boy was dead, so he saw to it himself. An hour later he was back at his station, the wind drying his hair, fulfilling a duty he'd always considered a sorrowful shackle of command.

Under a glorious blue sky, with a lilting breeze nipping at the sails, the crew stood at attention, clean-shaven, and neatly dressed for the burials. A plank was raised atop the starboard rail. Standing on either side, four men held the Union Jack high as a cloak of honor for each fallen comrade, save the pirates. Trevor recited a short prayer.

"I hereby commit these bodies to the deep. Ashes to ashes, dust to dust." He closed the Book of Common Prayer. At his instruction, the crew offered a final salute.

Wrapped in canvas, the remains were laid to rest. One by one, the shrouds slipped beneath the surface of the sea, disappearing into the indigo grave below.

Trevor noted his mistress had not witnessed the solemn ceremony. Having been informed she was asleep, he ordered she not be disturbed, because he thought it best to spare her any reminder of the deaths from the attack. The sun was beginning to set when she skittered toward the passageway leading to his cabin.

How he longed to go to her, to comfort her, to make love

to her. How he wanted Caroline, ached to hold her in his arms, if only to reassure himself that she was unharmed, that she was still very much alive. Despite his bloody good intentions, he was, once again, changing his tack. Hell and be damned, he would have her.

CHAPTER SIX

*R*insing the last soap from her skin, Caroline sighed and sank deeper beneath the water. It felt so good to wash away the dried blood and grime she had picked up from her makeshift infirmary. Resting her head against the back of the tub, she closed her eyes and wiggled her toes. Instantly, images of mayhem and carnage flashed. Once again, the tears burst forth.

She killed a man.

With legs bent, she pressed her forehead to her knees and succumbed to her despair, sobbing uncontrollably.

"Caroline."

Through the misery, her name came to her on a whisper, and she peered up to discover Trevor, standing in the cabin. She should have been embarrassed, but she wasn't. She should have made some attempt to cover herself, but she did not. Instead, without hesitation, she stood, stark naked and soaking wet, jumped from the bath, and ran straight into her captain's outstretched arms.

Desire danced as fire in the tumultuous depths of his emerald eyes, and she met his soul-searing kiss with a hunger to match his own, tearing his shirt aside to press her palms to his heated flesh. Incapable of rational thought, her responses were innate, as virgin fervor navigated her through erotic seas. She clutched his shoulders and then speared her fingers through his thick hair. It was as though her body had a will of its own, as if her life, her very existence were at stake.

And Trevor was her salvation.

Caroline was already in bed when she realized they had moved, and her captain hovered as a conqueror gazing on his latest spoils. Conscious of her nudity, she reached for the covers and began to slide beneath.

"Tonight," Trevor said as he pulled the sheets from her grasp and flung them aside, "let me be your blanket."

Oh, dear.

After divesting himself of his shirt, he sat at the edge of the mattress and pulled off his boots—the breeches soon followed. The tide had turned, and Caroline knew the time for going back had passed.

For a scarce moment, opposing emotions flickered. Honor, loyalty, responsibility to herself—and her family—welled. Only to be supplanted by unquenchable desire, impossible to abate. That was her chance, her golden opportunity.

Caroline would not shy away from love, and how she loved her captain.

Gathering her wits, she reminded herself he thought her an experienced paramour. Would not a woman of said profession enjoy the magnificent display of masculine physique? She hoped aggressive ogling would temper her shock at seeing the front of a naked adult male again. Nervous anticipation bloomed, and she prayed he would not notice. Though she knew little of the occupation, Caroline was certain no true ladybird would swoon at the sight of a—

And there it was, just as she had remembered.

To her relief, when Trevor faced her in all his fully aroused glory, his cocky grin evidenced that he had misinterpreted her reaction as a declaration of his unrivaled endowment. Perhaps he would understand if she fainted.

"Are you ready for me, darling?" he inquired in a tone that held more than a hint of mischief.

The man had to be joking, and how on earth was she supposed to answer?

I do not know where I end and the bed begins.

I feel as if I am about to be ill.

I am terrified.

Just as quick, Caroline corrected herself, because Trevor would never hurt her. Biting her lip, she nodded an affirmative, because she doubted her ability to utter coherent words.

With the exuberance of a boy, her seducer joined her on the bunk, stretched beside her, and claimed her mouth in fierce plunder. With his fingertips, he traipsed a sensuous trail from her hip to the curve of her waist, along her ribcage, and traced circles on her breast, setting her skin ablaze and her head spinning. When he pinched her nipple, she moaned her appreciation.

Trevor broke their kiss and caught her wrist. "Touch me." Guiding her hand, he led her to his hardened length.

As forged steel encased in the softest velvet, it was a miracle of flesh unlike any she had ever seen or felt. Unsure what to do, Caroline tightened her grip. "Show me...how you...want it."

His expression of bewilderment, her captain tutored her without complaint or comment. Then, to her amazement, he closed his eyes, set his forehead to hers, his face betraying unfettered ecstasy, and he groaned.

The mere sound of his pleasure tugged at her gut, inside her some unnamed force built, slowly at first, then charging to the fore. Raw hunger nipped at her senses, and sweet fire sang in her veins. That she could wield such power over him enthralled and inspired her, at once. With wanton abandon, Caroline drew imaginary figures around the swollen tip and caressed him in an urgent rhythm.

"Enough." Trevor halted her play. "Else this will be over before we get started."

But she could not stop.

Desperate to know his body, to learn more in the elusive realm of desire, Caroline ran her hands across his rippled chest and skimmed his ribs. To her abiding delight, Trevor took her breast into his mouth, licked and suckled, teasing her without mercy. Then he turned to the mate, and the decadent torment began anew. Slowly he eased down, worshipping every inch of her with his lips.

Offering herself with no inhibition, she arched into him. When Trevor reached her navel, he tickled her with his tongue until she squirmed and lauded his finesse with a sultry moan. He moved lower still, wedging between her legs. His fingers sifted through the curls at the apex of her thighs, bringing her alert. With light strokes, he parted her most intimate flesh and bent his head.

It was inconceivable to be kissed—there.

Fearing she would shatter into a million pieces, she held her breath. With eyes fixed on the wooden beams overhead, she stared, mouth agape, tears streaming her temples, as passion tasted her for the first time. To be wanted, to be desired, had been unknown—until now, and the experience was more beautiful than anything she could have imagined.

In that moment, Caroline truly surrendered.

Trevor could do with her as he wished, and she would not resist. When he probed her with a finger, she cried out, and her loins erupted in flames that spread as a firestorm, consuming her from head to feet. Wave upon wave of sumptuous heat sashayed over her skin, and a strange yet enticing hunger blossomed in her belly. Higher and higher, Caroline soared to a dizzying pinnacle.

And then it happened.

Reality suspended, time stood still. Then the world turned, and her last vestiges of sanity shifted with it. She screamed, but it came as a mere echo to her ears through a haze of lust. Drowning in a tide of sensuous pleasure, the gently reared society miss was reborn a woman through incomparable release.

As long as Trevor lived, he would never forget Caroline's face as it looked now. Dew-kissed, flushed, lips swollen, and eyes half-open, her expression so abandoned, so willing— and so trusting. Foreign emotions dammed his throat, threatening to choke him, and he was positive he had just discovered the unimaginable talent of the charming courtesan. She could make a man feel as if he were the most desirable creature in existence.

As if he were her first and last lover.

Never in his life had he wanted anyone so much. He had tried to deny her, tried to resist her. She had been aboard his ship for more than two weeks, sharing his cabin no less, and he had yet to bed her. But the more he spurned his desires, the stronger they grew. Now he was engulfed in need, a need only Mistress Caroline could fill.

Plagued by a burgeoning ache in his loins, he sought to ease his arousal in the way he knew best. But before he yielded his faculties, Trevor feasted once more on the pliant flesh between her legs. She was the sweetest morsel he had ever sampled, and the throaty hum of her appreciation spurred him. Flicking her taut nub with his tongue, he laved and suckled, until the last threads of control fled him, and he ravished her with his mouth.

Again, she cried out his name, and her body went rigid with completion. He could wait no longer, because he had to have her. In seconds, Trevor settled himself over her and lowered his hips. With one powerful thrust, he sheathed himself fully inside her. She screamed, but it was a wail of agony, not ecstasy, and his heart stopped.

It was impossible to miss the filmy barrier, proof of her virginity that he had breached.

He froze, his flesh held deep within hers. *"Caroline?"*

She lay motionless beneath him, and though her eyes were squeezed shut, tears seeped from the corners, evidencing her distress. And while his mind shouted denial, Trevor suspected he had just secured his place in hell.

But it was unthinkable.

Images played in his head, again and again. There was her shy grin that never failed to disarm him, foam teasing the rose-tipped peaks of her breasts as she had slumped forward in the bath, in an effort to shield herself from his gaze. He recalled the winsome blushes that colored her cheeks every time he undressed in front of her, the way she shivered in his embrace when he kissed her, and how she had swooned during his first attempt at seduction. Hints and indications of her innocence had been everywhere, had he chosen to see them.

An irrefutable certitude dawned on him slowly—no man had ever occupied the place where he now rested. Caroline was well and truly his, because he had claimed her virtue. The knowledge worked on him in ways Trevor could not understand.

In that instant, everything changed.

Obsessive possessiveness surged within him. Whatever their stations, whatever their lot in life, for eternity, he swore he would be the only man to touch her thus. When they returned to London, he would bestow on her gifts and a home worthy of the treasure she had given him. A contract would be drawn to ensure he remained her sole benefactor, because he would not share his bounty.

"Shh." Descending to his elbows, he framed her face in his hands. Pressing his lips to her forehead, he tried to calm her. "It is all right, love. I promise it will pass."

He kissed her eyelids, the tip of her nose, the apples of both cheeks, and then took her mouth in a gentle caress. Desperate to reassure Caroline that he would not hurt her anymore than he already had, Trevor waited with patience of which he had not thought himself capable.

After a few minutes, she relaxed, wound her arms about his neck, and twined her fingers in his hair. When Caroline pulled him close, returned his kiss, intensified it, he pumped his hips. In deference to her delicate state, Trevor withdrew, smooth and unhurried, flexing his spine, and repeated the same conservative cadence. Moving on her, inside her, in monotonous sweeps, he schooled her in an intimate invasion.

Primitive lust, raw desire gnawed at his senses and threatened to devour him. But something in the dark recesses of his conscience stayed the beast within. Like the finest French brandy, he savored her tender flesh, wallowing in the tightness of her succulent, untried sheath.

With a look of wonder, she said, "Oh, my."

"Oh, my, indeed." Trevor could not help but smile, as he reached for her knee.

Dipping her chin, Caroline followed his lead, and he was surprised to discover a woman could blush from her head to her toes. With his arms braced, he hovered and quickened the pace, thrusting deeper and harder. And she was right there with him, every step of the way, feeding his hunger, matching it with her own. As he was about to lose himself, he stopped.

"No." She scored her nails to his shoulders.

Trevor chuckled at her unabashed demand. "Enjoying yourself?"

"*Yes.*" She averted her gaze, heeled his flanks, and turned red as a tomato.

Since no gentleman would leave a lady wanting, Trevor gave her his weight and seized her lips in a savage attack. Wrapping his arms under her shoulders, he cradled her head in his hands. Holding her firm in his grip, he set a feverish pace, pumping his hips in an urgent measure. Beneath him, Caroline tensed as she peaked and gave her scream into his mouth.

The decadent ripples of her climax seduced him, and he teetered on the precipice of heaven on earth. Thrusting once more, he spilt his seed in what seemed an endless rush of pure, unadulterated pleasure.

A FEW HOURS LATER, Trevor woke to the flutter of delicate kisses on his skin. It took him a few seconds to marshal his wits and realize where he was and, more importantly, the identity of the woman sprawled underneath him. Propping himself on his elbows, he gazed into Mistress Caroline's baby blues.

"Hello." In the dim light of the few lanterns still burning, she favored him with a radiant smile.

"Well, hello, yourself." He chuckled.

"I am starved." She bit her lip, and he would wager his ship that her cheeks were flushed a captivating pink. "Are you hungry?"

"As a matter of fact, I am." He wrinkled his nose. "But I believe our dinner will be cold as ice."

"I do not care." Her eyes flared. "I am famished."

Despite inclinations to the contrary, Trevor withdrew from her body, eased from the bed, and retrieved his robe. A small, crimson stain on the sheets caught his attention. "Perhaps you should clean yourself."

Covering her breasts with her arms, Caroline scooted to the edge of the mattress, accepted the familiar swath of silk he held for her, stood and cinched the belt at her waist. "Oh, dear. I ache where I did not know I could ache." With tentative steps, she walked to the washstand, as he pulled on breeches.

"I am afraid that is a common occurrence." He lifted the lids and assessed the state of their dinner. As suspected, the fare had cooled. "Well, it was stew, but it does not look quite right."

"Try stirring it."

Frowning, Trevor picked up a spoon and swirled the congealed goo. "I do not think it is helping."

Caroline approached the table. "You are right." She giggled. "I have seen paste that appeared more appetizing. Here, separate the meat and vegetables from the gravy."

He pulled out a chair. "Shall we dine?"

Over a bland meal, they shared bits of conversation. And though his companion was as entertaining as ever, several questions reverberated in his brain, but Trevor was unsure how to broach the subject.

What had a naked virgin been doing aboard Dalton Randolph's ship?

He had believed Caroline was Randolph's mistress. After the events that had transpired between them, Trevor knew he had been wrong. Yet the lady had never refuted his assumption. Had her maidenhead been auctioned?

Who was she, in truth?

What was her background?

Why had she not confided in him?

The source of his conundrum stood, leaned forward to collect his empty plate, and the folds of her robe gaped, affording a splendid view of her bare bosom. A wicked erection roared to life, and his heartbeat quickened. He grasped her wrist and took the dish from her hand. "Leave it."

"Did you not have enough?" She blinked. "I have some potatoes."

"I do not want food." He lowered his chin.

Casting him a shy grin, she acquiesced as he steered her into his lap. With ruthless control of his faculties, Trevor had her naked and straddling his hips in less than a minute. As she eased down, he guided his length inside her, and a moan passed her lips.

He halted his play. "Did I hurt you?"

"No." Caroline gazed into his eyes. "I think you are lovely."

He nipped the tip of her nose. "Not half so lovely as you."

She shifted and sucked in a breath. "What do I do?"

"Pretend I am your favorite mount and ride."

True to form, and to their mutual benefit, Caroline applied herself with the same enthusiasm with which she took to her chores—not that he expected any different. As Trevor buried his face in her breasts, he recalled their unfinished business.

They could bloody well talk in the morning.

THE HINGES CREAKED on the door of his cabin, interrupting his slumber and signaling a most unwelcome intrusion. Trevor hugged the supple feminine body he had spent the better portion of the night exploring, made a mental note to speak with George about the need for discretion, because the first mate was the only crewmember who dared enter the captain's quarters without knocking, and yawned. Whatever the reason for the incursion, the entire French Navy could not coax him from his bunk.

The familiar hiss of unsheathed steel brought him awake and alert in an instant.

It was a sound every warrior perceived as a call to arms. Upon opening his eyes, he found himself staring down the pointed end of a sword. Thinking first of Caroline and her safety, he pulled her close, attempting to shield her from the unforeseen threat. Still asleep, she muttered incoherent babble and nuzzled his chest.

"Just what are you about?" he whispered with ire. "And who gave you permission to enter my cabin?"

Recognition dawned, confusion rode in its wake, and Trevor sat upright. Movement had him glancing toward the foot of the bed. In a state of complete bewilderment, he looked right, then left, and wondered if he were in the middle of some horrible nightmare.

The invaders were no strangers. In fact, they were nobles of his set, but that had done little to dispel his discomfort or explain why one was so provoking.

"What in bloody hell are you two doing here?" he asked.

Weapon unwavering, the interloper responded, "I have a better question. What in bloody hell is she doing here?"

"That is none of your damn business." He hugged his courtesan and cradled her head.

"On the contrary." His former naval comrade appeared quite put out. "She is my business."

"I beg to differ." Trevor would tolerate no interference where Mistress Caroline was concerned—not even from an old acquaintance. "If you believe you have a prior claim on my lady, hear me when I say it must perforce yield to mine."

"Is that so?" The flat of the blade shook as the captain of the *Tristan* appeared on the verge of a violent tantrum.

"It is, because I beat you to her prize. If she was meant for you, then I shall compensate you, whatever the price." Trevor held his challenger's stare, even as the dangerous metal docked within inches of his throat. "Careful, Rylan. I will not relinquish her without a fight."

"You will relinquish her with a fight." The notorious hothead seemed ready to explode. "I demand satisfaction."

"For what?" Trevor bared his teeth.

"As if you do not know."

The lady in question stirred in his embrace. The blanket dropped to her waist as Caroline stretched long and then nuzzled him. Trevor would have preferred she not bare her wares for the delectation of his adversaries.

"*Oh, my God!*" His expression one of fury, Rylan's face turned beetroot-red.

"Blake?" The former virgin rubbed her eyes. "Is that you?"

"Do not forget me, kitten." The partner in crime addressed her in a term of endearment, sending a shiver of dark foreboding that traipsed Trevor's spine.

"Damian?" She peered at the figure that had, until that moment, stood silent.

"*Kitten*?" Confusion settled as a lead ball in the pit of his belly, and Trevor arched his brows. Had he not claimed her maidenhead, he would have wondered if she had serviced both dukes. "You know them?"

She nodded. "Yes."

"For the love of Christ, Caroline, cover yourself." The man averted his gaze, as if he were embarrassed.

The cohort behaved in similar odd fashion, and Trevor was perplexed. "Were you meant to pleasure both these men?"

"Now see here—"

"Blake, I can explain." She snatched the sheet to her neck.

"You damn well will," the legendary mariner spat.

Trevor almost choked when his conquest used the aristocrat's Christian name, as it was clear the two had a history. "What is there to explain?" he asked, since nothing about the situation made sense.

"And you will remove yourself from that bed—now!" His foe behaved like an angry father, but Trevor knew that was not possible.

"Excuse me." He kissed her forehead. "Do not yell at my lady, chap, or I will call you out."

"Too late." Rylan focused on the floor. "I am calling you out."

"Give me a minute to put on some clothes, and I will be

happy to oblige you." He tossed the blankets aside.

"No." Caroline wrapped her arms tight about his waist. "Trevor, please, you must not fight him."

"What is it, darling? Are you afraid?" He cupped her cheek. "Worry not, because I will not let him take you."

"Oh, I beg you, do not hurt him." Tears pooled in her eyes, and desperation permeated her features. "If you care anything for me, do not raise your sword against him."

Nausea swept over him, as Trevor feared his bunkmate might have formed some silly female attachment to his longtime rival. Despite his better judgment, and bracing for her response, he asked, "Why?"

"Because he is my brother."

CHAPTER SEVEN

"*B*loody everlasting hell."

"What is it, Cap'n?" George peered from behind the wheel, where he had taken refuge since Trevor stormed the quarterdeck with not one, but two interloping nobles, hot as a hornet's nest, in tow. "I thought you would be happy to see them."

With a shudder of confusion, he stared at the engrossing figure that occupied the seat beside his during every session of Parliament. As acquaintances, they shared a love of the sea, fine cigars, well-aged brandy, and beautiful paramours. No mere mortal, the one-time naval commander, notorious for his short fuse, was known throughout the *ton* by many names. He was none other than Blake Thornton Deverell Elliott, fifth Duke of Rylan, Marquess of Balfour, Earl of Grafton, Viscount Pelham, Viscount Gladstone...oh, the list was endless.

And, if truth were told, elder sibling of Trevor's delectable cabin mate.

The prospect defied reason, yet he could not argue the validity of her personage, evidenced by her sword-wielding, curse-spitting relative. Which meant his sweet Caroline was not a courtesan-in-training but, rather, Lady Caroline Elliott, highborn gentlewoman and member of one of England's most respected families.

Had he not said he wanted answers as to her background? Trevor would have preferred she was an ill-experienced demirep, a blank canvas for him to tutor in the sensual arts, and not a blueblood in hiding. He had expected the former, never imagined the latter.

"George, please, shoot me." Under normal circumstances, he would be quite pleased to engage in a round of verbal fencing and pointed insults, neither facetious nor serious, with the ducal duo perched on the rail, at present. It was common knowledge that Damian Seymour, Duke of Weston, was Blake Elliott's constant companion. In a world where lust for land and power had brought warriors to the battlefield, their friendship was the stuff of legend. And Trevor's association with the pair, often described as a harmless rivalry of like-minded reprobates, extended back to his days at Oxford. Strange, he could not recall Blake ever mentioning a sister. "What, in God's name, possessed you to permit them free entry to my quarters?"

"Why would I not? If memory serves, you struck the last blow when you hired that toothless hag of a doxy, told her your name was Elliott, and pointed her in the direction of the *Tristan* and her captain." The first mate scratched his cheek. "Where were we? India?"

"That was a harmless prank." Trevor gazed at the impressive vessel anchored alongside the *Hera* and speared his fingers through his hair. "What you did may see me hanged from the highest yardarm."

"Nonsense." George chuckled. "Do not tell me the lads are in a fit over yer whore—"

"Will you be quiet." Trevor hissed. "Are you trying to get me keelhauled?"

"Keelhauled?" The old salt grinned. "Who guards her, Rylan or Weston?"

"She is none other than—"

"Blake." Trevor turned as the lady in question, who had been granted the privacy of his cabin to get dressed, ran into the formidable duke's waiting embrace.

"Caroline." Cradling her head in his hand, Blake closed his eyes. "I thought you lost to me."

Despite their familial connection, gut-twisting envy plagued Trevor as the siblings hugged. And his discomfort increased tenfold when she favored the other man with the same display of affection. But what struck him was the change in his line of thought. During his naked dance at the rude point of a blade, while tugging on breeches and boots, his singular focus had been how to wrangle himself out of his current predicament.

Because Caroline was a gently bred woman of character, honor demanded he restore her reputation. And it had not taken a genius to deduce the required reparation—a daunting prospect that scared the hell out of him. "George?"

"Aye, sir?" The first mate checked his timepiece.

"Clear the deck." Trevor stiffened his back.

"I do not understand your alarm." Caroline appeared puzzled. "Why did you think I was lost? Did you not get my letter?"

"I did." Blake compressed his lips. "Upon my return to London, I received an urgent summons from Mama. By the time I reached Elliott House, she was on the verge of hysterics. Nothing would appease her but that I depart for Jamaica and bring you home, posthaste."

"Oh, dear." She clasped her hands in front of her. "But Mama need not have worried. I explained my reasons for leaving, and she knew I was with Dalton."

"And you believe that made everything all right?" The elder brother shifted his weight. "I daresay my entire being shook as I read your missive. You cannot go gallivanting unescorted across the ocean on a ship filled with randy sailors. And considering what has happened, I do not see how you can argue your position."

"But nothing serious occurred." Caroline peered in his direction and smiled. "And Trevor has been a complete gentleman."

"A complete gentleman?" Blake's eyebrows almost reached his hairline, and he glanced at Trevor. "I found you *en flagrante delecto*, and you have the audacity to call him a gentleman?"

Although Trevor had known the inevitable would come, that he would have to face the music, he had not expected the pangs of guilt assailing his conscience.

"Explanations are in order." Pinning him with an icy stare, Blake brushed aside the folds of his greatcoat and set his hand to the hilt of his sword. "Enlighten me, Lockwood. Why did you kidnap my sister?"

Trevor opened his mouth to say something—anything—but Caroline cut him off.

"Lockwood?" Her blue eyes grew wide, and she clutched her throat. "Do you know each other?"

"Oh, we know each other very well," Blake replied, his voice dripping sarcasm. "And there is a reason he took you from Dalton's ship."

"I do not understand." With a familiar guileless countenance, Caroline turned to Trevor. "You told me that Dalton asked you to convey me to London. Is there something you neglected to mention?"

In that moment, he would have made a pact with the devil to disappear on the spot. He would have welcomed an attack by Cavalier, would have preferred to confront the entire French fleet than admit his indiscretion. In his quest to settle a grudge, Trevor had acted rashly. And in haste, he had injured an innocent.

"Come, Lockwood." Her brother arched a brow and tapped his fingers to the rail in an impatient rhythm. "Regale us with your tale."

For a scarce second, Trevor considered jumping ship and swimming for London. But he had never been accused of being a coward in his life and was not about to start now. "First, hear me when I say I did not know she was your sister —much less a woman of character."

"What do you mean you did not know?" Blake directed his attention to his sibling, and Trevor breathed a sigh of relief. "Did you not inform him of your name, of your connections? Did he not believe you?"

"I did not think it signified." Caroline paused, and though she spoke to her brother, it was Trevor she faced. "According to the Captain, he simply wanted company as he crossed the Atlantic. He said Dalton owed him money from a game of poker."

"You did not think it signified?" Blake slapped a fist to his open palm. "And you placed your confidence in him—a total stranger? How on earth could you be so naive?"

"He said he was a friend of Dalton's, and he mentioned Dirk, as well. They sailed together in the Navy. The men of the watch stood guard, and they never would have let him aboard, or in the captain's cabin, without permission." She shrugged. "There was no reason to fear him, as he stated, from the first, that he would not harm me."

"Did you see the note he left behind?" Blake asked. "It was quite provocative."

Uh, oh.

"Note?" she replied. "He left a note?"

"Indeed." The duke sneered. "And it will leave you in no doubt of his intent."

When Blake retrieved a folded piece of parchment from his waistcoat and handed it to his sister, Trevor thought he would swoon like a woman. He knew what she held, even without inspecting it, and his goose was jolly well cooked.

As Caroline scanned the missive, her shoulders sagged, and her mouth fell agape. When she lifted her chin and gazed at him, the agony marring her lovely features struck Trevor as a bolt of lightning, skewering his miserable hide.

"You wrote this," she stated in monotone. "You left this for Dalton?"

Though something inside him screamed a denial, he nodded once. "Aye."

"When I dropped anchor in Jamaica, Dalton was emptying his stores in preparation to race after you." Blake scowled. "As I carried nothing but ballast, I set sail at once. I have been chasing your wake for weeks and had almost given up hope of finding you when a storm hit. It was a lucky break, because the *Tristan* is a heavier ship and better suited to foul weather. With the canvas hardened in, I knew I would catch you."

"But, I do not understand." Caroline again read the missive. "Why would Trevor kidnap me? We were strangers."

"Do you recall Dalton's story involving a pilfered paramour?" Blake flared his nostrils.

"Yes, he was quite full of himself." She wrung her fingers.

"Well, *he* is the bounder Dalton crossed." Blake curled an arm about her waist. "Lockwood thought you a whore. In recompense, he drugged the crew and kidnapped you, with seduction as his sole objective. Did you not see their slack bodies strewn about the deck?"

"He wrapped me in a blanket for my protection—or so he claimed." She frowned, and Trevor felt it all the way to his toes. "I saw nothing."

He glanced at the sky, rolled his shoulders, and exhaled a breath in a failed attempt to alleviate the tension investing him. How was he ever going to escape the mess for which he bore sole responsibility? "I can assure you, had I known her connections, I *never* would have taken her." The last was said with a wealth of meaning he prayed Blake and Damian comprehended.

"What?" Caroline gasped, and she searched his eyes when their gazes met. "After everything we shared—" She bit her lip and appeared on the verge of tears. If she cried, Trevor was a dead man.

"Why did you not apprise him of your personage?" Blake asked with unveiled irritation.

At her sibling's prompt, she masked her sadness behind a haughty façade no actress on Drury Lane could best and thereby saved his skin. "I had sought to protect our good name and social status." Caroline swallowed hard and continued to stare, as if he had three heads. "If it were known that I had sailed without proper escort, with a man —friend or not—our family would be ruined."

As the brother and sister quarreled, Trevor wondered if the situation could get any worse.

"Of all the senseless, ridiculous, imbecilic...Caroline, do

you realize this situation might have been avoided had you simply revealed your identity?" Blake railed. "My God, woman, what were you thinking?"

"Well, that is fine. Blame me for everything." She glared at her brother and thrust her chin in the air. "I had been kidnapped. For all I knew, he could have held me for ransom. But he promised to deliver me safely to London, if only I agreed to be his mistress for the voyage."

"If only you agreed to be his mistress? Oh, I can guarantee you will be much more than his mistress." Blake stood as an impressive sentry. "He will make you an honorable offer, else I will stew his gullet."

Trevor tugged on his shirt collar, because his predicament had just worsened.

"You cannot mean that." Caroline fisted her hands in her brother's shirt. "I know you too well, and you would never force me to wed. And he is not suitable."

"I beg to differ." Her sibling scoffed. "He is an excellent candidate for a husband, given that he has claimed your maidenhead. It will not be the first time a groom enjoyed his honeymoon prior to the official, licensed ceremony."

"You must be joking." She teetered, and for a moment, Trevor thought she might faint. "He is a-a sailor."

"Aye." Blake inclined his head. "As am I. What is your point?"

"I refer to his station." Caroline averted her stare. "Or lack thereof."

Now that comment raised his hackles. How dare she attempt to cast a slur on his heritage? Just as fast, Trevor reminded himself that he had never apprised her of his background.

"Wait a minute." Her brother wiped his face. "Do you not know of his—"

"Your sister is not privy to my position." Trevor paused and contemplated how to phrase his reasons for keeping her in the dark, without insulting her. "Since I assumed she was a woman of loose morals, and she did not correct my assumption, I thought she might fence me for money."

"Unscrupulous reprobate." Eyes flaring, Caroline whirled on him in a flash. "How dare you say such a thing?"

Once more, Blake raised his sword.

In light of the current threats to his person, Trevor had not spoken wisely.

"Hold hard." Damian ventured into the fray. To Trevor, Weston said, "You really should quit while you are ahead."

"It was an honest mistake." He held up his palms in surrender. "And she never once gainsaid me."

"Let me at him." Blake hissed and curled his lip.

"Not until he restores her reputation." Damian peered over his shoulder. "That, I believe, is our primary intent."

"All right. He can speak his vows." Blake hugged his sister. "Then I will kill him."

"You make no sense, brother." Caroline blinked in an owlish fashion. "Papa will roll over in his grave if you force me to the altar. And Trevor has no wish to marry me." She cast him a curious glance. "Do you?"

"Well—"

"What he wants is of little consequence. He is governed by the same precepts, my dear," Damian explained. "As such, he must make amends, and there is only one remedy for his offense."

"You are a member of the peerage?" White as a sheet, she swayed. "But—that cannot be possible."

The quarterdeck grew quiet as a tomb, and unbearable tension festered in the silence.

"Perhaps I should do the honors." Damian swept an

arm in an exaggerated flourish. "Lockwood, may I present Lady Caroline Elliott."

Looking Caroline straight in the eye, he stood tall. "Trevor Reed Marshall, sixth Earl of Lockwood at your service, my lady." To make a good impression, if that were still a viable option, he sketched his most elegant bow.

"You are an earl?" Caroline covered her mouth and stumbled. "Oh, dear."

"Oh, dear? Is that the best you can manage?" Blake rested hands on hips. "I found you in his bed—naked. Tell me he forced you, and I shall dispatch him to his maker this instant."

"He did not force me. I gave myself of my own free will." Caroline stomped a foot to the deck. "And stop repeating everything I say."

For a scarce moment, Trevor thought of intervening on her behalf, but, in the interest of self-preservation, he remained quiet. The other duke on deck arched a brow and appeared to be fighting a smile, laughter, or both. He wondered what the man found so funny.

"I beg your pardon." Blake shuffled his feet and grimaced. "You allowed yourself to be compromised?"

"Yes." Caroline wrinkled her nose as she answered.

As though on the verge of an apoplectic fit, Blake contorted his expression. "For the love of all creation, why?"

"Because I wanted him," she declared with the unabashed forthrightness Trevor had always found attractive. "And he wanted me."

In that second, his respect for her grew by leaps and bounds. For some unknown reason, he could not stop grinning at her. But his confidence waned when he spied the pain etched in her taut visage. "Caroline, if you will hear me—"

"—Or so I thought." She chuckled, self-mockingly. "I should have known better than to invest the slightest measure of faith in him. I see now his only interest lay in the revenge he sought. He did not want me," Caroline stated with palpable bitterness, which scored a direct hit to his moral center. "Once again, I am a pawn in another man's game."

Recalling the conversation in his cabin, her heartbreak at the hands of an unknown blackguard, Trevor defined himself as the worst sort of heel. He ached to take her in his arms and apologize, to reassure her that, no matter what, everything would be fine.

"Good God, Caroline, tell me we are not back to that old tune." Blake rolled his eyes and sighed. "It was your first Season. You must put that mess out of your mind. One incident, neither trivial nor grave, can rule the remainder of your life. You are past due to move beyond it. And you should have let me kill Darwith."

"Darwith?" Trevor's mind raced. "That was you?"

With the cry of a banshee, Caroline leapt at him, but her brother simply lifted her from the deck and jerked her to his side.

"Let it go." Blake cupped her chin. "The bastard was never worthy of you."

Trevor may not have known Caroline as long as her brother, but he recognized what was shaping up to be a grand female tantrum.

"Do not tell me how to feel, as it is my life." Toe to toe with her sibling, hands on hips, Caroline frowned. "Besides, this is your fault."

"My fault?" Blake stared down his nose, his stance mirroring hers, and Trevor wondered if he should offer a bit of advice to the duke on how best to manage the iron-willed woman. "Nothing would have happened had you stayed home—where you belong."

"I decide where I do and do not belong, and you knew I could not abide another Season without you." She humphed. "You promised to be there for me."

"I fulfilled my pledge!" Blake roared.

"How so, as you had not docked when I set sail!" Caroline shouted, evidencing a temperament and lungs just as strong as her brother's.

"Had you not departed, you would know I returned, as vowed." Blake wagged a finger mere inches before her face, and Trevor thought to advise against such heavy handed tactics, lest the spirited lady render her brother one digit less than the standard five. "But no—you had to run like some scared rabbit."

"I beg your pardon." Caroline flinched and retreated a step. "Scared rabbit? You resort to name calling because I do not fancy dressing up and preening about as a mare for auction at Tattersall's?"

Blake shrugged. "Better that than parading naked on the high seas."

"Blast it all, Blake, stop shouting at me, as I am not a child." Caroline pounded his chest. "And I did not parade naked. He is the only man who saw me thus."

"If that was supposed to inspire confidence, you failed miserably." Blake compressed his lips.

"You are an old woman." She pouted.

"And you are a spoiled brat."

While the siblings continued their row, Damian advanced. "I should warn you, she has a bit of a temper."

"Aye." Trevor clucked his tongue. "We have met." Pressing his fingertips to his temples, he rubbed in light circles, because his head felt as if it would split in two at any moment. His evocative little temptress was the sister of a duke and some relation to another. And while Caroline battled a living legend that could make many a crusty salt quiver in his boots, invoking one rebuttal after another, rising to his defense in some circumstances, Trevor envisioned her, as she had looked that morning.

He recalled her chestnut locks splayed across his pillow and what he did to transform her lush tresses into a mass of wild tangles. He remembered the velvety softness of her ivory skin and the sweet cries of feminine release that passed her honey lips. What was a gentleman to do?

"*Enough!*" Trevor stepped forward. "Bring on the vicar. I will marry her."

TO SAVE a small measure of pride, if that were possible, Caroline had intentionally enacted a scene with her brother on the quarterdeck of the *Hera* to avoid crying in front of Trevor. But once she had gained her stateroom aboard the *Tristan*, she had shed a river of tears. The anguish, the utter disappointment was too much to bear.

Would no man ever want her?

Telltale pounding on the door made her jump. "Who is it?" she asked, as if she could not guess.

"Very funny." Blake stormed into her chamber. "Sooner or later, you are going to have to discuss the situation with me."

"I shall opt for later." Though she had not thought her self-imposed exile would forestall the inevitable until they docked in London, she had hoped for at least a night to prepare for the confrontation with her too insightful elder sibling.

"I am not leaving." He closed the door and leaned against the oak panel. "Out with it, little sister."

"By all means, do make yourself at home." Seated in a chair, dressed in a pale blue day gown, one of several items their mother had packed in haste for her return journey, Caroline lowered the book she had been attempting to read and prayed for strength.

The last thing she wanted was to collapse in a fit of hysteria before her brother, not to mention she had grown weary of weeping. With slippered feet tucked under her chair and hands clasped atop the leather bound tome, she met Blake's stare. "What is it you wish to discuss?"

"You cannot be serious." He arched a brow.

"On the contrary, I am very serious. The matter has ended, and there is nothing more to say." She folded her arms, to emphasize her point. "I do not want to marry him. Indeed, I do not wish to marry, ever. I will return for the Season and put on a brave face. When all is done I shall retire to the country, with Mama, and content myself with life as a spinster. I will have cherished memories to see me through the years, and I shall never regret one moment I spent aboard the *Hera*."

"It is not that simple." Blake approached and rested his hip against the back of her chair. "You have been compromised. Even now you could be carrying his child. You are my sister, and I will stand with you, come what may, but you must consider Mama. Your ruin will be borne by our entire family." He tapped the tip of her nose, a gesture that evoked many fond childhood memories. "Think, Caroline, not just us, but Mama, as well. You know her. She is quite the *grande dame*, and this will destroy her."

"I would rather you had forced me to wed." Caroline swallowed hard. In her desperation to flee London, she had not pondered how her actions might impact her family. She had always loathed the social strictures of the peerage, which had often dictated her life as if she were a marionette on a miniature stage. "You are disappointed in me, are you not?"

"I wish I could understand your rationale." With uncharacteristic stoicism, Blake had not met her gaze. "I wish I could sympathize with your motive and subsequent actions, as it might be easier to make sense of our predicament."

For a second, Caroline contemplated sharing her dilemma, her heartbreak. But there was nothing to be gained, other than inciting her brother further and placing Trevor's neck in greater peril. "Pray, continue."

"Yes, I am disappointed. I had thought you a woman of good judgment and character. I hold you in higher esteem than most men of my acquaintance. Have I overindulged you? Was I too lenient in your upbringing? Perhaps it was wrong of me to encourage your independent nature. Somehow I feel as though I have failed you." Blake rubbed his eyes, and she noted the lines of strain etched on his forehead. "I have always taken such pride in your self-reliance. It has been of great comfort while at sea that I did not have to worry about you. How could you act with such reckless disregard for your own safety? How could you put yourself in this untenable position?"

"For heaven's sake, Blake, you act as if I intended to be kidnapped." She stared at her clenched fists. "I meant only to avoid the Season. I do not see how you can blame me for my capture."

"Lord Lockwood must bear some, but not all, of the responsibility for what has happened, as you have made it clear, you did nothing against your will. While Lockwood's reputation with women is notorious, and you were indeed an innocent, I must admit I hold you equally culpable for what happened *after* he abducted you." He stood tall and inclined his head. "I know you, as I know myself. You are no weak simpleton to be easily led. I believe you when you tell me he did not force himself upon you, that you allowed yourself to be compromised. As such, you must accept the consequences of your actions."

Her heart pounded, her ears rang, and her mouth tasted dry as desert sand. "You want me to marry him."

"My dear, it is no longer a question of what I want." Blake knelt before her chair and covered her hands with his. "You were not meant to live alone. I wanted a love match for you, as our parents had. Hell, it is what I want for myself. But in truth, Lord Lockwood is your only option. I know him, as we served together in the Navy. Despite his recent actions, I remain convinced he is a man of honor. Given the chance, I believe he will make a fine husband and who knows, in time, you may come to love one another. However, I will not force you to accept him. The final decision is yours to make."

"I need to think this through." Caroline worried her lower lip and avoided his knowing gaze. "Please be assured I will endeavor to restore your good opinion of me. You shall have my answer upon our return to London."

"I had best leave you to it." Blake chucked her shoulder. "But remember that no matter the path you choose, you are still my sister, and I love you."

"Despite my ruin?" Again the tears beckoned.

"Of course." He grinned. "It is one of the perks of being a duke. I can tell everyone in polite society to go to the devil, and yet the laws of etiquette demand they bow at my every entrance."

"You are incorrigible," Caroline said to his back, as he made for the door.

"I am an Elliott." Blake cast her a mischievous glance. "As are you." Then he exited the cabin.

In the silence of her sanctuary, hours ticked away, signaled by the mantel clock in her quarters. The sun was setting when she ventured to the poop deck for a breath of fresh air.

Glorious streaks of orange and gold cut the encroaching night sky in a dazzling display of nature's omnipotence. But on her, the beauty was ill spent. Her thoughts centered on the ship following theirs at a close but safe distance. No doubt because her brother had declared he would blow the *Hera* out of the water should she stray from the *Tristan's* wake.

Caroline had made her decision, and she knew what she had to do. She would make Blake proud and that was important to her. She would accept responsibility for her actions—but she would do no more.

Long ago, she had vowed never to give her heart to any man. Never again would she fall prey to love. That was a mistake already made and a lesson obviously not learned, because Caroline had trusted Trevor. She had gifted him her body and soul.

She had fallen in love.

And he had used her to avenge the loss of his mistress.

He thought you a whore.

Her brother's words rang in her ears as a humiliating refrain.

"How could you, Trevor? With you I shared my past and my humiliation." The wind sifted through her hair. "Yet it did not dissuade you. You did not alter your course, and you played me false."

Imaginary walls barricaded her in a formidable defense. The door shut tight, and the bolt slid home. An illusory but nonetheless powerful rasp of steel shivered in her chest, as the impact of his betrayal eclipsed her in desolation and despair.

A cool breeze penetrated her light gown, drawing her from her melancholy meditation. Trembling, she wrapped her arms about herself and then scurried to the companion ladder. At the top rung, she paused and glanced over her shoulder.

"Well, Lord Lockwood, you shall have a wife. One who will serve you well." Tears pooled, blurring her vision, and Caroline swallowed a sob and lifted her chin. "But you will not have my heart."

CHAPTER EIGHT

A fortnight later, Damian informed Caroline they had just passed the North Foreland, the famous headland on the eastern coast of Kent marking the entry to the Thames estuary. In a flurry of activity, she packed the little trunk her mother had sent with a few belongings to sustain her through the trip home. Soon the *Tristan* would dock in London, and she would embark on her new life, the one inadvertently set in motion with a night of passion.

Her emotions flip-flopped as she wrestled with the decision she had made. One minute Caroline could not wait to see Trevor and announce their wedding date, and the next she determined to do whatever necessary to ensure she never laid eyes on him again. And whenever she slipped into a moment of weakness, allowing herself to believe he desired her, in truth, she recalled that his ardent attentions had been based on a ruse—on a lie. There she found strength in anger.

All the while, Caroline suffered the unshakeable certainty that once among the beauties of the *ton*, Trevor would no longer find her alluring—not that he ever had.

And then she wondered why she cared. If he chose another bride, her problem would be solved, and she would be free. Resolved to stay her course, she folded the last of her garments, closed her trunk, and joined her brother and Damian on deck as the ship anchored at Deptford.

"Our carriage is here, my dear. We will drop you at Elliott House." Blake offered his arm in escort. "By the by, Mama is at Pembroke. She circulated a rumor about town that you were ill and convalescing in the country. I will send for her posthaste and, upon her return, we shall discuss how to proceed—provided you have made a decision."

"I suppose she will have to be told everything?" They navigated the gangway with Damian in tow.

"I do not see how we can avoid it." Blake handed her into his carriage. "Her nose for trouble can best my finest hound."

"More's the pity." Caroline sank into the squabs and gazed out the window. "I had hoped to spare Mama any unnecessary torment."

"I think, perhaps, it is a tad late for that." He occupied the seat beside her, followed by Damian, who sat opposite them. "And you will have to explain the situation compelling you to act without delay. That is, if you have chosen your path."

"I have." Caroline bit her tongue. "Of course, you are right."

"Aren't I always?" Blake settled his greatcoat, then cast her a frown. "About what?"

"Despite my trepidation, I shall have to be quite frank with Mama." She shrugged. "Therefore, I will heed your advice."

"An excellent notion." He slid an arm about her shoulders and nudged her close. "We need to maintain the pretense of your condition. Remember? You are supposed to have been gravely ill. And do not forget, there is much to be planned depending on whether or not you have accepted Lord Lockwood."

"I understand." Caroline glanced at Damian, who smiled. "I believe I have considered every option."

"My chief concern is your continued happiness."

"I know, Blake."

"Your future is of paramount importance."

"Yes, Blake."

"It is my most fervent hope that you do not feel bullied into a precarious position."

"No, Blake."

"Because if you *do* feel pressured—"

"I do not feel pressured."

"Caroline, will you be serious?"

"I am being serious." She spied skepticism in his dour countenance. "I have considered the situation, from every angle, and know what must be done."

Blake arched a brow. "Well?"

"Well—what?" Panic rang clear in her voice. Caroline paused and attempted to calm herself. "I should think the answer obvious. If Lord Lockwood will have me, I shall marry him."

"Are you certain?"

"No." Why had he asked the one question guaranteed to unnerve her? "I have never felt so uncertain in my life. But as I said, I know what must needs, and I shall not fail our family."

Blake dipped his chin. "I promise to do everything in my power to protect you."

"Thank you, but, no, thank you." She covered his hand with hers and squeezed his fingers. "I am not a child, and this is not a simple matter of a scraped knee for you to kiss and make better."

His expression softened. For as long as she could recall, Blake had always been her champion, and it was evident he remembered, too. "Caroline, while I admire your determination, you should know Lord Lockwood is no babe in the woods."

She dusted her skirts. "Be that as it may, considering how you found us, I hesitate to point out that neither am I."

At her side, her brother stiffened. "My dear, Lockwood is no boy with which to be trifled. When it comes to women, he is a past master. And there is a vast difference between taking a woman to bed and courting a wife."

"Oh?" Caroline narrowed her stare. "Just what do you know of marriage?"

At that moment, Damian, who had remained silent as the dead for the past half-hour of their trip, succumbed to gales of laughter.

"Care to share what you find so amusing?" Blake tapped his fingers to his thigh.

She elbowed her brother in the ribs. "Do not rip at him."

"It appears your little sister is not so little anymore." Damian wiped a tear from his eye and snickered. "By God, but your mother could not best the look Caroline shot you."

"Mind your own business." Blake folded his arms and scowled. "I hope Alex gives you equal measure when it is her turn to wed."

"Haa." Damian snorted. "My Alex is an angel. I daresay she will set her cap for some boring viscount, move to the Lake District, and I will have nothing to do but whittle away my days recalling fonder times."

"You should be so lucky," her brother grumbled.

The carriage came to an abrupt halt.

Caroline peered beyond the window to the comforting sight of Elliott House. Located in Grosvenor Square, the elegant home, with a red brick façade and Corinthian columned entrance, was a grand gem among the more fashionable London residences. A trio of footmen sporting powdered wigs and the ducal colors hurried from the front door.

"In any case," Blake said as he disembarked, "I will speak with Lockwood and dictate our terms."

"Do not dare." Caroline frowned as her brother handed her down. "I have a plan and will handle Lord Lockwood, myself."

"Are you sure that is wise?" With an arched brow, Blake appeared unconvinced of her fortitude.

"Indeed. If I am to marry, I intend to start out as I mean to go on." A passing carriage caught her eye, and she was positive Trevor occupied the refined equipage. Caroline craned her neck and perched on her toes to get a better view.

It was her captain.

A funny feeling blossomed in her belly, salacious images danced in her head, and a host of delicious sensations shivered over her skin. She retreated, tripped, and landed hard on her bottom.

"That, my dear," Blake said as he lifted her from the pavement, "is precisely what I fear."

AFTER A MORNING VISIT FROM A TAILOR, Trevor spent his first full day in London reviewing estate affairs with a small contingent of agents and solicitors, each offering curious stares whenever he fell victim to unexplained chuckles. No doubt his household staff thought their lord and master bordered on lunacy, because once he concluded his business, he indulged in a fit of knee-slapping hilarity that echoed in the foyer of his home.

In his lifetime, Trevor had been accused of propelling many a faint-hearted woman into a melancholy state, a pit of despair, or an abyss of misery depending on the female penchant for hysterics. Never, at least to his knowledge, had he ever been charged with upending—in the literal sense—the fairer sex. But he could not deny what his eyes had seen.

After securing his ship and transferring command to George, he had boarded his carriage for the ride into London proper. As his equipage approached Mayfair, he had noted an impressive coach in the lane. The ducal coat of arms emblazoned on the side had brought him alert in an instant. It had been his hope to catch a glimpse of his bride-to-be and gauge her demeanor.

Throughout the remainder of the journey home, Trevor had wondered if Caroline would still possess the effortless effervescence he found so appealing, or if she would conceal her guileless nature behind a bilious curtain of conventional conduct. The mamas of the *ton* had a way of stifling any inherent qualities in young ladies that most men deemed conducive to a pleasant union. To his infinite thanks, it seemed his intended suffered no such deficiency.

Because the minute they locked gazes, Caroline had fallen flat on her derriere. Perhaps when next they met, he should offer to soothe what he considered a superior posterior. Staring out the window overlooking Park Lane, he chuckled. The chime of the mantel clock heralded the evening hour. After checking his appearance in the wall mirror, he headed for White's.

The private rooms were filled by the time he arrived at the popular gentlemen's club. Locating an empty chair in a quiet corner, Trevor procured a copy of *The Times*, ordered a brandy, and lit a cigar. He was half finished reading a lengthy article detailing the latest events from the front when a familiar baritone rang in his ears.

"Good God, my eyes must be deceiving me for I have yet to take a drink this night."

Peering beyond the edge of the paper, Trevor smiled at the friendly face of the lone person he could always count on to be happy to see him. "Markham, you devil, how are you?"

"So it is you, Lockwood?" Lord Everett Markham glanced left, then right. "I am not hallucinating?"

"Aye, it is I." They shared a hearty half-hug. "And in the flesh no less."

"Come now, how long has it been? Five years? Six?" Everett pressed a fist to his chest. "I say, I think I will have a drink. The shock, you know."

"Still possessing a flair for the dramatic I see." Trevor clucked his tongue. "Some things never change. You have not, by any chance, taken up a career on the stage?"

"Perish the thought." Everett grimaced. "Though I daresay my antics pale in comparison with those of my brother."

"Commiserations." He frowned, and then signaled a passing servant. "Shall I order you a brandy?"

"By all means." Markham commandeered a chair and hauled it to the corner. "Make it two."

His classmate from Eton had long suffered in the shadow of his elder sibling, Charles, Earl of Woverton and future Marquess of Talbot. As the second son, Everett existed as an invisible relation to his parents, who focused their attentions and affections on the heir apparent. For Trevor and Everett, abandonment functioned as common ground, and as such, they had been joined at the hip since they were in shortcoats.

"Tell me." Resettling himself in his seat, he stretched his legs. "Your parents, are they in good health?"

"I assume they are in very good health, but I do not have much contact with them nor do I care to—but let us leave that behind. So, what brings you to London? When last we spoke you swore off this town for eternity." Everett arched a brow and grinned. "I do not suppose you have decided to fulfill your duties as earl and get yourself leg-shackled?"

Lips compressed, Trevor bit his tongue and looked his friend straight in the eye. The jaw-dropping visage with which he was rewarded proclaimed the truth had dawned.

"Marriage? You?" Markham blinked. "You cannot be serious."

Trevor envisioned his lady and smiled. "But I am."

"Truly?" Everett rubbed the back of his neck.

"Indubitably." Trevor chucked his shoulder. "What say you, old friend? Will you stand with me as I take my vows?"

"Bloody hell." Everett drained his glass in a single healthy swallow and solicited a refill. "You have spent too much time at sea, and the salt water has corroded your brain. I should sooner summon a physician."

"Come now, wish me merry." He leaned forward, rested elbows to knees, and conjured bawdy images of his erstwhile Mistress Caroline. "I welcome the happy event."

"You have lost your mind, because I see the future, and it is littered with perfume and petticoats." Markham wrinkled his nose. "Forget about patronizing the gaming tables."

"I resent that, Everett, really I do." Trevor snorted, as his impending nuptials also required he apply himself with due diligence to the creation of the next generation of Marshalls. In that commitment, he would gladly succeed or die trying, given the lady in question. "And I promise I shall suffer no such demise."

"How is that?" His friend groaned and cast an expression of pure skepticism. "The vicar's noose has claimed bigger men than you, if you do not mind my saying."

"No similar fate shall befall me, because I have a plan." He examined the polished toes of his boots. "I have devised a strategy that will allow me to continue my life as I choose, despite taking a wife."

"You are serious." Everett drew a handkerchief from his coat pocket, patted his brow, and narrowed his stare. "What did you do, compromise the unfortunate bride-to-be?"

Oh, how the truth hurt. "Now wait a—"

"Lockwood, just the man I seek." Blake, with Damian bringing up the rear, folded his arms and glared at Trevor.

Cursing under his breath, Trevor stood and faced his soon-to-be-brother-in-law. "What in bloody hell do you want?"

"Come to dinner." Blake compressed his lips. "Tomorrow—at Elliott House."

"Perhaps I shall." Trevor inched forward, they ended up toe to toe, and he was determined not to flinch. Blake might have rank, but he had the benefit of age and experience on the arrogant duke. "Of course, I require an invitation."

Painfully quiet seconds ticked past.

"Ahem." Everett cleared his throat. "Trevor, are you not going to introduce us?"

～

THE FOLLOWING EVENING, Caroline reclined on a daybed in her sitting room at Elliott House. Having failed in every attempt to read the novel in her hands, she relented and closed the book. As she stared at the cover of the old tome, she pondered the outcome of the engagement she awaited with nervous anticipation.

Trevor was coming to dinner.

Clasping her trembling hands in her lap, she reminded herself he was the same man with whom she had shared a cabin aboard ship and in whose arms she had spent the most memorable night of her life.

A night that haunted her dreams.

At sea, she had considered him an ally, of sorts. A friend, if she applied the term loosely. Trevor had treated her with kindness and charmed his way into her heart. It hurt to discover his passionate pursuit had been nothing more than a well-played deception.

Now, reluctant suitor or not, he was her enemy.

Caroline waged war and, as such, had plotted her strategy with ruthless detail. In defiance of societal dictates, she would not obey her future husband, as had most wives of the *ton*. Despite the accepted constraints, she determined to remain her own person. And while her position required she produce an heir, she resolved not to enjoy the task.

"My lady, His Grace requests your presence in the study."

"Thank you, Annie." She nodded to her lady's maid. "I shall be right down."

Bolstering her defenses, Caroline stood, walked to the long mirror, and brushed imaginary wrinkles from the skirts of her pale pink gown. "Do not worry, as everything will be fine," she said to her reflection. "Trevor is just a man. And if all else fails, he can kill you, but he cannot eat you."

With shoulders squared, she marched from her room and straight to the door of her brother's domain. A footman set the oak panels wide, and she entered with the poise and ease one would expect of a duke's daughter, until she caught her slippered toe on the edge of the Aubusson rug and stumbled.

Sitting behind his desk, Blake bent his head and covered his face with his hand. Occupying a chair at his left, her mother, God bless her, managed to maintain the smile on her lips, even though her expression seemed a bit forced. Trevor, blast his handsome hide, stood upon her less than graceful approach and had the audacity to gurgle, which carried more than a hint of laughter.

Caroline was going to kill him.

At least she would were she not so distracted by the transformation of her rogue captain into a well-heeled English gentleman. Dressed in a precision tailored coat of charcoal gray Bath superfine, he looked only slightly dangerous, with an elegant diamond pin securing the folds of his cravat. Buckskin breeches encased his muscled thighs and disappeared into a pair of polished Hessians.

With an inward smile, she almost asked if Trevor slept in his boots. Then she recalled he had done no such thing. Before she could stop herself, the full extent of her knowledge of the man dawned, and her cheeks went up in flames. Cursing her own stupidity and those double-damned blushes, Caroline sought to conceal her malady in a proper curtsey. "Lord Lockwood, what a pleasure it is to see you again."

"My lady." Her intended swept her a refined bow, and

she could only envy his finesse. "May I say the pleasure is mine."

Blake shifted his weight and coughed. "Uh, Lockwood, Caroline, I hate to interrupt this heartfelt reunion, but we have much to discuss concerning your return to society and subsequent betrothal."

"After much consideration, it is my most fervent hope to spare you any taint of a scandal." Her mother possessed uncanny strength and tactical skill. "I believe such a rough beginning would bode ill for the union, given the already precarious position."

"Your pardon, Your Grace." Holding her gaze, Trevor raised his hand, as would a young fop seeking permission to speak at Eton. "But my offer of marriage has yet to be accepted."

"Indeed?" Caroline stood her ground and pinned his emerald eyes. Had he thought to intimidate her? Oh, her captain would find his challenge well met, because she would not falter so early in the games of love and war. "And I find it difficult to accept an offer of marriage that has yet to be made."

"My apologies on my oversight. It would seem you are correct." With a trace of a smile on his lips, and the devil in his countenance, her husband-to-be knelt before her, and she decided she preferred him on his knees. "My dear Lady Caroline Elliott, will you grant me the honor of being my wife, as I should be your lord and master? Will you consent to be my countess, my friend, my lover, my partner in all enterprises—and the mother of my children?"

Caroline almost choked on her tongue.

It was not the daunting list of responsibilities that terrified her but, rather, the effortless ability with which Trevor made his declaration. And though she had rehearsed her reply countless times, her articulate response eluded her at the moment she needed it most. She took a minute to remind herself of her situation, of the circumstances compelling her to wed.

The bitter pill of pride formed a lump in her throat, but Caroline swallowed her discomfit and shielded herself in anger. "Lord Lockwood, I would be honored to accept your proposal. I am well aware of the duties I shall assume as your wife, a station and charge I am prepared to fulfill, and pledge to do credit to your good name."

"Caroline, are you sure?" Blake rubbed the middle of his forehead. "I will support your decision, regardless of the consequences."

"Yes." She longed to hurl a string of invective at her future lord and master, but such behavior would reflect poorly on her mother.

"Rest easy, Rylan." Trevor tucked her into the crook of his shoulder. "I shall endeavor to make her happy and can assure she will want for nothing."

Caroline considered informing her intended that her hot-tempered sibling could not be so easily placated.

"And I guarantee you will make her a fine husband or a rich young widow." Blake pounded his desk with a fist. "The choice is yours."

Oh, how she loved her brother.

"Enough bickering." Her mother stood. "We need to discuss the marriage contract and disbursement of her dowry—"

"Keep it," Trevor stated with disdain.

"What?" Caroline glanced at him. "You cannot mean that."

"It is a good deal of money, Lockwood." Blake appeared on the verge of a fit. "I am not privy to your financial status, but my sister is an heiress. As the daughter of a duke, she must be cared for in a manner as befits her rank."

"I have no need of her money." Trevor lowered his chin. "If you insist I take the dowry, then let us put it in an account in her name, whereupon the funds can be held in trust for our children."

"A noble gesture, Lord Lockwood." Her mother reclaimed her seat. "May I assume you will conduct yourself in similar exemplary fashion throughout the courtship?"

Trevor nodded once. "You may."

A hint of a gasp slipped from her lips, and Caroline cursed herself in silence. Focusing on one of the high-back chairs facing her brother's desk, she wanted to flee, but if her enemy would take no quarter, neither would she.

"Very well." Her mother inclined her head in an affectation Caroline knew from experience meant business. "You may pay court for four weeks. We will announce your betrothal in *The Times*, and you can marry four weeks after that, with none the wiser. To accomplish our objective, you must cut a wide swath through the ballrooms of the *ton*. Fortunately for us, the Season is in full swing, so your courtship will take place in view of society and must be convincing. I trust it will not be too difficult a task, Lord Lockwood?"

"On the contrary, Your Grace." Trevor smiled a sly smile that gave Caroline gooseflesh. "I consider the opportunity to court your daughter a pleasure not to be missed. Furthermore, in all appearances, I shall be in earnest."

Caroline scrutinized her fiancé, as she knew not what to make of his odd proclamation.

"Mama, what about the family?" Blake inquired.

"As Damian and Dalton already know what has

happened, I think it best to include the others in our efforts. I really do not see how we can avoid it, and we could use their support. However, I do believe we can omit any reference to the fact that the relationship has been consummated." The mantel clock sounded the dinner hour. Her mother rose and accepted Blake's ready escort. "Now then, Lord Lockwood, it is time to introduce you to the rest of the family."

It was only when she felt faint from lack of oxygen that Caroline exhaled. Everything happened so fast, and control of her life seemed beyond her grasp. The next thing she knew, she assumed her customary place beside her mother in the foyer, with her fiancé at her right, and prepared to receive their guests. When the Douglas family crossed the threshold, she realized there was no retreat.

For good or ill, her course was set.

Later, while seated in the drawing room, Caroline inventoried their guests. Her lifelong friends were in full attendance save one, as Dalton remained in Jamaica.

Aside from Blake, Damian and his younger sister, Lady Alexandra Seymour, were punctual, as always. Dalton's older brother Dirk, Viscount Wainsbrough, had arrived with Lance Prescott, Marquess of Raynesford, and his cousin, Lady Elaine. Admiral Mark Douglas, Lady Amanda Douglas, and their two daughters, Cara and Sabrina, completed the odd extended family.

The introductions were made with polite decorum, and Caroline fidgeted in anxiety and dread, until Trevor took her hand and placed it in the crook of his arm. Setting his palm to her knuckles, he squeezed as if to reassure her. The thoughtful gesture scored a direct hit to her heart and both strengthened and unnerved her.

As predetermined, Blake explained the events necessitating the gathering, taking care to place details in the best possible light. The reactions were surprisingly reticent, as everyone promised to aid the couple in their ambitious proposal. When dinner was announced, Caroline sighed, as the weight of the world lifted from her shoulders.

~

TREVOR SIGHED, as the weight of the world settled on his shoulders.

He studied his bride-to-be, dressed in a pink confection, which brought out the charming blush of her cheeks. With her hair piled atop her head, she conveyed the picture of feminine elegance. In her current attire, no man—blind or otherwise—could ever mistake her for a doxy. On the thought, seductive images and sultry cries captured his senses. Transported into the past, he envisioned Caroline, highborn Englishwoman, warm and inviting in his bunk aboard the *Hera*. In an instant, he found the idea of marriage more appealing.

Seated beside his intended, he marveled at the group gathered at the large table. The ease with which they conversed, the inside jokes, the moments of companionable silence indicated familial intimacy unlike any he had ever known.

Which left Trevor quite the outsider.

The events after dinner only added to his distress. In most English homes, it was customary for men to remain in the dining room, to take their port or brandy. Later, they would join the women in the drawing room. He quickly learned that in the Elliot household, such was not the case. While the elders headed for the parlor, with Admiral

Douglas in tow, the younger group, male and female, made for the study.

"So you seized Caroline from under Dalton's nose?" Eyes twinkling, the youngest Douglas rocked on her heels. "Hells bells, but that is one I will never let him live down."

"Sabrina, you mustn't say such things." The older Douglas frowned. "I am sorry Caroline, Lord Lockwood."

"No need for apologies or formalities." Amused, he bowed before the two sisters. "You must call me Trevor."

Extending an arm, as would a gentleman, Sabrina appeared pleased when he took her hand in a firm grasp, instead of bestowing the usual chaste kiss to her gloved knuckles. "And you can call me Brie, like the cheese, you know."

The men in their group laughed, as though her peculiar behavior were a common occurrence. Likewise, the young ladies shook their heads in reproach.

"Are you truly blood relatives?" Trevor asked. "Or should I offer you my other leg?"

"Actually, I would say we are bound by blood." Damian drew near. "But you will have to get Caroline to share the story."

"Oh, no," his bride-to-be protested. "You tell it so much better than I."

"She is right, old man," Lance chimed. "Give it a go."

"All right." Damian unbuttoned his coat and perched on the edge of Blake's large desk. The others gathered round, settling to hear the tale to which it seemed they were privy. Unsure what to expect, Trevor leaned against the high-back chair Caroline occupied.

"If you are to understand the depth of our bond, I should start at the beginning." Damian sipped his brandy. "Our five families have been allied since the fourteenth century, and that allegiance is a tradition, of sorts. Where most would have gone their separate ways, over time, our ties have become stronger. Our parents raised us to respect family and friendship." His brow a mass of furrows, Damian stared into his glass.

"My father had an old captain's log, the first entry was in the year of our lord, 1309," the duke explained. "There is an ancient seafarer's oath written inside. On a moonlit night, at the twelfth hour, we came together in the gardens and pledged the same, as brothers and sisters, all. To solidify our pact, we mingled our blood with a tiny nick to the finger." Damian shrugged. "To the casual acquaintance, ours may seem a childhood fancy, but I warn you, do not take us lightly. I am her brother as Caroline is my sister. Do not think you can supplant us."

A palpable tension hung in the air. The mood in the room had taken a definite turn, and he had the distinct impression he had just been put on notice. The solitary figure on one side, Trevor swallowed hard, as Caroline and her family loomed as the opposition. The lines were drawn.

Trevor had never felt so alone in his life.

CHAPTER NINE

All is fair in love and war, or so Virgil wrote.

Caroline smiled as the familiar literary passage echoed in her ears, because tonight she would launch her campaign for independence against a certain arrogant earl. She had taken great pains to put her best foot forward for the evening, dressing in an ivory silk creation, which she wore as armor and Blake had teasingly said made her look like a Roman deity.

Perhaps Diana—goddess of the hunt?

The ballroom at Richmond House filled to capacity, and the *ton* was in full attendance. She clutched Blake's arm as he escorted her and their mother through the crush. Bursts of light flashed before her eyes, and Caroline realized she had forgotten to breathe in the last several seconds. Exhaling before she swooned, she craned her neck and searched for her quarry.

Desperate circumstances called for desperate measures, and she was going on the offensive. While she had agreed to marry her errant captain, theirs was a union born of social dictums, not a bloody allegiance of the heart. And from the moment he revealed his deception Trevor had become her adversary. When the night was over, he would know better than to toy with her heart again.

"Oh, my dears, I believe I see my little coterie." Her mother patted Caroline's cheek. "Have a lovely evening."

"I will, Mama." She dipped her chin. "And you, as well."

"Ready to face the music?" Blake winked. "I see our friends gathered at the back wall."

"No time like the present." With a roll of her shoulders, she compressed her lips.

Various notables offered their acknowledgements, many ladies vied for her brother's attention, and several former suitors solicited dances as the Elliott siblings navigated the throng. Approaching their group, Caroline spied Trevor. But to her chagrin, he snared her senses with yet another striking mutation. Garbed in black formalwear, with a diamond twinkling at the center of his cravat, he was devastatingly handsome. Her heart skipped a beat, and her pulse pounded.

Blast her traitorous body.

How was she supposed to appear confident when her cheeks burned as dry timber newly set aflame? In silence, she thanked God for Blake's escort, else she would have fallen flat on her face—or bottom. And to her good fortune, a lilting adagio covered her gasp of surprise when Trevor met her gaze. Why he startled her she neither knew or understood, since they were secretly engaged to wed it seemed a harmless gesture. Harmless if she ignored the gooseflesh prickling her arms. Perhaps it was because his eyes held more than a hint of mischief.

Summoning what could best be described as false courage, Caroline held pace with her brother and stopped only when she stood at Trevor's side. The men, engrossed in a dialogue of horse breeding, appeared not to notice she had arrived. Likewise, the ladies had their heads together, trading the latest *on-dits*.

"My lady." Trevor claimed her hand and placed a chaste kiss on the inside of her wrist. "Allow me to introduce an old friend of mine, Lord Everett Markham."

An imposing figure of a man stepped forward and bowed. "Pleased to make your acquaintance, Lady Caroline."

His lopsided grin raised her suspicions in an instant. Had Trevor shared the details of their relationship with Lord Markham? Almost in panic, she shot her husband-to-be a worried glance but gleaned nothing from his casual countenance.

Hoping for a little assistance from her friends, she stole a peek from left to right. To her abiding frustration, she realized Lady Richmond could have marched a purple elephant through her ballroom, and Caroline's lifelong companions would have feigned indifference.

"Care to dance, my lady?" She shivered as Trevor expelled his warm breath over her ear. "It would be my honor."

Why had he sounded so genuine?

Caroline was certain her efforts would be much easier if he were an insufferable boor.

"Oh—yes, but no, I mean not now—I was saving a waltz for you, my lord." For her plan to work, she had to reserve a waltz, because the country-dance would not suit her strategy.

"Why limit ourselves?" He inclined his head and grinned his wolf's grin. "We can always dance again."

Guilt nagged her conscience, and she worried her bottom lip. "Actually, we would rouse undue curiosity and speculation were we to indulge in excess of one turn on the floor this night. Anything more would be tantamount to a declaration."

Her prey frowned. "And it would be too soon to make such a statement?"

"Indeed." The disappointment in her voice seemed so sincere. Perhaps she possessed a talent she had never before tapped.

"Very well, until the waltz."

Caroline sighed her relief.

"Oh, I say." Everett stepped to the fore and offered his escort. "Allow me to indulge you this dance, my lady. I am sure Lord Lockwood will not mind."

She almost swallowed her tongue.

"You are too kind, Lord Markham." Her stomach clenched, and tension invested her spine as Trevor's friend led her to the dance floor.

"You must call me Everett." He bowed. "So, do tell, how are you acquainted with my old chum?"

Caroline just managed to stop herself from spilling the contents of her belly on his elegant coat. She searched her mind, a convenient explanation not too far from the truth formed in her brain. "Oh, I am not that familiar with Lord Lockwood. He served in the Navy with my brother. In fact, Blake introduced us." Pleased with the ease of her delivery, she relaxed.

"Really?" Everett smiled a little too sweet for her liking. "Trevor conversed with His Grace the other day at White's, and I got the distinct impression your sibling is not altogether too fond of him. Could it have something to do with your impending nuptials?"

Bloody hell, the blackguard knew the truth.

Because her betrothal had yet to be announced, there

was no other explanation. In a flash, she flushed, giddy with panic, tripped on her toes, and clutched his hand.

"Calm yourself."

The words fell over her in a whisper. When she inclined her head and peered at her partner, the rogue favored her with a cat-that-ate-the-canary-smile. The rake was positively—incorrigible.

"Fear not." Everett chuckled and arched a brow. "Your secret is safe with me."

In a valiant effort, Caroline tried to dispel his infuriating —but correct—assertion. "I do not know of any secret requiring such assurances."

"Of course not," Everett replied with glib supremacy. "That is why you are as white as a sheet, and my normally cool-headed friend is glaring at me as would a jealous husband."

"My lord, do you not think the decorations charming?" She focused on the wall, vowing not to meet the nosy noble's stare. But his mocking laughter filled her ears, and she bit her tongue against a slew of inventive curses.

The music ended, and Everett returned her to Trevor, who engaged in spirited conversation with her brother, Damian, Lance, and Dirk. He acknowledged her with a smile of cherubic innocence and resumed his discussion. Caroline was ready to hit him. How dare her fiancé leave her at the mercy of that annoying man?

An elbow to the ribs caught her attention. "Good heavens, Sabrina, stop it," she said.

"You know, Lord Lockwood is not half bad. He is very handsome in a rugged, robust sort of way. Do you suppose his friend is a captain, too? They are not at all like these perfumed dandy peacocks we have been forced to endure. I might have to hie myself off on someone's ship to find my own husband."

"Shhh." Caroline held a finger to her lips. "Careful, Brie, someone might hear you."

"Do not get snippy with me, and you are the one raising your voice." The youngest Douglas clasped her hands in front of her. "Do you really have to marry him?"

Just then, Alex, Cara, and Elaine joined the conversation.

"Have you kissed him yet?" Alex whispered, wide-eyed with wonder.

"Oh, do tell," Cara responded, as Elaine nodded her enthusiasm.

Since she was the first to embark on a betrothal, her friends no doubt had numerous inquiries. Problem was the Netherton's ballroom had not seemed an appropriate venue for such intimate dialogue. But in assessing her friends, Caroline realized there would be no avenue for escape.

"If you promise not to breathe a word of what I tell you, I shall entertain your queries."

After a quick glance, from side to side, Alex leaned to impart, "We shall be as silent as the grave."

The remaining ladies nodded their agreement.

Caroline shrugged and asked, "What is it you want to know?"

Like a military salvo, the questions came in rapid fire.

"Have you kissed him?"

"Did you enjoy it?"

"What is it like?"

"I have heard some men use their tongue."

"Where did you sleep aboard his ship?"

"Have you seen him naked?"

"Slow down, one at a time." Caroline paused and

inhaled deeply. "Yes, I have kissed Lord Lockwood—numerous times. And yes, I enjoyed it, although I cannot say why."

"How did it make you feel?" Cara asked, her voice tinged with nervous excitement.

Now that particular inquiry she had to ponder. Since the women were as sisters to her, Caroline was compelled to answer honestly. "My heart pounded in my ears, and a strange warmth permeated my body. It is rather similar to the first time you drink brandy—but without the choking."

"Ahem. I hate to intrude, but I believe I have this dance."

Good heavens, she had been so involved with her friends she had not recognized the first strains of the waltz. Her grand moment had arrived. Pressing her palm to Trevor's arm, she took one step and flinched. "Oh dear, I seem to have twisted my ankle." Caroline prayed her ruse was convincing. "Brie, would you be so kind as to act in my stead?"

"That is not necessary." He placed a hand at the small of her back. "If you are hurt, you should sit. Allow me to escort you to the *chaise*."

"Nonsense, I insist you go on without me." She glanced at Brie and winked. "Please, Sabrina."

"Are you sure?" Her lifelong friend appeared perplexed, and Caroline knew why.

"Positive." Retreating, Caroline stifled a giggle. "Besides, this will give you two an opportunity to become better acquainted."

"As you wish." Brie grabbed Trevor by the elbow and led him to the slaughter.

Trevor did not know what to make of his intended's curious behavior. Instead of taking her ease in the nearest seat, she strolled along the rear wall, sporting a grin that made the hair stand at the nape of his neck. Nothing made sense—until he engaged one Sabrina Douglas in a waltz.

The rather eccentric young woman had a devil of a unique talent. Every turn—hell, every step, she trounced his toes and any other inch of his feet she could reach. It would be a miracle if he ever walked limp-free again. And while he had never been partial to orchestra music, he found a new appreciation for the stuff in that it concealed his grunts and groans of discomfort.

"Sorry about your toes, Lord Lockwood." Sabrina cast him a knowing smile. "Cannot imagine why Caroline imperiled you so, given she intends to marry you. Everyone knows I dance with the grace and ease of a cow with its hooves stuck in the mud."

"Do not fret, Miss Douglas." The mental fog cleared, and Trevor chuckled. How could anyone not admire such frank honesty? "You are doing fine."

Her guileless admission told him she had been an unwitting accomplice in whatever game his fiancée played. Making a note to pair her with Everett at the first opportunity, he trudged forth. Upon his deliverance, he searched for his charming future wife, but his little angel remained noticeably absent. The dinner bell sounded, and he decided to adjourn to the dining room without his bride-to-be.

"Lord Lockwood."

Trevor turned to find Sabrina's elder sibling waiting for him. "Yes, Miss Douglas?"

Cara inclined her head and smiled. "Caroline asked me to accompany you to supper."

Suspicion nipped at his heels, and he braced for the next shot across his bow. "I hope she is not unwell?"

"Oh, it is nothing like that." With consummate grace, Cara accepted his proffered arm. "She is taking a breath of fresh air and will join us in a moment."

A brief scan of the thinning crowd in the ballroom confirmed his intended's conspicuous absence. He wondered what next Caroline had in store. "I am at your service, Miss Douglas."

Trevor soon found he was also at Cara's mercy.

Seated in pride of place at the end of a long table, the Douglas sisters flanked his left, while Alex and Elaine perched on the other side. In rapid succession, the charming but importuning ladies hurled question after question at him. And to his dismay, theirs was the sort of interrogation designed to bring a man to his knees—if not the brink of insanity.

"How old are you?" Elaine inquired.

"Have you ever been in love?" Cara asked.

Alex leaned forward. "Do you like to dance?"

"Are you a fisherman?" The last query came from Sabrina.

He shuddered. Were he aboard his ship in the middle of a raging storm and faced with such an examination, he would swim for shore. Movement at the opposite end of the table caught his eye.

With a gloating smile, Caroline raised a glass in what was no doubt a mocking toast.

So his delectable future wife had thrown down the gauntlet. Lucky for his bride-to-be, he was more than ready to meet her challenge. He shook his head and laughed. With the patience of a saint, he answered each and every inquiry. Then, he retrieved his balloon of brandy and saluted his fetching fiancée.

Let the games begin.

~

A FORTNIGHT LATER, Trevor had reached the end of his tether.

His stubborn future wife had resisted his every effort to woo her. How in bloody hell was he supposed to romance a woman he had not danced or dined with in a sennight? He had tried everything he could think of to put their relationship back on track, had even solicited Everett's assistance in cornering his quarry. But regardless of his attempts to curb Caroline's rebellion, she remained a step ahead of his game. Consequently, their courtship had digressed to a blundering comedy of errors.

Determined to strike an accord with a certain chestnut-haired termagant, he trudged up the stairs to Elliott House, with a peace offering, and raised a hand to knock on the door, when it opened suddenly. Faced by a rather stiff looking character, he suppressed a smirk and handed his card to the butler.

"This way, my lord." The voice held as much personality as a tabletop.

Trevor trailed the staid servant to the drawing room. In the doorway, the duchess stood as chaperone, and he paused for a last minute check of his appearance, because he so wished to make a good impression. Just then, his future in-law turned and flashed a dazzling smile, which he found inexpressibly arresting, given the resemblance to his fiancée.

Even at her age, Her Grace of Rylan was a striking

woman. As if by magic, the visage he studied transformed into that of an older, more mature Caroline. The duchess spoke, the image of his intended faded, and he snapped to attention.

"Lord Lockwood, it is kind of you to join us," she whispered. "I thought it best to maintain my daughter's social schedule in allowing these gentlemen to pay call, but you need not worry, because I daresay she has shown greater enthusiasm when faced with having a tooth extracted."

Nagging doubts yielded to smug satisfaction. Perhaps he had been mistaken, and it would not be so difficult to win her. But what if Caroline had planned another trick? Peering into the room, he spied the source of his confusion, dressed in lavender and seated on a sofa.

One of her many callers—and a clumsy buffoon at that —recounted a harrowing tale of hunting and horsemanship so utterly unbelievable as to make the stories by the Brothers Grimm pale in comparison. Trevor remained rooted in the doorway, positive he might be ill at any moment, thus necessitating a quick escape, and endured a truly painful ode to Caroline's blue eyes. As he struggled to ignore the syrupy sentimental ravings, he took note of the floral bouquets, offerings to his soon-to-be-wife's beauty, no doubt, perched atop various pedestals about the room. The unfortunate suitors had not a chance.

Caroline was his—already promised.

So why was he wound tight as a clock spring?

Glancing at the small box he held in his tremulous grasp, he wondered self-consciously if he had erred in his chosen gift. Thankfully, before another embarrassing and overzealous oratory could begin, she met his stare.

"Lord Lockwood?" Caroline rose from the sofa. "What a wonderful surprise."

As the center attraction, he cleared his throat, tugged at his cravat, and sketched his most polished bow. "My lady."

With noticeable aloofness, which set his nerves on edge, she inclined her head. "Do make yourself comfortable, my lord."

Had she intended for him to crouch on the floor? "I would love to, but every seat is occupied."

"Take a position beside Caroline," Her Grace suggested.

In that instant, Trevor decided he rather liked his mother-in-law-to-be.

"Of course." Caroline averted her gaze, resituated herself, and patted the cushion at her left.

A warmer reception would have boosted his flagging confidence, and the pack of hopeful suitors shot him sullen glares, as he navigated the crowd. He unbuttoned his coat and settled next to his lady. Then he recalled the present he had procured as a token of remembrance in honor of the treasure she had bestowed upon him that superb night in his bunk. "And this modest offering is for you, Lady Caroline."

Was it his imagination or had she bounced when she accepted the parcel. "You need not have gone to such trouble, Lord Lockwood."

"It was no trouble. And while I did not think of flowers, my selection has brought me many fond memories, and I hope it does the same for you." A chill shivered down his spine as she lifted the lid and peeked inside. He held his breath and exhaled only when her face colored a lovely shade of pink. Without doubt, she knew precisely to which memories he referred.

"Oh, my lord, it is lovely. What a thoughtful gift." Caroline lifted the delicate wooden miniature, complete with sails. In fact, the ship was an exact replica of the *Hera*. "Thank you. I shall treasure it always."

Bursting with pride, Trevor could summon no words of response so he merely nodded his head. No doubt their war of wills was at an end, and Caroline would once again welcome his suit. Yes, for a man who had never courted a woman, he was doing quite well.

TWO WEEKS LATER, Caroline stood amid her group in Lady Northcote's ballroom, pretending to listen as Alex shared some new bit of gossip. In reality, she mulled her—or should she say Trevor's—agenda for the night. Since embarking on her war of retribution, she had reveled in success after success.

The previous night had been her crowning achievement. She had managed to seat Trevor between the Hogart twins, commonly referred to as the braying asses, at supper. Even now she laughed as she recalled the expression of abject horror on his face as they returned to the ballroom after the meal. She had also noticed he had not eaten much. The Hogart twins had that effect on people.

What amazed her, however, was that he took her tortuous enterprises in stride. With good humor, he met every dance partner—even Brie. Her captain answered every question with a smile and managed to charm every single female in her lifelong group of friends.

Including Caroline.

She thought it the worst insult that she should be falling in love with Trevor all over again.

Of course, the replica of the *Hera* holding pride of place on her bedside table had not helped matters. Whenever she looked on the precious miniature, guilt wreaked havoc on her conscience. Perhaps she could relent just a bit. Perhaps she should grant him one waltz.

Glancing at the full dance card hanging from her wrist, she smiled as she considered her sudden popularity. Brie had teased Caroline mercilessly that it might have something to do with the radiant glow on her face, since she returned from Jamaica. Of course, Brie also intimated it had nothing to do with the sea air and everything to do with a certain sea captain, a fact Caroline denied to no avail.

But she had not wanted to glow with happiness. She had not wanted to hope. She had not wanted to believe Trevor had any real interest in her. Caroline feared the minute she invested the minutest amount of faith in him that he would disappoint her, once more.

And how he had disappointed her.

Yet she loved him. Never would she have shared her body with him, given herself to him, had she not first committed her heart, which made his betrayal far more grievous.

"You are woolgathering, my lady." Trevor chuckled. "Dare I ask if your thoughts are of me?"

Forcing a smile, she gazed from beneath her lashes at Trevor. "You may ask, my lord, but I shall never tell."

"I believe this is our dance." Oh, he was in a mood to play, and she was in a mood to indulge him.

Her resolve weakened, and she stepped forward without checking her card. "I believe you are correct."

"My back has been bothering me today." He wrinkled his nose and winced. "But I should be keelhauled before I allow you to suffer because of my malady, so I took the liberty of procuring an alternate partner, Sir Kleinfeld."

Caroline gulped.

Even Sabrina could not rival Sir Archibald Kleinfeld's talents on the dance floor. The mere mention of his name was enough to strike terror in the heart and feet of any debutante. "My lord, I would be willing to sit this one out and enjoy your company, instead."

"I should sooner walk the plank than deny you the simple pleasure of a waltz, my sweet Caroline." Trevor clucked his tongue. "Given your estimable efforts to ensure my warm welcome, upon my return to London after an extended absence, I consider it my solemn duty to reciprocate, in kind."

"Oh, I say. This is a treat." Wearing a fuchsia coat emblazoned with large gold buttons, Sir Kleinfeld clicked his heels and shot her a toothy grin. "It would be my honor, Lady Caroline."

To refuse the gawky peacock would be an unforgivable breach of decorum, so Caroline forced a smile to her lips and uttered a silent prayer for the health and welfare of her toes as she placed her hand in the crook of his elbow.

Hers was a useless endeavor.

One after another, the less-than-graceful males of the *ton*—all substitutions for her supposed partners—had approached and claimed her dances. By the time the dinner bell pealed, her poor feet throbbed. Without doubt, she realized her husband-to-be had exacted lethal recompense for her shenanigans, of late, and resolved to bear his abuse in the same sporting fashion as he had suffered hers. She supposed he was owed one good turn.

Caroline soon discovered Trevor's revenge had just begun.

While considering the selection of sweets offered after the meal, six full portions of lemon custard suddenly appeared before her. She had always thought lemon custard the ideal dessert to encourage moderate food consumption. With a consistency similar to the phlegm that pooled in one's throat when cursed with a wicked cold, and a taste to match, it was better suited to punishment for a recalcitrant child.

A glance over either shoulder revealed various smiling dance partners from earlier in the evening. "W-what have we here, gentlemen?"

"In a humbling display of gallantry, which I could only hope to imitate, Lord Lockwood shared with his potential rivals your particular affinity for lemon custard," Sir Kleinfeld stated with youthful enthusiasm. "Eat up, Lady Caroline."

Determined to persevere, and refusing to allow Trevor a measure of victory, Caroline clutched a spoon, shoveled a large amount of the vile concoction, and sucked it into her mouth. Shuddering, she closed her eyes and swallowed the clammy congeal, which stuck in her throat.

"She must be chilled," remarked one of her admirers. "I shall fetch her some ratafia."

Now that added insult to injury. "No."

With every consecutive bite, Caroline reminded herself she had asked for it. No doubt Trevor had conceived of her scheme and engaged in combat of his own contrivance. Summoning resilience of which she had not thought herself capable, she cleared the last dish of custard, when her nemesis appeared at the other end of the table. As she had done to him that first night of battle, he raised his glass in toast and smiled.

Just as she was about to return the gesture, a sick feeling came over her, and the ground teetered beneath her feet. With a hand to her mouth, she fled the dining room. As she navigated the ballroom at a furious speed, her slippers skidded on the polished marble. After running through the double doors at the center of the back wall, she hit the flagged surface of the terrace and just reached the hedge.

In the bushes, Caroline bent and revisited all six portions of lemon custard.

CHAPTER TEN

*A*fter the infamous lemon custard affair, Caroline made a concerted effort to blend into the background of the Lester's formidable ballroom, the following evening. She had learned her lesson and had no desire to attract attention. When fencing with one rogue sea captain, she was out of her league. If she were lucky, Trevor would accept the dessert disaster as suitable recompense and punish her no further.

Should he wish to commence the courtship, he would get no argument from her. As far as she was concerned, they had reached a tenuous détente. Pressing a palm to her still shaky belly, she prayed he felt the same. Hugging the shadow of a large bust seated atop a pedestal, she almost jumped out of her skin when the devil in question tapped her shoulder.

"Come." He caught her wrist. "Take a turn about the room with me."

Caroline's first instinct was to run.

"I warn you, I shall brook no refusal." As if reading her thoughts, Trevor clutched her elbow and anchored her at his side. "Any rejection will be considered a call to arms, and I am better than you at this game."

"Rejection, indeed." Though his smile conveyed his threat was in jest, Caroline could not muster sufficient confidence to gainsay him. "I should be honored to walk with you, my lord."

They strolled, unhurried and nonchalant, nodding acknowledgements to various notables, as they weaved left and then right through the crush. Conscious of the pointed stares and whispered comments, she rued the gossip spreading among the *ton*. Was it so inconceivable that an earl would be interested in the daughter of a duke or just one that was neither petite nor pretty? Perhaps the curious spectators believed her familial connections were her most promising assets.

They neared a sidewall, and he paused at a door. With a mischievous grin, he arched a brow. "Trust me?"

"Certainly not." If her eyes had not betrayed her fear, her voice underscored her trepidation. "You have given me ample reason to suspect you of the worst motives."

"Wise woman." He chuckled, pushed open the panel, and handed her over the threshold.

The small study presented a cozy sanctuary bathed in the silvery illumination of the moonlight filtering from the doors propped open to the terrace. Deserted but for the two of them, the chamber was cool and inviting, unlike the stifling warmth of the crowded ballroom.

Before she could protest, Trevor leaned against the closed portal, hauled her against him, and took possession of her mouth, plundering her flesh as would a starving man who had just found sustenance. For several minutes, he held her tight, while he skimmed her lower back before his hand came to rest on her bottom.

Ignoring the warning bells in her brain, Caroline wrapped her arms about his neck, twined her fingers in his hair, and held his lips to hers. Scorching heat poured through her veins, fire burned in her loins, and she melted into him. It was so lovely to taste her captain again. After a few heated, groping, desperately quiet minutes, his frenetic intensity eased. Trevor's caresses relaxed, when he at last lifted his head. When their gazes met, what she spied made her gasp in surprise.

Visible in his stare loomed the same raw hunger ravaging her senses.

But why should he be thus affected? Was it possible? Could it be that he wanted her? Perplexed by his reaction to their scandalous dalliance, she uttered the first thing that came to mind to break the uncomfortable silence. "You kissed me."

One day soon she was going to have to sit down and pen a series of suitable rejoinders that would keep her from appearing a complete idiot in similar instances.

"I could not help myself." Trevor grinned. "I have wanted to do that ever since we returned to London."

Caroline blinked. "You wanted to kiss me?"

"Aye." His grin widened into a boyish smile. "I have missed you."

"You have missed me?" Bloody hell, she sounded interested and bit her tongue.

"Caroline?"

"Yes?"

"Why do you keep repeating what I say?"

"I do not know." She shrugged. "Perhaps I am distracted."

"Then allow me to distract you further." Trevor bent his head and again set his mouth to hers and passion erupted.

Images from the past flooded her consciousness, a soupçon of alarm swirled about her feet, nipped at her nerves, and shivered over her skin, but Caroline languished amid a tidal wave of pleasure. His words of desire echoed in her ears—until the refrain mutated into unhinged mirth. Taunting. Mocking. Jolted to reality, she stiffened in his embrace.

"What is it, darling?" Trevor nuzzled her temple.

"Darling?" She vented a self-deprecating snort. "Why do you speak to me thus? You are no gentleman to feign an attachment we both know you do not harbor."

"I beg your pardon." Even in the dimness of the room, his shock was palpable.

"You do not want me. You never wanted me." She wrestled from his embrace. "I was nothing more than a convenient means to an end."

"What are you talking about?" Trevor reached for her. "We are going to be married."

"Only because you are forced to repair the damage to my reputation." Expressed aloud, the truth devastated her, and Caroline retreated. "I know I am not the sort of woman a man desires."

"You think I do not want you?" He lunged, caught her by the wrist, and pressed her hand to a firm bulge in his trousers. "Does that feel like I do not want you?" In an illicit rhythm, he rubbed her palm over his erection. "Do you remember holding this part of me inside you?"

Wicked images flooded her mind, ensnared her senses. Naked bodies sliding, pumping, and grinding to a chorus of masculine groans and feminine sighs playing a sensual accompaniment. The study seemed suddenly oppressive, and she could not breathe.

"Let me go." Caroline struggled to wrench free, but his iron grip imprisoned her.

"Do you think of me at night when you go to bed?" he asked, his voice husky. "When you slide between the sheets, do you envision me at your side?"

"No." She lied in a pathetic attempt to maintain the last portion of pride.

In her dreams, Trevor came to her without fail. In the realm of make-believe, she relived everything he had done to her, all they had shared, aboard the *Hera*. But in her fantasies, his seduction was always preceded by a pledge of everlasting love, and sometimes she woke to find a slick wetness where their bodies had come together. Surrendering just enough to trace his turgid length with her fingers, she gave herself to the temptation he manifested. To her surprise, Trevor let go her wrist and allowed her to stroke him, at will.

"I think of you every night," he said on a groan. "I taste your honey lips on mine."

Was it possible? Could he be telling the truth?

"I conjure your warm, soft body beneath me, taking my flesh deep within yours, again and again, until you cry in release." He sighed, a heavenly affectation she felt to her core.

Dare she hope? "Oh, Trevor."

"I want you, my sweet Caroline."

Out of nowhere, her brother's words revisited her: *He thought you a whore.*

The resultant heartbreak chilled her to the bone.

"No." She withdrew her hand as though she had been scalded. "You wanted Dalton's mistress. That is not the same as wanting me."

CONFUSED AND PAINFULLY AROUSED, Trevor did not pursue his fiancée as she fled the study via the terrace. Moments later, he connected his fist with the oak-paneled door, and the pain in his knuckles offered a welcome respite from the ache in his trousers. When he managed to compose himself, he returned to the ballroom in search of his intended. He had not far to look.

Caroline had taken refuge amid her lifelong friends.

Though none gave any indication they were aware of her tremulous state, he reminded himself they were her family —not his. If she hinted at their quarrel, though he doubted she would, he knew to whom they would ally. Alone and outnumbered, Trevor headed for the card room and a bottle of brandy.

IN WHAT HAD BECOME a frustrating routine, Trevor trudged up the entrance stairs to Elliott House. He had been seeking a private audience with his fiancée for three days and had yet to have any success. It had not taken a genius to surmise the little darling avoided him, a tactic that drove him to the edge of insanity. With renewed determination, he pounded the oak panels. When the granite-faced butler opened the door, Trevor shoved his way inside the grand residence. "I wish to see Lady Caroline, and I am not leaving until she grants me an audience."

"Her ladyship is out, sir." The manservant appeared terminally bored. "If you wish to leave a card, I shall convey your regard."

"Like bloody hell." Trevor strode to the opening of the

drawing room. "Caroline!" He shouted at the ceiling. "I am not leaving until you come out." Tapping an impatient beat with his booted foot, he put his hands on his hips and waited for a sign of his exasperating future wife. Seconds passed with nary a hint of his intended. When next they met, he was going to heat her posterior for such insolence. Lashing out with an arm, he emitted a primitive growl and stomped back into the foyer. "Caroline, I swear on our first-born, I will remain at this very spot until you face me."

"What on earth is going on here?" The duchess appeared at the landing and navigated the grand staircase. "Lord Lockwood? Are you trying to bring the whole house down about you?"

"Your Grace." Trevor bowed, and then stood upright, arms folded. "I demand to see Lady Caroline."

She waved to the butler, who made a fast exit. "I am afraid that is not possible."

"You refuse my request?" He slumped.

"I do not." His soon-to-be-mother-in-law smiled. "The simple fact is my daughter is not here. She is, at present, lunching with the Douglas sisters."

"Oh." It was as if someone had knocked the wind from his sails. Trevor stared at the marble floor, a wave of defeat weighed heavy on his shoulders. "I give up."

The duchess approached. "Perhaps I can be of service?"

After placing a chaste kiss on her proffered hand, he contemplated the estimable noblewoman. She was a nurturing parent, which in light of his formative years defied logic. Never had he seen a mother so devoted to her child, as his own had abandoned him for her lover, while his father had forsaken Trevor for comfort in a bottle. If there were anyone he could rely on to help him, that person would be Her Grace.

With a dip of her chin, the duchess seemed to sense his quandary. "Will you join me for tea, Lord Lockwood?"

"It would be an honor, Your Grace," he said before he realized he had spoken.

As he followed Caroline's mother into the drawing room, Trevor drowned in a dark vortex of indecision, as though he had cast off without a map and a compass. For him, asking anyone for help manifested a cold swim in unfamiliar waters.

"May I offer you a refreshment, Lord Lockwood?" She settled on a sofa and lifted a silver teapot from a matching service.

Trevor shook his head. He opened his mouth, rethought his words, and resumed his repetitive stride. Finally, he whirled in a half circle. "Why does Caroline think herself unattractive?"

"Well—"

"She is beautiful—stunning in my estimation. Yet she believes herself unappealing." He splayed his arms wide. "I ask you why?"

"Perhaps because—"

"It is too ridiculous. I have never found a woman half so pleasing to the eye." Trevor huffed a breath in frustration. "And she calls herself undesirable. How can that be possible?"

"Lord Lockwood." She appeared to be staving off laughter.

"Yes, Your Grace?" He nodded once.

"I give you leave to address me as Sarah, and please be seated. It is quite difficult to hold a conversation with someone who will not stand still." She retrieved a square of shortbread from a plate. "I feel as though I am attempting to speak with a racehorse."

"My apologies." Trevor plopped himself into an over-stuffed chair, propped his elbows on his knees, and cradled his chin in his hands. "Help me to understand Caroline." He narrowed his stare. "Surely this low opinion of herself stems from something more than the incident with the Darwiths?"

"Much as it pains me to admit it, I must bear some of the responsibility for her situation." Sarah brought a cup to her mouth but paused, and an expression of sadness marred her elegant features. "Caroline was her father's daughter. Charles doted on her, raising her in much the same crude fashion as Blake. I may have indulged their unusual relationship to the point of neglect."

Her Grace's revelations offered invaluable insight. He inclined his head and arched a brow. "How so?"

"When Caroline attended finishing school, she had a terrible time adjusting. She was a bit of a Long Meg, more athletic than graceful, as I am sure you have discovered. Her marks for deportment were always her worst." Sarah pursed her lips. "The business with the Darwiths was the final straw, I am afraid."

"How can I make it better." Sitting up straight, he slapped a hand to his thigh. "And an apology is past due for the unfortunate circumstances surrounding our acquaintance. While I cannot undo what has already occurred, please know that I have only your daughter's best interests, at heart."

"Indeed." For an uncomfortable few minutes, she scrutinized him, and he shifted beneath the weight of her examination. "From my understanding, you shared a cabin with Caroline, aboard your ship. What do you think of her, Lord Lockwood?"

"Please, call me Trevor. And, if you must know, I find my

lady the most frustrating, willful, difficult woman of my existence." Then he recalled fonder times and smiled. "But she risked her life to repair a sail, spent hours mending my men's clothes, and devoted herself to improving the galley fare. She is a credit to her sex. Deuced near faced a bloody mutiny when my crew thought I had hurt her."

"So you generously proposed a betrothal?" The duchess tapped a finger to her chin. "Given our connections, I can secure an amenable match for my daughter, should you reconsider your sacrifice. Caroline is—"

"No." Trevor gritted his teeth and composed himself to ward against further spontaneous outburst. "Forgive my forthrightness, but, as I have claimed her bride's prize, it is my duty to make amends. And Caroline and I got on well before I learned of her personage, so it stands to reason we will enjoy such equanimity after the vows are spoken."

"Delighted to hear it."

"She will make an excellent countess."

"Of that I have no doubt."

"And I am, to a degree, fond of her."

"Yes, I believe you are incomparably suited." The duchess giggled, and she gave him collywobbles.

To his delight, and unimaginable good fortune, Her Grace of Rylan proved to be a veritable treasure trove of information concerning his difficult bride-to-be. As he would were he studying for exams at Oxford, Trevor made a mental list and checked it twice while simultaneously devising a counterattack.

By the time his affable hostess walked him into the foyer, Trevor was energized with a renewed sense of purpose. "Words cannot adequately express my gratitude for your assistance, Your Grace. I fear I owe you a debt I can never repay."

"Think nothing of it." Sarah patted his cheek, and he struggled to suppress a flinch. "Make my daughter happy, and you may consider the debt paid in full."

"I—that is to say—" Unaccustomed to such innocent displays of affection, he searched for a suitable rejoinder.

"Dear man, you will make Caroline a fine husband." She stumped him again with a squeeze of his hand. "Why do we not look on this afternoon as a simple meeting of like minds?"

"As you wish." He bowed.

The familiar granite-faced butler opened the door, Trevor turned to the threshold—and stopped dead in his tracks.

Oh, yes.

THE SUN blinded Caroline as she emerged from the Rylan town carriage, and she shielded her eyes from the bright rays. Settling her skirts, she climbed the stairs to her home. Her stomach was a lead ball of jumbled nerves, as memories of the previous night assailed her emotions. How she managed to partake of lunch with Cara and Sabrina without reliving the meal soon afterward would be one of life's great mysteries. With a none-too-graceful yawn, she pondered a nap. Shadows enveloped her as she entered the foyer.

And walked straight into Trevor's arms.

Her gasp of surprise passed from her lips to his. As he suckled her flesh, he thrust his tongue in an obvious rhythm, bold and illicit—wild and inciting. She responded in kind, engaging her captain in a sensuous duel. Wool tickled her palms as she clutched his arms through his coat, and the rock hard muscle beneath her hands tensed in an enthralling display of masculine physique.

It seemed ages since Trevor last kissed her.

But as Caroline found her passionate pace, he released her. Without a greeting or a goodbye, Trevor left her standing in the foyer. Eyes wide and mouth agape, she touched her fingertips to her lips and exhaled. "Good heavens."

Slowly, she turned and barely stifled a scream.

At the foot of the grand staircase, her mother stood, sporting an expression Caroline was not certain she trusted. "How was your engagement, my dear?"

"It was lovely." The annoying warmth of a blush permeated her cheeks, and she wished she could sever her head. "Um, that was Lord Lockwood."

The smile her mother adopted gave Caroline gooseflesh. "Indeed, it was."

IT WAS THE FASHIONABLE HOUR, later that same day, and Caroline strolled with her mother, nodding acknowledgements to Lady Jersey and Lady Sefton. Wearing a long, grey twill sarsnet pelisse, *á la militaire*, with clasps of mother-of-pearl set in old gold, and kid half boots, she adjusted her crème Limerick gloves and mulled the earlier events. To all appearances, she was nothing more than a blushing debutante, participating in another dreaded social spectacle known as the Promenade. Yet her mind a mass of confusion, and on more than one occasion, she had to be prompted to offer a greeting or risk cutting an important member of the *ton*. As her world spiraled beyond her control, her body seemed a foreign entity, because she never knew it was possible to be hot and cold, at once.

Damn Trevor and his kiss.

If she closed her eyes, she could taste his lips on hers, sense his tongue rousing hers, and thrill to the fiery heat of his embrace.

So she had not closed her eyes.

"Lord Lockwood, how lovely to see you."

Oh, no. She winced. Not again.

As her mother welcomed the lethal adversary, Caroline fidgeted and averted her stare. Of course, propriety forbade her to ignore her fiancé, but why had he come to the park? For all the years she had joined in the ridiculous parade, never had she encountered the Earl of Lockwood.

"Would you be so kind as to escort Caroline?" her mother inquired. "I must speak with Lady Northcote."

Bloody hell, her mother was a turncoat.

Against efforts to the contrary, Caroline stiffened her spine and gritted her teeth. Could she not remain relaxed and composed around that man? In silence, she uttered a quick plea to the Almighty, asking that her future husband be struck dumb in that instant.

"It would be my honor, Your Grace."

Her prayer went unanswered.

"My lady." His voice was smooth as silk and shivered over her from head to toe.

Questioning her sanity, Caroline lit her gaze upon her nemesis. "Lord Lockwood." She dipped her chin in a proper address. But she paid no heed to the fluttering in her belly and the pounding of her heart. How could she wage war against him when she could not ally her body and mind?

Trevor offered his arm. "May I say you look very lovely this evening?"

"What are you doing here?" she snapped.

"Smile, my dear." He cast her a lazy grin. "Else you will give the scandalmongers a juicy tidbit for tomorrow's sheet."

Though it seemed an insurmountable feat, Caroline managed a suitable expression. Together, they toured the park and, to her displeasure, snared the avid attention of the *ton*, as evidenced by the pointed stares. She could kill her mother.

"Why are you here?" Her tone was pure ice and more than conveyed her suspicions.

"I thought it obvious." The bounder had the audacity to wink. "I am courting you, darling."

"That is not necessary," she replied, as she acknowledged Countess Lieven.

"But it is," Trevor purred. "And I consider it a treat not to be missed.

"You are being ridiculous." Lady Ainsworth waved, and Caroline responded, in kind. "You do not want to marry me."

"I beg your pardon." Her escort stopped mid-stride. "Who said I did not want to marry you?"

Anger seared a path from her brain to her fist, and before she brought shame to her entire family, she resisted the urge to punch her husband-to-be in the nose. Could an injured snout be passed to an heir? "Tell me truthfully. Before you discovered my identity, were you intending to propose upon our return to London?"

FACED with a question he was certain had no safe escape, Trevor hesitated. Lying was not an option. If it were anyone else, he would have done just that, but not with Caroline. Expecting—demanding—honesty from her, he was compelled to surrender the same. Braced for her reaction, he said, "Well, I would have proposed something, just not marriage."

"As I suspected." She let go his arm and stormed toward Park Lane.

Mindful of their audience, of their situation, he gave a tempered chase. At the roadside, his bride-to-be looked left, then right. Despite her unveiled ire, she possessed the good sense to wait for traffic to clear. Though his gaze focused on the flirty flounce of her brown curls, a rumble of carriage wheels caught his ear. He turned and spied an unmarked rig barreling down the thoroughfare. Clad in black, a scarf shielding his face, the driver flicked the reins, as if spurring his horses.

"My lady." Though he could not fathom why, a chill of unease traipsed his spine. By his second step, Trevor was running. "Caroline."

"Watch out!" Passersby shouted in unison.

The ominous equipage lurched onto the pavement, and his future wife screamed. He expected her to leap clear of the danger, but she appeared dazed, as she stood stock-still. At the last possible second, he snaked an arm about her waist and lifted her from harm's way.

The brisk wind from the runaway carriage rustled his hair as Trevor shielded her with his body. Nearby strollers, shaking fists in the air, barked admonishments at the careless coachman. But the rig returned to the lane and sped off, disappearing as fast as it had materialized.

With a sob, Caroline buried her face in his chest and trembled in his embrace.

"Shh," he crooned as he cradled her head. "You are all right, love."

With an expression of worry mixed with fear, the duchess approached. "What happened?"

"Nothing. It was an accident." Touched by her concern for her daughter, he was not sure he would ever become accustomed to such displays of affection. "With your permission, I will walk Lady Caroline home."

"Of course." His soon-to-be-mother-in-law cast him a timid smile. "I should come with you."

"That is not necessary, Mama." The lady of the moment inched from his hold. "As Lord Lockwood said, I am fine. A bit dusty, perhaps, but none the worse for wear."

"If you are certain you are unharmed." The duchess cupped her daughter's cheek. "I shall be along shortly. Ring for a bath, and I shall send word to the Hogarts that you are not feeling well. And I will have Cook prepare your favorite dessert of strawberries and cream."

"That sounds lovely." His intended clutched his arm. "Enjoy the promenade, and do not hurry on my account."

In silence, Trevor squired Caroline to Elliott House, but his mind was anything but quiet.

Unanswered questions swirled in his brain, and uneasy conjectures and suppositions nipped at his heels. Was he panicking? Was he making too much of something that amounted to nothing more than a minor mishap?

The ever-aloof butler set the doors wide as they ascended the entrance stairs.

In the foyer, Trevor asked, "Is Rylan in residence?"

"His Grace is in the study, your lordship." The manservant bowed. "If you will follow—"

"I will show Lord Lockwood to the study." Caroline tugged at his elbow. "Why do you want to see Blake?"

As she steered him into the hall to the right, he pondered the situation. Since he had not wanted to alarm her, he needed a distraction. "We are supposed to meet at White's, and in light of your unfortunate accident, I expect to be late."

"You cannot be serious." Caroline arched a brow and wrinkled her nose. "There is no need to fuss. As you told Mama, I am fine. Yes, I am a bit shaken, but it is nothing that a long soak in a hot bath will not cure."

What he would give to join her in a bath, to scrub her back, but Trevor wanted to caution his bride-to-be. Wanted to warn her of a danger of which he had not known. He was not sure what motivated his sense of urgency, his well-honed instincts. But something within him stirred, and a prevailing foreboding of dread portended danger.

Words, the echo of an angry threat, reverberated in his ears. An image of a masked coachman, the scoundrel's gaze fixed on Caroline, flashed before his eyes.

"Here we are—"

The sharp edge of desire lanced through his belly, and Trevor pulled her into a little alcove just outside the door she had indicated. He was not certain why he had done it, what had moved him to attack, but he pounced on his intended right there in her home.

On a groan, he covered her lips with his in a communion of soul-deep passion. With implicit caresses, he skimmed her curves. Desire shivered over his flesh as Caroline pressed herself to the evidence of his arousal in untutored wantonness. When he settled a palm to the swell of her breast, she gave a gasp of surprise into his mouth. Her hands fisted in his hair, holding him to her in a frantic embrace. How he ached to lift her skirts and take her against the wall, to savor her cries of pleasure—

"*What in bloody hell is going on here?*"

His lady flinched and tried to retreat at the bark of her brother's booming baritone, but Trevor tightened his hold and cradled her head with his hand. Driven by a wave of almost obsessive protectiveness, he made no attempt to hide the fact that they had been kissing. For some reason he could not fathom, he compounded his breach of decorum and stroked her cheek with his thumb in a scandalous display of affection.

"We need to talk." He met the hotheaded duke's stare. "Now."

"What are you about?" His eyes flared, and Blake lowered his chin. "By all that is holy, I swear if you were not betrothed to my sister, I would see you at dawn on Paddington Green."

"Stop shouting, Blake." Caroline inched from Trevor's grasp and, with admirable courage, faced her elder sibling. "I was simply showing Lord Lockwood to your study."

"Via the path to ruin?" her brash relation retorted.

"I beg your pardon?" In a gesture that was becoming quite familiar, his future wife folded her arms and compressed her lips. "As you pointed out, we are betrothed. And Lord Lockwood can hardly spoil that of which he has already partaken."

At her bold rejoinder, Trevor just managed to suppress a snort of pride.

Her brother stood, mouth agape, and shock evident in his visage.

"Go upstairs and have your bath, my lady." He pressed a chaste kiss to her forehead. "Blake and I have business to discuss."

"As you wish." Caroline smiled. "I will leave the telling of the incident in the park to you."

"What incident?" the duke inquired.

"Pray, a moment." Trevor studied the elegant sway of her hips as she strolled down the hall. At the end of the corridor, his fiancée cast him a glance before disappearing around the corner. Good God, had she not known how she affected him when she looked at him like that?

"Lockwood, if you are finished ogling my sister, I would appreciate an explanation."

"Of course." Trevor blinked. "Might I trouble you for a brandy?"

"Indeed." Blake ushered him into the ducal domain. "Make yourself comfortable, as you are so cozy with my family."

Ignoring the barb, Trevor settled into a chair before the large desk at the back of the sumptuously appointed study, as his soon-to-be-in-law lifted a decanter and filled two glasses.

Blake offered him a balloon and perched on the edge of the desk. "What has brought you here, Lockwood?"

After a healthy gulp of brandy, Trevor detailed the sword fight aboard the *Hera* and the death of Henri Cavalier at Caroline's hands.

"You exposed her to Cavalier?" Blake slapped a palm to his thigh. "Bloody nasty business."

"Not willingly. I left her in my cabin with orders to lock the door behind me." Trevor rolled his eyes and shook his head. "The next thing I knew she was dancing across the decks with a pirate."

"And she killed him." Blake stood upright and speared his fingers through his hair. "That is not good."

"But that is only half of it." Trevor sighed.

The duke narrowed his stare. "There is more?"

As the nobleman's demeanor grew darker by the minute, Trevor relayed the event in the park. "Blake, I can see that you are concerned, but you must know Cavalier would have to be insane to venture to London. It is too ridiculous to believe he will carry out his threat to Caroline's person."

"And yet your first instinct was to seek my counsel." Downing the contents of his glass in one impressive swallow, Blake poured himself another brandy. "Caroline was very young when our family first clashed with the Cavaliers. She would not understand the significance of her actions and the danger in which she has placed herself."

"What have you not told me?" Tension invested his frame, and Trevor rubbed the back of neck. "Do you suspect the accident with the carriage was intentional?"

"Aye," Blake responded. "As do you, or you would not have thought it important enough to mention. Jean Marc Cavalier is as driven as he is ruthless. If he has discovered my sister's identity, I have no doubt he will seek his revenge, at any cost."

"But he is the most wanted blackguard on the seas. Were he caught on our shores, he would be given a fair trial and hanged." Trevor set his balloon on a side table and rested his elbows on his knees. "The man is without honor. And I cannot imagine his brother's life is worth so great a price."

"His brother *and* his father." Blake swore.

Trevor leapt from his chair. "What?"

"You see our sire killed his."

CHAPTER ELEVEN

The following morning, Caroline pondered the actions of one handsome sea captain. What was she to make of Trevor's odd behavior the previous evening? After the impromptu tryst in the hall outside Blake's study, and their subsequent discovery by her hotheaded brother, Trevor consented to join the family for dinner. How shocked she had been when she entered the drawing room and found her fiancé waiting to greet her. He had been attentive, charming, and quite like the affable host whose company she had enjoyed aboard the *Hera*. The experience left her uncertain of her chosen path. A knock on the door interrupted her thoughts. "Come."

She was surprised when her mother peeked around the edge of the oak panel. "Have you any prior engagements for today?"

"None." In a single brisk move, Caroline closed the book she was not reading and settled the musty tome in her lap. "I had thought to catch up on my study of court portraiture."

"Excellent." Smiling the sort of smile that made the hair

stand on the back of Caroline's neck, her mother entered the room and shut the door. "Though I regret taking you away from what I am certain is a stimulating endeavor, you and I are overdue for a chat."

In an instant, Caroline's suspicions were confirmed, and she stood. "Mama, what have you done?"

"Come with me." Her prying parent swiped the book from her grasp and tossed it on the chair Caroline had occupied, then caught her by the wrist and led her into the sitting room adjoining the bedchamber.

"All right, Mama." It was too late when Caroline realized she had plunked down, in a rather unladylike fashion, in the cushions on the *chaise* near the window overlooking the gardens below. In an attempt to reclaim a scrap of proper deportment, she smoothed imaginary wrinkles from her skirts. "What is it you wish to discuss?"

"I must confess my true motive in insisting Lord Lockwood court you in public." As usual, in taking her seat, her mother adopted an elegant posture one would expect of a duchess and had, no doubt, on many occasions moved those in the *ton* to question the authenticity of their blood connections. "It was my intent to determine the depth of his affection for you, as I have always hoped you would marry for love."

"But what about the scandal?" The conversation was unexpected and unwelcomed. Despite the shock, Caroline masked her discomfort in a question. "I have been compromised."

"My dear, I do not give a whit about scandal." Her mother arched a brow. "This family is made of sterner stuff, as are you."

"Do not worry about me." Caroline tugged a small piece of lint from the hem of her sleeve. "I am fine."

"I do not think you are being honest with me or yourself." Her mother huffed a breath. "Do you love Lord Lockwood?"

Why had she asked the one query guaranteed to stump Caroline?

"I have given Lord Lockwood my declaration, which you witnessed." Lifting her chin, Caroline looked her mother in the eyes. With teeth clamped on her bottom lip, she promised herself she would not cry for Trevor, at least no more than she had already. "What I feel is irrelevant."

"I see." She gazed out the window. "It is a pity, really, because I believe Lord Lockwood has developed a tendre for you."

"Mama, Lord Lockwood is marrying me because Blake will kill him if he does not restore my honor." She snorted. "He neither wants me nor loves me."

"Can you be so sure?" her mother inquired in a soft tone.

"No. In light of my recent lapses in judgment, I am not sure of anything anymore. But after all that has happened, how can I make up my mind?" Her hands fisted in her skirts, Caroline gulped. "Am I not allowed a measure of indecision? Everything is so confusing."

"That is because you are trying to rationalize that which is irrational. Love defies reason, my dear. It is a nebulous emotion intended to be recognized, accepted, and cherished —not understood. When you are in love, you take your mate as he is, imperfections and all." A whimsical expression invested her patrician features. "You might say you love Lord Lockwood in spite of himself. No doubt, when it comes to Trevor, you find yourself tolerating behavior that would move you to violence if committed by another suitor."

"Yes." Caroline nodded her agreement. "How did you know?"

"I felt the same about your father," she explained with a chuckle. "And I am positive Lord Lockwood cares for you, just as I am equally certain he is not happy about it."

"I do not understand." How she wanted to believe her mother.

"Your father, rest him, used to say I was his greatest strength and his worst weakness. I practically dragged the great *Nautionnier Knight*, kicking and screaming, to the altar." Her mother smiled wistfully. "Caroline, love can leave a man feeling extremely vulnerable, something to which I assure you they are unaccustomed. Most men find the stuff of poetry an incoherent language and, in some respects, a threat."

"I am terrible where men are concerned." With nervous agitation, she wrung her fingers. "Everything I do seems so awkward. I know I am not attractive, and he could find someone a vast deal more appealing."

"My dear, you do yourself a grave disservice." Without a word, her mother stood and paced the floor. "I shoulder the blame for not recognizing how deeply the incident with Lord Darwith affected you, but you must know he was never worthy of your hand. I would wager he regrets choosing that harridan he married."

"Would that I could presume that, Mama." Yet Lady Darwith presented Caroline's opposite, in every way. "But I will not lie to myself."

"Darling, you are a beautiful, intelligent, strong-willed woman." Her mother returned to the *chaise*, sat at Caroline's side, and clasped hands. "Any number of men would count themselves fortunate to have you for a wife. Who would be so brave as to stow away on a ship full of strange men headed for a foreign land? And how many men can wield a sword as well as you?"

Ill at ease with such praise, Caroline shifted her weight. "Mama, you know very well that *ton*nish men do not consider those qualities desirous when seeking a suitable bride."

"All right." Her mother clucked her tongue. "Then let us focus on what has already occurred. As you have made it clear, you willingly gave yourself to Lord Lockwood."

At the bold declaration, Caroline's cheeks burned with a ferocious blush. "I did."

"Tell me, did he take your maidenhead soon after he kidnapped you from Dalton's ship?" She lowered her chin. "Or did he wait to do the deed?"

To convince herself she was fully *compos mentis* and engaging in such highly improper dialogue with her mother, Caroline pinched herself, and the sting distracted her from the embarrassment. "We did not...come together...until weeks later." In haste, she added, "But it makes no difference. He only wanted me because he thought I was Dalton's mistress."

"Why, then, did he delay his revenge if that was all-important?" she inquired, much to Caroline's dismay.

"Because of the terms we negotiated." Caroline recalled the conversation aboard the *Hera*. "I asked that he not compel me to surrender, else he would have had his way much sooner."

"I disagree." Her mother shook her head. "Had Lord Lockwood forced his attentions on you, immediately, I would concur with your conclusion, and we would not be planning a wedding. However, since he did not, then he must have made love to you because he wanted you. My guess is that he postponed the seduction because he hoped you would come to feel the same for him."

Caroline shrugged. "It does not signify."

"Actually, it does." Her mother caught her in a piercing stare. "Be honest with me, darling. Do you care for Lord Lockwood?"

What she would have given to voice a denial. But she refused to lie to the woman who gave her life, so she had to admit the truth. As the pain of Trevor's deception revisited her senses, Caroline could only manage a curt nod.

"Then go after him." Her mother waved a fist as though rallying the troops. "Take Lord Lockwood in hand, and make it work. I know you are hurt, but if you give yourself half a chance, I believe you will find love. And, afterward, you can teach him to fear your wrath."

"You make it sound so simple." Drowning in a sea of confusion and skepticism, Caroline shivered, ignoring the nausea welling in her throat, and frowned. "But I do not even know where to begin."

"You must define your place in his world, else he will do it for you." Her mother frowned. "And I would wager you will not appreciate what little he grants you."

"How am I to do that?" Nothing in her world seemed fixed. "As it stands, I cannot decide whether I love or hate him, from one minute to the next."

"In short, that is marriage." Her mother giggled. "My dear, men are no real mystery or challenge. All you have to do is be the bold, beautiful woman I raised, and Lord Lockwood will fall at your feet. You are a fighter, darling, and I know you can do this, but having been burned once, I fear you are a tad battle-shy."

Puzzled by her mother's rationale, Caroline hugged herself. "Mama, what are you thinking?"

Tapping a finger to her chin, her mother walked to the armoire and pulled the doors wide. Hands on hips, she whirled about and caught Caroline in her sights. "My dear, it might be time for new armor."

The next thing Caroline knew, she huddled in the Rylan town carriage with her mother, making the rounds between the milliner's, the hosier's, and the corsetiere's. While being measured for a wide array of new gowns for every possible occasion, she fidgeted under the scrutiny of the seamstress as fabric was draped, situated, and pinned. Gone were the conservative, girlish pinks and pastels that made up her current wardrobe. Her new apparel embraced bold neck-lines and svelte cuts, all done in vivid, but tasteful, jewel tones.

Once her mother deemed that particular aspect of their mission accomplished, they returned to Elliott House for their afternoon repast and were finishing their meal when the hairdresser arrived.

As Caroline sat still as a statue, the diminutive coiffeur studied her as if he were Michelangelo and she his model. The severe chignon she usually favored was loosened and her ends trimmed. Her rich brown mane was piled in care-free curls atop her head, with soft wisps teasing the back of her neck, and whimsical ringlets artfully framed her face.

And all the while, Caroline wondered what had possessed her to stand before her mother and proclaim, "I will do it."

IT HAS OFTEN BEEN SAID that trial by fire is the best test of a new idea. The next evening, as she sat at her vanity, Caroline studied her reflection in the mirror and questioned her sanity. With her hair perfectly coifed, she almost had not recognized the woman staring back at her. Made of plush crimson velvet, her gown boasted a plunging neckline and a cut that hugged her curves in a tantalizing display of feminine prowess. It was common knowledge that some of the more brazen women of the *ton* often wet their chemises in order to achieve the same effect her skilled seamstress had attained.

"Oh, I say. Lord Lockwood will swallow his tongue once he sees you in your finery, my lady."

"Thank you, Annie." Facing her maid, Caroline grinned. "I do so hope you are right."

When she descended the stairs of her family home, further reassurance was found in the gaping mouthed, wide-eyed stare her brother sported upon spying her.

"Thank you, Blake." She kissed his cheek. "I needed that."

He blinked one, twice. "A-are you going out in public d-dressed like that?" The stuttering evidenced his stupefied state.

"Indeed, I am." She could only hope her rogue captain was similarly afflicted.

"But I can see your—" Blake held his hands to his chest.

"They are called breasts, my dear son." Their mother, dressed in violet silk satin, glided regally to Caroline's rescue.

"I know that." Her brother appeared on the verge of an apoplectic fit. "But you can see her bosom."

Her cheeks burned, and Caroline bit her bottom lip to keep from laughing and thus incur his wrath.

"Do not be a boor, Blake." Her mother tugged on her gloves. "Your sister looks stunning, and she has a lovely figure. I daresay she gets it from me."

"Mama, *you* did this?" Blake scowled.

With cool elegance and well-honed hauteur, mother approached son. "Do not take that tone with me, Blake Thornton Deverell Elliott."

Caroline winced. It was not smart for her elder sibling to tangle with their mother when she invoked the full compliment of his given names.

"While you may forever see Caroline as your baby sister, you must remember she is now a grown woman, soon to be married and a countess, at that. It is imperative she dress as befits her station." With a pat of his cheek, she said, "It is time to let her go, my son."

"As you wish." Though his response implied consent, the glance Blake shot Caroline conveyed a wealth of meaning to the contrary.

When their mother strolled out the door, she added, "And if you find yourself lacking for things to do, I suggest you follow your sister's example and get yourself a wife."

With a wicked shudder, he peered at the ceiling, as if in silent plea for divine intervention. "Caroline, I am beginning to think it would have been much less complicated to run Lockwood through with my best sword." He helped her put on her cloak, then offered his arm.

"Nonsense." She clutched the crook of his elbow. "And how often have you remarked that blood forever ruins the shine on the blade?"

"You are quite right." Blake handed her into the coach. "I say, it is a cool night. Perhaps you should retain your cloak for the evening? I would not want you to catch a cold."

"Fret not, brother mine." Caroline sank into the squabs beside her mother and grinned. "Should I become chilled, I shall inform Lord Lockwood of my discomfit, and you may rely on him to remedy the situation and warm my person, posthaste."

Now if only she could maintain the false bravado for the evening. During the ride, she mentally girded herself for the fight that was to ensue. Though her objective had changed, as had her original plan, her method of attack was the same for any goal she hoped to attain. When the carriage stopped before the main entrance to Trantham House, Caroline resolved to dive in, headfirst.

Shadows played on the Italian marble floor, as couples danced under the light of glittering crystal chandeliers, in the ballroom at Lady Trantham's opulent London mansion. As was her duty, she stood behind her mother and brother as they were announced. When her name was called, she stepped into the arena where many a man had been felled by delicate, but nonetheless lethal, weapons of silk, satin, and lace.

After bidding their mother a pleasant evening, Caroline held tight to Blake as he forged a path through the crush. In silence, she prayed she would be up to the task she had set for herself. That somehow, she would win her future husband's heart. But she knew it was going to take a lot more than a new gown and hairstyle, given her fragile confidence.

Nearing the far wall of the massive ballroom, her brother indicated he had found their group. Just then she caught sight of Trevor standing amid their friends. A collective of jaws dropped when the gathering took note of her new battle gear. With head held high, she smiled and walked into the fray with seemingly unimpaired aplomb. But she laughed aloud when she overheard Damian telling Alex, "Do not even think about it."

THROUGH A HAZE OF RAW LUST, Trevor struggled to restore the self-control that had been shredded by the mere appearance of a goddess in red velvet, or as she was more commonly known, his future wife. What he had previously considered a chore of courtship now seemed the perfect venue for seduction. With nervous anxiety, he cleared his throat and took extra care not to swallow his tongue. His skin tingled from head to toe, and his palms itched at the thought of roaming her shapely curves.

With the face of an angel and the body of a sylph, his bride-to-be had caught the attention of every inch of him, and a handful in particular. At the same time, he attempted to recall the suggestions on wooing a lady of character, which Everett had laughingly provided. Of course, his friend had said nothing about courting a highborn beauty while fighting a rampant erection. At that rate, he was going to be hard until Christmas.

"My lord, a penny for your thoughts." Caroline stood before him with an expression of cherubic innocence, and the combination she presented was well nigh irresistible.

"A thousand pardons, my lady, that I should neglect you so." He bowed and, upon straightening, raised her gloved hand to his lips. "May I say your beauty held me entranced from the moment I first saw you?"

"You may," she replied, staring at him through her flirty lashes.

"May I also say that gown is an inspiration." And he would give his ship to peel the fetching garment from her figure.

"You may." She giggled.

"May I say that your hair is—good heavens." Trevor

wrinkled his nose. "What have you done with your hair? Is this a new fashion? Surely you have not cut it?"

"Only a little." Pressing a hand to her temple, Caroline retreated a step, and her smile faltered. "Do you not like it?"

He frowned. "Well, I suppose it will grow back."

"Perhaps, and then I might speak with you again," Caroline stated in an icy tone that told him he had committed another egregious error. Holding his gaze, she added, "Dirk, would you care to dance?"

He almost pointed out that it was his waltz, but in the interest of keeping his head on his shoulders, Trevor acquiesced as the elder Randolph, with a sheepish backward glance, led her to the dance floor.

Blake rolled his eyes. Dalton, having recently returned from Jamaica, chuckled and rocked on his heels. Damian pretended not to notice Trevor's mistake. Lance leaned close and whispered something in Cara's ear, and her countenance bespoke dreadful ire. Alex, Elaine, and Sabrina adopted identical stances, with arms folded and glowers that would make the saltiest sailor quiver in his breeches.

"You seem to have an affinity for digging your own grave, my friend." Lord Markham snickered.

"Everett, I am not in the mood for your quips." Trevor craned his neck to keep his lady in view. "Somehow, I have upset Caroline."

"Of course you have, you addled ass." Markham clucked his tongue. "You never tell a woman her coiffure is *démodé*. Have I taught you nothing?"

"Bloody hell." The fog lifted. "I was only trying to pay her a compliment. I preferred her hair as it was, is that so bad?"

"When it comes to the fairer sex, indubitably." Everett winked. "They are a mystery and a challenge. And that is what keeps us interested, but I submit you are done for the night, if not a sennight, after your less than stellar performance."

"But I have never had trouble with doxies." Trevor tugged at his shirt collar.

"You would equate your lady with a whore?" Everett arched a brow.

"I get your point. But what sort of shark infested waters is this game polite society has the unmitigated audacity to call courtship?" Had they not been in the middle of a crowded ballroom, Trevor would have dearly loved to lop off Everett's head, if only to wipe the smirk from his face. "Give me a ship, and I would much prefer to sail the Horn than navigate this sphere, for it is truly a shallow pass with hidden shoals, and there are no maps or charts to ensure survival."

"Do not be so hard on yourself." Everett smacked him on the shoulder. "I suspect you have been too long at sea, and London is neither kind nor accommodating to a sailor's life."

The waltz ended, and Trevor was not surprised when his future wife sought refuge amid her friends, who favored him with a lethal mix of icy glares and wicked scowls. "The air has turned cold, has it not?"

"Indeed, but you brought it on yourself." His only friend nodded once. "What say we adjourn to the card room and a bottle of brandy?"

Trevor had hoped to strengthen the tenuous bonds with his future extended family, as they were an odd assortment of characters he still could not understand. In their circles, he was an outsider and remained consciously aware of the fact. At first, he could not see how he would ever find his place in their clique, yet of late he had gained some small measure of ground. But it was evident that whatever inroads he had made were now blocked by his unintended insult.

"Perhaps you are right." He sighed. "Tonight is a loss."

"And speaking of losses, I promise to keep yours to a few thousand pounds." Everett grinned.

"How generous of you."

THE ELLIOTT TOWN coach bobbled through the streets of London, bound for Chatham House the following night. The fête was one of the premiere events of the Season, and everyone who was anyone would be in attendance. Judging from the queue of carriages waiting to deposit their consignment at the entrance to the columned, Palladian style mansion, the *ton* had put in a good show.

Twiddling her gloved thumbs, Caroline sat across from her mother and mulled her day. Blake had sent word that he intended to spend the night at his bachelor lodgings and would meet them at the ball. She knew what that meant, and when he arrived that afternoon for an unscheduled fencing session, she had taunted and teased her brother, until she yielded her foil to his vicious riposte.

Of course, she was grateful for Blake's company. He served as primary distraction from the other man in her life who had neglected to pay call. In anticipation of Trevor's visit, she had composed a conciliatory speech to be delivered prior to accepting whatever gift he had chosen to convey his regrets concerning his thoughtless comments at the Trantham's ball. To her dismay, her fiancé had not shown his face during the prescribed hours, and Caroline would have gone in search of another ship on which to stow away had it not been for Blake.

After fencing for an hour, he admitted he had seen Trevor at his boxing gym and ascertained that no such visit was forthcoming. It seemed Lord Lockwood was unsure of his welcome and thought better of making an appearance. Blake had suggested she give Trevor a chance to make amends and display ample gratitude for any apology he might extend. He also implied that Trevor was every bit as frightened by the prospect of their impending marriage as was she. Strange, she could not recall ever discussing her fears with her elder sibling. Brothers could be so bothersome and, sometimes, annoyingly intuitive.

Dressed in a gold embroidered gown of burgundy tulle, Caroline stood at her mother's side, as they were announced. With head held high, she scanned the ballroom in hopes of catching a glimpse of her brother or Trevor. As if from nowhere, Blake appeared and escorted their mother, but he seemed to have forgotten his younger sister, and she spiraled in a chasmal vortex of indecision and self-consciousness.

And then she saw Trevor.

Bedecked in black formalwear and sporting a boyish grin, he was devastatingly handsome. Her heart skipped a beat, and a fluttery sensation tickled her belly. In an instant, the transgressions of the past were forgotten. Why could she not stay angry with the infernal man? Casting a side-long glance at her brother, she caught his wink. There were times when Caroline could just kiss Blake.

"My lady." Drawing her from a bottomless pit of trepidation, her captain anchored her at his right. "May I say you look quite lovely this evening."

"You may, my lord." Oh, dear. Were they going down

that road again? "And I daresay you are rather dashing, yourself."

"Praise, indeed." Raising her gloved hand to his lips, Trevor flipped her wrist and placed a kiss on her bare flesh, then settled her palm in the crook of his arm. "Allow me the honor of escorting you this night."

As the strings of the orchestra sounded the first waltz of the evening, Caroline whirled about the dance floor in Trevor's vise-like embrace, gaining confidence with each successive turn. He held her close, too close, and she marveled at what she felt.

When the bell pealed, signaling supper, he led her into the dining hall and to a small table for two tucked in a corner, which allowed them a minute measure of privacy. Later, her attentive fiancé made his excuses, only to return with a strawberry tart.

To her abiding delight, her shameless future husband leaned and whispered in her ear. "I would give my ship to have you naked in my bed, as I fed you strawberries, sweet Caroline."

Good heavens, her green-eyed dragon had returned with a vengeance. "Would you?"

Smiling seductively, he reached for her hand, slipped his thumb inside her glove, and caressed the center of her palm in maddening circles. "I must confess, as of this moment, it is my fondest wish."

"My lord, were it in my power to grant such a request, rest assured I would do so without delay." Oh, how nice it was to see him blush for a change.

For the first time since their courtship had commenced, Caroline truly enjoyed herself. She almost forgot the circumstances necessitating their engagement and the relentless self-doubt. As Trevor broke small bites of the tart and fed them into her mouth, checking to make sure there were none the wiser, he serenaded her with ribald suggestions involving her body and his tongue, starting at the crest of her ear and traversing a sumptuous path to her toes. His demeanor was reminiscent of fonder days aboard the *Hera*, and she developed a new appreciation for his verbal ravishment.

It seemed too soon when the pleasant meal ended, and with great reluctance they joined the crush of revelers inching toward the ballroom. Trevor and Caroline, with Brie and Everett in tow, were caught in a crush of bodies. In the crowd ahead, a familiar voice rose above the chatter.

"Oh, no, my dears. I assure you he could not be serious about Lady Caroline. Lord Lockwood told me he has no interest in any of our young debutantes," crowed Lady Darwith, Caroline's archenemy. "A man like that needs a real woman to satisfy him."

A chorus of giggles rent the air, the earth tilted beneath her feet, and Caroline swayed. Years of engrained inhibition charged the field, as staccato flashes of painful memories beat her into submission, and she slumped her shoulders.

"Are you all right?" Trevor asked. "What is wrong?"

"Does she speak the truth?" Humiliation dammed her throat, and unshed tears stung her eyes.

He blinked. "I beg your pardon?"

"Lady Darwith." She swallowed hard. "Did you talk to her? Have you no partiality to a debutante?"

HELL AND THE REAPER, there was no retreat.

Trevor needed no explanation to discern the motives behind Caroline's query. He revisited his conversation with the duchess, recalled the history and the devastation caused by one barracuda known as Lady Darwith. "Aye, I said it. But—"

With a plaintive cry, his fiancée tore from his side and plunged into the sea of partygoers.

"—You are not like any debutante I have ever known." Stunned, Trevor glanced at Everett and Sabrina, who eyed him with unveiled sympathy.

"No offense, old chap, but your wooing is becoming awfully painful to watch." Everett arched a brow. "Too bad I am not in need of a wife, else I would be happy to show you how it is done."

"Take my advice, do not try it. Courtship is a race you cannot win." Trevor scratched his temple. "Well then, would someone like to tell me whether or not I should go after her?"

"Pray, a moment." Elbowing Sabrina, Everett said, "Perhaps all our lovebirds need is a little friendly interference from a master and his protégé. What say you, my dear Miss Douglas?"

Sabrina favored him with a conspiratorial grin that gave Trevor gooseflesh from head to foot. "My lord, I do love a good intrigue."

CHAPTER TWELVE

"*M*iss Douglas, I do not presume to understand whatever nonsense you and Everett are about. Really, I must find Caroline." Trevor dug his heels into the graveled path in the rose garden. "I insist you tell me where we are going."

Sabrina peered over her shoulder and pressed a finger to her lips. "Shh, damn fool man. Do you want to announce to the whole world we are here?" She faced forward and tugged hard on his wrist. "If you wish to see Caroline, then follow me. And, blast it all, keep your voice down."

Despite inclinations to the contrary, he trailed his less-than-graceful guide around a tall hedge. In the clearing, secluded and well hidden from the main house, sat a petite orangery. As they approached the door, Trevor heard voices inside and paused.

With a haughty air of determination, Sabrina let go his arm, marched to the entrance, and turned the knob. With a backward glance, she inclined her head. "Well, are you coming?"

"I suppose I have nothing to lose." Trevor uttered a

prayer in silence and stepped into the tiny structure.

Pale blue light from the moon streamed through the glass panels overhead, illuminating the diminutive hothouse. Tucked among the plants of various tropical varieties were a *chaise* and a tapestry frame. And making a thorough examination of an exotic orchid, while engaging in polite conversation with Everett, was Caroline.

When Everett spied him, he stood upright. "Right. Well, I believe my work here is finished." He strolled toward the entrance and offered Sabrina his escort. "Come along, Miss Douglas."

To wit the younger Douglas blinked. "I beg your pardon? Where do you think we are going?"

"Allay your fears, my dear." His friend chuckled. "My thoughts were of a decidedly noble endeavor."

"Indeed?" Sabrina appeared skeptical. "You—noble?"

"Indubitably." Everett grinned. "Do you dance, Miss Douglas?"

Her eyes flared. "Of course I do, you ass."

Markham pressed her hand into the crook of his elbow. "Tell me, my dear Miss Douglas, has anyone ever mistaken you for a lady?"

She humphed. "I am sure no more than have mistaken you for a gentleman."

As the two continued their playful banter, Trevor stared surreptitiously at Caroline. She seemed determined to focus on anything but him, and he knew not what to make of her indifference. A palm settled on the small of his back.

"Get in there, old boy." Everett gave him a gentle nudge.

With a tentative step forward, he slipped a finger in his coat pocket and toyed with the bauble he intended to give his fiancée. Once the voices of his bickering accomplices faded, he made his move.

"That is a lovely bloom you have there." God help him, he was discussing flowers. Could anything be more humiliating for a man of the sea? "Is it your favorite variety?"

"No." She gave him her back. "I prefer roses."

"Well, roses are nice, I suppose." Trevor shuffled his feet and inched closer. How he wished she would look at him. "I shall have to remember that and gift you a bouquet on special occasions."

"Please, do not trouble yourself." Something in her tone gave him collywobbles.

"I assure you, my dear, it will be no trouble to shower you with trinkets and the like." Her response puzzled him. Had not all wives expected copious amounts of gifts, especially roses? Trevor forced a chuckle. "Else I may not survive our courtship."

"My lord, you have just touched on the topic uppermost in my mind." Caroline rotated a half-turn, providing him a glimpse of her profile. "I believe it is time for us to end our charade."

Somewhere, fate must be smiling. Trevor rolled his shoulders and sighed his relief, because he had not wanted to delay their nuptials any longer than necessary. "My dear, I could not agree more."

"Then we are agreed." She sniffed. "I hereby release you from any and all obligation with respect to our betrothal. You are free to pursue other viable candidates for a wife."

It was as though the world beneath him had opened up and swallowed him whole. The warm and inviting walls of the orangery gave way to a bottomless chasm, dark and dreary. His ears rang, and his gut clenched. Held in suspense somewhere between heaven and hell, an echo from the past played a mocking tune, haunting and taunting. A memory that still cut sharp as a razor sliced through him.

In a flash, he stood in a luxuriously appointed drawing room. The site was his ancestral pile, a place he had not visited in years but had not forgotten. A little boy loomed before his father, begging to be allowed to remain at home, rather than be sent to school. He had sought acceptance. Validation. His pleas had been ignored, and he had been rejected.

As he teetered on the edge of a precarious precipice, Trevor realized he had forgotten to breathe. The shock of her declaration shivered over his flesh, and he revisited her words in his head.

"Pray forgive me, but did I hear correctly?" Despite his efforts, his voice held a wealth of surprise. "You no longer wish to wed me?"

"My lord, I believe if our courtship has accomplished anything, it has shown us we do not suit." She shrugged, as though she were dismissing a lowly servant. "And you have my solemn vow that what occurred aboard the *Hera* will never pass my lips."

He should have been pleased, should have been grateful that Caroline had thrown him a lifeline. While only the worst cad would have refused to restore her honor after claiming her maidenhead, she was well within her rights to spurn his offer. But in that moment, Trevor was deluged by emotions quite the contrary. Anger and resentment gnawed at his senses. In desperation, he grasped for the best rebuttal to her rebuff. "But...I compromised you."

"I am as much to blame for that situation." Calm and composed, she clasped her hands in front of her. "It is unfair of me to exact so high a price."

"Caroline, stop." Unable to remain still, he paced. "If

this is about Lady Darwith—"

"Lady Darwith spoke the truth, do you deny it?" she inquired.

The question fell as a very real barrier between them.

He stopped in his tracks. "She spoke the truth, but—"

"Well then, we concur," she said, with something between a sob and a sigh. "Our betrothal is broken, and I suspect you will depart London, soon. I wish you safe journey."

That was it?

He had been tossed aside?

Thrown over?

Without so much as a by your leave, he was dismissed?

Like bloody hell.

"So you wish to be rid of me? Do you think me beneath your standards? Am I not polished enough to satisfy the daughter of a duke?" Ire poured forth as a vicious riptide, driven by years of paternal abandonment. Trevor was in his element now, and he wielded his tongue, as would a master swordsman toying with his opponent. He used his knowledge of her faltering confidence to his advantage. Heaping insult after insult on her head, he delighted in each successive slump of her shoulders, until her chin rested on her chest. Yet she took his abuse with an annoyingly polite demeanor and garnered newfound respect. "If memory serves, I was man enough aboard the *Hera*."

"Lord Lockwood." Covering her mouth with her hands, Caroline gasped. "Please, do not be vulgar."

So the society maiden was offended?

Good.

He wanted her to ache as he ached.

To suffer as he suffered.

"I recall a night when you did not find me vulgar. In

fact, you shouted my name, again and again, in the throes of passion. Tell me you do not desire me, Caroline. Look in my eyes, and tell me you do not dream of me, late at night, in your bed." At the end of his tirade, Trevor exhaled audibly. Purged of his fury, he speared his fingers through his hair and pinned her with his gaze, but his efforts were wasted. She remained silent and aloof, as she had since he entered the orangery.

"Fine. Is this how you wish to end our agreement? Do not fret, love." He stomped toward the exit. "I am going. You have my word that you shall never have to suffer my presence again."

His former fiancée appeared rooted to the floor. How dare she ignore him? He spun on his heel and took two steps in her direction. "I intend to set sail on the morning tide."

Caroline portrayed a rousing impersonation of a statue.

"I mean what I say." He smacked a fist to a palm.

He thought she might have blinked.

When it became clear that his ex-bride-to-be would not relent, Trevor studied the betrothal ring in his hand. A combination of two separate pieces, it had taken him the better part of three hours to make the final selection. In the end, much to the consternation of the jeweler, he had chosen to fit the band of one ring to the setting of another, because he wanted something as unique as the woman who would be his future wife.

Since he doubted their paths would cross again, Trevor took one last glance at Caroline.

And then it happened.

A traitorous tear slid slowly down her cheek, belying her apathy.

How strange was it that a single drop could wash away

his hurt?   But she had betrayed her true state.   Despite attempts to convince him otherwise, she was not so detached, as she would have him believe. For good or ill, he walked straight to his difficult bride-to-be and knelt at her feet. And when she finally met his stare, his uncertainty was mirrored in her turbulent, watery gaze.

Bereft of the polished proposal he had composed with great care, he uttered the first words that came to mind. "My dear, I know I am not the best match you could have made—"

"You cannot be serious." Caroline flinched.

"Oh, but I am." He nodded once.

"That is absurd."   Incredulity permeated her lovely features. "For I feel the same can be said for me in regard to you."

"Darling, you are too kind." He tugged off the glove on her left hand. "I am only an earl and not a very successful one. It is common knowledge among my peers that your connections far surpass mine. Your dowry, while not so great as to encompass my fortune, is a sizable sum many a rake would kill to possess."

"What is this?" She cast him a half-smile. "You think yourself inadequate?"

"Not inadequate—but definitely not a prize." With a gentle caress, Trevor slipped the glittering jewel to her finger, then bent his head and brushed his lips across her bare knuckles.

"What is that?" she inquired with a hiccup.

"Your betrothal ring." He could not help but chuckle. "What say you, my sweet Caroline? Will you marry me?"

Caroline seemed spellbound by the gem. "Where did you get it?" she asked, with a shaky voice, as she studied the large marquise-cut diamond.

"Well, I did not steal it, if that is what you imply." The weight of the world perched on his shoulders.

"I infer no such thing." Tears streamed her face. "But...it is beautiful."

"I had it fashioned just for you, and it is an exclusive design, much as my lady." He inclined his head and ignored his aching knees. "I have been carrying the bauble in my waistcoat pocket for days, while trying to find an opportune moment to present it to you. I cannot conceive of a more auspicious occasion to gift your ring than now, when you are trying to give me the old heave-ho."

Caroline all but glowed. Waving her hand in the moonlight, she appeared thrilled with the significance of the sparkling jewel. "But you could marry anyone."

"Perhaps." Trevor rolled his eyes. "Yet I am on my knees before you."

"Did you tell Lady Darwith you were not interested in a debutante?" She shuffled her feet. "Be honest, please."

"I did—present company excepted." He winked. "Because you are unlike any debutante I have ever met."

"True." She giggled. "And you are unlike any earl I have ever met. Are we not a fine pair?"

"Indeed, I think so. And as I recall, you said something similar aboard the *Hera*." The pain in his legs heightened his urgency, as had the beast below his belly button. "Caroline, I will have your answer."

Biting her bottom lip, she struck a coy pose. "You know, I rather fancy you on your knees, Captain."

"Do not get used to it, love." Stiff muscles aside, he was on his feet in seconds. "Though I rather fancy having you on yours."

"Scandalous, my lord." When she made to turn away, he caught her around the waist and hauled her into his arms.

"Trevor, we must be careful. Think of the shame were we to be caught dallying."

"Rot the lot of them." He nudged her with his hips and knew the moment she noted his raging erection, as she rewarded him with a soft gasp and a look of wonder. "Your answer, *now*."

"Yes." Framing his face with her hands, their noses less than an inch apart, she whispered, "Forever, yes."

Had she hesitated, he feared he might swoon. Lady luck smiled benevolently upon him now.

Just how they got to the *chaise*, Trevor had not known or cared. For a man, being ravished by an uncharacteristically aggressive young woman, and his fiancée at that, was a treat not to be missed. Though her caresses were wild and still untutored, Caroline more than compensated with a tidal wave of enthusiasm. But before his charming intended got carried away—and carried him with her—he decided it was time for the master to take the reins of passion.

With his accommodating future bride stretched across his lap, he reached for one hand, then the other. But it was as if she had sprouted additional limbs because nothing on his body escaped her touch.

Caroline twined her fingers in his hair and bit his lip. "My lord, can we not do something?"

"Er—darling." She loosened the fastenings of his breeches, and he just managed to avert emancipation of his Jolly Roger, which was overly jolly and only too happy to weigh anchor in her harbor. "As you pointed out, it would not do to be caught in a compromising position."

"Is there not a way?" As she straddled his thighs and wiggled dangerously close, she nipped his chin. "I mean, my dear Captain, you are so resourceful."

Tempted by her offer, Trevor reminded himself that they

were not yet wed, and his eager but naïve seductress was no dockside doxy. But he recalled his earlier assault on her confidence and realized she needed more than a piece of jewelry to repair the damage. And there were means to satisfy the sensuous appetites without actually doing the deed.

So when he slipped his fingers beneath the edge of her velvet gown, easing down the bodice and baring her breasts, he comforted himself in the knowledge that he was only doing it for Caroline. In full control of the situation, he could stop in an instant.

And he would…in a minute.

Using his arm for support, he leaned her back and feasted at the tantalizing crevice between her breasts. As he ran his tongue over her sensitive flesh, she moaned a sultry invitation he was all too ready to accept and held his head to her bosom. With the tip of his tongue, he flicked a nipple, bringing it to turgid arousal.

Caroline cried out, and he quickly covered her mouth with his palm.

"Shh, darling. As much as I would love to hear your screams of pleasure, tonight, that cannot be, as we dare not risk discovery." He kissed her nose. "Perhaps we should return to the ballroom."

Even in the dim light, he could not miss the flare of her gaze. "If you stop now, I swear, I shall scream."

Clutching the lapels of his coat, she set her lips to his and devoured his flesh. The warmth of her response was a potent elixir, yet he maintained a death grip on his faculties. Their licentious engagement was for her enjoyment, thus he forced himself to remain detached, until she grasped his wrist and slid his hand under her skirts.

The succulent territory between her thighs was an erotic

trap he had contrived to avoid—at least, for now. Of course, a rake of his caliber had nothing to fear from a barely ex-virgin. Relying on his wealth of experience, Trevor was confident he could pleasure her without surrendering to the lust waging a fierce battle within him. Were their little tryst in danger of being uncovered, he could cease their amorous pursuit.

And he intended to...in a minute.

But, good heavens, the woman was sweet. He suckled and laved the twin peaks so amply displayed for his delecta-tion. Surely it would be neglectful of him to favor one breast over the other? Against his better judgment, he blazed a naughty path beneath her skirts to the thatch of curls he remembered with frightening detail. But the first touch of her moist folds nearly sent him into the abyss. And that was as far as he would venture, because once he brought her to fulfillment he would halt their dalliance.

Which he would do...in a minute.

"Oh, Trevor." With a lusty sigh, Caroline squirmed in his lap.

Well, perhaps he would need more than a minute.

The taut bud of her desire was enough to entice a groan and a shudder, but when he slipped a finger inside her passage, her molten honey was enough to make him cry. And that shredded the bonds of his self-control.

Trevor was undone.

He would take his soon-to-be-wife, right there in the orangery. As if she sensed the urgency, understood his pain, Caroline pressed her palm to his aching erection and squeezed.

"Are you sure?" he asked, even as he released the hooks at his waistband.

"Hurry." She fiddled with the opening to his breeches.

"I can bear it no longer."

He thought to say something of propriety and prudence, but when she freed his length and kissed his neck as she stroked him, Trevor surrendered. The hunger, a raw lust rode hard in his veins. Inching down on the *chaise*, he grasped her hips and lifted. In one swift move, he impaled his society miss.

For a scarce second, shock pervaded her expression. Inhaling sharply, she met his gaze. Slowly, Caroline closed her eyes, and relief washed over her face. He set his forehead to hers.

Together, they exhaled.

For a while, they simply sat there, his flesh held deep within hers. Strange, it had never occurred to him that she could want him as much as he wanted her. Had she fantasized about him as he had her? He wondered if he occupied her thoughts in the quiet hours, as he obsessed of her.

In his dreams, he always claimed her swift and hard, plundering her softness, as would a marauding barbarian. Yet, in reality, when he put his hands on her body, something inside him, a mystical restraint that defied recognition, never failed to temper his invasion. Enrapt, ensorcelled by a power too great to deny, Trevor was driven by a need to draw out the experience, to savor her lush curves, and to languish in her delicious warmth. For him, with her, the physical union represented an affirmation for which he would fight the devil, himself.

When he seized her mouth, he thrust. Again and again, they danced in a rhythm as old as time. Desire flared, burning bright as the moon. Passion shimmered as a multitude of stars, blanketing them in a tender embrace. When Caroline brought him to the precipice of heaven on earth— too quickly for his male ego to allow—he held her still.

"What is it?" She tried to move, but he kept her at rest. "What is wrong?"

"Nothing, love. You unman me, as no woman has done since I was a green lad." Once he bridled his baser instincts, he lifted her until the plum-shaped tip of his arousal teased her opening. Then, painfully slowly, he navigated her descent. Fully seated, Caroline bit her lip and sobbed a sweet exhalation.

"All right, my saucy debutante. It is your turn." He dropped his hands to his sides and held tight to the *chaise*. "Let us see what you can do."

It was as though he had heeled an unbroken mare.

The shot rang out, and Lady Caroline Elliott, highborn daughter of a duke and society miss, rode him, wild and wanton, in a voluptuous race to a robust finish. Rigid in the throes of fulfillment, his stunning fiancée reached for the spoils of victory with unabashed ardor and a scream that would have summoned the entire crowd of partygoers had he not covered her mouth with his.

The sheer magnificence of her completion drove him straight into the realm of rapture. Burying his face in her neck, Trevor groaned, "Oh, God."

Her heart beat a rapid salvo, which mirrored the pulse pounding in his ears and soothed the savage within him. He pressed a kiss to her velvety flesh and nuzzled her chin.

"My, but that was delightful." She squeezed him.

At her charming admission, he chuckled. "You know, I believe marriage may not be quite so torturous, after all."

"What?" She sat back and cast him an irresistible pout. "Do you consider matrimony punishment?"

"Relax, darling." He pinched her bottom, and she humphed. "No man in his right mind would confess to being happily leg-shackled."

"Why?" She folded her arms in a manner that suggested reproach, which might have been successful, if not for her current position in his lap. "Is it so unfashionable to love one's wife?"

Love?

Bloody hell, he had never said anything about committing his heart. Myriad responses raced through his addled brain. In the end, he opted for the unvarnished truth. Trevor shrugged. "Because it simply is not done."

"That is absurd." Caroline swatted playfully at his chest and eased from his embrace. When they parted their bodies, she glanced down and froze. "Oh."

"Here, my dear." In a reflex action born of years of experience, he withdrew his handkerchief and offered the lace-trimmed square. "Take this for your needs."

"Thank you." Although he had seen her naked as the day she entered the world, his future wife skittered behind a large-leafed plant.

"By the by, I suggest you settle yourself." After righting his clothes, he ran his fingers through his hair and stood. "We had better return to the ballroom before your brother comes in search of you."

"Do not worry about Blake." She emerged from the foliage looking every bit as prim and proper as she had prior to their tempestuous liaison. "I happen to know he has an assignation with a certain lady and will be rather occupied with the chase."

"Indeed?" Trevor offered his escort. "I can relate."

She elbowed him in the ribs. "You, sir, are a cad."

"Yes, but I am your cad." For him, truer words were never spoken.

They strolled through the gardens, and he could not resist whispering lewd praise of her performance in the

orangery. By the time they entered the main house, Caroline's cheeks were red as a tomato. He prayed no one would
suspect the cause of her flustered state and hoped the smug
satisfaction soothing his senses was not evident in his
expression.

To his infinite gratitude, it appeared that her friends
were none the wiser. None, that is, but Sabrina and Everett.

Upon spying her friend, the innocent Douglas clucked
her tongue and rocked on her heels. "Goodness, you two
must have had a ripping argument."

Though he had not thought it possible, his intended's
blush intensified. "You could say that," Caroline replied, as
she averted her stare.

With a noticeable swagger, Everett charged the field and
whispered, "Enjoyed yourself, did you?"

Trevor pretended to find something interesting in the
crowd. "I am in your debt."

"Indeed, it appears you are most assuredly obliged."
Markham gloated.

Trevor rolled his eyes and huffed in frustration. Never
would he hear the end of that night. As he mulled a series
of pointed rejoinders, his betrothed summoned her cadre of
female friends.

"So, do tell." Everett chucked his shoulder. "Does all
that spirit lend itself to other pursuits, or can you freeze
water on her derriere?"

"Watch yourself, Markham." Trevor tugged on his cravat
and grinned as Alex jerked Caroline's hand and gawked at
the betrothal ring. "That is my future wife you disparage."

"My humblest apologies. I meant no offense. You have
my best wishes for eternal happiness." Everett leaned close.
"But you had better stop seducing her with your gaze, else
her guardians will hang you from the nearest yardarm."

Trevor winced.

Peering to his left, he discerned he was the sole subject of the most inauspicious regard of the men in his soon-to-be extended family, rakes whose experience and understanding of the sensuous arts no doubt rivaled his own. As such, Caroline's demeanor provided every proof of a well-pleasured woman. The sea of frowns and arched brows conveyed that their secret rendezvous was not so secret.

"Oh, my friend." Everett snorted. "You are done for, yet the lady does not favor the svelte physique of your usual candidates, though I am not criticizing your change in taste, as I much prefer curves."

"Will you cease your prattle?" With clenched fists, Trevor gritted his teeth. "I am beginning to think you were a chit in another life, for your endless chatter. And Caroline is exactly as I want her."

"Now, now." Everett smirked. "Do not be—"

"I beg your pardon, my lord." As a Botticelli angel, Caroline stood before them.

"Heaven forbid." His voice oozed characteristic charisma, and Everett wagged a finger. "One so lovely should never beg."

Trevor was certain he was going to be ill at any second.

"I merely wish to thank you for your assistance in our difficulty." Caroline pressed her hand to her lips, and then set her palm to Everett's cheek. "Dear man, you are a romantic at heart."

To Trevor's perpetual delight, the ever-suave, always imperturbable Lord Everett Markham blushed.

"Well, look at his high and mighty lordship." Sabrina slapped him on the back. "All pink in the face."

"Oh, shut up," Everett snapped.

CHAPTER THIRTEEN

*W*hen she entered the dining room the following morning, Caroline was nonplussed to find Trevor seated at the table, conversing with Blake and her mother. "My lord, what a pleasant surprise."

Her incredibly handsome intended and her sour-faced sibling stood. Curious in an instant, she struggled to maintain a calm façade, while an insatiable hunger, which had nothing to do with food, burgeoned in her belly.

"And I did not expect to see you so bright and early, my dear brother." She kissed his cheek. "I had thought you were staying at your bachelor lodgings."

"You thought correct," Blake groused with an equally dour frown. "And I would still be there now, tucked amid warm sheets, had not Mama sent for me at the crack of dawn."

"It seemed a nice idea to break our fast as a family." Her mother winked. "Especially in light of our new addition."

"Ah, yes." Blake reclaimed his place and sipped his coffee. "You are right as always, Mama."

How Caroline had managed to stifle her laughter, as she considered the selections on the sideboard, she had not known or cared. No doubt her brother had left behind more than a cozy bed, and it was obvious His Grumpiness of Rylan was in no mood with which to be trifled. Just then, an impressive growl rumbled from her empty stomach. Good heavens, she was famished, and her unusually voracious appetite seemed boundless. After retrieving a plate, she opted to forgo her typical morning fare of dried toast and, instead, served herself generous portions of eggs, kippers, and bacon.

When she turned toward the table, she discovered Trevor had pulled out a chair. As she neared, he dipped his chin and smiled. His wicked expression gave her goose-flesh, images from their tumultuous tryst the previous evening flashed before her eyes, and she shivered.

With a grace and ease of which her sire would be proud, she settled her plate with nary a stumble. A newfound level of feminine deportment invested her none too petite frame as she draped a napkin in her lap and picked up her fork. "I trust you passed a pleasant night, brother mine?"

"Indubitably," Blake declared with a smug smirk, then stabbed a mound of meat pie and paused. He glanced at his plate, peered at Trevor's, and then Caroline's. A brow arched in question, and he studied her with unveiled interest. "What is this? No toast?"

"I find I am quite starved, though I do not know why." She shifted in her seat and scooped a pile of eggs. "I feel as if I have not eaten in a sennight."

"Indeed?" Blake narrowed his stare and inclined his head. "Tell me, my charming sister, just where did you two hie off to during the ball? You were gone for quite a while."

Caroline choked on a half-chewed piece of bacon and

gulped down a river of water. Trevor, who had been devouring his breakfast like a ravenous wolf, faced her. In unison, they blinked.

"We took a turn about the garden."

"We toured the Chatham's library."

A loud chink pierced the quiet as Blake's silverware hit the elegant china. With an ominous scowl, he asked, "Really? The garden *and the library*?"

Did she detect a note of sarcasm?

"Yes." Caroline bit her tongue against the panic welling in her chest. "You know how fond I am of books. And I wanted to show Lord Lockwood some rosebush varieties I believe would make an excellent addition to his family estate in—"

"—Althrup," Trevor inserted.

"That is it." Thank goodness the man could think on his feet. "Althrup."

"Mmm hmm." Blake sat back in his chair and tapped his fingers on the table. "Books and roses, Lockwood?"

"You should have been there, Rylan." Trevor cast her a naughty grin. "It was quite...stimulating."

Caroline's cheeks went up in flames.

On an exhale, Blake said, "Mama, we need to get these two married, and the sooner the better."

"My son, I could not agree more." Was her mother smiling?

"But, I thought you did not want to raise suspicion among the *ton*." Caroline chewed her lower lip and wondered if her relations had guessed what occurred between her and Trevor at the Chatham ball. "What of the scandal?"

"Have you considered what could have happened had

you been caught playing in the bushes?" Blake inquired with a snort.

"Forgive me for being forward, but anyone with a pair of eyes in their head could see the tendre developing between you." Her mother dabbed the corners of her mouth and set her napkin on her plate. "I daresay there is already a running wager at White's as to the birth date of the earl's heir. Have you any objections to hastening your nuptials, Lord Lockwood?"

Caroline feared she might swoon.

"None, Your Grace," her soon-to-be-husband replied without hesitation.

Now she was certain she was going to swoon.

"Mama, do you really believe the situation merits such drastic measures?" Were there not an audience present, Caroline was positive she would have consumed her finger-nails and gnawed all the way to her knuckles.

"What is the matter?" Trevor leaned close. "Do you not wish to marry me?"

"No—yes—that is to say...I thought our original plan one of sound judgment." Was it her imagination, wishful think-ing, or had he looked disappointed by her initial response? "Of course, if you agree that a quick marriage would be best, then who am I to say otherwise?"

If it seemed as though her life had spun out of control, prior to that moment, and Caroline was positively adrift as her future was plotted with a precision that Wellington, himself, would envy. Her mother decided they should forego a large wedding in favor of a small, private ceremony at St. George's Church. Blake was tasked with writing the Archbishop to request a special license, which would allow Trevor and Caroline to marry within a fortnight. By the time the quartet adjourned their odd assembly, everyone had a list of items to be completed in the next few days.

Caroline and her mother shopped on Bond Street for her trousseau, they planned the menus for the wedding breakfast that would follow the ceremony, and they dutifully made the rounds of afternoon tea parties. Soon, the *haut ton* was abuzz with the impending nuptials of Lady Caroline Elliott to the man society had long referred to as the Elusive Earl.

But for Caroline, Trevor was anything but elusive.

He called on her every day, a different hothouse bouquet in hand. She knew the flowers were intended as a subtle reminder of the tryst they had shared in the orangery at Chatham House. However, she was certain she would die of embarrassment when her mother commented on his fondness for flowers and suggested they erect their own hothouse.

To which her incorrigible husband-to-be replied, "Actually, I have just arranged to have one built at my ancestral pile." He studied Caroline with a shameless gleam in his eyes. "I have only recently discovered the simple pleasures to be had in an orangery."

There were other gifts, as well. He brought her a small tin of sugared candies, a box of chocolates, an elegant gold gilt jewelry box embossed with the Lockwood family crest, and a pair of diamond stud earrings. But it was the first present he had bestowed upon her, the wooden replica of the *Hera*, which she kept on the night table beside her bed. On a sunny afternoon, he took her for a drive in the park, where they sat under the maple trees in Berkley Square and ate flavored ices from Gunter's, then promenaded through Hyde Park. Another evening, he appeared on her doorstep with tickets to a play on Drury Lane.

Before she knew it, the eve of her wedding had arrived.

As HE STOOD in front of the elegant townhome marked 24 Upper Brooke Street, Trevor studied the gold embossed summons he had received only that morning. Pressed in wax, the imprint of an intriguing seal bore the shape of an eight-point wind-star. And the Latin phrase, *Nulli Secundus*, Second to None, held pride of place.

> *Lord Lockwood,*
> *The honor of your presence is requested at six o'clock, 24 Upper Brooke Street. Be prompt and discreet.*
> *The Brethren*

Trevor reached for the knocker and was startled when the door opened to reveal none other than Admiral Mark Douglas, father of Cara and Sabrina, and a legend in the British Navy.

"Ah, Lord Lockwood, and on time." As if they were old friends, Admiral Douglas set the oak panels wide in welcome. "But we are gathered in the study."

When he strolled into the foyer of the palatial residence, Trevor searched his mind for some clue to the purpose of the perplexing invitation. Everything seemed to be in its proper place, except for the fact that there were no servants or staff present.

"Please, follow me." Admiral Douglas led him down a side hall and to another entrance. "After you."

The door rested slightly ajar. Trevor pushed open the panel and stepped inside the spacious study of mahogany walls, which boasted leather inserts. The air smelled of cigar smoke, which declared the room a man's domain. An intricately carved bookcase filled with old tomes and account ledgers occupied the wall behind a matching desk, and a leather high-back chair sat at the rear. In the center of the room positioned a half-circle of identical chairs, all of which were occupied, save one in the middle.

Blake, Damian, Dirk, Dalton, and Lance, the full compliment of his wife's male family members, posited a curious audience. It was evident that something of importance was about to take place, but Trevor had no inclination to participate in their impromptu drama, however harmless. As he considered making a hasty retreat, the latch clicked and the bolt set behind him. In other words, he was locked in and going nowhere.

"Will you have a seat?" Admiral Douglas gave him a slight prod. "Can I offer you a brandy?"

"Uh—yes, thank you, sir." Bloody hell, he might need a whole bottle, since the faces before him revealed nothing in regard to the circumstances necessitating such a secretive summons.

At that moment, the elder Randolph stood. "Will you not join us, Lockwood?"

"Yes—" And then he saw it, the same extraordinary insignia embellished on the breast of Dirk's navy blue coat. Unlike any symbol Trevor had ever seen, the seal, fashioned of gold, featured the same wind-star design and Latin phrase as the curious missive. But a large blue diamond twinkled at the center.

"Your brandy, Lord Lockwood." The admiral smiled.

Trevor accepted the glass and swallowed the contents in a single gulp. The hair stood on the back of his neck, and a chill of unease shivered over his flesh.

"Are you all right, Lockwood?" Dalton inquired with a grin.

"You look quite pale," Blake said as he snatched the empty brandy balloon from Trevor's grasp.

Trevor cleared his throat. "Would someone care to tell me—"

Without warning, Blake unleashed a vicious punch to Trevor's gut. "There it is. Now that we have dispensed with the honor punch, in honest payment for my sister's virtue, we can put that nasty business behind us."

"How very big of you. Anyone else care to have a go while I have a mind to allow it?" Hunched over, Trevor braced for another sneak attack. As he assessed each naval man in the study, he noticed they sported the same magnificent badge of order.

But what order?

"Relax, Lockwood." Admiral Douglas settled behind his desk. "We are all friends here."

"Are we?" On guard for another assault, Trevor shifted his weight. "I am not so sure."

"Perhaps this will allay your trepidation." The admiral placed a box covered in indigo velvet atop the blotter.

"What is it?" Given the chilly reception, Trevor expected the bloody package to explode.

Admiral Douglas merely arched a brow.

"Oh, all right." Despite thoughts to the contrary, he snatched the parcel and lifted the lid. Inside, on a bed of pure white satin, sat the same mysterious seal.

"It is the badge for the Order of the Brethren of the Coast," the admiral stated.

"*The Brethren of the Coast*?" Trevor almost dropped the container. God, help him, he feared he might faint. "But—

they are the stuff of legend. You do not expect me to believe
they actually exist, do you?"

The Brethren of the Coast was a secret society of daring
sea captains, and he had heard countless stories of the
fabled order. What naval man had not? Nautionnier
Knights rumored to have descended from the Order of the
Knights Templar, the warriors of the Crusades, their
exploits were widely circulated throughout the seafaring
ranks, and glorified in bawdy shanties, but the Brethren
were considered nothing more than exaggerated lore, for
there had never been any proof of their existence. It was oft
speculated that Vice Admiral Nelson, himself, had been one
of their league, but that was just a child's fancy, was it not?

"Ah, yes, the stuff of legend. But what is a legend,
without a kernel of truth? In 1307, King Philip IV of France
sought to dissolve the Order of the Knights Templar.
Denied entrance to the Order, and in debt to the Templars
for an enormous sum of which he was unable to repay, King
Philip plotted to destroy the Order and seize the vast wealth
and property it possessed. In connivance with Pope
Clement V, the Templars were accused of heresy, sorcery,
and sexual perversion, and arrested and tortured in an effort
to gain confessions," Admiral Douglas explained in a
melancholy tone.

"Of the estimated two thousand Templars, many were
killed or committed suicide as a result of the Inquisition."
Lance continued the tale as he inclined his head and
frowned. "Only a handful of Templar mariners escaped
persecution by sailing for England, where torture had been
outlawed. Seeking the protection of Edward II, the English
Templars were spared the fate of their French brother
knights."

"The Order of the Brethren of the Coast was formed in

1312, by the surviving Templar mariners, after their order was banned by papal decree." Damian stretched his booted feet. "Since that time, our forefathers have logged a distinguished history of service to the Crown."

"Pull my other leg." Trevor tugged at his cravat and perched on the edge of his seat. "The Brethren are nothing more than an old seaman's tale."

"I assure you, this is no joke." With a grim expression, Dirk rested his elbows on his knees. "You are marrying into our family. Caroline's father was a Knight of the Order, as was his father before him. As you shall now serve."

"Wait a minute." Trevor's grip on reality slipped, and he leaned forward to set the little box on the desk. "And what if I refuse, as this sounds more than a bit farfetched—"

The unmistakable rasp of unsheathed steel brought him out of his chair in a heartbeat. Just as quick, Blake and Damian caught him by the arms and forced him to the floor.

"On your knees, Lockwood," said his soon-to-be-brother-in-law.

"Hold hard." Trevor struggled to break free without success. "I completed my commission and am no longer in the Navy."

"Indeed, you have." The admiral rounded his desk, sword in hand. "And had you not served honorably, we would neither allow your marriage nor extend an invitation to join the Order."

"You call this an invitation?" Trevor snorted. "So I have a choice in the matter?"

"Of course." The admiral chuckled. "And it must be freely made."

"But if you refuse, we shall have to kill you," Dalton added, as though daring Trevor to reject the privilege.

And it was an honor, one that had not escaped his

notice. What young midshipman had not dreamed of the day that he might call himself a Nautionnier Knight, while roaming the Royal Naval Academy halls in Greenwich, as no other military order afforded the distinction? Yet never once in his wildest, youthful imaginings had he thought such estimable seamen actually existed. But would he belong? They had been born into the Order. He had been admitted by default through marriage. Again, he felt the outsider, the misfit, and the one who had not deserved a place in such elite company.

"Were your military record undistinguished, we would not offer you this recognition," the admiral said, as if he had guessed the reason for Trevor's hesitation. "Believe me, Lord Lockwood, you are worthy."

Unnerved by the admiral's unfailing insight, Trevor studied the floor. "I do not know what to say."

"You need only embrace your fate." The admiral paused, and the room grew silent as a tomb.

How long had he wanted to belong to anything—to exist as something more than himself, and a Nautionnier Knight at that? But would he ever truly be a member of their family? It would be so easy to refuse, to sail on the next high water, and leave London in his wake. But that decision meant he would never see Caroline again, either. "I accept."

The tip of the antique sword grazed his left shoulder, then his right, as Admiral Douglas wasted no time bestowing the knighthood. "Rise, Lord Sir Lockwood."

"Well done," said Blake, while he hauled Trevor to his feet and unceremoniously slapped him on the back. "You are one of us."

"Of course, there will be no appearance at court, because we serve in silence. However, there will be a notation made in your naval file." Admiral Douglas gave him a fatherly hug. "Welcome, brother."

Each man, in turn, repeated the same greeting. Dalton included a chuck on the shoulder, and Dirk informed Trevor he would be accompanying him on his first mission for the Brethren.

At last, Blake approached. "You have no idea how difficult it has been for my little sister to keep our secret."

"Caroline knows what has happened?" Trevor asked.

"Indeed, but it was not her place to mention it to you." Blake clucked his tongue. "Though I must say, she is very proud."

Mortified by an uncharacteristic burn in his cheeks, Trevor lowered his chin. Never in his life could he recall anyone taking pride in his accomplishments. "Caroline is very emotional."

"Let us come to order, gentlemen." Admiral Douglas pounded his fist to the desk. "We must finish our business so you lads may be about your celebrations." He handed Trevor a parcel of documents. "These are your new Letters of Marque issued by the Lord High Admiral, himself. From this day forward, you shall sail under special commission, and your missions will come from the Lord High Admiral, through me. Though I am sure it is unnecessary to impress the point, I shall simply remind you that our dealings must always be held in the strictest of confidence."

"I understand, but what are my duties? What is expected of me?" Trevor accepted the rolled parchment, and a smaller seal for authenticating correspondence, and promptly tucked the packet into his coat pocket. "I only ask because, as of tomorrow, I shall have a wife to consider."

"Your concern for Caroline is commendable." Admiral Douglas perched on the edge of his desk. "However, our first priority is the war, and she understands that it must be so. You see, although Wellington defeated Joseph at Talavera, his losses were enormous. With Soult threatening to cut the road to Portugal, Wellington was forced to fall back. He and his men have been secretly constructing a defensive system, a line of trenches and redoubts north of Lisbon stretching from the Atlantic to the Tagus, known as Torres Vedras. The Brethren have been tasked with supporting this effort by delivering reinforcements and supplies, as marked military vessels are too easy to track."

"Of that I have no doubt." Trevor ran a series of shipping routes through his head and plotted an imaginary course that would enable him to elude enemy ships. "I take it the French are, as yet, unaware of this development?"

"As far as we can tell," said Blake. "Our information has been solid. An elite operative, a member of the Counterintelligence Corps, code-named *L'araignee*, has proven quite reliable."

"*L'araignee*?" Trevor narrowed his stare.

"The spider," Blake explained. "Whoever he is, the man is very good at what he does, because his reports have been quite revealing."

"Now then, enough talk of war." Admiral Douglas slapped his hands to his thighs. "This is a time for celebration. Lance, bring the decanter and refill our glasses. I believe a toast is in order."

The men gathered in a circle, and Trevor assumed his place between Blake and Damian.

Admiral Douglas raised his glass high. "*Nulli Secundus.*"

Trevor had barely tasted his brandy, when his fellow knights hustled him out the door, down the hall, and into the cool evening air.

"Where are you taking me?" The expressions with

which Blake and Damian favored him made his skin crawl, and he stumbled as they attempted to shove him into an unmarked carriage. "Wait, what about my rig?"

"Do not worry, as it will be sent to Elliott House. And you will not need it tonight, because you will stay at our bachelor lodgings. Tomorrow, we shall see you to your wedding, safe and sound, lest you forget your way to the church." Blake gave Trevor a push. "Now get in there."

"All right." He crawled to the bench and considered escaping through the opposite door. "Where are we going?"

"To celebrate your getting leg-shackled," Damian declared as he settled his coat.

"Bloody hell." Trevor rolled his eyes.

"Right." Blake rapped the roof, and the coach lurched forward. "There is nothing like a night of drinking and wenching to send you into matrimonial bliss."

"Just a minute, brother," Damian interrupted. "Caroline will have our heads if we take him wenching the night before he gets shackled. Not to mention your mother, my sister, and the rest of the women."

"Hang it all, I had not thought of that." Blake rubbed his chin and furrowed his brow. "But how the devil would they find out?"

"I do not know." Damian shrugged. "But somehow they always do. I would swear they have a spy keeping watch on our bachelor lodgings."

"Well, we shall have to get him foxed, instead," Blake announced, as if making an imperial decree.

Damian wrinkled his nose. "Do you think Caroline will appreciate a bridegroom with a headache?"

"Blister it, Damian, if you are going to be prudish, you may as well hie yourself to Elliott House and spend the evening with the women." Head cocked to the side, Blake said in a girlish, high-pitched voice, "If you hurry, you may learn to sew or pour tea, or some other wifely endeavor."

As a spectator to the bungling comedy of errors, Trevor chuckled. "Do I have a say in the matter?"

In unison, Blake and Damian shouted, "No!"

The carriage slowed to a halt, and Trevor realized they had journeyed to the docks. As he stepped down, another carriage rolled up behind theirs, and Dalton, Dirk, Lance, and Everett descended. Together, they entered the Muddy Rudder, a dank, smoke-filled, crowded tavern frequented by veteran naval officers and sea hardened crewmen. The strange accompaniment of noblemen straddled wooden benches, which looked as if they would collapse at any moment under the combined weight. A rough barmaid took their order and quickly delivered a tray laden with mugs.

Trevor downed a healthy gulp of ale and studied the men who, for all intents and purposes, were now his family. But despite what had occurred in the admiral's study, he still felt very much an outsider. Thank heavens his friend had been included in his farewell to bachelorhood. At that moment, Everett met his gaze from across the table and offered a mock salute.

"What?" Trevor grimaced.

"This does not seem real." Everett shook his head. "Never thought I would live to see the day that you would be felled by a woman."

"That makes two of us." Trevor touched his mug to Everett's.

"So you admit it?" Everett waved off a passing doxy. "You have been conquered by the weaker sex?"

"I admit nothing." He signaled for another ale. "But I am not displeased by my impending nuptials."

"Oh, come now." His friend appeared exceedingly skeptical.

"It is true." Trevor emptied his mug. "Consider this, I shall never again have to chase a skirt to fill my bed."

"I will grant you that." Everett smirked. "But will that not be like eating the same fare for dinner, night after night?"

"Perhaps." Trevor envisioned his lady, warm and inviting on his wedding night. "But she is a prime dish."

"You have me there." Everett nodded once.

"And what is this sudden revulsion toward marriage?" Trevor tapped a finger to his chin. "If memory serves, you have long desired a wife and a family."

"I beg your pardon?" Everett choked and cleared his throat. "You are mistaken, sir."

"When we were in shortcoats, you spoke of nothing else." He leaned close and said, "What was it you used to wish for? Ah, yes, I remember now. You wanted a quiet little thing, with no opinions of her own, much less a desire to express them, to fetch your pipe and slippers, every night, and sit at your feet while you read to her."

"Go to the devil." Markham cast a mighty scowl.

Trevor burst out laughing. "Mark my words, old friend. When you least expect it, the preacher's noose will snare you."

"Perish the thought." Everett scoffed. "It would take a creature of unimaginable spirit to get me to the altar."

"You know, I said the same thing myself." Trevor laughed, in a remarkably light-hearted exultation. "And although I squired her from Dalton's ship, Caroline swept me off my feet."

CHAPTER FOURTEEN

$\mathcal{T}$he sun shone bright through the windows at Elliott House, bathing Caroline in soothing saffron warmth, as she trailed her palm down the oak balustrade of the grand staircase. Dressed in ivory satin trimmed in old gold, she fancied herself a princess and prayed Trevor would think himself a fortunate man for marrying her.

Blake stood in the foyer, looking splendid in an elegant grey morning coat, and smiled as she approached. "You are stunning, my most cherished sister." He bent and kissed her forehead. "Are you ready?"

The question seemed a double-edged sword.

Despite her qualms, Caroline had decided to let bygones be bygones and wipe the slate clean. She would begin anew with her rogue captain because, in light of their impending nuptials, there was no use dwelling on the past. If she wanted to claim the future she had dreamed of as a child, a fairy tale wedding and a husband who loved her, she had to tweak her strategy. And although Caroline accepted the fact that she loved Trevor, she hated to admit he had not shared her devotion. However, for her sake and sanity, that could not mean he never would.

"I suppose it is now or never," she said with a shrug.

"Are you sure you wish to go through with this? I love you, and I would not secure your eternal unhappiness with a betrothal ring—society be damned." Her elder sibling tipped her chin. "Say the word, and I will hie you off to the Caribbean. On my honor, I swear Lockwood would never find you."

"Stop being so serious, and I love you, too." She clutched his wrist and squeezed a reassurance. "My darling big brother, thank you for caring, as you always have, but I know what I am doing."

"All right." Blake settled her hand in the crook of his elbow. "If your course is fixed, then let us away."

They boarded the gleaming black Rylan town coach, the ducal coat of arms emblazoned on the door, and journeyed to St. George's at Hanover Square. Nervous anxiety shivered beneath her skin when the six-columned entrance came into view. She held tight to Blake's arm as she descended the coach, entered the church, and navigated the long aisle with fashionable society in full attendance.

And hoped she had made the right decision.

At the altar, at the Archbishop's instruction, Caroline made her vows, with Trevor at her side and Everett standing as first groomsman. Tears welled in her eyes when Trevor turned to her and pledged, "My heart will be your shelter, and my arms will be your home."

They were only words, but Caroline resolved that someday his oath would accurately portray his commitment and their life.

The next thing she knew the ceremony had ended, and her new husband reached for her. Cupping her cheek, he lowered his head and their lips met. Theirs was not a passionate kiss but a corporeal affirmation filled with a silent promise and faith in the future for which she dared wish.

With clasped hands, they strolled the aisle amid marked applause and rousing cheers. Outside, the Lockwood town carriage waited, and Caroline skipped aboard. Easing into the cushions, she had barely settled her skirts when Trevor hauled her into his lap and put her thoughts into expression.

"Lady Lockwood." He licked the crest of her ear.

"Good heavens," Caroline exclaimed in disbelief. "We are married."

"And not a moment too soon." He chuckled and hugged her so tight she feared she might split in two. "Another week of courtship, and I would have lost my mind."

"Poor aggrieved husband." She cast him a pout. "Was it that bad?"

"Worse." Trevor nipped her nose. "And I shall have my due—tonight, in recompense for that awkward exercise in lunacy. But for now, as you pledged to obey me, before God and everyone, I issue your first command. Kiss me, *wife*."

That was an order to which Caroline happily yielded, and as a duteous spouse, she put all her heart into her charge. It was no small wonder she had no recollection of the remainder of the brief journey to Elliott House.

Later, she stood, prim and poised, beside her husband in the receiving line, but her toes wiggled a salvo of nervous energy in her slippers. Carriages wheeled down the graveled drive, stopping beneath the portico to allow invited revelers to disembark, and the wedding reception began as guests assembled in the drawing room for refreshments.

The celebration was a harried affair, because Trevor had

stated it was necessary for them to embark on the wedding trip prior to sundown. Thus her mother had planned a small meal for their extended family at four, after the well-wishers departed.

The great table in the dining room of Elliott House was cloaked in ivory damask, exquisite Sèvres china, and brilliant silver placed with expert precision. Numerous vases, bursting with delicate white roses, perched atop pedestals about the room, and a lilting aroma wafted through the air.

As she scooted a fried oyster across her plate, Caroline peered at her husband, who seemed to be unusually interested in her eating habits. "What?"

Trevor smiled the sort of smile that gave her gooseflesh. "Would you care for more oysters, my darling wife?"

"No, thank you." Had the man a strange predilection for shellfish? "I daresay I had better stop. At this rate, you will have to roll me to the carriage." Then she recalled he had not shared the destination of their honeymoon. "Where did you say we are headed?"

"I did not say." He narrowed his stare and tapped a finger to the tip of her nose. "Patience, my dear. I have planned a surprise for you, and it is one to which I am looking forward. Now, I suggest you fill your belly, because you will need all your strength for the night that is to come."

Oh, dear.

While his last words were hushed, Caroline could not mistake his meaning. And his devilish chuckle conveyed he had noted the blush burning in her cheeks. "You, sir, are a devil."

"Yes." He waggled his brows. "But I am your devil."

Shortly thereafter, she adjourned to her room to change into an emerald green traveling gown. After checking her appearance in the long mirror, she paused in the doorway of her bedchamber. Casting a misty glance about what had been her sanctuary, she revisited not the physical furnishings but the memories of her life. The little girl who played pirate games with her brother and always saved him the last lemon tart was now a married woman, and a countess at that. Gone were the days when Blake could kiss away her pain. She would have to rely on herself to endure the trials of tomorrow.

"Buck up, Caroline." She stood, straight and tall, and lifted her chin. "Like Mama said, Trevor is only a man. He pulls on his breeches one leg at a time."

With a silent farewell, she marched forth into the hall, turned right, and then left. At the landing of the grand staircase, she halted, as a new future beckoned.

Trevor waited halfway down the steps. Spying her, he held out a hand and flicked an entreaty. "Come, love. If we do not depart soon, we are going to be late."

She gulped. "Late for what?"

Clutching her bridal bouquet of white roses mixed with daisies, Caroline descended, accepted his proffered escort, and approached the balustrade.

In the foyer below, the unmarried ladies assembled. Hope danced in their expressions because, according to popular superstition, the fortunate, or unfortunate, bouquet catcher, depending on their perspective, should be the next to wed. Cara waved a greeting, then stepped out of view, only to return with a pouting Sabrina in tow.

Once she was certain everyone was present, Caroline raised the bouquet, inhaled the sweet scent, and gave her back to the crowd. A murmur of excitement from the female throng filled her ears, as she heaved the arrangement over her shoulder. The guests roared, and she whirled about in time to see Sabrina, shock investing her features, holding the flowers to her bosom.

"She will never forgive me for that." Caroline laughed and blew a kiss to her dear friend, who frowned and shook her fist.

"Ready to greet the masses?" Trevor asked.

"I am." She nodded once.

Together, they ran the gauntlet of rice and glad tidings. At the carriage, a footman stood at attention, and she paused to wave goodbye to her mother and brother. Wiping a stray tear from her cheek, she stepped inside the equipage that would carry her from her family and all that was comforting and familiar. Cheers erupted at their departure, and she rested her head against Trevor's shoulder. When they passed through the formidable gates of Elliott House, she closed her eyes and bit back the fear gnawing at her gut.

"Any regrets?" Trevor nuzzled her temple. "You can tell me, you know."

As she shifted and met his stare, Caroline realized her husband spoke in earnest. But there was something else in his gaze, something she could not quite identify or comprehend. Yet she sensed his need for approval, for validation. Could it be possible? Was he just as intimidated by their change in status? "Not a one."

"Excellent," he said against her lips.

An encouraging desire, an aching hunger, supplanted the trepidation and nervous knots in her belly when their tongues danced. Caroline moaned her appreciation as he settled a palm to her clothed breast. In what seemed a natural response, she caressed the fast rising bulge in his wool breeches, rubbing a repetitive rhythm, until he groaned deep in his throat.

They had been in the carriage for no more than an hour when it came to an abrupt halt.

Trevor broke their kiss. "We have arrived."

Still simmering from their heated embrace, she blinked in surprise. "Already?"

"Indeed." He grasped the latch, opened the door, and exited the coach.

"But—what are we doing here?" she asked as Trevor handed her down. "Are we sailing?"

With a mischievous grin, he merely shrugged.

Curiosity set in, deeper and deeper, as they walked amid the shadows of the mighty vessels berthed at Deptford, the private dockyards of the East Indiamen. Since Trevor had accepted a Nautionnier knighthood, he now anchored with the family shipping business, which had been incorporated into the East India Company and provided a ruse for the Brethren, so the *Hera* should be docked in the vicinity.

When Caroline spotted his ship, what listed in the rigging gave her pause, and she froze in her tracks. If she harbored any lingering doubts concerning her decision to marry Trevor, they disappeared in an instant. Because hoisted to the main topgallant stay swayed a festoon of evergreens. A wedding garland was a centuries-old custom of the British Navy to announce the marriage of a crewmember. As a child, she had seen countless such expressions and had always pretended they were for her.

But that wedding garland was truly hers.

Her vision blurred by happy tears, Caroline peered at Trevor. "My lord, you did this?"

"Aye." He dipped his chin. "I hope you are pleased."

Before she embarrassed herself, she buried her face in his coat and mumbled, "Thank you."

T REVOR BENT his head and kissed the crown of his wife's chestnut hair. The apprehension gripping his shoulders eased, as it appeared his bride would not be offended by a shipboard wedding night. Though he had wrested with his chosen accommodations, the gesture was purely symbolic.

Since they had first made love aboard the *Hera*, it seemed a good omen to commence married life there, too. His cabin was familiar, comfortable, and might do much to help Caroline relax. His trusty bunk would bloody well go far to help him relax. What was it about bedding a married woman—his own wife—that had him shaking in his boots as he ushered her up the gangplank?

A small contingent of his crew, some accompanied by their spouses, stood in attention at the waist of the main deck. George clicked his heels and saluted. "Welcome aboard, Cap'n."

While his first mate made the introductions, Trevor looked on in pride. Exhibiting characteristic altruism, Caroline greeted and thanked each woman who had assisted with the preparations for their stay, and he counted himself the most fortunate of men that she had not considered such business beneath her station. After checking with the watch, which would guard the ship for the night, Trevor whisked his bride into his arms and set a course for his quarters.

He had some consummating to enjoy.

C ANDLES BATHED the cabin Caroline knew so well in soft light, and a vase filled with roses sat on the small dining table. On the massive bed in which they had shared one memorable night, a burgundy counterpane had been turned down to reveal pure white linens. At the soft click of the latch, gooseflesh covered her from head to foot.

"Alone at last, Lady Lockwood." Trevor's arms encircled her waist, and he nibbled the crest of her ear.

"Yes, we are," she said with a shiver. "What would you like to do first?"

"I beg your pardon?" His lips blazed a trail to her neck.

"We could play a game of cards." Despite her efforts, she failed to wrench her gaze from the bed. "Or perhaps you are hungry? Should I go to the galley and—"

"I think not." He began untying her laces, leaving her in no doubt of his preferred activity.

"Trevor?"

"Yes?"

"What are you doing?"

"Is it not obvious?" He slipped the wool from her shoulders. "I am undressing you."

"I gathered that." The fabric bunched at her hips, and he skimmed his palms along her curves. "But—why?"

"My dear, you ask the most perplexing questions." The gown fell in a pool of green on the floor. "Just how do you propose we consummate our marriage?"

"The same as other properly wed couples." Caroline whispered, though she knew not why. "In our nightclothes, beneath the covers. And do not forget to douse the lamps."

"Where on earth did you ever get such revolting notions?" Trevor chuckled as he tugged the ribbon of her chemise and sent it to join her gown.

Clad only in her stockings and garters, she kicked off her slippers. "Well, Alex has a book—"

"A book?" Trevor grasped her shoulders and turned her

to face him. "Just what has my blushing bride been reading?" he inquired with a naughty smirk.

"Do not dare laugh at me." She folded her arms and tried to forget that she was, for all intents and purposes, naked. "This is serious."

"What is serious?" He pinched her bottom and winked.

"Etiquette." Caroline swatted his hand and retreated to the center of the cabin. "According to our social standing, we must engage in marital relations as would any other noble duo."

"How boring." Trevor followed in her wake. "And impossible."

"Why impossible?" She took two steps back. "Can you not see? I am only trying to be a good countess."

"Do me a favor." He doffed his coat, then untied and tugged off his cravat. "Just concentrate on being my countess."

"I do not understand." The shirt hit the floor, and Caroline sought to further the distance between them but discovered herself trapped against the bed frame. And although she tried not to stare at his bare chest, she inclined her head and ogled him anyway. "You wish me to be bad?"

"Yes." His voice was thick with passion and poured over her like marmalade on a hot scone. "But only with me."

"Oh?" As he bent to pull off his boots, the muscles in his arms flexed. Good heavens, she had forgotten how beautiful her husband was without clothes. "And how do you define bad, my lusty lord?"

"As you so kindly pointed out, we are married." Trevor rested his hands on his hips. "Therefore, we are licensed to do as we choose, especially in private."

"So we may engage in improper conduct?" She licked her lips. "Really?"

"Truly." He leveled his chin. "And right now, I am in the mood for some good, clean, naughty fun."

"Then what are we waiting for?" Caroline flew at her captain, speared her fingers through his hair, hugged him tight, and bit his shoulder.

"Slow down." Trevor chuckled, scooped her up, and eased her to the mattress. "We have all night, Lady Lockwood."

"How I love the sound of that." She heeled his flanks. "Say it again."

"Lady Lockwood." Trevor kissed her neck. "Lady Lockwood." He laved her bare breasts. "Lady Lockwood." Inching lower, he dipped his tongue in her belly button. "Lady Lockwood."

As his lips brushed the inside of her thigh, Caroline parted her legs. In an instant, she recalled that singular night at sea and what he had done to her. But when her husband suckled her most intimate flesh, she thought she would shatter into a million pieces. Fire danced in her veins as he draped her knees over his shoulders and gripped her bottom. And while he seemed calm and composed, she longed to scream but feared the crew might burst into the chamber and interrupt his spectacular brand of ravishment. Instead, she sank her teeth into the fleshy side of her hand.

Oh, it was wonderful to be a wife.

A MUFFLED feminine cry sounded the alarm, and Trevor prepared to wage a sumptuous war. Caroline was the most succulent confection he had ever tasted, and her pleasure song drove him to the edge of insanity. Slowly, deliberately, he devoured her skin, soft and sweet as a ripe peach. Retracing his earlier path, he unfastened his breeches, hooked his arms behind her knees, covered her mouth with his, and penetrated his bride in a single swift thrust.

And stopped.

Once again, a mysterious restraint reined him in, held him at bay and kept him from ravaging his wife. An enigmatic force he could neither identify nor fathom, an unrecognizable power from within, held him in check, compelled him to savor her body as if for the last time. When she scored her nails across his back and wiggled her hips, Trevor shivered and could have cried. Was it possible that Caroline desired him as he desired her?

On a languorous refrain of slip and slide, he released her legs and reared on his elbows. As her breasts jostled in rhythm, a subtle gasp sounded in concert with his thrusts. Some day very soon, he was going to ride hell bent for leather between Caroline's thighs. But for now, he would relish the bounty in his arms as he would a fine port.

And make love to her until she screamed.

IT WAS in the wee hours when Trevor next stirred, and while some lamps still burned in his cabin, most of the candles had guttered. Relaxed, sated to his toes, he inhaled deeply. Then he realized a plush female body stretched beneath him and recalled the identity of the woman. Rolling to his side, he gazed at Caroline's sleeping form and frowned.

How had he forgotten to remove her garters and stockings?

Had they not twice consummated their vows—in case the first one had not sufficed? He was certain he had stripped her bare, and it was obvious from the wrinkled mass at one ankle that he had attempted to complete the task. Worse, a check of his person revealed he had only succeeded in inching his breeches to his knees.

With great care so as not to wake his wife, Trevor stole from the bed. After ridding himself of his breeches and divesting her of the remaining unmentionables, he turned out the lamps. When he returned to the bunk, the mattress dipped from his weight, and Caroline rolled into his side.

An incoherent mumble passed her lips, and she rested her head on his shoulder and a palm to his chest. Soothing warmth pervaded his senses and caressed his skin, and he required no light or mirror to tell him he grinned as a giddy schoolboy. Had anyone ever professed that the mere act of embracing his bride, holding her lush feminine form, could be as potent an intoxicant every bit as satisfying as lovemaking, he would have called that person a liar.

Just as quick, the gnawing hand of fear gripped his belly, and Trevor shuddered.

Something had blossomed between them, and he would be a fool to ignore it.

An attachment unlike any he had ever known grew, despite his efforts to the contrary; snaring him in a trap he neither desired nor appreciated. He had known it, had felt it before he stood at the altar with Caroline. Born of the same endless torment that had devastated him when she climbed the rigging and when Cavalier had threatened her, the nameless connection captured him in some ethereal prison he seemed helpless to evade or escape. He spied the mystical attachment in her eyes whenever she looked at him and wondered if the same emotion reflected in his. The prospect bloody well scared the hell out of him.

While he liked Caroline, admired her even, he could not

love her. Trevor had seen, firsthand, what relationships based on sentiment wreaked on a man, and he wanted no part of such evil. Never would he surrender so much unchecked power to a woman. He would provide for his wife, delight in her body, and get children on her, but he would not share his heart.

Nor was he interested in hers.

Caroline snuggled closer and nuzzled his neck. "I love you."

At her proclamation, freely bestowed, his ears rang with shock, his palms dampened, and gooseflesh spread as an unforgiving plague. To her credit, she made her declaration with no hesitation. Trepidation spawned raw terror.

Trevor desperately wanted to run.

CHAPTER FIFTEEN

The carriage rolled along the turnpike bound for Althrup, a quaint little village in Sussex and home of the Lockwood family estate. Caroline stared out the window but saw nothing of the countryside extending beyond her inner thoughts. At her side, the source of her quandary dozed.

Although they had welcomed the day with a memorable breakfast that involved a predatory sea captain and fresh strawberries with cream, Trevor had not uttered a word since they enjoyed an afternoon repast at a coach inn. His mood suddenly sullen, he had perched in the corner, folded his arms, and drifted off as they resumed their journey. Caroline frowned at her reflection in the glass.

Perhaps the honeymoon had ended.

Prior to their wedding, her chief concerns had centered on the fact that her future spouse had been forced to the altar. Now that the deed had been done, her mind wandered in an alternate direction.

How was she supposed to make Trevor fall in love with her?

To her detriment, her lone experience with a man in the romantic realm involved an insincere declaration and an illusory courtship. Flirty glances, stolen caresses, and sweet nothings had been exchanged, and the chase had been unremarkable.

And that was the problem.

Caroline had been duped by the deception and had not guessed the truth behind the charade until it was too late. She had gifted her heart to an undeserving suitor and had been devastated and shamed, with polite society as an audience.

But that time was different.

The depth of devotion she harbored for Trevor was unshakable, rock solid. Never had her emotions been engaged in so forceful an attack—not even for Lord Darwith. Of late, she had realized her feelings for the one who held the distinction as her first love amounted to nothing more than a girlish crush, a fancy.

Yes, that time was different.

Trevor might not be in love with her yet, but she would win him. He would offer his heart on a silver platter, or her name was not Caroline Patience Elliott Marshall, Countess of Lockwood.

"Why so serious, sweet?"

She flinched. "I thought you were sleeping."

"I was." He slipped an arm about her shoulders and pulled her near. "But, as you see, I am awake."

"Indeed." As he nuzzled her temple, she giggled in gratitude for his improved spirits.

"Did you manage to rest?" Trevor inquired, as he rubbed his eyes.

"No." Caroline shook her head and mustered a smile. "The prospect of arriving at my new home is exciting and a tad disconcerting. You have an army of servants, and I wish to make a good impression."

"Darling, Althrup was built over a century ago, so it is hardly new. And as mistress of the manor, you have nothing to fear." With a peck to her cheek, he lifted her to his lap. "Besides, you have already met some of my staff, so there is no need for concern. And you did not get much sleep last night."

He was correct, and the recollection burned a path of embarrassment to her face. "My lord, you are incorrigible."

"You knew that when you married me." Before she could respond, her husband gave his attention to the passing landscape, let down the window, and shouted to the coachman. "Oy, Thornton. Stop here."

"What is it?" Confused, Caroline scooted to her seat. "Is there something wrong?"

"Come with me." A footman opened the door. Trevor exited and then turned to provide assistance. "I hope you do not mind, but this vantage shows the estate at its best."

Smoothing the wrinkles from her skirts, she lifted her chin.

And her jaw dropped.

Trevor escorted her to the verge. "Lady Lockwood, I give you Althrup."

"Oh, my." Caroline swallowed hard. "It is lovely."

An emerald valley spread wide before her, and nestled in a crescent of mighty oaks was a charming village. Marked by thatched rooftops and a majestic Wren steeple, the rural community conveyed an invitation of which no words were required to welcome a recent addition.

But the *pièce de résistance* commanded a hilltop just beyond the village, as a spectacular sentry, and quite took her breath away. An opulent residence constructed of red sandstone with mullioned windows spanning the front, Althrup soared to life as clouds reflected in the glass, lending the manmade structure an ethereal quality that was the stuff of dreams.

"The grounds are ringed by a Saxon moat, and a topiary garden sits amid the boxed hedges." With child-like enthusiasm, Trevor pointed as he spoke. "Over there are the rose gardens, with arches and pergolas encircling a lily pond. The waters of the Channel are visible from the rear of the main house, and our chambers have a stunning view." With a countenance that begged approval, he asked, "Well, what do you think? Can you make it a home, a place to raise our family?"

As Caroline recalled the sadness that marked his childhood, she thought it incredibly unfair for such glorious beauty to be overshadowed by unimaginable pain. "Althrup is more than I could have hoped for, as are you."

Trevor cupped her chin and brought her gaze to his. At length, he searched her eyes. "Can you be happy here?"

Ghosts from the past marred his handsome visage, and Caroline stretched on her toes and pressed on him a kiss filled with promise. "I am already a vast deal happier than I ever thought possible, as long as I have you."

After returning to the coach, they continued their journey. In silence, she ticked off a mental list. While supervising the redecoration of her chambers in their London residence, she had met the housekeeper, Mrs. Porter, and the cook, Mrs. Coomb, matronly figures she adored in an instant. Roberts, his butler, had been hired before Trevor's father died. Winton, his valet, was a grey-haired stodgy character that reminded her of Jennings, the butler at Elliott House. There was Thornton, the coachman, and Jones, the groom. And she had not yet been introduced to the gardener, the undergrooms, and the footmen, not to mention the housemaids. And in the event her memory failed, tucked inside her reticule was a sheet of paper on which she had written several names.

When the coach passed through the gates of Althrup proper, she bit her lip and squeezed her fingers.

"Stop worrying." With an arched brow, Trevor covered her hands with his. "You will do fine."

"I pray you are correct." In the forecourt the coach halted, and the countess of Lockwood disembarked with her earl.

The servants stood in line, waiting to greet their master and new mistress. As she crossed the threshold into the grand foyer, Caroline gazed at the high moulded ceiling and, at its center, a magnificent crystal chandelier. An oakwell staircase opened to a wide landing, and she spied what appeared to be an immense gallery. Mrs. Porter and Roberts made the introductions, and she expended considerable effort to address those she could remember by name.

"Your ladyship, perhaps you would like to freshen up after the long ride and take your ease before dinner?" the housekeeper inquired once the staff had been dismissed. "May I show you to your room?"

"An excellent notion, Mrs. Porter. Please, ring for a bath." Caroline turned to her unusually quiet husband. "My lord?"

As a Greek statue, Trevor seemed fixated on a large portrait of a proud looking nobleman that she surmised, from the noticeable resemblance, was his father.

With tentative steps, she approached. "Lord Lockwood?"

His brow a mass of furrows, he said nothing. As though

chiseled in stone, his features appeared tense and his back stiff, and he clenched his jaw.

"Trevor?" Perplexed by his abrupt change in demeanor, she inched closer and tugged on his coat sleeve. "Are you all right?"

"What!" He winced and then scowled. "What do you want?"

"Forgive my interruption." Startled by his harsh outburst, she jumped. "Are you unwell?"

"No." His tone was pure acid.

"I beg your pardon, my lord." Anger radiated from his body, and she was confused to find herself the target of his ire. "If you have no need of me, I should like to retire to my apartments."

Nodding once, Trevor said, "Go."

Shock shivered over her flesh, as she had not incurred his wrath since the day she climbed into the *Hera*'s rigging. Caroline hugged herself and made for the stairs. "Lead the way, Mrs. Porter."

The housekeeper cast her a sympathetic glance, then averted her stare. "Perhaps I should have the painting removed to the gallery, your ladyship."

At the landing, they turned left and navigated a long hall. Caroline asked in a low voice, "Has his lordship not made such a request before?"

"I beg your pardon, my lady. Before—what?" the servant inquired as she opened a door.

"I refer to one of his lordship's previous visits." Caroline swept into a chamber that immediately made her feel at home and doffed her gloves. The countess's suite had been decorated in the same creamy white and deep blue, the latter chosen because it reminded her of the sea and her captain, which she had selected for her quarters in London. "Has he not already declared an objection to the portrait?"

"I do not follow, your ladyship." Standing at the center of the sitting room, Mrs. Porter appeared surprised. "I mean no disrespect, my lady, but the present Earl of Lockwood has not been in residence at Althrup for over twenty years."

AFTER WASHING AWAY the road dust, and donning a fresh shirt and buckskin breeches, Trevor stalked the earl's apartments. As he paced along the sidewall, the chamber seemed to collapse on him from every angle, and his knees weakened. Everywhere he looked, memories evoked his father's visage. Echoes of rejections, the vehemence of an embittered and broken sire, haunted his every step. Raking a hand through his wet hair, he lowered his chin and stared at the floor. The successful sea captain still carried the wounds of the little boy who had departed Althrup, unwanted and unloved, so long ago.

And he hated himself for it.

"Why did I come back to this hell on earth?" He closed his eyes against the pain.

Gooseflesh pricked his arms, and he stomped toward the bed and flung himself onto the mattress. For a few minutes, Trevor studied the ceiling, until it spun out of control, swirling into a black chasm that mirrored his hollow existence. Hideous laughter, mocking and taunting, roared in his ears, nausea rolled his belly like the evening tide, and his palms dampened with perspiration.

When he had given his bride a brief overview of his ancestral home from a distance, he had thought the fiery ache in his heart, torments of his youth, had been extinguished by years of hard work, loose women, and bad ale. But the second he had entered the foyer and faced his father, albeit via a portrait, the agony of his childhood struck him as a bullet between the eyes.

"I need to get out of here." He leaped from the large four-poster and stopped. "But where could I go?"

His gaze lit on the door adjoining his suite with his wife's. A balm for his soul was always to be had in her warm embrace, and a tumble might be just what he needed. Trevor was already in her room when he realized he had moved.

By the window, Caroline reclined on a *chaise*. As he approached, he discovered she slept. With her cheek resting against her palm, and classic features sublime in repose, she could pass for one of Botticelli's angels. Though a quilt covered her body, his imagination supplied a vivid picture of the voluptuous form he had spent the better part of the night surveying with his tongue. Careful not to disturb her slumber, he eased to the foot of the *chaise*. Slipping a hand beneath the blanket, he stroked a shapely calf.

"You never should have married me." Memories, dark moments from his past flashed a rapid-fire assault.

Guileless, unafraid of her own raw vulnerability; he could not fathom why she wanted him. Beautiful, sweet, and generous, she deserved more than a shell of a man, yet that knowledge had not dulled his desire to sate his senses in her velvety flesh, nor had it kept him from the altar.

Walking his fingers along the curve of her leg, he caressed the back of her knee. "You do not know what I am, and I am unworthy of you."

Caroline shifted, and he froze. With a moan, she wrinkled her nose, and then appeared to relax.

"One day I will hurt you." In an unconventional warning, Trevor gripped her ankle. "And you will leave me as has everyone else."

A soft cry passed her lips, and he released her just as she opened her eyes.

"My lord, is something wrong?" Caroline sat upright and yawned. "You look quite pale."

The quilt dropped to her waist, and, to his delight and much needed distraction, his wife was clothed only in a sheer robe. "What have we here?"

"Hmm?" His blushing bride peered at her state of dress, or lack thereof, and reached for the quilt. "Oh, dear."

"No, do not hide from me." He clutched the end of the blanket and tugged in the opposite direction. "I relish the view."

"Trevor." With a half-hearted kick, more playful than serious, she yanked on the cover. "What will the servants say?"

"Who cares?" The lusty feminine cry with which she never failed to herald her release would provide his staff with plenty of juicy gossip. He wanted to hear her shout with ecstasy—now. After wrestling the quilt from her grasp, he tossed it to the floor. "We are married."

"But, is it proper?" Caroline licked her lips and appeared to have noted that his shirt hung open. "We always have...relations in the dark. Should we not wait for night?"

"You little fraud." In one swift move, he scooped her into his arms. "You do not want to wait, do you?"

As he carried her into his chamber, she shook her head.

"I thought as much." Trevor chuckled and deposited her in his bed. How was it possible for a woman to blush from head to toe, he wondered as he divested Caroline of the robe? "My dear, if you must offer some excuse to those who would inquire, though I doubt anyone will, as this is our home, simply say that we took a nap."

"But I have already napped." With palpable skepticism, she blinked.

"Then you are going to keep me warm." After stripping off his shirt, Trevor unfastened his breeches and marveled at her innocence, despite the fact that he had claimed her virginity months ago.

"My lord, you are almost twice my size." Inclining her head, she clucked her tongue. "Who would believe such nonsense?"

"Caroline, are you going to argue with me for the remainder of the afternoon?" With his breeches at his thighs, he sat on the edge of the mattress and dropped his drawers.

"I was only—"

Her mouth fell agape, and her protest died when he stood and faced her in fully aroused glory. How he enjoyed flustering his highborn bride. "You were saying, my dear?"

"Y-you are insatiable," Caroline whispered while averting her stare.

"Get used to it." On all fours, Trevor climbed atop the bed, nudged her knees apart, and settled his hips to hers. Although he could not love his wife, and never would, he could make love to her as fifty men. "Because for the next couple of hours, you shall be my pillow."

WHEN CAROLINE CHECKED her appearance in the vanity mirror prior to dinner, the subtle flush in her cheeks from an afternoon of vigorous lovemaking was still evident. Dressed in a low-cut red gown, chosen to bolster her arsenal as she prepared to launch an offensive, she descended the main staircase and strolled into the drawing room. An impressive rumble in her belly signaled a voracious hunger, or a wicked case of nerves, and she was glad her husband had not yet presented himself.

Tonight signaled a new beginning in the campaign to win Trevor's heart. In order to have any chance of success, she had to persuade him to allow a monumental breach of etiquette. At issue was a centuries old practice, a stricture governing the marital household.

Hands settled at her waist, and warm lips caressed the top of her ear. "That was a memorable nap."

"Nap?" Inclining her head, she gazed at the man foremost on her mind. "But you did not sleep."

"Those are the best kind, darling." Through her dress, he pinched her bottom. "Shall we schedule a repeat performance for tomorrow?"

Oh, dear.

"My lord, that sounds lovely." Passion battled with a genuine desire for food, and Caroline feared she might waste away if he would not let her eat. "But there is something I need to discuss with you."

"Fire away." At the hearth, Trevor checked his watch and adjusted the clock on the mantelpiece. "You have my undivided attention."

For good or ill, she had to make a stand. "Well, it is about your bed—"

"Really?" The quick change in his demeanor, from nobleman to barbarian, gave her gooseflesh, and he returned to her side in an instant. "And you think me insatiable."

Great heavens, her wolf prepared to pounce. Caroline

realized she had erred and sought to clarify her position. "Trevor, I want—"

"Shall I have a tray sent to my chambers?" Taking her hands in his, he brought her fingers to his lips. "I will feed you, myself. But I may feast on you."

Oh, no. Now he distracted her.

"I beg your pardon, your lordship." In the doorway, Roberts bowed. "Dinner is served."

Saved by the butler.

"Wonderful." Yes, Caroline retreated, but only for the moment. Accepting her husband's proffered escort, she said, "I am famished."

"Indeed?" As they navigated the oak-paneled hall, Trevor bent his head and whispered, "I do not know why, since you already had dessert."

"My lord." She elbowed him in the ribs. "You are shameless."

"You knew that aboard the *Hera*." He winked. "So what else is new?"

Upon entering the dining room, she cursed her bad luck. Footmen perched in every corner, so her intimate proposition would have to wait. Heaping platters evidenced Mrs. Coomb's culinary acumen, and Caroline wished she possessed the patience to savor the delectable fare. But she plowed through five courses like a farmer during the fall harvest.

"Would you care for another helping, my dear?" her husband asked with unabashed amusement.

"No, thank you." With a hand to her full but unsteady belly, she reclined in her chair. "I believe I have eaten enough."

In silence, Trevor draped his napkin over his plate, stood, and again offered his arm. "In the future, I shall have the cook prepare an additional afternoon meal. I will not have my countess looking wan."

Touched by his concern, Caroline's confidence soared. But as they reached the foyer, she could summon no words to initiate the conversation in which she was desperate to engage.

Gazing at the marble floor, she shuffled her feet.

Trevor cleared his throat.

"Have you—"

"I suppose—"

Her husband smiled, and Caroline responded in kind.

"Ladies first." He nodded once.

"No, please." Curling her toes in her slippers, she clasped her hands. "You were saying?"

"There must be...I am sure...no doubt you have some needlepoint that requires your attention." With a mighty frown, he shifted his weight.

The gruff demeanor had returned with a vengeance, and she changed her tack. "Actually, I had thought to peruse the library."

"Oh?" His eyes lit up as a child on Christmas morn. "Perhaps you would consent to keep company with me in the study? Would you care for a brandy?"

And there it was again, the nagging suspicion resurfaced.

Was it possible?

Had Trevor thought she would reject him?

"My lord, that is a wonderful idea." Though his sugges-tion played right into her pocket, his obvious relief at her acquiescence acted as a salve to her conscience.

Once they were ensconced in the study, her husband dragged two chairs in front of the hearth. At a side table, he lifted a decanter and filled two glasses, then joined her before the fire.

"Have you any plans for tomorrow?" He unbuttoned his coat and sat.

"Mrs. Porter wants to review the household accounts. Everything appears to be efficiently run, but there is always room for improvement." Fortified with a healthy gulp of liquid courage, Caroline peered at her perplexing spouse. "Why do you ask?"

"I should like, very much, to show you the estate. Perhaps we could tour the village? If memory serves, there is a tavern that dishes exceptional fare. We could have lunch." With an expression that cried for acceptance, he said, "If you are too busy, we can do it some other time."

"I shall postpone my meeting for the day after tomorrow." Her heart sang, as she dared not refuse his offer, and she smiled. "Because there is nothing I would rather do than spend the day with you."

"Excellent." With undisguised enthusiasm, Trevor all but bounced from his seat. "We shall depart after breakfast."

The long-case clock signaled the hour.

Intuition told Caroline that was the opportunity for which she had been waiting. "I have need of a favor."

"Of course, love." At the side table, he refilled his glass. "Whatever I have is yours to command."

Staring at the flames in the fireplace, she uttered a silent prayer. "I was wondering about your bed. I mean—my bed. That is to say—our bed."

Bloody hell, she retired the field without firing a single shot.

Save the crackling wood in the hearth, the room grew as quiet as a tomb.

"Caroline, was that a question?"

The lines had been drawn, the gauntlet thrown. Slowly, she stood and faced her adversary, the possessor of the prize she wanted most. Delight danced in his stare, and she crossed her arms. "Do not dare laugh at me. This is important."

"What is important?" he inquired with hands in the air.

The cat was out of the bag, so she refused to retreat now. "Where we sleep."

"I am missing something." With a groan, Trevor rolled his eyes. "What is so important about our accommodations? Are you displeased with yours?"

"No—yes." Embarrassment gnawed at the tangled nerves in her gut, but she remained firm. "It is just—my parents shared a bed."

"No doubt they did, love." With a devilish grin and an exaggerated swagger, he closed the distance between them. "Else you would not exist."

"You misunderstand." Caroline searched for the words, the correct phrases to reinforce her cause. "My mother and father slept together even when they were not begetting children. I want us to do the same."

"What?" Trevor paused, mid-stride. "Am I to understand you wish to pass every night in my chamber?"

Let the battle ensue.

"Yes."

"But—it simply is not done." Her usually cocky captain appeared quite flummoxed, but not so much as to render him incapable of flanking her argument. "Surely polite society frowns on such an arrangement."

Ah, there was the flaw in his defenses.

"Are you not the same man who delights in breaking the dictates of the *ton*?" She took a single step forward. "I had thought you would revel in the chance to thumb your nose at propriety."

"You have me there." He mirrored her move. "Be warned, I snore."

"As I recall, I tolerated that aboard the *Hera*." Mama, God bless her, had been right. The male sex was an easy mark, and she took careful aim. "Do you not want me?"

"We both know I do." Trevor grasped her waist, brought them toe-to-toe, and proof of his desire beckoned even now.

With oh-so delicious victory in sight, she lifted her chin and wiggled closer. "Then what is your objection?"

He shrugged. "I suppose I have none."

"So it is settled." She wound her arms about his neck.

"Aye." He skimmed her hips with his palms and cupped her bottom. "Hereafter, you shall share my bed."

"Very good, my lord."

And in the game of love: advantage, Countess of Lockwood.

CHAPTER SIXTEEN

*S*eptember gave way to October, the wind blew from the north, and the leaves turned in a dazzling autumn collage of orange, gold, and brown. Having opted to remain in the country, rather than return to London for the end of the Season, Trevor fell haphazardly into a somewhat comfortable coexistence with his wife.

For the most part, his priorities revolved around two passions. The first, a secret love of agricultural management, surprised his bride because he had devoted so much time to the sea. He spent hours studying crop reports with various land agents, read books on tilling and fertilizing, and had even presided over regular meetings with the tenant farmers. Perched atop his favorite stallion, he became a frequent fixture in the estate fields. But it was his second passion, involving the cultivation of decidedly more feminine terrain, which often occupied his thoughts to the detriment of all else.

Easing back in his chair, Trevor propped his feet on the desk and smiled.

Although Caroline possessed a sensuous nature that

rivaled his own, she had yet to break free of the societal dictates under which she had been reared. Innocence and inhibition combined to stifle innate curiosity, and her desires were often conveyed in shy whispers and hesitant gestures. Tonight, if she allowed it, he was going to show her how to—

"Trevor?"

"Yes?" He nearly fell out of his seat. "What is it?"

"This just arrived by messenger." Pretty as a picture, the lady of his fantasies loomed before the desk and handed him an envelope. "I am sorry if I startled you, but it looks important."

"Through with your meeting?" Trevor asked as he broke the familiar seal and unfolded the correspondence.

"Yes." She nodded with unabashed enthusiasm. "And I am pleased to announce that I have been elected chairperson for this year's Harvest Moon Festival."

"Indeed?" As Caroline spouted details, he digested the contents of the letter. After several minutes, he realized the study had grown eerily silent. When he glanced up, he discovered himself the object of intense scrutiny.

"So, how goes the unpacking?" Caroline opened a large trunk filled with his belongings. "Do you need any help?"

"If you have nothing better to do, be my guest." She had not fooled him for a second.

"I suppose the lot will fall to me, should there be a matter of importance to which you must attend." She bent and retrieved a stack of bound ledgers. "Where shall I put these?"

"On the second shelf." He motioned to a bookcase on the sidewall.

"Of course, if you require privacy, I can enlist the aid of the staff and organize your study when you take your afternoon ride." A parcel of worn documents in tow, she inclined her head. "And these?"

"Fourth shelf and on the left." He tossed the parchment on the blotter, steepled his hands, and wondered how far she would venture with her poorly executed ruse. "And I have no intention of leaving you alone in my personal domain, love."

"But I do not wish to keep you from...whatever you may be about." On her next fishing expedition, she vented a groan of exertion and straightened with a leather bound tome in her clutches. "Good heavens, but this is heavy."

Bloody hell, his wife had just stumbled upon his collection of etchings.

Trevor bolted from his chair. "I have received my first assignment from Admiral Douglas."

"Just as I feared." She gazed in his direction but maintained a tight grip on the licentious volume. "When do you depart?"

"I ship out in a sennight." Acquired during his last visit to India, the erotic art depicted sexual acts, some of which even the most hardened seaman would hesitate to ask of a doxy, in vivid detail and would no doubt send his highborn bride into an apoplectic fit.

"Oh, dear." Easing the book to her lap, Caroline propped her elbows atop the cover and rested her chin in her palms. "I knew it would happen eventually, but I had not expected you to be called into action so soon."

"Since the run on Buçaco, the war has intensified." Perhaps under the guise of conversation he could wrestle the startling pictures from her fingers without piquing her interest. "Wellington is locked in a standoff with Massena. The French Army has withdrawn from the lines of Torres

Vedras and taken a position between Santarém and Rio Maíor."

"Such nasty business." An expression of concern invested her delicate features. "What is your mission?"

"I shall transport members of the Counterintelligence Corps to the Continent—"

"How terrible." She buried her face in her hands. "You will be carrying spies."

"Darling, I accepted the responsibility. And while I lure the French Navy from Portugal, Damian and Lance will deliver supplies and reinforcements." He sat beside her. "Even now, your brother braves treacherous seas to support the cause."

"I know." Caroline lifted her head and gazed at him through tear-filled eyes. "But, somehow, this feels different."

"Do not fret. Dirk will accompany me, per the admiral's orders." Spying an opportunity, Trevor reached for the tome. "Here, let me take that from you."

"No. I can manage." She brushed aside his offer of assistance. "I promised to help organize your study, and that is what I shall do."

"If you insist, you may put the book on the third shelf." Exhaling in relief, he slapped his thighs, stood, and lent his support as she rose from the daybed. "So, your preparations are going well for the festival, I presume?"

"Yes, they progress nicely." Her gaze widened and, to his chagrin, she returned to her seat. "And I have a favor to ask."

"I am all ears." And he should have been keelhauled for exposing her to such prurient material.

"I should like, very much, to invite our family to stay with us the weekend of the festival, as an impromptu house party." Clutching the volume to her chest, Caroline set her chin on the edge of the cover. "They are your relations, too, and it will only be for two days."

"I have no objections." Trevor uttered a silent prayer for divine intervention. If he had to, he would burn the expensive bachelor's indulgence, posthaste. "But remember, we shall return to London shortly thereafter."

"Splendid. I will send the invitations, at once." Just then, she peered at the heavy book and trailed her fingers along the gold embossed binding. "My, what incredible craftsmanship."

Trevor was positive his goose was cooked. "Yes, it is quite rare."

To his good fortune, however, Caroline inched from the daybed, appearing none the wiser. As she strolled to the sidewall, she smiled. "Then I shall be extra careful." With an unladylike grunt, his wife hoisted the erotic anthology to the shelf.

She retreated a step—and halted. "Upon my word."

Blast his miserable hide. The location Trevor had designated put the bloody collection, with a bawdy picture front and center, right before her nose. "Caroline, dearest. Would you ring for—"

"Are they doing what I think they are doing?" She retrieved the lascivious catalogue. "What is this?"

"Nothing. It is not fit for my countess." He attempted to flank her inquiry but was too late. "Darling, you do not want to look at that."

"Yes, I do." She regained the daybed, deposited the damning work in her lap, and opened to a marked page featuring a particular position he had previously studied for sheer inventiveness.

Expecting shock and disapproval, Trevor was nonplussed when Caroline continued to peruse the lurid depictions. With each successive illustration, her breath grew rapid, and she tugged at the lace collar of her gown. For him, the subtle rise and fall of her bosom, coupled with furtive glances in his direction, proved an affecting experience. It was as though he was viewing the pictures for the first time, and a vicious erection roared to life in his breeches.

He leaned close and stared over her shoulder. "They are called etchings."

"Yes, I know." She nodded.

"You do?" For the umpteenth time, she surprised him with her characteristic derring-do.

"Of course." She gasped, as she turned the page. "Blake has an impressive store, but he favors Gillray."

"As do most men of my acquaintance." How he wanted her. "These are foreign."

"I have never seen any so colorful. And you have done that to me." Her emphasis held a hint of excitement. "And that, too."

"I have, many times." How he ached to claim her, right there on the daybed. "And if memory serves, you liked it."

"That does not look very comfortable. But what about this?" She pointed to the opposite page, which featured a woman performing a similar act on a man. "I would never have conceived of putting *that* in my mouth."

"Some men find it very pleasurable." At her guileless admission, Trevor could not help but chuckle. "Do not gainsay it until you have tried it."

"You want me to try it with you? You would enjoy it?" Was it wishful thinking on his part, or was Caroline a willing pupil? "Do you trust me to hold you between my teeth?"

"Aye," he responded without hesitation. "I would enjoy

it very much, but I would not recommend using your teeth, love."

"Then you must show me." She licked her lips. "How does one go about it?"

Now that was a lesson Trevor was ready to provide. "Do you recall the afternoon I took you to Gunter's?"

"I do." Inclining her head, Caroline narrowed her stare. "We sat beneath the maples and ate ices."

"Well?" When he said nothing more, she blinked. He arched a brow, and her cheeks turned a lovely shade of red.

"I believe I understand." In a deflating move he felt all the way to his loins, she slammed the book shut and stood. "Are you quite busy, my lord?"

"No." Disappointment was a bitter pill in his throat, and he frowned as she handed him the volume. "Why?"

She strolled toward the door. "Join me for a nap?"

Frustration evaporated in an instant. If he was not careful, he was going to drool. "That is an offer I dare not refuse."

In the entryway, she averted her stare and said, "And bring the etchings."

"SPREAD YOUR LEGS A LITTLE WIDER, and center your hips. Much better." Trevor parried and deflected Caroline's button-tipped foil. "Keep your knees bent, but not too much."

"Like this?" Silently vowing not to repeat the same mistake, she checked her place on the terrace and thrust again. To her chagrin, he evaded her attack and followed with a perfect riposte, which clipped her arm. "Bloody hell."

"Stay low to the ground." Her husband chuckled and then engaged her once more. "You are weaker than I am, but more agile, so try to capitalize on your advantage."

"All right." As Caroline assumed the correct stance, she studied the foil Trevor had designed especially for her and grimaced. "Ouch."

He halted. "What is it, love?"

"A nasty carpet burn on my...lower back." She compressed her lips. "You were quite energetic this afternoon."

"Sorry, darling," he said, though he looked not the least bit repentant.

"No apologies necessary." She giggled. "We shall simply be more careful the next time."

To wit her incorrigible green-eyed dragon wiggled his brows. "My lady, I can make no promises."

After passing the afternoon in his chambers recreating several acts depicted in the book of etchings—on the bed, in the chair, on the floor, and against the wall, he had gifted her the sleek weapon. But what thrilled her most was his declared intent to share something with her outside his private quarters.

"You are doing quite well," he stated as they crossed swords. "It was my hope that a lighter foil would enable you to fence with a more competitive edge. And I believe I prefer you in breeches."

At his admission, she tripped. "My lord, you are scandalous. Now if only I could find a pair of lighter feet."

"Do not get discouraged." With a boyish grin, he adopted a defensive posture. "This time, see if you can recover faster."

She nodded once and charged. "*En garde!*"

"Excellent. Your technique is superb." Trevor lunged,

but she managed to outmaneuver his attack. "Wonderful. I daresay you could defeat many a man twice your size."

"Truly?" Caroline laughed, and he winked. How she loved the nuances of his unconventional character. "Including Cavalier?"

No sooner had she uttered the words than Caroline knew she had made a horrible mistake. In less than a second, Trevor's demeanor changed in much the same fashion as it had the day they arrived at Althrup. As though rooted to the tile floor, he paled before her eyes. Yet the reason for his discomfort eluded her.

"What did you say?" He furrowed his brow.

"It really does not signify." She swallowed hard and cursed her loose tongue.

"Has something happened?" The brooding expression that heralded a vicious mood swing returned with a vengeance. "What are you not telling me?"

"Nothing, I swear." Despite the pleasant hours spent in their chambers and all her hard work, it was evident the spell had been broken. And she was at a loss in regard to the situation. "My apologies. I did not mean to upset you."

"I am not upset," he barked, then lowered his chin. "But I suggest you defend yourself as though I were your worst enemy. Let us see what you have learned."

Chilled to the marrow, she raked the sleeve of her shirt across her forehead. She would not ignore his warning. "As you wish."

The clash of steel meeting steel sliced through the air, and in an instant, she knew she had pricked his temper. With a well-placed thrust, he launched a vigorous offensive, and Caroline soon found herself cornered.

"Parry." Trevor evaded her safeguards and tapped her shoulder. "Again."

"My lord, this is practice." She stumbled, and he prodded her elbow with the end of his foil. "I am not your adversary."

"But what if I am yours?" He assumed an attack stance. "Pretend I am Cavalier and fight."

She backed away. "Trevor, I have had enough for today."

"Do as I say." He lunged, and she parried.

"Please, I am tired." And Caroline was a little scared.

"Come at me." His gaze was wild, animalistic. "Do it now."

At his command, she thrust.

With masterful precision he deflected the blow, and her practice sword slipped from her grasp. Just as fast, he brought the tip of his foil to her throat. Resting her arms at either side, she met his turbulent stare and managed not to scream.

"How could I—you are so—what would I do without you—" Her husband opened, and then closed his mouth. And looked unbelievably lost.

"Do not fear." In an attempt to calm, to soothe, Caroline set her palm to the flat of the blade and pushed it aside. She had to reassure him. Had to dispel his palpable terror. "I will never leave you."

"I beg your pardon?" Trevor threw his sword to the ground, stormed forward, clutched her shoulders, and shook her once. "You think to make me an emotional cripple, to bend me to your will like some addled fop from the schoolroom?"

"No." Realizing her mistake too late, that he misread her actions as manipulation, she framed his face with her hands. "I only want to be your wife."

"Hear me well." He speared his fingers through her hair,

and their noses were mere inches apart. "I had a good life before I met you, and I do not need you."

"All right." Determined not to flinch, resolved to stand for love and marriage, Caroline met him, toe to toe. But inside, she ached for her husband.

"I will not yield." To the contrary, his grip loosened.

"I understand, my lord."

Desperate seconds ticked past.

In a flash, Trevor claimed her mouth in a searing kiss and released her just as fast. Before she could respond, he turned on his heel and stomped into the house. Alone on the terrace, she searched her mind, grasping at clues in regard to his peculiar behavior. Suddenly, her mother's words of wisdom shimmered as hope on the horizon.

Love does not come easy for men.

Was it possible?

Could it be true?

Stunned by the revelation her captain had unwittingly laid bare, Caroline folded her arms and considered her next move. There would be no tears shed today, because the evidence was irrefutable. He might not like it, might even deny it.

Trevor cared for her.

THE SUN BLAZED BRILLIANTLY against a backdrop of cloudless azure sky on the morn of the Harvest Moon Festival. Villagers arrived in droves for the event, their curiosity apparent as they waited to meet the long absent earl and his bride. Their odd extended family was the talk of the town, for never had Althrup hosted so many members of the peerage, and Caroline beamed, as would a proud mother.

The air was heavy with the aroma of roasted ham and beef flowing from the taverns, which mingled with the scent of fresh-baked goods from the cake houses. A long line formed at the apple stall before noon. A team of acrobats, which Trevor had generously hired, thrilled audiences with daring feats. Later, a crowd gathered in front of the platform erected to showcase local musicians and a small dance troupe. Children eagerly awaited rides on the swings and the roundabout. At three, the races began, with Blake, Dirk, and Damian acting as judges. Afterward, Lance and Dalton supervised the archery contest and the axe throwing competition.

For their part, the Earl and Countess of Lockwood made an effort to meet and greet everyone. Caroline fought hard to suppress a twinge of jealousy when a group of smitten young ladies surrounded her handsome husband. Until she retreated to the sidewalk and was mobbed by local dandies who appeared happy to serve as her escort. Only seconds had passed when Trevor, sporting a nasty scowl, elbowed his way to her side and dispatched the eager bucks with a lethal stare.

"Damn bloody scamps," he said with a pout. "Who will protect you when I am at sea?"

"You need not worry on that account." She could not help but giggle. "What care I for boys when I have you?"

"Spoken like a Lockwood." Though he smiled, his brow was a mass of furrows. "Well, my dear countess, your festival is a success."

"Yes, we have had nary a glitch." Caroline gazed at the sky, which evidenced that night fast approached. "But the day seems to have flown."

"Perhaps." Trevor tapped her nose. "But there is still one surprise left."

"Oh?" She clucked her tongue. "Just what are you about?"

"You shall see." A man on a mission, he steered her through the crowd.

When he paused at the entrance to the inn, she pulled up short. "My lord, you cannot be serious...I mean...not here. We have guests. Can you not wait until we return home?"

"What a dirty mind you have, love." He opened the door and ushered her inside with a pat on her bottom. "And I promise to make ample use of your imagination, tonight."

"Good evening, your lordship," said a man behind the counter.

"Mr. Ridley." Trevor snaked an arm about her waist. "Would you be so kind as to give the word?"

"Aye, sir." The innkeeper nodded.

"What word?" Inclining her head, she peered at her husband. "And where are you taking me?"

"Patience, my dear." He led her to a small staircase. "After you."

Hiking her skirts, Caroline ascended to the top, and then paused before a little door. When she glanced over her shoulder, Trevor simply smiled, reached around, and turned the knob. The tiny portal opened to reveal a rooftop access, probably used by the chimney sweep. Darkness enveloped her as she stepped to the platform. Stars twinkled, and moonlight illuminated his face.

"All right." Not since his angry display on the terrace had she been so perplexed by her spouse, and she folded her arms. "Would you care to tell me why I am here?"

Trevor shifted his weight, slipped his hands into his coat pockets, then reversed his stance and set his palms to her waist. "Because I owe you an apology."

"Oh?" Dare she hope?

"My behavior of late has not been very noble." He pulled her close. "My conduct has been unforgivable, and I am sorry."

In that moment, Caroline let her heart sing. But before she could bask in the glory of his expression of regret, a thunderous roar pierced the quiet, and a starburst of color exploded in the night sky. *"Fireworks."*

Trevor nuzzled her temple. "They are for you, my beautiful wife."

Another rumble sounded, and light flickered over the village as a cascade of radiant sparkles showered from high above the treetops.

"How marvelous." Wrapped in her husband's warm embrace, Caroline relished each successive spectacle.

Volley after volley rocked the building beneath her feet, and the crowd gathered on the thoroughfare below signaled their approval with a concert of shouts and applause. The finale commenced with a rapid barrage, and she held tight to Trevor as fiery streams turned night into day. And when the last aerial blaze extinguished, he pressed on her an impossibly sweet kiss.

"My lord, you are forgiven." She nibbled his lower lip.

"Is that all I get for my hard work, love?" he asked, in his playful voice.

"Of course not." Nervous anticipation sparked in her belly. "Rest assured that I should endeavor to convey the depth of my appreciation of your efforts upon our arrival at home."

"But what about your family?" He grimaced.

"They are *our* family, and I will plead a headache." She giggled. "Trust me, they will understand."

"Then what are we waiting for?" He opened the little

door, and they retraced their steps. As they crossed the lobby, Trevor saluted the innkeeper. "Thank you, for the use of your facilities, Mr. Ridley."

The man dipped his chin. "A pleasure to be of service, your lordship."

On the street, the crowds had dispersed, and only a few people lingered. Trevor looked left and then right. "I do not see our coach." He glanced at her and frowned. "And you are without a wrap. Perhaps you should stay in the lobby, while I locate our rig."

"But the stable yard is not far." The wind blew, and she shivered. "I can come with you."

Arching a brow, he doffed his coat and draped it over her shoulders. "Thornton may have to harness the horses, and I will not risk you catching a chill."

Thrilled by his show of concern for her welfare, Caroline decided that was one battle she could afford to surrender. "In that case, I shall do as you ask and remain here."

Tucked, safe and warm, in the inn, she stared out the window as her husband searched for their equipage. A lad smiled as he swept refuse from the sidewalk, and she responded in kind. Shortly thereafter, a steady clip-clop caught her ear. When she stepped outside, she spied the Lockwood coach coming down the lane and started in that direction.

Near a tavern, Caroline heard a noise and paused at the entrance to an alley. A mountain of casks blocked the narrow passage. "Hello?" Wood creaked and groaned. "Is someone there?"

A cat shot from the stack.

≈

WHEN HE SPOTTED his wife standing at the roadside, Trevor waved a greeting. Since Althrup was situated just east of the town, the driver had to turn the rig around. As they came to a halt, he exited the coach. The wall behind her appeared to shift, he narrowed his stare and realized the wall was not a solid surface but was in fact—

"Caroline, *look out!*"

Breaking into a full sprint, he lunged and reached her in the nick of time. With only seconds to spare, they landed hard on the street and skidded on the gravel. The barrels crashed on the walkway, sending splintered wood flying, and missed them by a hairsbreadth. As the commotion echoed on nearby buildings, a few villagers darted from their homes, and liveried footmen rushed to their aid.

Trevor shook his head in an attempt to gather his wits, and his wife lay eerily still. "Darling, are you hurt?"

After what seemed an eternity, her eyelids fluttered, and she gasped. "I believe I am fine."

"Be careful." A quick assessment showed her dress was torn and dirty, and her elbows bled. Providing support, he helped her to her feet. "Here, lean on me."

"Oh, dear." Caroline buckled.

Conscious of her injuries, he scooped her into his arms and carried her to the coach.

"Does her ladyship require a doctor?" someone asked.

"Yes." He covered his wife with his tattered coat. "Have him meet us at Althrup."

"Aye, sir."

A small crowd gathered along the fringe of the mangled mass, and Trevor approached a man holding a length of rope.

"I do not understand it, your lordship. As the barkeep, it is my responsibility to secure the empty casks." The poor soul shifted his weight. "I swear those barrels were properly tied down."

"No doubt it was a terrible accident." Trevor accepted the section of twine and inspected the ends. The hair rose on the back of his neck, and he shuddered.

The original knot remained, and the protruding ends had frayed with age. The rope had failed in a different segment, and the twine looked clean-cut, as though severed by a knife. Coiling the section, he returned to the coach and shouted, "Home, Thornton."

An image of Caroline, crushed beneath the rubble, flashed before him, and he gained a measure of relief when she snuggled close. But inside him, something shattered.

Someone tried to kill his wife.

CHAPTER SEVENTEEN

*M*uch to her displeasure, Caroline returned to London with her husband the following Monday. Since Trevor was scheduled to sail in a sennight, she politely refused all social invitations and opted to remain in their townhouse, so as not to miss a single minute with him. Preparations for Trevor's impending mission consumed precious hours, and his maiden voyage as a Knight of the Brethren weighed heavy on her heart and mind. So, while he passed his days organizing his crew, ordering provisions, and readying the *Hera*, she busied herself devising different ways to show her captain how much she cared for him.

After commissioning a miniature portrait of herself from a noted artist, Caroline paid an extra fifty pounds to ensure the painting would be completed before Trevor departed England. She devoted an entire morning to the creation of a design incorporating their initials into a unique monogram, which she lovingly embroidered on his handkerchiefs. And at the corner of each lace-edged cotton square, she placed a small drop of her perfume.

On Tuesday, they rose from bed in the pre-dawn hours to welcome the sun. Wednesday, Trevor spent a half-hour brushing her brown locks, only to devote three hours mussing them again, and she was not about to complain. And Thursday, ah Thursday, now that was a memorable afternoon made special when her rogue captain made love to her on the desktop in his study. Poor Mrs. Porter had been unable to remove the large ink stain on the back of Caroline's dress.

"A penny for your thoughts."

"I do not believe that time flies when you are having fun." Standing on the dock at Deptford, she peered at her brother and frowned. "Rather, time flies as danger nears."

"Do not worry." Blake chucked her chin. "Lockwood is a devil of a seaman, and Dirk will be with him. Heaven help the French if they stumble upon those two."

"I pray you are right." Inside her ermine muff, Caroline clenched her hands.

The rising sun warmed the earth, quelling the chill of the brisk November morning. Waves splashed against the pilings, and tiny ripples formed a delicate mosaic of water in motion. The decks of the *Hera* were alive with the activity one would expect of a ship preparing to sail, and, at the helm, Trevor shouted orders to the crew. Mentally, Caroline rehearsed the speech that might help her discern, once and for all, whether or not her husband loved her. It was clear Trevor wrestled with inner demons, but the cause was not equally clear. Could he love her, or was his constancy more akin to the attachment one mustered for a favored hound?

"Will they be gone long?" she inquired.

At that moment, six cloaked figures, their faces shielded by black hoods, boarded the ship. As members of the secretive Counterintelligence Corps exchanged greetings with Trevor, she shivered.

"Little sister, you know well enough that is a question for which there is no answer." Blake scratched his cheek.

"I ask because I shall miss him." And she desperately hoped her husband would share her affliction.

"Your devotion is commendable." Her elder sibling caught her in a half-hug and playfully tugged her ear lobe. "Perhaps I can provide suitable diversions to keep your mind from wandering to less pleasant thoughts while Lockwood is at sea. What say we take in a play?"

"You must be joking." Trevor glanced in her direction, and Caroline smiled. "Your dislike for the theatre is surpassed only by your aversion to opera."

"Be that as it may, I am willing to put your happiness before my own." Blake rocked on his heels. "And it has been too long since we enjoyed a brother-sister outing."

"How magnanimous of you." Men scrambled into the rigging, which signaled her husband would soon depart. Was he not going to bid her farewell? "Blake?"

"Yes?" He arched a brow.

"Would you kindly inform his lordship that I should like to speak with him before he takes leave of these shores?" She had a declaration to make.

"As you wish." Blake chuckled.

THE INSTANT his brother-in-law started in his direction, Trevor realized he was not going to escape the duty he most dreaded. Of course, he had not intended to sail without stealing one last kiss from his wife. "It appears I have been summoned."

"Indeed." At his side, Dirk chuckled. "And at this moment, I must confess I do not envy you."

"Lockwood." Blake stood tall and clicked his heels. "My sister begs an audience, and you would do best to ally yourself with Bony should you refuse her request."

"Bloody hell." A chorus of snorts and snickers pricked his pride, and Trevor set down his charts. "You will watch over her while I am gone?"

"As promised." The estimable duke leaned on the railing and folded his arms. "I have already invited her to the theatre, and Weston will accompany her to a musicale."

"Weston? A musicale?" Whistling in monotone, Dirk slapped a thigh. "How much did that set you back?"

"A case of my finest brandy." Blake gazed at the sky and shook his head. "And the widow Tremaine."

"You chased her skirts for a month." Dirk wrinkled his nose. "That had to hurt."

"As must needs." Blake scowled.

"But Caroline is none the wiser?" Trevor inquired as he stared at the lady in question. Upon arrival in London, he had gathered the Brethren and relayed the full details—and his suspicions—of the incident involving the fallen casks. "Although Cavalier has not shown his face, I do not believe we can be too careful."

"I concur." With his brow furrowed, Blake sighed. "And I agree that we should not inform my sister of your concerns. Such revelations would, no doubt, incite brazen defiance of our safeguards."

"No doubt." Trevor rolled his eyes and walked toward the companion ladder. "Gentlemen, on that note, I shall make my farewells."

Men scurried in all directions, singing bawdy shanties as they worked, when he crossed the main deck. "Check the foremost ropes," Trevor said to the boatswain, who barked new orders to the crew. At the bottom of the gangplank, his wife stood. As he approached, she curtseyed.

"My lord, the weather is fair." She stuck her tongue in her cheek. "Surely that bodes well for your mission?"

"It should." He resisted the urge to toss Caroline over his shoulder and convey her to his cabin. "But the tide awaits no man, and I must cast off." Expecting a river of tears, Trevor steeled himself for the deluge, but her expression bore no hint of distress.

"Then I wish you safe journey." She extended a gloved hand.

Like an idiot, he accepted her gesture, as would a proper gentleman. "Thank you."

"You are most welcome."

He stared at her.

She stared at him.

"I have something—"

"I wanted to give you—"

Blast his clumsy hide, it was as though Trevor had returned to courtship hell. "Ladies first."

"After you." Caroline bit her lip. "I insist."

"All right." He retrieved a small parcel from his pocket. "This is not much, just a token of my esteem."

"Oh?" She accepted the gift and unfolded the brown paper. "Why, it is lovely."

And then his wife burst into laughter.

"Would you care to tell me what about my painted image is cause for convulsive hilarity?" He shuffled his feet.

"My lord, you misunderstand my reaction to your surprise," she said through a few lingering giggles. "You see it appears we are on the same page."

He arched a brow. "I do not follow."

"Perhaps this will make things clearer." Caroline produced a similar-sized package.

When he unwrapped the framed miniature of his bride, Trevor chuckled. "Which artist did you use?"

"Mr. Bainbridge." With his portrait clutched to her bosom, she sidled near. "And yours?"

"The same." Tension eased from his shoulders, and he met her inquisitive stare. "But even a master could not do justice to the genuine article, love."

"Oh, Trevor." The dam broke, Caroline trembled, and she seemed fragile as a porcelain doll. "I miss you already."

And his current state mirrored her sentiment. Despite the inclination to hold her in his arms and offer a modicum of comfort, he could not move. Clinging to the reins of self-restraint, he turned toward the ship. "I shall see you soon, dearest."

"Wait." She caught his wrist. "You will be careful? You will come back to me?"

Sunlight flickered on the water, and he gave his attention to the silvery shimmer. He had made many journeys, so why should that one be any different? "Depend upon it."

"Know that you carry my heart with you," she said in a shaky voice.

And he looked her straight in the eyes. "What?"

With admirable strength, his wife lifted her chin. "I love you."

Hers was the sweetest confession he had ever heard.

Although Caroline had uttered the words on their wedding night, never had she declared herself to his face, before God and everyone present. The combination of her charming expression and statement embodied the solution to his quandary. His departure was unique because, prior to that day, no one had ever bothered to care whether or not he returned. The implications were overpowering.

Bereft of speech, and his pulse racing, Trevor struggled to breathe. Operating on instinct, he enveloped Caroline; as would a drowning man grasp a lifeline. And just as fast, he set her at arm's length. Not until he gained the quarterdeck had he chanced a glance at his bride. The emotions ravaging his senses would not abate, and he waged war against himself. Trevor could not be more adrift were he in the middle of the open ocean without a ship.

Caroline truly loved him.

"She does not look happy," Dirk whispered as the first mate bellowed the order to make sail. "You should have provided some reassurance."

"I am not a man of maudlin romanticism." On the dock, she blew him a kiss, and he waved. "I would rather be keel-hauled."

"That can be arranged."

THE DRAWING ROOM at Marlborough House was warm and inviting, and ladies filed into the area after a lavish six-course meal. Caroline pressed her palm to her very full belly and peered at her brother, who whispered in a young conquest's ear. No doubt the blushing woman was the current prize in his passionate pursuits and the reason he kept stealing Caroline's opera glasses during their earlier outing.

To his credit, Blake called on her every morning, making breakfast at Elliott House a regular walk down memory lane. Together, along with Damian, and sometimes Lance and Dalton, they rode through Hyde Park and raced along Rotten Row. True to his word, her elder sibling escorted her to the Adelphi on Drury Lane on Wednesday. And tonight, he had obtained a box for the production of *Don Giovanni*. But despite the companionship from her friends and family, she was lonely. And worse, a mere sennight had passed since Trevor sailed.

Due to the end of the Season, most of fashionable society, including her mother, resided in the country. So when the invitation to the Marlborough's dinner party arrived, she posted her acceptance in a flurry of anticipation and excitement. Had she known the Viscount and Viscountess Darwith were also on the list of attendees, she might have reconsidered.

At that moment, the butler rolled in the tea trolley, and Lady Marlborough drew nigh, with Caroline's sworn enemy in tow. "Lady Lockwood, I believe you are acquainted with Lady Darwith?"

With a smile, Caroline lifted her chin and waited.

Slowly, very slowly, her nemesis curtseyed. "Countess."

"But of course." A surge of triumph roared through her veins, newfound confidence strengthened every muscle, and Caroline wanted to shout for joy. How satisfying it was to be recognized as the hag's noble better, and she averted her stare. "Lady Darwith and I are old friends."

"Excellent." The hostess poured two cups of tea. "Then I shall leave you to enjoy your refreshments and conversation."

"So unfortunate that Lord Lockwood could not join us." The serpent slithered. "What did you say has kept him from our gathering?"

"I did not say." Sensing an attack, Caroline raised her

defenses but held her ground. "But if you must know, he is at sea."

"Really? So soon after your wedding?" With a smug expression, the shrew compressed her lips. "One might assume marriage does not agree with his lordship."

"Such is the price for the wife of a sea captain." The witch may have thought herself the victor, but Caroline had yet to fire her guns. Taking careful aim, she let fly her answering salvo. "Oh, I forgot. You did not wed such a man, so you would not understand."

"*Well.*" Eyes as wide as the saucer in her hand, the termagant retreated two steps. "I beg your pardon, Lady Lockwood."

"No pardon necessary, Lady Darwith." The sweet taste of success danced on her tongue, and Caroline moved in for the kill. "You are dismissed."

As the de-fanged and defeated she-wolf stormed toward the sofa, a group of women engaged in gossip nearby exchanged what appeared to be looks of approval and dipped their chins in unison. And across the room, Blake raised his glass and winked.

Indeed, love was an invincible shield.

Yes, Caroline considered Trevor the source of her mettle and vigor. Even now, from far away in some unknown location, his presence reached out and warmed her heart, touched her soul. An unfailing support, an invisible fortification protected her from every conceivable danger. Should fear beckon, a single glance at his miniature could banish the chill of trepidation. And although her husband had yet to voice his declaration, something on which she refused to dwell, she had not lost faith. Hope burned bright as the sun in the match and the man.

On the thought, Caroline mingled among the guests.

"Countess." After executing a stiff curtsey, Lady Trowbridge backed Caroline into a corner. "What is this nonsense I hear? Your husband has gone to sea?"

"He has." She nodded once. "But it was a business matter of much importance."

"Humph." The old widow adjusted the fuchsia turban on her head. "There is nothing so important as providing an heir to the earldom."

Embarrassment burned in her cheeks, and Caroline cleared her throat. "You have my solemn vow that I shall endeavor to address the deficiency upon his lordship's return."

"See that you do." Lady Trowbridge peered at the empty cup in her hands and frowned. "I need more tea. If you will excuse me, Lady Lockwood."

"Of course." As the quirky character headed in the direction of the trolley, Caroline laughed and started toward the windows.

And walked straight into Lord Darwith.

Blue eyes, with a few more wrinkles at the corners but no less animated, twinkled. With guinea-gold hair and austere, deadly handsome features, her onetime love had changed little since their ill-fated courtship. But now, a man with chestnut locks kissed with more shades of brown than she ever knew existed stirred her blood. And she preferred green eyes that shimmered like precious emeralds.

"Good heavens." Somehow, she managed not to spill her tea. "Forgive me, my lord."

"But I am to blame." Clutching her forearms, her former suitor kept them from falling to the carpeted floor. "A thousand pardons, Lady Lockwood."

"The fault is entirely mine." She noticed her brother, a

stern look on his face, approaching and stayed him with a quick wave. "I did not watch where I was going."

"My lady, you are too kind." After righting his coat, Lord Darwith bowed with an elegant flair she remembered well. "Countess, it is a pleasure to see you again."

"And you, Lord Darwith." The nervousness that marked their previous encounters remained curiously absent, and Caroline gave vent to a sigh of relief. "Are you enjoying the evening?"

"Indeed, I am. And allow me to belatedly congratulate you on your wedding." Her gloved hand in his grasp, he brought her fingers to his lips, then met her gaze. "Lord Lockwood is a fortunate man."

The once notorious rake could still melt butter with his stare, and she clucked her tongue. "I hope he shares your view."

"No doubt he does." Although Lord Darwith smiled, a hint of sadness seeped through his suave facade. "The duchess, she is in good health?"

"Yes, my mother is quite well, thank you." No bitterness, no hurt feelings loomed as a black cloud over her heart. "And your family?"

"The same, thank you." Lord Darwith shifted his weight, tugged on his coat sleeves, pulled a kerchief from his pocket, and wiped his brow. Suddenly, the calm confidence dissipated, and his demeanor changed. "Lady Lockwood—Caroline, if I may be so bold. Please accept a long overdue apology in regard to our failed courtship. Were I half a man, I should have offered some expression of regret months ago."

He could have knocked her over with the feather from Lady Trowbridge's turban.

On occasions too numerous to count, Caroline had

dreamed of that moment. In her fantasies, she had acted aloof, had even cut Lord Darwith in full view of the *ton*. Glorious vindication and smug satisfaction would at last be hers. Instead, she felt only sympathy.

Because she had married Trevor, and basked in the glow of true love every day of her life, she could summon nothing beyond pity for the melancholy viscount. At the very least, he had earned everlasting mercy for willingly shackling himself to the cold-hearted wretch he called wife.

The irons of the past loosened, and her heart broke free of the pain, humiliation, and distrust. Gone was the bone-gnawing sorrow and self-disgust. In its place remained blissful relief and a spirit of forgiveness unlike any she had known since childhood.

And in that second, Caroline realized she had never loved that man. "My lord, an apology is not necessary. What happened between us has been forgotten."

"Dearest lady." He shook his head and chuckled. "The ignorance of my youth blinded me to the qualities most important in a mate."

"You must not say such things." She checked to make sure no one had overheard the discussion. "And I am a happily wedded woman."

"Have no fear on my account." The charismatic viscount snared a brandy from a passing maid. "I should sooner sever my right arm than hurt you again."

"My, but you sound gloomy." Caroline grinned, which he returned, measure for measure. "Let us leave behind such depressing matters. Tell me what you have been doing with yourself."

"Well, I have just procured a rare Egyptian artifact," he stated with boyish enthusiasm. "It is from the eighteenth dynasty."

"Really?" A marvelous idea occurred to her. "You are still collecting?"

"Indubitably." He quirked a corner of his mouth. "Hunting antiquities is my sole passion in life."

"Oh, Lord Darwith." Bubbling with excitement, Caroline could barely contain herself. "I wonder if you might help me with a personal enterprise?"

"Countess, I am your servant to command." He clicked his heels.

"Excellent, but you must promise to keep our secret from my husband."

THE BUNK PITCHED, Trevor rolled to one side and came awake. When a flash of light spilled through the stern windows, he tossed his legs over the edge of the mattress and stood. An ominous rumble shattered the quiet of his cabin, and the ship heeled hard a-starboard. He ended up back in bed. "Bloody hell."

Using his hands, feeling his way inch by inch, Trevor located his breeches, boots, and shirt. In a strange waltz across the boards, he stumbled in the direction of his locker and pulled on his wool coat and oilskin raingear. The *Hera* bucked, and he lunged for the door. "Christ Jesus!"

Metal was cold to his palm as he twisted the knob, held tight to the frame, and sidled into the hall.

In similar fashion, hugging the wall, Dirk exited his quarters. "I would say we have encountered a nasty storm."

"What was your first clue?" Trevor asked as they crawled on deck.

Chaos blew a violent welcome of wind and rain, and the men of the middle watch struggled to secure a sail.

Through the downpour, he located the boatswain clinging to the mainmast. "Mr. Boyle, get the crew below at once."

"Aye, sir. The tempest caught us off guard, and we barely managed to take in the canvas." The old salt pointed skyward. "And I have one ensnared high in the rigging, Cap'n."

A wave crashed over the bow, dousing Trevor in bone chilling seawater. Bursts of lightning illuminated the hectic scene, and he spied the outline of a body dangling in the ropes. Could the situation get any worse? "Bloody everlasting hell."

"Make for the quarterdeck," Dirk shouted. "I will get your man down."

"This is my ship and crew, you head for the helm." Trevor grabbed a fistful of Dirk's gear. "Steer into the wind, or we will be sleeping with sharks."

"Do I look like a virgin?" The viscount wrenched free. "Save your sailor, I know what to do."

The motion of the ocean sent Trevor flying into the shrouds. With a death grip on the ratlines, he began his ascent. Raindrops rode the mighty gale, and his face and eyes burned beneath nature's assault. Higher and higher, he climbed as the world around him erupted in an awesome display of raw power. When he slipped, he sucked in a breath and uttered a silent prayer. "Caroline."

As soon as he said her name, Trevor questioned his sanity. Hell and the Reaper nipped at his heels, and all he could think of was his wife. The taste of her sweet tongue lingered on his lips, the velvety softness of her hair played on his fingertips, and the sumptuous warmth of her body comforted him even now.

From somewhere deep inside him, he found the courage to climb.

Time seemed to stand still as he navigated the ropes. At the platform where the topmast capped the lower masthead, he regrouped. With a leg tangled in the line, the crewman listed upside down in the wind.

"Can you hear me?" Trevor caught his attention.

"Cap'n, you should not be here," the sailor hollered in response.

At least the poor soul was conscious. "Have you any broken bones?"

"No, sir. Just a rope burn."

Thank heaven for small favors. But the real trick would be freeing the tar without sending both of them tumbling into the sea. A possible solution dawned, and he shimmied to the topmast stay. From his precarious perch, he leaned forward, caught hold of the mariner's coat, and pulled hard.

The ship lurched, and Trevor lost his footing.

With one hand, he clutched the stay. All of a sudden, the captain was in greater peril than the subordinate, who remained trapped in the rigging. Gusts of air buffeted his body, and the mast mutated into a cruel whipping post. On the howling gale, a familiar voice delivered a plea.

Come back to me.

Trevor closed his eyes and envisioned his bride. An image of her smiling face formed in his mind, and his memory supplied the rest of her curvaceous figure. Unfailing honesty and unshakeable support shimmered in her gaze. Caroline lifted her arms and reached for him.

I love you.

The strength of a hundred men invested his fatigued frame, and Trevor opened his eyes and crawled to the platform. The *Hera* sailed into the wind and sliced through the waves. As the bow crested, he wedged a foot in the topmast shrouds and arced with the movement of the ship. Grasping a fistful of the sailor's coat, he jerked the sea dog upright as the stern lifted. When the bow again crested, he released his charge, and the mariner dropped safely to the platform.

While the trip up the mast had seemed endless, the descent took only a few minutes. After dispatching the injured tar, he plotted a course for the quarterdeck and relieved Dirk from the helm.

"That was some rescue," said the viscount, clutching the rail. "Had I not witnessed it for myself, I would not have believed your report."

"I do not follow." Trevor made a futile attempt to dry his face.

"I am referring to your mission summary." A wave crashed over the larboard side, and Dirk grabbed the wheel and helped maintain their heading. "Admiral Douglas will be quite impressed with your performance."

"I do not intend to mention it." Trevor groaned as the tempest delivered another saltwater bath. "I did my duty."

"Lockwood, you are a better man than you let on."

"Can you steer with your mouth closed?"

The annoying nobleman laughed and said nothing more.

In the wee hours of the morning, the storm abated, and they anchored twenty miles off the coast of Lisbon to await further orders. While he sent Dirk below decks, Trevor refused to be relieved by the first watch. Although he was dead tired, he knew sleep would not come easy, if it came at all.

When a sliver of gold divided sea from sky, he relinquished the helm to the first mate and assumed a post at the stern rail. Smooth as satin was the calm ocean, but inside him an emotional torrent raged. His mind raced with denials, but he had lost the battle. Fear settled as a lead ball in his belly, and relentless trepidation nestled on his shoulders. While he might lie to himself, no longer could he ignore his heart.

Trevor was in love with his wife.

CHAPTER EIGHTEEN

"Countess, I am honored by your presence at my little gathering." Lady Darrow smiled and ushered Caroline into the well-appointed townhouse.

"And I am equally honored by your gracious invitation." A butler accepted her wrap, and Caroline strolled through a double-door entrance that opened into the drawing room.

After enduring over a fortnight of curious outings with her brother and Damian, and their rakish shenanigans, she had sent a note informing Blake that she could not attend the Hogart's musicale. Pleading a severe case of megrims, Caroline had sought to stretch her independent wings and partake of an evening at the theatre on her own.

A chorus of whispers greeted her arrival at the stately residence, which seemed odd in light of the innocuous affair. Had no one thought her capable of contributing an educated opinion to the cultural review group? Of course, the fact that she could claim only the slightest acquaintance with those present might have had something to do with the chilly reception.

"Lady Lockwood, Lord Sheldon has expressed an

interest in your company," the hostess said with a peculiar gleam in her eye. "If you will allow me to make the introductions."

A sinfully beautiful man sketched a dramatic bow and cast her a brazen glance as though he knew how she looked in her chemise. "Countess, this is pleasure."

"You are most kind, Lord Sheldon." She extended her hand and shivered with unease when his lips lingered scandalously at her wrist. "S-so, you are a fan of the theatre, my lord?"

"Good God, no." Lord Sheldon escorted her to a green damask covered sofa. "Must confess I cannot stomach such drivel."

"Oh?" Gooseflesh encompassed her from top to toe, though she could not comprehend the cause of her distress. "Then why are you here?"

"The same reason as everyone else, for a bit of companionship to pass the time." The audacious lord hovered inappropriately nigh. "May I call you Caroline?"

"You are too bold, sir." Panic traipsed her spine, and she inched to one end of the sofa.

"And you are a delight, my dear." In less than a second, he closed the distance.

"When will we get started?" she asked in a high-pitched voice, hoping to find refuge, from the unwanted advances, in intelligent discourse.

"Sweet lady, we can begin right now." The nobleman chuckled and stood. "Come. I believe Lady Darrow has prepared my usual accommodations."

"I do not follow." Caroline swallowed hard as he brought her to her feet. "Why can we not do it here?"

"A woman after my own heart." Lord Sheldon tapped a finger to her nose. "You are a naughty girl."

"There must be...I am not sure...I do not understand." Something in his expression drew her up short, and she dug her heels into the rich carpet. But the insufferable man would brook no refusal. With an arm at her waist, he led her into the foyer.

And a familiar face embodied the escape for which she had prayed. "Lord Markham, what a wonderful surprise."

"What on earth are you doing here?" Everett blinked, as would an owl.

"Are you a member of Lady Darrow's theatre group, too?" Lord Sheldon's grip on her elbow tightened, and Caroline inclined her head. "Pray a moment, sir. His lordship and I are old friends."

"Theatre group?" Everett's brows almost reached his hairline. He opened and then closed his mouth. "You cannot be serious. Did the blackguard lure you here under false pretenses? In the name of Lord Lockwood, I demand satisfaction."

As it appeared the two men planned to duel in the foyer, Caroline intervened. "My lord, I came here of my own volition." She readily accepted Everett's proffered escort. "But I am confused. What usually occurs at these cultural reviews?"

"Cultural reviews—" Lord Markham choked. "Is that what you thought?"

"Of course." She shrugged. "Why else would I be here?"

"Walk with me." Everett steered her along the sidewall. "You should not have ventured into this lair of wolves. If Trevor finds out, he will hang us both from the nearest yardarm."

"Lord Markham, you talk in riddles." A dark sense of foreboding nipped at her heels.

"Look around." He whispered into her ear. "Do you not see the men and ladies pairing?"

She scanned the vicinity. "But they are wives of—"

"Marital vows matter not when one seeks divertissements of a carnal nature." Everett drew her to his side.

The intimation of his words, the crude education, opened her eyes. Only then had she recognized the loaded stares and illicit caresses of the mating dance.

"Oh, dear." Caroline stopped dead in her tracks. "I have made a dreadful mistake."

"Shall I retrieve your belongings?" Everett inquired in a hushed tone.

"Please, do so." The urge to run, to depart Lady Darrow's and never return charged every nerve and consumed every muscle.

But Lord Sheldon loomed in the foyer, a barrier to her flight. "Going somewhere?"

To avoid a scene, Caroline stayed Everett with a squeeze of his fingers. "Lord Markham, would you be so kind as to send for my carriage?"

Everett peered at her, then glanced at Lord Sheldon. "As you wish."

Clasping her hands, she lifted her chin and looked the intrusive lord straight in the eye. "My presence here is the result of a gross error for which I am entirely to blame. Had the true purpose of this gathering been known to me prior to my arrival, I would never have come."

"A faithful wife? How exceedingly cruel of you, Countess." Lord Sheldon bent his head and placed a chaste kiss to her cheek. "I bid you a restful night."

"And the same to you, my lord." The heat of his stare weighed heavy on her conscience, and she marched down the hall, claimed her wrap from the butler, and crossed the threshold.

Everett stood like a sentry at the carriage door. When she sank, safe and snug, in the squabs, he fastened the latch and shouted, "Make haste!"

Though the streets of London were quiet, her insides were anything but, and Caroline had not breathed a sigh of relief until she entered Mayfair proper. The rig turned onto Park Lane, and her home came into view. The carriage halted, and the footman handed her to the sidewalk. Roberts flung open the door, but a strange noise caught her ear.

"Hello?" She peered beyond the wrought iron rail at the area stairs below. The servant's passage was shrouded in darkness, and she could see nothing. "Is someone there?"

"May I be of assistance, your ladyship?" asked the butler.

"No." She narrowed her stare and rubbed the back of her neck. "I am sure it is nothing."

Hiking her skirts, she skipped across the marbled foyer, up to the second floor, and down the hall to her apartments. Ensconced in her bedchamber, she folded her arms in an attempt to cease her trembling.

"What is the matter with me?" With a hard yank on the bellpull, Caroline summoned her lady's maid. "Mine was a harmless error. And I was only at Lady Darrow's for a few minutes."

Despite concern for her reputation, her real conundrum centered on honesty and whether or not she should apprise Trevor of her ill-fated outing. His mother's infidelity had burned scars on his heart and mind, and a confession, even one based on good intentions, might serve to cause him undeserved torment.

But should she lie to Trevor and thus compound her blunder?

"I cannot do it, as the issue does not signify." She sat at her vanity and buried her face in her hands. Other than Everett, there was no one to which she could turn for advice. "Can no one help me?"

Fingers speared through her hair, and pins scattered about her lap. "Perhaps I may be of service?"

Caroline blinked into the mirror and gasped in shock. "*You are home!*"

The chair toppled onto its side when she stood and flew into Trevor's arms.

"When did you drop anchor?" She nipped his chin. "And why did you not send word?"

"I beg your pardon, my lady wife." He grazed her nose with his teeth and hugged her impossibly tight. "I dispatched a messenger upon my arrival at Deptford but was disappointed to receive a reply from Roberts informing me that you were unavailable. Where—"

"Oh, how I missed you," Caroline said as she scored her nails on the back of his neck.

"And I you," he declared with a grin, and then nuzzled her temple.

Amid her flirty giggles and his hearty chuckles, she showered Trevor's cheeks with kisses. But as their lips met, the laughter ceased. Fiery passion spun a delicate web, encircling them in a cocoon of desire.

"Shall we adjourn to my chamber?" he inquired, shuffling her in his embrace.

"To your bed," Caroline stated with unrestrained enthusiasm. "Hurry."

"Darling, I like the way you think." Trevor sidled into

the little corridor joining their rooms. "By the by, I dismissed your lady's maid for the night."

"Scoundrel." In less than a minute, she untied his cravat and discarded it on the floor.

"Indeed, I consider the opportunity to undress you a pleasure not to be overlooked." He bent his head and licked her throat. "But, at this moment, I am not certain I can withstand the torture."

"Then why wait?" Caroline kicked off her slippers as they entered his suite. "I want you so much it hurts."

Trevor stopped right there and kissed her.

And kept kissing her.

She was not sure how they got to his four-poster, but in the blink of an eye, he deposited her at the center of the mattress. With a flick of his wrist, he lifted her skirts. Boots and all, he climbed onto the bed, and she parted her thighs in implicit surrender. Fumbling with the fastening of his breeches, he finally managed to free the proof of his arousal. On a groan, he came into her hard and fast.

The welcome weight of his body, the erotic dance of his hips, and the intimate thrust of his flesh deep inside hers combined in exquisite invasion. Again and again, he assaulted her senses, claimed her corporeal self in the most elemental infiltration known to man. Delicious fire simmered beneath her skin, and a decadent tension marked the entrance to her personal pleasure dome. The gates of heaven on earth approached, Caroline reached for the sumptuous pinnacle to their union and—

Trevor opened his mouth in a silent scream and froze.

Afterwards, he collapsed atop her.

Puzzled, aching from an as yet unfulfilled hunger, she tapped his shoulder. "My lord?"

"Mmm hmm?" He mumbled incoherently.

"Are you finished?" She gazed at the ceiling.

"For now." With a chuckle, Trevor raised his head and stared at her. His smug expression and self-satisfied smile faltered. "Did you—"

"No." And how she ached.

"Bloody hell." He collapsed once more. "Sorry, love. I promise to do better if you will give me a few minutes to recover."

"Well, if a few minutes is all you require, I suppose I can be patient." Playfully, she slapped his bare bottom and wiggled her hips. "But whatever am I to do in the meantime?"

"You could tell me what you were about at so late an hour." Trevor propped himself on his elbows and frowned. "Imagine my disappointment when I entered the foyer and discovered the one face I most wanted to see not present."

Caroline almost swallowed her tongue.

"My lord, I attended a play." Searching for a convenient explanation, she stumbled upon a haphazard excuse for her absence. "There was a delay involving the actors, and you know how terrible traffic in the lanes can be after a performance has ended."

"Ah." He nodded once. "So, what did you see?"

"It was an independent production." At least in that she had not lied. "A comedy called *Daisy Pulls It Off*."

"And with whom did you share the entertainment?" he queried and then arched a brow.

Would his questions never cease?

But how could she avoid his interrogation without arousing suspicion?

"Blake." And then a flash of brilliance sparked in her brain, and Caroline knew just how to distract her rogue captain. "But surely we have other more pressing business to complete, which takes precedence over theatre fare?"

"Darling, I am not yet—"

She drew him near and whispered against his lips, "Perhaps this will inspire you."

IN A PRIVATE ROOM at White's, the Brethren of the Coast gathered to celebrate Trevor's maiden mission as a Nautionnier Knight. While the men traded the latest bawdy jokes circulating the more fashionable London clubs, he replayed the pleasant night spent in the arms—and between the thighs—of his wife. Over and over, he revisited certain sweet moments, mentally savoring the succulent fruits of their fiery couplings. But what captured his thoughts was what he had not achieved.

Namely, Trevor had failed to profess his love.

"I read your report, and it was quite thorough." Admiral Douglas sipped his brandy and arched a brow. "However, Dirk's summary included the harrowing tale of a heroic rescue, involving a member of your crew tangled in the rigging, high atop the mainmast, during a raging tempest. Yet, curiously enough, your account neglected to mention said rescue."

"Bloody hell."

In the process of downing the contents of his glass, Blake spewed the amber intoxicant across the table. "You climbed into the rigging during a storm? Are you insane? Do you wish to leave my sister a young widow?"

"Watch it, brother." Damian produced a handkerchief, wiped his face, and then dabbed his lapels. "This is a new coat."

Trevor could have killed his shipmate. He pinned Dirk with his stare and said, "I thought we were not going to mention that particular incident."

"I never made any promises I did not intend to keep." Dirk shrugged. "But I do recall warning you that reports must divulge all that occurs during missions for the Crown."

"Excuse me." Frustration evident in his expression, Lance pounded a fist on the table. "Would one of you care to enlighten the rest of us?"

"I have no wish to relive an event I would describe as unremarkable." Standing, Trevor emptied his glass in one healthy gulp. "I shall leave the telling to Dirk while I seek out my bride."

"Making up for lost time?" inquired Dalton with a toss of a coin and a shameless grin.

"You know it." Trevor glanced at the admiral. "If I may, sir?"

To wit the venerable naval legend replied, "Carry on."

As he strolled through the reading room, Trevor wondered if he could muster the courage to declare himself in the light of day.

"Ho there, Lord Lockwood. I did not know you had returned to London."

The voice was familiar and, unfortunately, so was the face. Trevor accepted the outstretched hand with suspicion. "Lord Sheldon. Have you some interest in my affairs of which I am unaware?"

"None, other than to express my sincerest congratulations on your recent nuptials." Lord Sheldon inclined his head and smiled the sort of smile that left Trevor feeling in dire need of a bath. "I met your lovely wife. She is a charming creature."

The hair rose on the back of his neck.

"Indeed, I agree with your assessment." Against his better judgment, Trevor asked, "Where did you happen upon my countess?"

Seconds ticked past.

Was it his imagination or was the insufferable ass pausing for effect?

"Last night, at Lady Darrow's."

"Nonsense, you are mistaken." No rake worth his salt had not indulged in the infamous, so-called cultural reviews. Trevor wanted to hit the arrogant aristocrat for besmirching Caroline's reputation. "My wife took in a play."

"Of course, your countess did just that." Sheldon had the audacity to smirk. "How fetching she looked in her blue gown and an alluring blush when she joined our group. And if memory serves, it was rather late when Lady Lockwood departed."

It was as though the world had opened up and swallowed him whole. Terror gripped his shoulders, clenched his gut. Laughter echoed in his ears, and a cold emptiness settled in his chest. In that instant, Trevor was no longer a man but a lost little boy—rejected and unloved again. And at his feet, his heart scattered in countless pieces, as autumn leaves after the first freeze.

"Are you unwell, Lockwood?" Lord Sheldon touched his arm. "You are quite pale."

"Your concern is unnecessary." Trevor flinched and retreated. "I beg your pardon, but I must be on my way."

The cool November air offered a welcome relief from the smoke-filled club as he stepped outside. Myriad tortuous thoughts swirled in his head, and he leaned against the wall for support. Denial charged his senses and bolstered his resolve. Why had he taken Lord Sheldon, a rake of the worst caliber, at his word? The troublemaker had to be wrong. And Trevor would not convict his wife without testimony to the contrary.

After collecting his rig, he made for home. Like a madman, he drove his team through the crowded streets. As he pulled in front of the townhouse he shared with Caroline, footmen rushed forth to take the reins. The foyer was quiet as he entered, and Trevor realized his wife would not expect him so early in the day. Roberts appeared and collected his hat, coat, and gloves.

"Is the countess in residence?"

"Yes, my lord." The butler bowed. "Her ladyship is in the study. Shall I inform her of your arrival, your lordship?"

"No." He was already walking toward his domain. "I will announce myself."

As he approached the study, Trevor noted the door was ajar. Voices emanated from within, and he halted when a decidedly masculine chuckle filtered into the hall. Hugging the baseboards, he crept closer—and almost shouted alarm when he spied his reflection in the mirror on the opposite wall.

"We must be careful now that Trevor has returned to London."

At Caroline's warning, a wave of nausea rocked his belly, and he feared he might be ill.

"Does he suspect anything?" the stranger inquired.

"No, and I intend to keep it so," his wife replied.

The remainder of their conversation was lost in a haze of confusion and rage. Stealthily, he slipped into an alcove in hopes of discovering the identity of the interloper.

The door to the study opened, and Caroline entered the hall. "Same time next week?"

None other than Lord Darwith gave chase. "If it is convenient."

"Let us plan on it, barring any interference from my husband." Caroline pressed a hand to her chest. "I am so excited, I fear I shall not sleep a wink until then."

"Then you are pleased with our enterprise?" his rival inquired.

"Oh, yes." The smile she offered her former suitor brought Trevor to the brink of tears. "Now, allow me to show you out."

Once the happy couple disappeared from sight, he calmly walked down the hall and ascended the back stairs to the second floor. Neither a maid nor a footman lingered, and to his infinite thanks, he crept into his private chambers unnoticed.

There, free from prying eyes, Trevor sank to the carpet and wept.

THE CLOCK CHIMED the midnight hour, and Caroline set her book in her lap and stared at the door of the corridor leading to her husband's suite. According to the butler, Trevor had taken to his bed, pleading a sour stomach, early that evening. Although she had attempted to check his condition after dinner, a footman posted in front of his receiving room refused to grant her entry—per the earl's orders. Worried, concerned for his health, she decided to ignore his wishes and inched from her bed. After pulling on a robe, she slipped into the diminutive passage. At the other end, she turned the knob and cursed when the hinges creaked.

The earl's apartment was dark save the light from the fireplace. Caroline peered at the four-poster and was nonplussed to find it empty.

"What do you want?"

She jumped.

"Trevor?" She gazed at nothing. "Is that you?"

"Of course. This is, after all, my home."

Following the sound of his voice, she located him, brandy balloon in hand, fully dressed, and sitting in an overstuffed chair before the hearth. "Are you much improved?"

"Never better." As he set his glass on a side table, his sinister chuckle gave her gooseflesh. "Enlightened even."

"Enlightened?" Caroline tiptoed to a position that afforded a view of his illuminated profile. "I do not understand."

"No?" He stood and stormed toward her. "You do not understand, my innocent wife?"

"Trevor, what is wrong? You are frightening me." Folding her arms, she shivered. "Roberts said you were ill. Shall I summon a doctor?"

"Darling, there is no cure for what ails me." Anger poured as molten lava from his impressive frame. "Except to rid myself of the source of my distress."

"And that would be—"

"You."

Whatever Caroline had expected him to say that was not it. Grasping the back of a chair, she steadied herself. "My lord, it is obvious you are upset—"

"Upset?" He gripped her shoulders and shook once. "I am bloody well furious."

"So I g-gather," she stuttered as he shoved her aside. "What have I done to displease you? What is my crime?"

"Where were you last night?" Trevor raked a hand through his hair and lowered his chin. "Why were you not home when I arrived?"

"I told you, I saw a play." She bit her lip and added, "But I would rather have been here to welcome you than any place else in the world."

"How touching." His demeanor dripped sarcasm. "So you attended the theatre—*and nothing more.*"

The ugly reality of her situation hit Caroline between the eyes. "There is more."

"What? Speak up, love." He cupped an ear and leaned close. "I did not hear you."

On an exhale, she virtually shouted, "I said there is more."

"The truth, at last." Trevor sketched a dramatic bow. "Pray, continue."

"During an intermission, Lady Darrow invited me to participate in what she called a cultural review." Caroline took a tentative step forward. "But I swear, once I discerned the purpose of the gathering, I left."

"And why did you not tell me?" he asked too calmly for her liking.

She crossed and uncrossed her arms. "Because I had hoped to spare you any unnecessary embarrassment in regard to my mistake."

"How thoughtful of you." He narrowed his stare. "Shall I describe how I danced a jig when Lord Sheldon informed me of your *mistake*?"

"No." The mystery was solved, panic rang in her ears, and Caroline shook her head. "You should have learned of it from me. And you have my solemn promise, in the future, I will apprise you of all my activities."

"How reassuring." Trevor retrieved his glass, downed the contents, and poured himself a refill. "But why do I not believe you?"

She recalled his past and his mother's deception. "My lord, you have my word as a lady—"

"Your word as a lady?" Venting a primal roar, he hurled the brandy balloon into the hearth. Flames flared when the intoxicant ignited. "You may have the face of an angel and the garb of a noblewoman, but you are nothing more than a common harlot."

Afraid, confused, Caroline skittered behind a chair and sank her fingers into the cushion. "Trevor, please—"

"What? Have I hurt you?" Like a jungle cat preparing to strike, he circled. "Enjoy the farce you have made of our marriage, for you have no one to blame but yourself."

Though she wanted desperately to assume the sum of her transgressions had been aired, she replayed the hours since his return. What had she missed? What piece of the puzzle that piqued her husband's ire eluded her grasp? "My lord, I sincerely apologize for venturing into Lady Darrow's residence. But I cannot imagine that my brief appearance warrants such harsh treatment."

"You think not?" He sneered.

"No." She held her ground.

"And what of Lord Darwith?" With his back to her, Trevor rested his hands on the mantel. "Did you tell him of your foray, or was he in attendance, as well?"

The world shifted beneath her feet, and Caroline swayed. She tried to respond, to voice a defense, but could summon no rebuttal.

Slowly, her angry spouse rotated and pinned her with an icy glare. "Guilt is etched all over your pretty face."

"I can explain," she whispered. "Give me a chance to explain."

"Make it good." With hands on hips, he arched a brow. "Your last effort was quite tedious."

"Despite our past, Lord Darwith and I have forged a friendship."   Her mind raced to compose a suitable rejoinder.

"And you enjoy his company?"   He speared his fingers through his hair, which spiked.

"I do."   She dipped her chin.   "But there is nothing illicit in reference to our relationship."

"*Your relationship!*"   Trevor turned and, with a single sweep of his arm, sent the mantel clock, a framed portrait, and two candlesticks flying.   "I will listen to no more of your lies."

"But I am telling the truth."   Despite attempts to the contrary, Caroline sobbed uncontrollably.   "Please, you must believe me.   Nothing untoward occurred."

"Nothing untoward occurred?"   He laughed, evoking a comparison to Cavalier's sinister cackle, and she fought nausea.   "You have made me a cuckold."

"No."   She reached for him, but he evaded her grasp.   " I am innocent."

"I can take no more."   Trevor veered for the door, and she followed in his wake.

"Wait."   She clutched his elbow, but he wrenched free.   "Where are you going?"

"I intend to seek comfort from this house of misery in a *cultural review*."   Oh, how he mocked her.

"Do you...am I to understand...you would break our wedding vows?"   A weight settled on her chest, and she could not breathe.   "You would take another to your bed?"

"I will do as I damn well choose."   He set the oak panels wide but halted when she tugged hard on his coat sleeve.

"Please, I swear—"

"You swear?"   He snorted.   "You are in no position to make promises."

"Do not do this, I beg you," she said as he loosened her hold with a flick of his wrist. "I shall never forgive you."

"Should I convey your regards to Lady Darrow?" he called over his shoulder while he strolled down the hall.

At his caustic remark, she emitted a plaintive cry and ran after him. "Trevor, if you involve yourself with another woman, your ship will never again dock in my harbor."

"As you wish." He descended the grand staircase without a backward glance.

"I mean it." Caroline clung to the balustrade. "You may go to the devil."

At the bottom of the stairs, Trevor turned and smiled. "Madame wife, I am already there."

CHAPTER NINETEEN

"*Y*ou know, there are eleven rooms in this residence, not counting my own, and each has a remarkably comfortable contraption called a bed." Everett chuckled. "Did you find it necessary to compound your misery by sleeping on the sofa?"

Trevor peered beyond the edge of his coat, which he had used as a blanket to buffer the chill of his friend's study. "How would you like to live out the remainder of your days without benefit of teeth?"

"No improvement on your mood, I see." After tying back the drapes, Markham rocked on his heels and clucked his tongue. "Do tell, what offense landed you on my doorstep last night?"

Sitting upright, Trevor shielded his eyes from the sunlight and yawned. "What makes you think I did something wrong?"

"Why else would you be here but for trouble in connubial paradise?" Everett plopped into a high-back chair, rested his elbows on his thighs, and grinned. "Come now, confession is good for the soul, or so some say, and I could use a little levity this morning. Besides, your wife is the sort of woman who brings out the worst in a man—his conscience. So, what have you done?"

"Not that it is any of your business, but Caroline is no saint." He pulled on his top boots. "I am the injured party."

"And I am a virgin queen." With an expression of unveiled skepticism, Everett rolled his eyes. "Give over."

"Blister it, Markham, cease your prattle." Standing, Trevor walked to the windows and gazed at the sidewalks below. "I am without blame and would much prefer to suffer in silence."

"Easy there, mate. But you are in a state." His friend's chuckle bubbled over into gales of laughter. "Did you hear that? I am a poet, and I did not know it."

"A regular Shakespeare." Trevor winced as his impromptu host collapsed in a fit of hilarity. "I should have stayed aboard the *Hera*."

"Why did you not?" Everett cocked his head. "Or is my humble abode the preferred substitute for the proverbial dog house?"

For a split second, Trevor considered admitting he had first sought refuge on his ship but thought better of it. Just how ridiculous would he appear if he conceded the fact that his sea accommodations served as a hellish reminder of his wife? In the solitude of his cabin, memories of Caroline's lusty cries of completion reverberated on the walls and filled his ears. The silken sheets on his bunk evoked a sensation similar to the brush of her velvety skin against his, and the scent of her perfume lingered on the pillows as a sultry summons his body was only too eager to answer. What on earth had possessed him to spend his wedding night dockside?

"Trevor?" Everett placed a hand on his shoulder, all humor aside. "What has happened, old friend?"

Betrayal left a bitter taste in his mouth, and he swallowed hard and peered at his lone ally. "While I was at sea, my wife ventured into the realm of the *demimonde*."

Markham averted his stare.

"Everett?" They had been as brothers for years, and Trevor could read his chum like a book. "You know something."

It was a statement, not a question.

"No, I know nothing." Everett strolled to his desk.

Trevor followed in his wake. "Liar."

"Now, see here." With both palms atop the blotter, his friend leaned forward. "What has or has not occurred in your marriage is none of my business."

"It is if you possess information pertinent to my situation." Trevor folded his arms and planted his feet. "Tell me what you know. Did you see them together?"

"If you are referring to what I think you are referring, then—yes." Everett grimaced.

Without a word, Trevor dragged a chair to the center of the Aubusson rug and settled himself. "I am listening."

Likewise, Everett sat behind the desk and scowled. "I am not a bloody scandalmonger."

"Would you rather be mum in your grave?" Trevor was all out of patience.

"What?" His countenance sobered, Markham appeared genuinely hurt. "Are you truly threatening me?"

"No." Trevor huffed out a breath and shook his head. "You are the only friend I have."

"Come now. You are making too much of this." Everett steepled his fingers and furrowed his brow. "Caroline was at Lady Darrow's for, at most, a half-hour."

"You were at Lady Darrow's?" He leapt to his feet. "What, in God's name, were you doing there?"

Markham narrowed his stare and compressed his lips. "The same thing you have done on many previous occasions."

Trevor opened and then closed his mouth and returned to his seat. "Sorry, old chap. Forgot myself."

"I should say so." Everett tugged at the folds of his cravat and cleared his throat. "If I may continue—"

"Please do—"

"*Uninterrupted.*" The usually composed nobleman produced a handkerchief and dabbed his temples. "Pray, indulge me. Upon my arrival at Lady Darrow's, your countess posited a misinformed, though altogether more virtuous, motivation for attending our inauspicious gathering."

Trevor rubbed his chin. "I do not follow."

"Do you not?" Everett smiled. "Your naïve bride had not the faintest notion in regard to the purposive nature of our *cultural reviews.*"

A glimmer of hope shimmered on the horizon. "How can you be certain of her confusion?"

"Because the look on her face when I revealed the truth was somewhat similar to the expression you are sporting right now." Everett fidgeted.

A meager portion of the weight on his chest lifted, and Trevor sighed. "Go on."

"In any case, she set Lord Sheldon on his heels, and I rather fancy the arrogant ass is still smarting from the sting of her rejection." Everett grinned.

"You heard this?" Was it possible? Had Trevor misjudged his wife?

"With my own ears." Markham surrendered to a series of guffaws. "Bloody hell, but you would have been proud."

"Perhaps." Had he leapt to unsupported conclusions? "What happened next?"

Everett met his stare. "She bade me summon her carriage, which I did."

"And?" Trevor perched on the verge of his seat.

"After an apology to Lady Darrow, your countess departed, reputation intact, posthaste."

Trevor pressed a fist to his mouth and traced the pattern on the carpet with his gaze. So Caroline had not defiled their vows on that particular night. Concerning Lady Darrow's party, his wife had not lied.

But what about Lord Darwith?

"All right, with that settled, why so gloomy?"

Trevor glanced at his inquisitive friend. "I beg your pardon?"

"You appear as if you have just lost your best hound." Everett reclined in his chair and propped his boots on the edge of the desk. "What have I omitted?"

"Nothing."

"Out with it, Lockwood."

What could he say?

How much should he share?

"My wife is having an affair." The mere act of voicing his concern provided a small measure of relief. When Everett flapped his arms in the air, then toppled to the floor, Trevor enjoyed a smidgen of humor.

"Are you daft?" Markham scrambled to his feet and righted his coat. "The woman is in love with you, although such reasoning defies the limits of perspicacity, but there it is."

"Wonderful." Trevor slapped his thighs, stood, and

paced before the fireplace. "I have been disgraced, cuckolded, and you make jokes."

"Wait a minute, old boy." Everett stepped in his path. "Are you serious?"

"Unfortunately, I am." Despite the humiliation and anger, Trevor detailed the events of the previous day, focusing on the discovery of his wife with Lord Darwith.

"So neither of them was aware of your presence." Everett scratched his head and frowned. "And yet their conversation, if it occurred as you described, remained decidedly innocuous."

"I find nothing innocuous about it."

"That is because you are emotionally invested, my friend."

Trevor vented a snort of disgust. "I do not—"

"Please, no denials." Everett waved his hand. "Allow me to make a suggestion."

"I await your advice with baited breath."

"Well, if you are going to get snippy—"

"Christ, you are a chatty chit." Trevor groaned and speared his fingers through his hair. "Just tell me what you have in mind."

"Meet with Darwith, and let him plead his cause." Markham shrugged and with a devilish smirk said, "Then you may kill the blackguard with a clear conscience."

"I am so happy to provide fodder for your amusement." Yet Trevor found nothing funny in his circumstances.

"If I find sport in your predicament, it is because I do not believe the situation is as grave as you paint it." Everett chucked Trevor's shoulder.

"I hope you are right." Because Trevor feared he could not survive her betrayal.

The long-case clock in the hall signaled the noon hour.

"The time for breakfast has passed." Everett strolled toward the door. "Why do you not have a bath while I order lunch?"

"I shall be along in a moment." Trevor retrieved a pen and a sheet of stationary from the desk. "Would you send in your man?"

"As you wish." Everett nodded once and exited the study.

After composing a brief missive, Trevor folded the paper and slipped it into an envelope. On the front, he inscribed an address.

"May I be of service, your lordship?" the stodgy butler inquired.

With the correspondence in his grasp, Trevor crossed the room. "Have this delivered directly into Lord Darwith's hands."

TREVOR'S DATE with destiny could not have come soon enough.

The following morning, in another stately residence, in another gentleman's study, he perused the selections on a large bookcase. Behind him, the door opened.

"Ah, Lord Lockwood." His nemesis entered with the innocence of a cherub. "Welcome to my home."

"Thank you for seeing me on such short notice, Lord Darwith." Trevor swallowed the urge to punch the man in the nose.

"Do not mention it. Please, have a seat." Darwith indicated a small sofa. "May I offer you a refreshment?"

"You are too kind, sir." Exchanging pleasantries with his mortal enemy pricked his pride, and Trevor gritted his teeth. "But as I have already impinged on your hospitality, perhaps we should proceed with our business."

"Indeed." With childlike enthusiasm, the rival rubbed his hands together. "You know, your wife has provided the penultimate victory of my greatest passion in life."

Incensed by the shameless disclosure, Trevor clenched his jaw. "She has?"

"Oh, yes." The blonde-haired, blue-eyed lord propped an elbow on an armrest and dipped his chin. "Lady Lockwood possesses a rare talent for spreading happiness wherever she goes."

Trevor dug his fingers into the sofa cushion. "And you have benefited from that talent?"

"You have me there, as I am her servant." Darwith cast a half-smile. "It appears my bad luck was your good fortune."

"How so?" Doubt gnawed at his conscience.

"Had I devoted more attention to the selection of a mate, I should have chosen better." The fair-skinned nobleman averted his gaze. "I should have married Caroline."

Enduring the spontaneous confession proved more difficult than Trevor had anticipated. The curse of infidelity burned as salt in an open wound, and a riptide of rejection drowned his senses.

"Well then, shall we get to the heart of the matter?" Darwith stood. "I must say I am not surprised Lady Lockwood found our secret hard to maintain."

The moment of truth arrived, and fear paralyzed Trevor as he braced for the final revelation. "Secrets have a way of outing themselves." And he wondered how many members of the *ton* were aware of his disgrace.

"Though I am thrilled with the results of our little enterprise, I must admit I am disappointed that the journey has ended." From an armoire, Lord Darwith produced a large wooden box. "At last, I shall be relieved of this precious burden, and yet it does not seem fair for one man to claim two priceless treasures."

Through a haze of anger and confusion, Trevor rose. "I beg your pardon?"

"Your countess divulged part of the history, and at the risk of sounding insensitive, the tale was fascinating." Darwith moved aside a stack of ledgers, an inkwell and pen, and positioned the elongated crate atop the desk. "When we embarked on our endeavor, Lady Lockwood demanded discretion, as I suspect she intended to surprise you."

Befuddled, Trevor drew nigh. "She did?"

"Of course." His adversary opened the lid. "But, true to her sex, she is incapable of keeping a confidence. Perhaps her inability stems from an innate purity of the heart."

The sentimental drivel struck him as cold water in the face. With renewed resolve, he trudged forth. His tormentor parted the brown paper, and Trevor peered inside the box.

For the second time in a mere week, the world tilted beneath his feet.

"It is a remarkable weapon." Lord Darwith trailed a finger along the flat of the blade. "Stunning workmanship."

The bronze hilt and incised motifs depicting the original inhabitants of the Garden of Eden mirrored those of the ancient sword that hung on the wall in his cabin aboard the *Hera*. At the base of the hilt, a decidedly female image distinguished one from the other.

"Eve." Trevor shuddered. "You found Eve."

"Nay, my lord. Your wife found Eve." The man he no longer considered an enemy lifted the long lost heirloom from a bed of hay. "She suggested that your mother may have sold the artifact in order to purchase passage to

France. I believe your man searched the Continent. Fate smiled upon us, because my contact located the item in the Highlands. And her written plea compelled the laird to surrender the old armament."

"It was on the isle?" Trevor teetered on the brink of overwhelming shame.

"Amazing, is it not? You should have seen your wife's reaction when I delivered the news of our success." Darwith chuckled. "She practically danced a jig."

But Trevor had seen Caroline's reaction, had witnessed her excitement from the shadows and had woven unsustainable conclusions from whole cloth. She had conspired only to mend his family legacy; she had restored the sword to its rightful owner. And he had turned it against her, had used her gift to cut her where she was most vulnerable.

"Lord Darwith, I am in your debt." And he owed Caroline an apology.

"Nonsense." The aristocrat passed him the heavy weapon. "Completion of this task discharges my debt to your charming bride."

"How were you obligated to my wife?" Trevor asked as he studied the luster of the blade.

"She has not told you of our history?" Darwith's mouth fell agape.

"If you are referring to the disingenuous courtship, I know the whole of it." He set the heirloom in the nest of hay and secured the lid.

"In exchange for forgiveness, I consented to act as solicitor on her behalf, but Caroline had already absolved me of my sin." Darwith stared Trevor in the eye. "It seems your countess has found consolation and sweet vindication in the match she has made."

"Indeed." Trevor picked up the box. "I know just how she feels."

"Take care, Lord Lockwood." The viscount extended a hand, which he took in friendship. "Perhaps some day soon you will show me the mate?"

"Count on it." He started toward the door. "Now, if you will excuse me, I have an important appointment."

"Give my regards to Caroline."

"You may depend upon it," he called over his shoulder.

And in that he was not lying, because Trevor was going home.

As he entered the foyer of the townhouse he shared with Caroline, Trevor paused in expectation of the pitter-patter that usually heralded the arrival of his wife. Of course, in light of the manner of his departure, and the controversial statements he had made, she might welcome him with a potted plant over the head, and it was nothing less than he deserved. Seconds ticked past in silence, and it occurred to him that she might have left him.

Swallowing his pride and fear, he turned to Roberts. "Where is her ladyship?"

"At the park, my lord." The butler bowed and then accepted the large box. "Shall I convey this to your study, my lord?"

"Please, do so." He caught a glimpse of his haggard appearance in the wall mirror and decided a bath and fresh attire might be just the thing to prepare him for a round of compensatory groveling.

Yes, he had jumped to conclusions.

Yes, he was an ignorant ass.

And, yes, he would get her back.

He took the stairs, double-time, veered left at the landing, and all but ran down the hall. Ensconced in his chambers, he spied a swath of silk at the foot of his bed. Even before he held the sumptuous garment in his grasp, Trevor knew to whom it belonged. Since their wedding, his countess had appropriated the four-poster in the earl's suite.

"What is to become of us?" he asked as he inhaled the subtle scent of her perfume. "Is the damage I have done to our marriage irreparable, when I have, at last, given my heart?"

He had been afraid, yet now he was fearless.

He had been distrustful, yet now he trusted.

He had been unloved, yet now he was loved.

So how could Trevor make Caroline understand his position when he could make no sense of it himself?

After a soak in the bath that soothed the ache in his lower back from two nights spent on Markham's sofa, he donned what he deemed gentlemen's garb and tied his cravat in a precise mathematical. With one final check of his hair, he retraced his earlier steps.

The sidewalks were alive with activity, and the promenade was in full swing. Amid the throng in the park, he spied his brother-in-law sitting atop an imposing white stallion. A survey of the immediate surroundings revealed the rest of the odd extended family in attendance, and he wondered at the reception he would receive.

Had Caroline apprised her friends of their brief separation?

As if on cue, Blake looked up and waved a greeting, which the group mimicked. At that instant, the lady in question faced him, and the force of her stare pinned him on the spot. In a smile and a nod, he offered an olive branch and awaited her response.

Poised and unhurried, she strolled to the curb on the opposite side. Inclining her head, the corners of her mouth lifted, and she stepped into the road. "Good afternoon, my lord."

Traffic kept Trevor at bay, but he moved onto the street edge and called out, "The same to you, love."

Thunderous hoof beats shook the ground, and he glanced right. At least seventeen hands, the black stallion had a commanding presence, but it was the rider who captured Trevor's attention. Cloaked in black, with a mask shielding his identity, the curious stranger spurred his mount despite the tangle of equipages on Park Lane, and Trevor questioned the man's sanity.

Until the horse drew nigh and, in one swift swoop, the mysterious rider stole Caroline from the thoroughfare.

"You there, *stand fast!*" Trevor charged into the road and was almost trounced by another set of hooves. "That is my wife!"

"Hurry, Lockwood." Blake reined in. "Climb aboard."

The villain continued down Park Lane, pursued by Blake, Trevor, and the other Brethren on horseback. At Curzon Street, the stallion galloped in the direction of Berkley Square, increasing the lead.

"Faster, Rylan." Trevor clutched the nobleman's lapels. "They are getting away."

"I could go faster without your added weight," the duke replied. "Would you care to shove off?"

"Trevor, *help me!*" Ahead, Caroline struggled with the unknown abductor. But her cries were muffled when the blackguard blanketed her in the merino pelisse she wore.

"Bloody hell." Trevor heeled the flanks of his brother-in-law's steed. "The bastard will suffocate her."

Through a wild series of turns, they raced the streets of Mayfair, sending innocent passersby fleeing for their lives. The party sped around Grosvenor Square, up Duke Street, along Oxford Street, retraced Park Lane, continued down the middle of Green Park, and onto St. James's. And somewhere during the chase, a cavalryman and three Bow Street Runners joined the collective of would-be rescuers.

A carriage pulled in front of the villain on the Strand, and Blake and Trevor gained ground. "Stop that man!" they shouted in unison.

But the scoundrel recovered and steered his mount into the pedestrian traffic on the sidewalk. Ladies shrieked as they scrambled for safety, and gentlemen hurled a slew of curses. Despite the people in his path, the kidnapper had not slowed his pace as he navigated Fleet Street and veered south on Blackfriars Road.

In the distance, Blackfriars Bridge loomed as the specter of doom. "Blake, if he crosses the Thames—"

"I know."

Until that moment, Trevor had not let himself ponder the identity of the individual who had snatched his wife from Hyde Park. But as the waters of the river came into view, he had to wonder if his worst enemy had made good on his threat.

At the bridge, Caroline freed herself from the pelisse and screamed.

"We are here," he cried in an attempt to reassure her that she was not alone. Her fists flew as she fought her attacker, and he prayed she would survive the ordeal. "Careful, darling," he said under his breath.

Once the masked rider reached the other shore, he gave the horse his head. In similar fashion, Blake let go the reins, and familiar structures passed in a blur. Trevor was certain of the abductor's destination before he entered the docks at Deptford.

The mighty stallion charged the boards, and officers of the Marine Police signaled the alarm. The rogue charted a course toward a schooner, and as the horse dashed up the gangplank, a slew of filthy sailors navigated the ratlines.

"She is going to cast off."

"Not without us," Blake replied.

There was something peculiar about the ship, and Trevor took a second look at the canvas and rails. And then it hit him. Despite of the fresh paint and new name, she was none other than *The Black Morass*.

And he would wager his first-born that Caroline's abductor was the captain. The same man who had vowed to kill every Elliott in existence. The brother of the lad Trevor's wife had slain.

A thief.

A rapist.

A murderer.

The most ruthless pirate to sail the seas.

Jean Marc Cavalier.

CHAPTER TWENTY

*T*he sun sat below the yardarm on the western horizon, and the London fog crawled into the docks at Deptford. At the stern rail, guarded by two filthy pirates, Caroline shrieked in horror as Trevor lunged at Cavalier. A telltale rumble of cannon fire heralded the arrival of the Marine Police, and the blast rippled through the air. A spray of water blanketed the starboard bow, and the ship trembled beneath her feet. A naval vessel crept within striking distance, and she spied a platoon of lobsters preparing to board *The Black Morass*.

On the main deck, Blake, Lance, and Dirk commandeered weapons from three unfortunate villains. Her brother charged the companion ladder, and her friends provided flanking support. Just then, her husband and Cavalier locked blades. The pirate captain produced a small dagger and thrust the pointed end into Trevor's forearm.

"Blake, help Trevor," Caroline screamed.

"I am fine," her husband responded angrily, as he danced a deadly waltz with his enemy. "Get my wife out of here."

At that moment, Cavalier shot a glance at her and shouted, "*Kill the wench!* A king's treasure to the man that slits her gullet."

The action came to a grinding halt.

An unnatural quiet settled over the ship as all eyes leveled on Caroline. The focus of unwanted attention, she retreated until the backs of her knees connected with the stern rail. Her breath came in a rush of pants, and her heart pounded in her ears. "Oh, dear."

Another barrage sounded, and everyone moved at once. But that time, the shot tore through the rigging, showering the combatants in canvas, rope, and splintered wood. The mizenmast creaked, then toppled toward her. The towering structure knocked one of her pirate keepers into the Thames, and the other dropped his sword and jumped for safety. Quick as a flash, she retrieved the discarded weapon and attempted to launch a defense against a rapidly nearing assailant.

"Come now, lovey." A toothless blackguard smiled and inched closer. "You might hurt yourself."

"Mind your distance." With a flick of her wrist, she caught the scoundrel across the cheek when he lunged for her. "Heed my warning."

"Bitch." The villain sneered as he pressed a hand to his skin. He licked the blood from his fingers and said, "You are going to pay for that."

Her adversary let fly a vicious offensive and, although she tried to protect herself, Caroline's attire hindered her efforts. To put it simply, her dress was made for walking, not fighting. Step by step, she lost precious ground and again found herself pressed to the rail. With nowhere to go, she clutched the stern lantern and climbed atop the rail.

"Blake, hurry." She waved the weapon to repel another attack. "Else I shall founder."

"Hold on." Her brother dispatched two pirates and gained the quarterdeck. "I am almost there."

Dirk and Lance navigated the companion ladder and, with Blake, finished off three additional enemy combatants. Her adversary turned, formed a line with his remaining allies, and issued a bold challenge to the trio of highly skilled swordsmen. Blake shared a silent exchange with his brothers in arms, assuming a familiar stance, and she almost felt sorry for her captors. As the battle ensued, she exhaled her relief and searched for a way down from her precarious perch. As she bent to reach for the rail, a cannon shot rippled overhead.

And scored a direct hit.

The Black Morass shuddered violently. Caroline teetered, dropped her weapon, and tried to maintain her balance, but her slippered feet tangled in her skirts. In a hairsbreadth of a second, she wobbled backwards. A single word passed her lips when she realized what was happening.

"Trevor."

WITH A BURST OF ENERGY, Trevor charged his blade, lunged, and caught Cavalier in the chest.

The pirate glanced at himself, at the red stain spreading on his white shirt, and then looked Trevor in the eyes. "Victory is yours, *mon ami*. Until we meet again." The villain sketched a mock salute and leapt into the river.

Trevor turned and searched for his wife. When he found her, his gut seized. For the briefest moment, they locked gazes. Terror functioned as a cruel link, and her fear ensnared his senses. With both arms extended, Caroline beckoned before disappearing into the fog.

"*No!*"

Denial mixed with rage, igniting every nerve, rousing every muscle. Like a madman, Trevor cut the throat of a pirate that foolishly got in his way, and then sliced open the gut of another. Moving, swift and sure, he severed the royal backstay and, with a steely grip on the rope and a running jump, propelled himself atop the quarterdeck. After discarding his sword, he doffed his coat and dove overboard.

The icy depths of the Thames enveloped his body and left him gasping for air. Strong undercurrents tugged at his feet, and he fought to tread water. "Caroline."

The yellow glow of lanterns played eerily in the fog, but Trevor neither heard nor saw any sign of his wife. Certain the layers of velvet and lace she wore would act as an anchor, he had to work fast. She could not—would not—outlast the deadly summons.

"Ahoy, Lockwood, are you there?" Blake called through the darkness from the opposite direction. "The Marine Police have launched several skiffs."

"I am here," he responded. "Fan out and search for Caroline."

Trevor continued his efforts in silence, mindful that any noise might muffle sounds of his bride. Finally, he relaxed and let the river take him, hoping the natural motion would reunite them. It took all his strength to keep his head above the surface.

A definite slosh caught his ear.

With renewed vigor, Trevor swam toward the slight noise in the aqueous mire. "Caroline, is that you?"

There was no response, so he trod water once again. Despair penetrated his heart as the Thames had penetrated his clothes. Gloom thick as the fog chilled his mind and soul.

And then something brushed his ankle.

He submerged into the frigid river and blindly reached with his hands. A strange sensation tickled his fingers. He kicked hard and grasped what he realized was Caroline's hair. In his excitement, Trevor forgot his locale, opened his mouth to shout the alarm, and almost drowned them both. When he regained the surface, he choked and sputtered before summoning assistance.

"I have her." He struggled with the weight of his wife's limp body, then slipped an arm under hers and held her to his side. "Someone—anyone—help us."

"Stand fast, Lockwood," Dirk replied immediately. "Give me another shout so that I may fix your location."

"We are here." After what seemed hours, but was only a few seconds, Trevor noted the distinct splash of oars, and a skiff came into view. "Thank God."

With utmost care, he gave an unresponsive Caroline into Dirk and Lance's custody. As the latter began attempts to resuscitate her, Trevor fell into the tiny boat. Just as fast, he bent over the side and heaved the foul river water he had ingested. He was wiping his face when the first feminine cough broke the tense quiet. Soon, Caroline mirrored his stance as she returned that which would have killed her to the Thames.

"Relax, darling." He rubbed her shoulders and whispered words of reassurance while Dirk took up the oars. "Do not fight it."

"Trevor." Shivering, her teeth chattering, his bride turned and buried her face in his chest. "I thought I would never see you again."

"Lockwood saved you," Lance said. "He went in without hesitation."

"Bloody ridiculous fool." Caroline wrapped her arms around his waist and hugged him tight. "I want to go home."

Home.

The word had held no meaning prior to his marriage. Now, home meant everything to Trevor. Home was wherever he was with his wife. However, he was no fool. Despite his lady's apparent happiness to see him, much unfinished business remained as a very real chasm between them. And he was willing to do whatever necessary to get her back.

"Anything for you, love." Trevor pressed his lips to her damp hair. "Anything for you."

WITH CAROLINE IN HIS ARMS, Trevor took the stairs two at a time. At the landing, he turned left and steered for their apartments. In the hall, he paused and stared at the door to her chambers. Frowning, he headed for his suite. As Trevor neared, a footman set the oak panel wide. He stomped through his receiving room and strode straight to his bedchamber.

"I can walk." She sneezed. "You should see me, I have been doing it for years."

"I beg your pardon?" He glanced at his bride, noted her smile, and set her feet on the rug before his four-poster. "You had a rough day. I thought to spare you the strain."

"Trevor, you must not worry." She patted his cheek. "I am fine."

"You could have drowned." He cupped her chin.

"But I did not." Caroline tugged on her wet gown. "Will

you help me undress? I want a hot bath and a fresh night rail."

"Here, allow me." He grabbed fistfuls of the tattered garment, ripped it apart from the bodice, and tried not to ogle her lovely breasts. A commotion in the hall had him peering over his shoulder. "What in bloody hell—"

Blake charged into the room with Dirk, Lance, and Damian in tow. "Lockwood, I want to see my...sister."

His brother-in-law looked at Trevor, then Caroline.

"You animal." Blake clenched and unclenched his hands. "She just survived a kidnapping and near-drowning. Can you not give her a measure of uninterrupted rest?"

"Rylan, I have had enough of your meddling in my marriage." Before Trevor could utter another word, the interfering duke pounced.

Blake caught him by the throat. "Was it worth it, Lockwood?"

He gripped Blake's neck, in turn, ruining the elegantly folded cravat. "Was what worth it?"

"What happened tonight was your fault." Blake shoved him back two steps. "You put her at risk."

"This is none of your affair, Rylan." Trevor regained his ground.

"The hell it is not." The arrogant lord shook him hard. "Caroline is my sister."

"And she is my wife." Trevor eased the lady in question out of harm's way and then lunged at her brother. "You saw to that."

"Blackguard." Blake's fist connected with Trevor's jaw and a wicked brawl ensued.

∾

As her husband and her only sibling tumbled on the carpet, Caroline skittered into the dressing room and wiggled out of her ruined gown. A loud crash reverberated on the walls, and she almost jumped out of her skin. Quickly, she draped Trevor's favorite black satin robe over her shoulders and cinched the belt at her waist. She hurried into the bedchamber before one of the two most important men in her life killed the other. And if anyone was going to send Trevor to the hereafter, she claimed first rights.

"Do your best," Trevor bit off between punches. "As long as I have Caroline, you cannot hurt me."

His impromptu declaration, although lacking charm and romance, was nonetheless compelling.

Seeking assistance in parting the imbeciles, she motioned for her friends to intercede. To her dismay, Dirk, Lance, and Damian stood placing wages on the eventual winner. When the battling boors knocked over a table bearing a brandy decanter and matching glasses, a lone unbroken balloon rolled to her feet. Caroline picked up the delicate crystal and hurled it at the hearth. It shattered on impact and the immense crack stopped the fight.

"*Enough.*" For the second time that night, she confronted an impressive compliment of the male sex. Mindful of shards, she faced her brother and pointed toward the door. "Get out."

Blake's eyes grew wide. "I beg your pardon?"

"You heard me." She tapped her foot.

"But—I am defending you." Blake wiped blood from his lip.

"And being pigheaded and ungrateful in the process." She folded her arms. "Out. All of you."

"Caroline?" Her ill-tempered elder sibling set hands on hips. "Are you choosing him over me?"

She bared her teeth. "Blake Thornton Deverell Elliott, so help me—"

"Are you sure, sister?" He stumbled.

"Out!" Now she stomped the floor.

"All right." Astonishment evident in his gaze, he raised both palms in implied surrender. "I am leaving."

"Perhaps we should bow to the lady's wishes. Come, brothers." Whistling in monotone, Damian inclined his head. "Bloody hell, she sounded just like your mother."

"Oh, shut up." With a lethal scowl, Blake ushered Dirk and Lance into the hall.

"She even did that thing with her chin. It was scary," Lance said just before he closed the door.

Peaceful solitude fell on the earl's suite.

Caroline had much to say to her husband. She had so many questions. Until she had the answers she needed, their future, and that of their marriage, was hostage to uncertainty. "Trevor?"

"Aye?" He rubbed the back of his neck.

"Did you mean what you said?" His answer would dictate her next move.

"What?" He wrinkled his nose, and she was positive he knew exactly what she meant.

"That as long as you have me, you cannot be hurt?" Caroline twined her thumbs and tamped her agitation. "Tell me truly."

"Yes," he stated with a grimace.

She would have danced a jig if there were not so much more to be discussed. But now she had hope as a shield. "Then where have you slept the past few nights?" She held her breath and promised herself she would react with the dignity befitting a countess.

He swallowed hard. "At Lord Markham's."

"Oh?" Caroline sighed in relief. "Did you not take a mistress?"

"No." He cast a mighty scowl.

All right. The man could live—with his most prized protuberance intact. "Why not?"

"Because you are the only woman I have any interest in touching." He shuffled his feet and gazed at the floor. "Or having touch me."

At that moment, her heart sang. Yet there was no time to celebrate, because she had one more query to pose. "If that is the case, then why did you leave me?"

He compressed his lips and furrowed his brow. "I thought you were having an affair with Lord Darwith."

The force of his statement hit Caroline as the cold waters of the Thames. Dumbfounded, she stared at her husband. "Have you so little faith in me?"

Trevor looked her straight in the eyes. "It is not a question of faith."

"Pray, explain yourself." How could he be so obtuse?

"You are not the problem." He raked his fingers through his hair. "I am. And I know you were not involved with Darwith. I am ashamed I doubted you. Thank you for returning the sword."

The room teetered. "How did you—"

"I met with him and discovered my error." Trevor wrung his fingers.

"I see." She gulped. "What else?"

"Your family." He lowered his chin. "Your friends."

"What about them?" She fumbled with the belt at her waist.

"I do not belong." His frowned deepened. "I am an outsider."

"Nonsense, they adore you." At his expression of skepticism, she shrugged. "Well, these things take some getting used to."

"No longer will I tolerate their interference in our marriage." Trevor walked to her. "It is humiliating and insulting."

"Perhaps you should depart London." A multitude of thoughts raced through her brain. "If you are beyond their influence, they cannot interject their opinions."

"You wish to be rid of me?" he inquired, as would a lost little boy.

Silly man. Had he really believed she would send him away? She would have laughed had he not appeared so sad. Obviously, they still had issues to resolve. As Caroline made to clarify her statement, a knock at the door brought her up short.

"Come," her husband barked.

"I beg your pardon, my lord." The butler bowed. "Doctor Handley has arrived."

"Excellent." She nodded. "Show him to my sitting room."

"Yes, my lady."

"Also, send for my maid and ring for a bath." She wiped a stray lock of hair from Trevor's forehead.

"At once, your ladyship."

"And, Roberts?"

"Yes, my lady."

"Have Annie pack my trunk. His lordship and I shall journey to—" She glanced at Trevor. "Where did you say we were going?"

With manifest surprise, her spouse uttered, "Sussex."

"We depart for Sussex before dawn."

"ARE WE THERE YET?" Caroline rubbed her eyes and shifted in the cushions as the coach halted.

Trevor gazed out the window and wondered what had possessed him to bring his wife to his old hideout. "Aye."

A footman opened the door, and Trevor stepped down. "I have owned this cottage for years, though it has been some time since I last stayed here."

Built of stone with a thatched roof, the structure sported a front door covered in peeling paint. Overgrown grass and weeds shrouded a cobblestone walkway, and the enclosing fence was in a state of disrepair. When he unlatched the gate, the panel fell from its hinges.

"Perhaps this is not a good idea." He propped the gate against the fence.

"Nonsense." At his side, his wife tugged at the strings of her bonnet and surveyed the tiny structure. "Brethren women persevere."

With high steps, Trevor tromped through the tall grass, pulled a key from his pocket, and unlocked the door. Inside, the place was in shambles.

Because he had never brought servants to the cottage, nothing had been protected with slipcovers. Thus a white film coated every piece of furniture. A sudden noise sent Caroline into his arms, and he spied several birds exiting the dwelling through a gaping hole in the roof. No doubt they were the source of the foul odor that welcomed them at the threshold.

"This is a disaster." Trevor cupped her chin. "Perhaps we can take a room at the coach inn in the village?"

She seemed to consider his offer, and then asked, "Why did you bring me here?"

"I want to be alone with you." He heaved a sigh and trailed a finger along the curve of her cheek. "Your family could easily travel to Althrup, but they do not know about this place."

Her answering smile soothed his injured pride. "Well, if we enlist the aid of the footmen and the driver, the roof could be repaired before nightfall. And I can clean the cottage, as it is not very big."

"You cannot be serious." He choked on the ripe stench.

But his bride was already recruiting the servants.

After unloading the coach, they made a quick trip into the nearby town. While Trevor purchased supplies needed to fix the hole, his wife bought a slew of comfort items from a local merchant. Upon returning to their seaside abode, they divided the work. He picked up a hammer, and she grabbed a mop and bucket.

His gentler half whistled while she cleaned, and he was eternally grateful to whatever benevolent fate bestowed on him such a remarkable woman. The damage to the roof was not as bad as he had thought, and with assistance from two footmen, he completed his task in a couple of hours. Finally, after issuing orders to return in a sennight, he dispatched the servants.

Later that evening, when he entered the cottage, a tempting aroma filled the great room. Trevor stood at the threshold and noted the changes. A thick rug lent warmth to the now clean wood floor, a makeshift drapery framed the large window overlooking the beach, and the furniture no longer appeared ghostly. Everything had been moved to a more functional arrangement, and fluffy pillows perched at both ends of the sofa. A small table had been righted and bore several lit candles. In the hearth, a roaring blaze bathed the dining area in soft gold.

"Do you like it?" To his left, Caroline stood at the range.

The transformation was impressive. "How did you manage all this?"

"Actually, there was not much to be done." She smiled and shrugged. "Although this room was very dirty, the two small bedchambers were relatively clean. Once I swept and mopped, and beat the cushions, the rest was just décor."

"And the curtains?" His private retreat was just as he had always imagined it, but it had taken his wife to achieve the desired results.

"The tiebacks are strings that I cut from an apron. The panels are bed linens, and they are pinned." She gave her attention to a pot, picked up a spoon, and stirred what appeared to be stew. "I thought I could hem them during our stay. I will take measurements and order new drapes from my favorite purveyor in London."

She could have knocked him over with a feather. "You wish to come here again?"

"Of course." Caroline added a pinch of seasoning to the stew and sampled the results. "It is lovely. And the extra bedchamber would make a wonderful nursery."

Trevor almost fainted. "N-nursery?"

"Indeed." She sprinkled spices from another tin into the pot. "This is the perfect place to bring our children. They can make sandcastles during the day and, when they are older, study the stars at night."

"I see." He swallowed the panic rising in his throat. "Have we much time—before dinner—that is? Is there water for washing?"

"Yes." She set the spoon down and wiped her hands on her apron. "A hipbath has been prepared in the extra chamber, and I have already bathed. Also, I set out some clothes for you."

"Excellent. Give me five minutes, and I shall be ready to eat," he said as he strolled down the hall. Free from her insightful gaze, Trevor stripped off his soiled garments and discovered the hipbath was too small for his large frame. Half sitting, he made a mental note to purchase a new tub and managed to clean himself. After donning fresh attire, he returned to the great room and found Caroline setting a basket, filled with chunks of bread, at the center of the table.

"Good heavens." He fingered a napkin, pulled out a chair, and sat. "This looks just like home."

"Really?" Caroline inclined her head, and her face was radiant beneath his praise. "I had hoped you would think so."

"You have outdone yourself, love." He picked up a fork and stabbed a morsel of beef in the bowl she had put before him.

Compliments, words of encouragement and applause, danced on his tongue, but Trevor lacked the courage to say what he knew his wife wanted to hear. So they passed the meal in deafening silence. Afterward, he helped clear the dishes.

"Shall we retire?" Caroline asked as she put away the last utensil.

"I suppose." He walked into the sitting area. "I thought I would give you the bed. I can sleep on the sofa."

"You do not wish to keep company with me?" Her query, softly spoken, belied her shock and pain.

"Caroline, the springs are old." He clenched his jaw. "The entire frame would probably collapse beneath our combined weight."

"Then let us put the mattress on the floor." Her chin

quivered, betraying her fragile state. "Later, we can buy a new—"

"No." Trevor pursed his lips and wondered why he was so afraid of his wife. "You would be more comfortable without my presence."

"Do not shift your preference for separate accommodations to my shoulders." With tear-filled eyes, she frowned. "The truth is you no longer desire me."

"You are mistaken." How was he going to get himself out of the mess he had made of their marriage? How could he make her understand what he could not fathom? "This has nothing to do with you."

"Then explain yourself." Caroline closed the distance between them. "You rescued me from Cavalier. You saved my life, yet it appears you do not want me."

Trevor could only stand there and stare.

"I have tried to be a dutiful wife. I have done all that is in my power, committed myself body and soul." She splayed her arms. "Why will you not love me?"

Her plea echoed in his mind, and he pressed his palms to his ears as if doing so would shut out the pain. The sentiment formed a familiar refrain of desperation and anguish. Caroline wrenched his elbow, and he grasped her forearms and backed her into the sidewall.

"Have you any idea how many times I have uttered the same words?" he asked through gritted teeth.

With a whimper, she shook her head.

"I begged my father to love me, but he never did. My mother had used his heart to destroy him, you see. And I sought to avoid the same fate." He gave vent to a self-mocking snort. "How ironic is it that, despite my efforts, I am my sire's son. I am exactly like him, but not as I had envisioned. I am a fool for not declaring myself, and I deserve to lose you."

IT WAS TOO much to hope for, too much to believe.

"Trevor, am I assuming too much?" Stunned by his revelations, Caroline gripped his wrists and braced herself. "Is it possible—do you love me?"

"Aye." He made a sour face no woman in her right mind could resist. "But I do not want to."

"Darling, you have nothing to fear, and I promise it will get easier." She giggled at his sweet admission and cried happy tears. "Love is a gift, not an obligation."

"It is a curse that defies logic, and you have turned me into a milquetoast." He set his forehead to hers, shifted, and pulled her into a snug embrace. "Caroline, please tell me you love me, because I desperately need to hear it."

"I love you." Rising on her toes, she nipped his nose. "I love you." She pressed her lips to his cheek. "I love you." Summoning the force of her devotion, evoking the vigor of her adoration, she bestowed on him a kiss filled with promises she fully intended to keep.

After a few heated, groping, hip grinding minutes, Trevor lifted his head and smiled his wolf's smile. "Perhaps we should adjourn to our bedchamber?"

Ah, it was good to be a woman.

Caroline started toward the hall but paused. "Dearest, though I would give anything to share a bed with you tonight, I do not want to rush you. If you require a period of adjustment, I will not complain."

"You are not rushing me, and I bloody will complain if

you leave my side." With a chuckle, he swept her into his arms, strode down the hall, sidled into the little chamber, and laid her on the bed. Just as fast, he all but jumped on her.

The frame collapsed and crashed to the floor, depositing the mattress, Caroline, and Trevor in a heap. They could only laugh at their predicament.

"Are you all right?" the green-eyed dragon asked with a devilish grin.

"Indeed." She locked her arms behind his head. "And you? Are you hurt?"

"I am, but it is an injury I willingly bear and hope never heals, because you scored a direct hit to my heart." Trevor framed her face and rubbed his nose to hers. "And I am so in love with you."

EPILOGUE

"*H*urry, darling." Trevor boosted Caroline into her saddle. "We do not want to miss the sunrise."

"Relax." She reached out and caught his gloved hand in hers. "We will get there in time."

He squeezed her fingers, and then climbed atop his favorite horse. "Ready?"

She nodded. "Follow me."

To his surprise, she heeled the flanks of her mare and set a blazing pace. He grabbed the reins and mirrored her movements. "*Yaa.*"

Although he was still a tad unaccustomed to the game called marriage, Trevor looked forward to the usual morning rides with his wife. It was their time to exchange trivialities, discuss plans for their future, or simply enjoy each other's company beyond the sensual realm of their connubial bed, something he cherished far and away more than he would have previously thought. And today, he was doubly grateful for what had become an intimate ritual because the Brethren had invaded Althrup for the weekend.

The brandy flowed and a tournament of billiards commenced. They played cards, charades, and a ridiculously competitive game of Pall Mall. Despite the profundity of back slaps and ribald male jokes, all intended to foster brotherly affection, no doubt, Trevor hated to admit that he still felt quite the outsider. And it was not because anyone had made comments to such effect, but rather because he just did not believe he was truly a member of their family.

Caroline peered over her shoulder and waved. "Come on."

The crisp December air should have chilled him to the bone, but a single glance from his wife warmed him inside and out. He urged his mount faster. When she steered south, he grinned. There was a spot that boasted an incredible view of the Channel, and he had come to think of it as their special place. They cleared the trees, and suspicion nipped at his senses.

At the edge of the cliffs, nine cloaked figures stood in the morning mist.

Trevor did not need to see their faces to guess their identities. Intrigued, he arched a brow and gazed at Caroline. She merely smiled. Disappointment shrouded him as a wet blanket, because he had not wanted to share his wife just then. They reined in and dismounted, leaving their horses to graze with the others. For a second, he considered swimming for safety, but Caroline took hold of his hand and led him to the Brethren.

"Do not be afraid," she said in a whisper. "I am with you."

"You are not the one that concerns me." He frowned.

"Morning, Lockwood." Damian appeared to stand as

leader of the pack. "Years ago, we pledged an oath in order to ensure that none of us would ever be alone. It is the same vow that joined our five ancestors, after they fled France and certain death."

Dirk chuckled and said, "To many, our pact may seem a childhood fancy. But as we grew older, and sorrow randomly touched our lives, that youthful promise evolved into something much more. It became an allegiance."

"Douglas, Elliott, Prescott, Randolph, Seymour." Blake dipped his chin. "Our ascendants, our five families, comprised the original Brethren of the Coast, and we have stood together for over six centuries. In our generation, Caroline is the first to marry."

"We had thought we welcomed you properly into our fold." Lance rocked on his heels. "We have since discovered we were wrong."

"In this family, no one is excluded. No one is left behind." Dalton inclined his head and grinned. "And although we did not abandon you, we did not exactly make you feel at home. Allow us to rectify our mistake, brother."

Caroline ushered him forward, and Trevor inhaled deeply. The Brethren and their female support formed a semi-circle, and Damian held up a worn, leather-bound book.

"This log belonged to my ancestors. My father carried it wherever he sailed, as did his father before him. As I do now. The oath that is written on these ancient pages is the vow we took on a dark night by candlelight. And it is the same promise we make to you, if you will join us."

In concert, the Brethren said, "Love, honor, and devotion were the beginning of our Order. Bonds of kinship and friendship all-important. We uphold these principles embrace for embrace, desire for desire, for one, for all. For King and Country we stand, for love and comradeship we live."

Damian closed the tome and extended a hand. "On my honor."

The simple phrase was repeated, and an additional palm added to the pact, until only Caroline and Trevor remained. Looking him straight in the eyes, his wife followed the example set by her friends.

He knew what they expected, was aware of his role to play, but he waited. Gulls keened in the distance, and a gentle breeze blew in from the Channel. And although he was not cold, Trevor shuddered.

The odd extended family, characters all, offered him something he had never believed existed, and he still could not quite understand them. They pledged to stand with him, for him. He had been alone for the better portion of his life and, in those solitary years, had always yearned to be part of something more than himself.

Trevor wanted to be a husband.

Wanted to be a father.

And he wanted to be a member of their family.

Placing his hand atop the stack, he winked at Caroline and said, "On my honor."

A chorus of cheers erupted, and they shared heartfelt hugs and robust back slaps. After mounting their horses, they rode hell bent for leather along the cliffs.

Trevor cast a glance at his wife, and she blew him a kiss. He laughed and realized that, for the first time in his life, he belonged to something more than himself. He was a husband, a lover, a friend, and a brother. And someday soon, if he applied himself in earnest, he would be a father.

Indeed, life was filled with promise.

The sun shimmered on the ocean, marking the dawn of a new day—and a new Nautionnier Knight.

ABOUT BARBARA DEVLIN

A proud Latina, USA Today bestselling author Barbara Devlin was born a storyteller, but it was a weeklong vacation to Bethany Beach, Delaware that forever changed her life. The little house her parents rented had a collection of books by Kathleen Woodiwiss, which exposed Barbara to the world of romance, and *Shanna* remains a personal favorite.

Barbara writes heartfelt historical romances that feature not so perfect heroes who may know how to seduce a woman but know nothing of marriage. And she prefers feisty but smart heroines who sometimes save the hero before they find their happily ever after.

Barbara is a disabled-in-the-line-of-duty retired police officer, and she earned an MA in English and continued a course of study for a Doctorate in Literature and Rhetoric. She happily considered herself an exceedingly eccentric English professor, until success in Indie publishing lured her into writing, full-time, featuring her fictional knighthood, the Brethren of the Coast.

Connect with Barbara Devlin at BarbaraDevlin.com, where you can sign up for her newsletter, The Knightly News.

ALSO BY BARBARA DEVLIN

BRETHREN OF THE COAST

Loving Lieutenant Douglas

Enter the Brethren

My Lady, the Spy

The Most Unlikely Lady

One-Knight Stand

Captain of Her Heart

The Lucky One

Love with an Improper Stranger

To Catch a Fallen Spy

Hold Me, Thrill Me, Kiss Me

The Duke Wears Nada

A Very Brethren Christmas

Owner of a Lonely Heart

BRETHREN ORIGINS

Arucard

Demetrius

Aristide

Morgan

Geoffrey

PIRATES OF THE COAST

The Black Morass

The Iron Corsair

The Buccaneer

The Stablemaster's Daughter

The Marooner

Once Upon a Christmas Knight

The Reaper

WORLD OF DE WOLFE PACK

Lone Wolfe

The Big Bad De Wolfe

Tall, Dark & De Wolfe

MAGICK TRILOGY

Magick, Straight Up

A Taste of Magick

Magick in the Air

PIRATES OF BRITANNIA

The Blood Reaver

THE MAD MATCHMAKING MEN OF WATERLOO

The Accidental Duke

The Accidental Groom